ADVANCE PRAISE

"It gallops along with scarcely a dull moment."
    Lisa Tutt

DATE DUE

"A fantasy w.... the same magnificence of conception, the same sense of looming presences whose purposes are not ours to apprehend. Fragments of old stories that stud and sometimes drive his narrative are not just there as decoration or machinery. They are there to make this world seem deeper and darker than Lloyd's gloom-ridden narrative allows."
    Time Out

"*Stormcaller*'s magical land is far from the cosy backwater we've become so used to of late. A pretty confident first novel."
    Dreamwatch

"The world that Lloyd has created seems much more real than that of most fantasy books. He has created a fantasy world that has believable politics and is inhabited by large numbers of ordinary people. . . ."
    Emerald City

THE
STORMCALLER

THE LAND

Xomejx
Merlat
Perlir
White Isle
Canar Chrit
Vanach
Tirah
Lomin
ELVEN WASTE
Tor Milist
Scree
Helrect
Mantil
Narkang
Raland
Canar Fell
Aroth
The CircleCity
Embere
Tor Salan
Denei
Castle Keriabral
Ter Nol
Mustet
Chotel
Sautin
ELVEN WASTE
Vijgen
Lochet
Mekray
Verech
Cholos
Tserol
TioHe
Lenei

N

DS '05

THE
STORMCALLER

BOOK ONE OF THE
TWILIGHT REIGN

TOM LLOYD

an imprint of **Prometheus Books**
Amherst, NY

Published 2008 by Pyr®, an imprint of Prometheus Books

Inquiries should be addressed to
Pyr
59 John Glenn Drive
Amherst, New York 14228–2119
VOICE: 716–691–0133, ext. 210
FAX: 716–691–0137
WWW.PYRSF.COM

12 11 10 09 08   5 4 3 2 1

Library of Congress Cataloging-in-Publication Data

Lloyd, Tom, 1979–
    The stormcaller / by Tom Lloyd.
        p. cm. — (Twilight reign ; bk. 1)
    Originally published: London : Gollancz, an imprint of the Orion Publishing Group,
2006.
    ISBN 978–1–59102–693–8 (acid-free paper)
    1. Gods—Fiction. I. Title.

PR6112.L697S76 2008
823'.92—dc22

                                                                                2008035328

Printed in the United States on acid-free paper

For my parents

ACKNOWLEDGMENTS

As WITH ANY FIRST NOVEL there are lots of people who deserve thanks, either for direct involvement in the project or for simply tolerating my eccentricities. My family's support over the years has been invaluable, while without the years of enthusiasm, encouragement, and advice from all corners, most notably Robin Morero and Ryan Morini, I might never have struggled through to finish the book.

Every writer needs to catch a break when he starts out and mine came when John Parker agreed to represent me, something I remain hugely grateful for, while Sensei Dale also did me a great service in helping the book end up in the hands of Lou Anders. The last word, however, must be in particular praise of Jo Fletcher, beloved editor and aristocracy expert whose commitment has surpassed all expectations. There really was none of the usual literary agent exaggeration when I was told that Jo was one of the very best editors in the business.

CHAPTER 1

IN THE DARK CORNERS OF THE NIGHT he dreams of the silent palace by the shore: a place where harsh sunlight and leaden shadows are cast over the white marble of its corridors. Without the cries of seabirds or the whistle of wind over flagstones the silence here is profound, broken only by the occasional faint break of a wave on the rocks outside and his own hurried heartbeat.

He finds himself in an immense hexagonal hall, looking down at incomprehensible script carved into the floor. The strange words corkscrew slowly in from a dark doorway to the foot of a spiral staircase, the hall's only other feature. It rises up from the floor, twisting thirty yards up through the air, then somehow fails to quite meet the hall's flat ceiling, stopping less than a yard short.

Prayer or curse, he follows the oblique path of writing around and around until finally he reaches the staircase. Each step has a symbol cut into its centre, runes he has never seen before. After a pause he places his foot squarely on the first and continues in that way, eyes moving always to the next shape, until he reaches the top. The air feels thinner up here. It looks a dizzying drop to the floor below when he leans over the balustrade. Then he squeezes through a hatchway in the ceiling and finds himself staring up from the floor of a cavernous domed shrine.

The palace is a shell, an unfinished work of altarless temples and blank crumbling memorials. In every direction he can see high halls, empty of everything but countless statues carved from the same ancient stone as the walls. Through the vaulted windows, even the waves lapping at the sun-blasted beach appear unreal. He has never ventured out to dip his fingers in that ocean or tasted the salt on the air or felt the touch of the sun on his skin.

Drifting down the yard-deep steps of an oval assembly hall, he feels exposed and vulnerable. An old woman once told him that the Gods decide your fate in such a chamber; they argue and debate over your birth until the course of your entire life is set. But there are no compassionate voices to speak for him here, no sound other than that of his bare feet on stone, muted, like the echo of a dead song.

He knows where his path will eventually take him. It's the same place every time, but still he walks through unknown rooms and down hanging walkways, always hoping that the next turning will be the way out. Once more he finds himself in a gigantic chamber, where a stretch of wall fifty yards long has been savagely ripped open. Picking his way over the rubble he enters the forest of statues inside. Monsters and heroes stand in stony readiness, waiting for the day they will be revived for some final cataclysm. A terrace lies through the pillars on the other side of the immense space. After the miles he's walked, another few hundred yards is too far for his legs to carry him. Fear liquefies his muscles and drags him down to hide behind the heel of some brave dead warrior, watching and waiting.

He sees a large man standing in the centre of the hall, terrible and powerful, as if the greatest of these statues has somehow come to life. He knows the man will die—that enormous strength means nothing to what stalks this place—even before a black-armoured knight appears from nowhere to attack the man. He sees a huge fanged blade tear at the man's flesh, watches it sever the head. Terror smoulders deep in his gut: he knows the blade will one day rip into his own frail body. And then he sees something horrific in the killer's face—the curse he shares. The palace fades. The blood pales. All that remains is the burning light of that gaze.

Isak lay motionless, tracing the familiar cracks and veins in the roof struts while his legs protested the lack of space in the cramped caravan. These dreams, though infrequent, had haunted his nights for as long as he could remember. Even though he was, in all other things, a stoical youth, they could still reduce him to a cowering child. The visions were so real he sometimes woke retching in dread. Shame crept over him at the thought. He was older now, old enough to be called an adult, and yet his dreams frightened him more than any man could. For a time he remained still, tracing the grain of the wood above to calm his pounding heart.

The clutter and dirt were reassuringly normal, and welcome for once. Finally sitting upright, Isak stretched and massaged the sleep from his long limbs until the tingle of a jolting wooden bed had receded. He tugged his ragged shirt into some semblance of order and pushed long fingers through his black, matted hair. He ignored the worn, filthy shoes that lay discarded in one corner. Looking out through the rear curtains he could see the warm weather continued. A scavenger bird hung limp in the deliciously blue sky, while swallows swooped and rose after the last of the morning's prey. Back home, summer would be long dead, but here it took the Land longer to accept that autumn had arrived. For the moment, insects and beaming flowers still reigned.

Through the fug of the enclosed room came a faint breeze, bringing with it a scent that was as different as the weather. Here the warm smell of clay-rich earth and wild thyme pervaded everything, though the damp resinous odour of home lingered in his mind. The dark loamy soil of the Great Forest to the north bore no resemblance to this sticky red dirt. They still had far to travel; he guessed another week at least would pass before the view started to change, so until then, he'd just enjoy the weather.

Isak poked his head out to where his father, Horman, sat with the reins swinging casually from his hand and one leg braced up over the footplate as usual. Dressed in similarly rough and patched clothes, Isak's father bore little resemblance to his son beyond the dark hair and pale complexion common to all of their tribe. He was smaller, with a scrappy beard that failed to conceal his perpetual scowl; Horman looked aged beyond his physical years, as if spite had drained his youth as well as his joy. Rusty earth stained his breeches and loose shirt. His black eyes flickered at the sound of Isak's movement but narrowed when he saw his son's face. He flicked up his coiled whip, but Isak dodged out of habit and it caught only air. There was nothing he could do to avoid the look of resentment that followed.

"So you decided to stir at last? It must be three hours since dawn. You're here to work, not to spend the night running the wilds. Sometimes I wonder why I keep you around at all." His father hawked and spat into the parched dust of the road, then returned his gaze to the distant horizon.

Isak answered bitterly, "and then you remember that I'm as good as a slave to you. In any case, it's not as if you could manage yourself."

This time the whip was wielded with purpose; Isak's retort was rewarded with an angry welt down his cheek.

"Shut your mouth, unless you want worse. And don't think you're getting any breakfast, not when I had to set the traces myself this morning. You didn't even catch anything last night—you're even more useless than the rest of your damn kind." Horman sighed. "Merciful Nartis, save us from white-eyes. No doubt Carel's fool enough to feed you, so get out of my sight or you'll get more of this." He twitched his whip and returned his attention to the road.

Isak vaulted the rail and leapt effortlessly on to the dusty ground. It was only as he trotted past similar wagons, ignoring the stares of their occupants, that he realised the pace of the whole train had been increased. They were two weeks behind deadline. Obviously the wagon-master preferred to punish the horses for his own drunken stupidity.

A long-dead river had carved this mighty path through the Land, stirring life for miles around, but that had been in another age. Now the summer heat baked everything to the same dusty brown and it took an effort to find the hidden beauty of this place: the strange nocturnal creatures, the scented mosses concealed under rocks, the camouflaged plants bursting with colour underneath. All Isak's father saw was the desiccated channel they drove down. It was too much effort to drag his damaged leg up the bank so the only things to break his horizon were the twin mountains to the south.

Isak ran over to one of the lead caravans and leapt up on to the driving seat with the carelessness of familiarity. The driver, like Isak himself, was a man apart from the rest of this inbred community. Carel made no comment other than to smile wearily at Isak's arrival. His crinkled face belied his strength and age—Carel was close in years to Isak's father, but where bile had aged one, experience had marked the other.

His black hair, now heavily seamed with white, was long, plaited three times, and tied back with copper wire, which declared to the world that he was a mercenary—but the white embroidery on his collar and the white leather threaded through the plaits set him above being a mere sword for hire. Carel—Sergeant Betyn Carelfolden—was a Ghost, a legend within their small group. He had retired from the Palace Guard of Lord Bahl, the Lord of the Farlan, a handful of summers after Isak's birth. Membership of that élite regiment guaranteed a position in society that could not be bought. Everyone respected the Ghosts of Tirah.

"Horman not in the best of moods today, then? Here, take the reins, I could do with a break."

Isak took the reins from Carel's hand and watched as the man stretched, then fumbled for his pipe. The horse, unimpressed, snorted scorn at its new handler.

Carel was the only person in the wagon train to treat Isak as if he were normal. Being born to parents who had been servants on a suzerain's estate, coupled with years of hard soldiering, had taught the mercenary to look beyond appearance, something for which Isak was always grateful.

"He's never in the best of moods," Isak grumbled. "Yesterday he pushed a knife right into my hand, just for touching that green ring of mother's." He held up his hand, displaying the ugly, dark-red scab.

"Well then, you deserved it." Carel wasn't going to let his fondness for the boy stand in the way of a lesson. "You know perfectly well what that ring means to him. Just leave her things alone. It's all he has left. At least you heal much faster than the rest of us. Be grateful for that."

"He has more of her than I do. All I have is the blame for her death." Isak sighed.

"And such is life," replied the mercenary without a trace of sympathy. He was Isak's friend, but that didn't mean Isak got special treatment. "You are what you are—that in itself is enough for most, and more for Horman. He really loved your mother. Why antagonise him?"

There was no reply. Isak just sat there looking sullen, unable to admit defeat.

"Fine, enough talk of your father. Are you looking forward to joining the Palace Guard? After Silvernight you can take the trials without your father's permission."

"What's the point?" Isak ran a fingernail along a groove in the wood. "I'll never be a Ghost—why would they want someone like me?"

"You won't be an outcast all your life, I promise you that. Do you think I would bother to waste my time teaching you to fight despite what that lot think?" Carel jabbed a thumb back at the wagons following. "These people aren't like most Farlan. You might never be popular, but the tribe has a use for you, sure enough. I've fought side-by-side with your kind, and there's far worse than your childish temper in the ranks of the Ghosts—men who'd have been hanged years back if they weren't so happy to be in the front line. You're all a dangerous lot, but you've more of a mind than most and the Swordmasters will see that. Just remember me when you become General Isak."

The veteran smiled and Isak smiled back. Carel didn't suffer fools or time wasters. There had to be something to his words, or all the hours of drilling and sparring would have been for nothing. Isak knew he could best Carel with a weapon—even a weighted training stick against a sword—but that wasn't the problem. All white-eyes were preternaturally fast, and strong, but it was this very power that scared normal people. Isak had had that demonstrated to him almost every day of his life.

Carel insisted there were others like him in the Guard, but no one ever saw them. If it were true, clearly they were not trusted with keeping the peace on Tirah's streets; they were used only in the slaughter of battle.

"I suppose you're right," Isak admitted. "I just daren't allow myself to hope. But I'll take any chance to get away from this lot, even if I have to break Father in two to do it."

This disrespect earned him a clip round the ear, one that would have been painful to anyone else, but Isak bore it without flinching. Every child in the train had felt the back of Carel's hand at one time or another, but it made no difference: they all loved him—and his stories. But no one else in the train understood Carel's obvious affection for the wild white-eye, and all Carel would say was that in Isak he recognised the angry young man he himself had been.

The wagoners were a community held together by blood ties as much as poverty. Most of the year was spent on the road and even in Farlan territory they kept to themselves. The caravan was the only home Isak had ever known, but it was not where he was welcome; only in the wild places did he find some comfort of belonging. The presence of others always reminded him that he was blessed and cursed in equal measure—and that men feared both. White-eyes were born to be protectors of the Seven Tribes, but jealousy and fear had demonised his kind and now many saw them as symbols of the Land's polluted soul.

Carel grimaced at the boy. "You're as sulky and bad-tempered as your father. I think you've inherited more than you lot normally do."

"Perhaps he's just particularly unpleasant," retorted Isak sourly.

"Perhaps so, but he's not too bad a man to others. Your problem is that you have the look of your mother. He sees her in your face, and that brings out the worst in him. If you didn't get at him so, you might not have to spend your life trying to stop yourself fighting back."

Isak turned his head sharply to meet the mercenary's knowing expression. As he looked into those dark eyes he saw the twinkle of humour that had brightened his childhood and relaxed. Carel might be the only one who could see his internal struggle, but he was also the only one who understood it.

"White-eyes are pretty much the same, whatever the tribe," he continued, tapping out his pipe on the rail beside him. The curl of a smile hung on his lips as he fixed a fond gaze on the youth. "You remember I told you about Sergeant Kulet? Now that one was a bastard, the worst white-eye I've ever met. Man killed his entire family when he was sixteen—well, 'cept his mother of course, but we can't blame any of you white-eyes for the size you were as a baby. The ones to blame are the Gods, and most folk aren't that stupid.

"Anyway, the Swordmaster wasn't allowed to execute Kulet. The high priest of Nartis stepped in and said a birthmark on his face showed Kulet'd been touched by Nartis." Carel gave a snort of scorn. "Touched by a daemon more like, if you ask me, but that birthmark was as blue as a temple door, no doubt about it. We kept him just drunk enough to spend most of the day telling jokes—the bugger could make me laugh even more than your foolery can—otherwise he'd get bored and start a fight in the barracks. But when you saw him on the battlefield—well, merciful Death! If you had Kulet next to you, you were glad. He fought like a man possessed, never gave ground, never left the man next to him vulnerable. You knew you were safe in his lee."

Carel took a long pull on his pipe, then tapped Isak on the head with it. "Smile; you're one of the blessed. You're all violent, insolent, brooding, and heartless. You make the best soldiers because you're twice as strong and half as caring. Don't take that wrong, you're like a son to me, but I've known many. Behind the eyes you've all got something barely under control. P'raps it's worse for you—your father never was good at taking orders either—but no white-eye was ever as meek as a lamb. Obey your father till the spring and then you're free, I promise. Just keep your temper until then."

"I hardly feel like I'm blessed."

"Ah boy, the Land is harsh. It's a cruel place and it needs white-eyes to tame it. The Gods knew that when they made the first of you to be born. The last of the Farlan line was their model, and scripture tells he was no court jester." Carel clapped a hand on Isak's shoulder and tugged him round to look him in the eye. There was an almost wistful tone to his voice when he spoke again. "Our Gods might be great and powerful, but they've never needed to be subtle."

Isak recognised the words: an old soldier's favourite mantra.

The veteran smiled. "Come on now, get that scowl off your face. The lecture's over." He put his feet up and leaned against the wooden frame of the caravan, content in the sunshine that they wouldn't see for months once they arrived home.

Isak shifted in his seat and settled down for a long and uncomfortable day. As his mind wandered, he tried to count the months until he reached adulthood. Whether he was good enough to join the Ghosts or not, next year he would be able to do as he pleased; not to be dragged back like a rogue mule when he left. His father had made the most of the law regarding childhood, but he couldn't hold on to Isak forever.

Becoming a Ghost was still a dream to Isak, but one thing *was* sure: he could better Carel with a sword. He had nothing more to learn. If the Swordmasters were like the wagoners, he would go elsewhere—perhaps become a mercenary like Carel was now and travel to distant cities. Many of his kind did that, and some never found employment to be proud of, but white-eyes didn't become hermits and live in quiet humility. Their nature was not so peaceful.

Isak was still lost in daydreams of military glory when a sound up ahead broke through his reverie. Heads appeared from almost every caravan and wagon in the train, anticipating something to break the monotony of the journey. The spiced breeze was still detectable, but it did nothing to cool faces red under the onslaught of the sun. Most people wore wide-brimmed hats of some kind, but Isak rarely bothered. His skin was as fair as anyone's, but it never peeled or burned, just as any injuries healed quickly. In those ways he *knew* he was blessed. It was the rest of it that made people nervous.

Off to the left Isak saw a pair of wood pigeons perched on a branch, eyeing the wagon train with lazy interest. He started to reach for the crossbow slung behind him but stopped when the sound came again. It was a voice calling. He pulled himself to his feet on the wooden seat for a better look.

From his vantage point Isak could see a horseman approaching, plaits swinging in the air and a spear held aloft. The signal asked for Carel, who had spotted the rider too and already slipped on to the back of his own steed, which trotted patiently alongside the wagon. The stock pony was nothing like as impressive as the horses he had ridden in the Ghosts, and it bore little decoration bar the tattoos of breed and a charm to Nyphal, the Goddess of travellers, but it had served well over the years. With one hand on the pommel of his sword, Carel indicated for Isak to rein in before urging his stock pony forward.

The wagon train ground to an eventual halt behind them as an uneasy silence descended. This was untamed land for the greater part, and people mixed curiosity with caution. As Carel reached the horseman, figures appeared from behind the bend in the road. Six men were coming towards them, five of them the train's guards, mounted on stock ponies like Carel's own, and one man, a stranger, on foot. The five on horseback towered above the newcomer, but they looked curiously cowed in his presence.

Carel stopped and dismounted once he was past the lead wagon. While he waited for the man to reach him he looked around, scanning the terrain. He didn't see anyone else, but he kept his hand on his hilt as the man approached—he appeared calm, but a stranger alone and on foot was more than unusual out here.

Isak found himself digging his nails into his palm in apprehension. The stranger was taller even than Isak, who himself looked down on the rest of the wagon train occupants. He was clad in black from head to toe, and the hardened leather and heavy, scaled armour he wore showed that he was not a native of these warm parts, where the guards wore little or no protection. Despite his height, the man was clearly not Farlan, nor from any other tribe Isak had seen on their travels.

Worryingly, the man had his sword drawn, yet Carel paid it no attention. He left his own weapon sheathed as he moved in close to speak to the man.

Isak realised suddenly that his attention had been caught by the blade itself, not the man who held it, which went against *everything* Carel had taught him. *The sword tells you nothing about what your enemy is going to do; keep your eyes on it and you'll watch it all the way into your belly.* Even knowing this, he couldn't tear his eyes away from the weapon: its shape and colour were unlike any he had seen before. Faint bursts of light pricked the black surface so gently that he almost dismissed them as fancy. Just the sight of that blade made Isak shiver, as if some primal fear stirred inside.

The stranger said something, too quietly for Isak to hear.

"We're just traders returning to Tirah. We don't want trouble, but we are prepared for it." Carel replied in a loud voice, so that those wagoners with weapons would reach for them. Isak could see that Carel looked puzzled, and a little apprehensive: this situation didn't make much sense—who travelled alone and on foot out here? Was this an ambush of some kind? He glanced back inside Carel's caravan to make sure that the mercenary's spear was within reach.

The stranger was hairless, and terribly lean, but there was no sign of illness; rather, he had about him an unnatural vitality. Pale parchment skin looked stretched to fit the skull underneath, and his eyes were completely black. For the first time Isak saw why people feared the differences in his own face.

"There is one here who is not like you, one who should come with me." The man spoke clearly this time.

"We have a white-eye with us; what of him? He's young. What use would you have of him?" Carel sounded dismissive.

"He should come with me to seek his future."

Carel stepped back, away from the stranger. "You think I'm just going to hand him over to you? You look like a sorcerer to me." He took hold of the charm around his neck, carved with the rune of Nyphal, protector of travellers, and muttered a short mantra under his breath.

"Get back into the wagon, Isak. Keep out of sight," hissed Horman, a concerned look on his face. He had approached Carel's caravan out of sight of the stranger; now he motioned his son off the driver's seat. Isak climbed down quietly and slid back into the dark interior without a word while his father cocked his crossbow.

"What does he want with me?" he whispered.

"I don't know, but whatever it is, I'll give you to him if you don't shut up." Horman scowled at his son and turned his attention back to Carel.

Isak did as he was told, fearing the stranger and his father's anger equally. Horman had never been a patient man; he blamed much of his misfortune on his supernatural son, from the inevitable death of his wife giving birth to Isak to his exit from the cavalry following an accident. Horman had no tales of heroic battle and near-fatal injuries overcome with which to enthrall his grandchildren by the fireside. Instead, he had lost his livelihood thanks to a simple drill manoeuvre gone wrong the day he learned of his wife's death. Now even ants crawling on the supplies were Isak's fault.

The stranger looked over at the wagons, his eyes moving down the line until Isak felt his gaze lock on to him. Suddenly a cold presence was all around, as if bitter winter had just invaded, and Isak fell back in surprise and alarm. He felt a surge of panic at the alien mind filling his thoughts and, inexplicably, hatred beyond anything he'd ever known before. In the next instant, the contact was broken off, so abruptly that Isak flinched in surprise.

"He'll kill me," Isak moaned, his hands trembling uncontrollably. "He'll kill us all."

Horman turned with a frown and gave Isak a clip around the head to shut him up. "He'll have to get in line then, now quiet!"

Isak ducked down as the stranger's gaze rested on the western horizon for a moment before turning back to Carel. "My name is Aracnan. I am just a mercenary, like you. My task was twofold; the second part was to deliver a message to the boy if he would not come. Tell your men to put their bows away. My employer is more powerful than you can ever imagine. Here is the message."

Carel found his hand full, and then Aracnan leapt up on to the rocky bank above him. It was a jump far beyond the capability of any street acrobat, but he landed so lightly that not a stone nor chunk of dirt was dislodged onto the stunned men below. Then he was gone.

They tried to track him, but once they had scrambled up the bank they couldn't even guess at which direction Aracnan had taken, and the ground held no clues that any man had walked there. Finally, unwilling to waste much more time chasing ghosts, the wagon master called off the futile hunt and they recommenced their journey in near silence, everyone lost in their own thoughts.

Isak jumped when Carel leaned over to whisper in his ear, some hours later, "Nyphal was looking down upon us, I'm sure; I felt her presence."

"Was that what I felt? A Goddess?" asked Isak, unsure whether he would have described what he had felt as divine.

The mercenary nodded, his eyes fixed on the western horizon, where the Gods lived. He'd seen Aracnan's anger, contained though it was, and had no doubt the Goddess had intervened for them. "We'll stop at the next shrine and sacrifice there. I'm not sure what Aracnan wanted with you, but he meant you no good—of that I'm certain."

He kept his frown for a moment, then shook it off and nudged Isak with a laugh. "The Gods were looking down on you, boy, so maybe they've plans for you after all. You might find out there are worse things in life than bales of cloth."

Isak sat with his lips firmly set, determinedly looking north to the cool, wooded valleys and mist-shrouded mountains the tribe called home: the land where the God Nartis raged in the sky above a city of soaring spires and the dark-haired Farlan tribe; north, to the Lord of Storms.

CHAPTER 2

TIRAH, THE SEAT AND HEART OF AN AUTOCRAT'S POWER: a city that slumbered warily at the heart of the Spiderweb Mountains. Crowned by seven great towers and wreathed in curling mist, Tirah was famed throughout the Land as the oldest of human cities, and one of the most beautiful. Dark cobbled streets led directly into the tendrils of forest that reached down from the mountain line. The rangers who patrolled up in the mountains described the grey mass of Tirah as besieged, a great standing stone slowly succumbing to the creep of moss. No one else went up there—it was a place where Gods and monsters walked. In three thousand years, the Farlan had spread well beyond Tirah's streets and into the dense expanse of the Great Forest, but it was far from tame.

This night, a creature far from home had ventured onto those streets, driven there by desperation and hunger. As a hero of the Western Tunnels, the most vicious battleground of a long-standing war, he'd been chosen as a seeker, for only the strongest could survive the rituals that entailed. Despite the risk posed by humans, the seekers were sent out in small bands to all corners of the Land, following the trail of magical artefacts their people needed so badly. Whatever spells the priests of home had burned into his flesh, they had made him aware of magic, leaving him as tormented as an addict by its bitter perfume drifting on the wind. Barely thinking, he'd trudged on, intent on his search, even as his comrades fell to the creatures of the forest.

It was loyalty that had taken them north in the first place, and it was loyalty that brought them, enfeebled and afraid, to their deaths in a land of cloying scent, numbing cold, and constant rain. No God would claim their souls and he feared that this place was so distant it would be impossible for any of them to join their forebears in the Temple of Ancestors, to guard over the next generation.

The daemons stalking him had caught the scent once more. Their chilling calls went up even as he found cobbles underfoot. The child in him wanted to turn and shout, beg for some respite, even as his aching heart strained to keep tired limbs moving. The warrior in him said *run or die*. The

blanket of fog brought their wail from every direction, and from an indeter-
minate distance. But they were close. He could feel them.

He ran, blindly—but it was a dead end, and at last there was nowhere
else to go. Blank stone walls rose up on either side; the only window he could
see was too high to reach. A low wooden storehouse hugged the left-hand
wall, but he was too exhausted to climb. The time had come. Panting, trying
to fill his tortured lungs in the choking, sodden air they had here, he allowed
himself one moment to remember the warm taste of home, then readied his
claws for battle. Drawing himself up to his full height, he called out his
battle-honours with what strength he could muster. The long list declared
his prowess even as it summoned the beasts to him.

Then he crouched, his withered limbs tense and ready, and a sibilant
snarl cut the night's mist. It scarcely had time to die as three leapt on him as
one and bore him down. So much for his pride. Now empty eyes ignored his
limp body being torn apart; unhearing ears were deaf to the guttural snorts
as his flesh was devoured, his blood licked up.

A figure watched the dying, but he felt nothing for the outmatched and
pitiful creature. He knew nothing of the Siblis race except that that they were
unsuited to these parts. A long cloak billowed out behind him as he ghosted
over the cobbled ground. But *something* had compelled the Siblis to come so
far, into so inhospitable a place. Curiosity stirred. Gliding over to the jerking
body he threw back the huge wolves with ease and bent down to inspect what
remained.

The beasts, baulked of their prey, snarled as they retreated a step, hackles
raised and ready to attack. Then they realised what he was, and that recognition elicited a whimper of fear, but the man ignored them. With heads down,
and bellies brushing the ground, the wolves backed away until, at a safe distance, they turned and fled back to the forest. They had melted into the mist
before they even made the tree line.

The man knelt down and placed the bow he was carrying to one side. It
was a beautiful weapon, fully six feet in length—the man was extraordinarily
big and could draw it with ease—and slightly recurved, with an intricately
painted design down its entire length. The grip and tips were finished in

silver but it was the hunting scene traced with infinite care in blue and white that made the bow a work of art.

"The last of the Siblis." He was glad to make some noise again after a day of silent tracking, even if he was speaking only to the night. He had found other bodies during the past week. "And this one was the seeker," he went on to himself. "The war must be going badly if they have revived this practice, but what in the name of the Dark Place brought it here?"

He knew the Siblis were engaged in an almost eternal war with the Chetse, a slow, bitter struggle that drained both sides and left no one a winner. Now it appeared the Siblis were desperate enough to curse their own soldiers with a craving for magic, a craving that would drive them to the brink of death as they sought weapons for their outnumbered warriors. There were runes cut into the corpse's torso, still open and weeping, kept that way by magic. Did they understand the agony they were putting their servants through?

"I think you go hungry tonight," he called out suddenly, looking up sharply at a form watching from the rooftop. A mutter cut through the mist—soft, but certainly not human—and then it was gone. Whatever had been watching would not return; seeing him was enough to guarantee that. He turned the corpse over, noting the length of the sharp bony protrusions extending from each wrist. A prod revealed how little meat was on the creature. They had all been starving in this alien environment. Its skin was rough and scaled like a lizard's, much tougher than human skin, but he could still count at least a dozen cuts and abrasions that had only half healed.

Picking the corpse up by the ankle, he threw it on to the roof of the small storehouse the Siblis had died against. The corpse wouldn't be disturbed tonight, at least. Gargoyles were mainly territorial, and hunted by sight, not scent: that one would not return soon, and no others would be drawn into claimed territory.

A muffled cry came from the main building as the owner heard the commotion outside. A weak light flickered in the window above and then a round face appeared, a man's, his several chins shaking in anger. A woman was shouting in the background.

"What in Bahl's name is going on out here?" The man blinked the sleep from his eyes and peered down at the street, a candle in one hand and a club in the other. "You, what are you doing? Get away, before I call a patrol!"

The giant slipped back the hood of his cape to reveal the blue mask underneath. His eyes blazed suddenly as he brought the bow up from the floor with a thought. The merchant gasped and dropped the club on to the floor, wincing as it fell on his bare toes.

"My Lord, forgive me, I did not realise—"

The giant held up a hand for silence. He was not in the mood for conversation.

"Return to your bed. If that wife of yours continues to screech, I'll have the Ghosts cut her tongue out."

Lord Bahl, Duke of Tirah and ruler of the Farlan tribe, marked the wall so a night patrol could retrieve the corpse later and continued on his way. This night was special to him. He didn't want anything to intrude on his memories of a birthday long forgotten by others, just to be alone with the past in his beloved city. Outside, he forgot his loneliness and bathed in the night, remembering the happier time before he had become Lord of the Farlan, when duty had not been his only purpose.

A low moan escaped his lips; it grew and rose up into the night sky. "Only one thing I have ever asked, only one," he prayed through the sudden waves of choking grief that rolled over him. "I have ever been loyal, but—" His voice trailed off. Forsaking the Gods would not bring her back; all that would achieve was harm to the nation that was now his life's purpose. He stood and made a conscious effort to subjugate those feelings, drive them back into the deepest reaches of his heart. On this night only, the date of her birth and her death, the Lord of the Farlan allowed his dreams to be of her.

Off to the north, the Golden Tower caught his eye. The half-ruined landmark still shone in daylight, but now it was little more than a black presence that Bahl felt as much as saw against the night sky. Squatting near the tower's base was a tavern, the only glimmer of happiness in the entire district. Bahl could hear a dulled chatter coming from within. This was a poor district nowadays; the warehouses and workshops meant few people actually lived here. The patrons of the tavern would be labourers and wagon drivers, men without homes who followed the work. They were always amongst the first to hear news from abroad.

He eyed the drab, graceless tavern. It backed up against a larger building and faced into a crossroads, a good position even in this mean quarter of the city. A statue stood at the centre of the crossroads, probably for no reason other than that there was space. Bahl wondered how many men these days would recognise that the statue before him was a monument to Veriole Farlan, the first king of their tribe. How many would truly care? The city was covered in statues of lords and Gods, as well as scowling faces said to ward off evil spirits. Though there were very few creatures like the gargoyle watching the people below, the city's grim and ancient grandeur meant tales persisted.

Taken by a sudden thirst for beer and cheerful voices on such a dismal night, Bahl drifted towards the tavern, changing his appearance as he did so. He felt the clammy night air on his scalp as he pulled off the close-fitting silk mask he wore. A simple glamour gave him dark hair with three copper-bound plaits. No magic could alter the colour of his eyes, but a mercenary white-eye would probably be ignored. Lifting the hem of his cloak, Bahl gave it a quick violent twitch; when it fell back to touch his calves it was a dull green—only the rich wore white cloaks. The simple enchantments left behind a familiar rushing tingle, a seductive reminder of how little he used his prodigious skills.

The combination of age and dirt obscured whatever picture adorned the sign that moved stiffly in the night air, but if Bahl's memory served correctly, this was The Hood and Cape. At least it was not one of the many taverns in Tirah that liked to have his head swinging in the breeze. The tavern was dingy, but light shone merrily enough through the window, an invitation to passersby to leave the chill open air. Bahl didn't think the welcome would extend to him, but he thumbed the latch and pulled open the door anyway.

Pipe smoke tickled at his eyes as he ducked through the doorway into a large room illuminated by two fires and several oil lamps. Rough tables stood in no real order and the ground was sticky with spilt beer and mud. A short bar opposite the door was manned by a drowsy man who had a paunch fitting to a barkeep and a scowl for the new arrival.

A man of about fifty summers sitting by the fire was apparently the centre of attention in the room. Rather dirty, with unkempt hair and his right leg resting on a stool, he was obviously in the middle of regaling his audience with a story, something about an encounter on the road to the Circle City. The tall white-eye kept his head bowed as he crossed over to the bar. He picked up the tankard of beer that was placed wordlessly before him and dropped a silver coin in return. The barkeep frowned at the coin for a moment, then swept it up and went in search of change.

Bahl hunched down over the bar, leaning heavily on his elbows to make his great height less obvious and facing away from the focus of the room. When the barkeep returned with his change, a motley collection of copper pieces, Bahl gave the man a nod and found a bench on the furthest side of the room from the storyteller. There he could sit and listen in peace.

Bahl almost laughed at himself. Here he was, sitting and sipping at his beer—surprisingly good for such an establishment—but what *was* he doing? Sitting alone in a tavern in one of the city's less salubrious districts, scarcely half an hour's walk from his palace—perhaps he'd finally gone mad? Then he heard his own name mentioned by the storyteller, and Aracnan's, and every nerve in his body came alive. He'd not been paying the man much attention, so all he caught was that Aracnan had demanded to speak to the teller's son. Now why would that be?

He sipped the beer, no longer tasting it. There was something in the air that disquieted him: first the seeker, following his death to Tirah, then the casual mention of Aracnan. Bahl could almost see a thread weaving its way through the streets, snagging on his shoulder and drawing him into its web. It was a string of unlikely or inexplicable events . . . some agency was at work here.

The man holding court claimed that he had seen the mercenary slipping into the palace when he had been a member of the cavalry there. Then, with a self-important ring to his voice, he added that he had been told to forget the whole incident by the Chief Steward himself when he raised the matter with him.

Bahl wrinkled his nose, unconvinced. He doubted even the most alert guard could notice Aracnan's passage if Aracnan didn't wish to be seen, and his Chief Steward tended to threaten his subordinates in a more direct fashion. It was strange to hear the storyteller use Aracnan's name, though: Bahl had been acquainted with Aracnan for more than a hundred years, yet he knew almost nothing about the man. Even the rumour that Aracnan had been the one to teach Kasi Farlan, the first white-eye and last of King Veriole's line, how to use a sword was unconfirmed. That was before the Great War, seven thousand years ago. Bahl could believe it. Immortals kept their secrets close, and no mortal had eyes like Aracnan's.

The little Bahl had picked up about this current story was enough for him to want to meet the boy Aracnan had apparently wanted to talk to. Aracnan had his own agenda, but sometimes he was commanded by the Gods themselves; whatever his purpose, it was always worth investigating his actions.

An old man sitting by the fireside coughed obviously. Bahl guessed he was the usual storyteller in this tavern and had not taken kindly to some dirty wagoner taking centre stage. A love of stories and mysteries was at the heart of Farlan culture: a Farlan liked nothing so much as to tell all manner of grand tales, washed down with a drink or four. It was a poor tavern indeed that couldn't afford a resident storyteller to entertain the customers.

The elderly man smoothed his beard and shuffled in his seat as he played his audience. Bahl smiled inwardly; Aracnan's *greatest* feats were known to only a handful of people, and there might well be even greater exploits that had gone completely unnoticed by history.

"Aracnan is as mysterious as the Gods themselves," the old man began, his voice pitched low to make his audience listen the more closely. "Some say he fought at the Last Battle. Perhaps he is one of the cursed Vukotic family."

He paused, allowing a mutter to pass around the room as men frowned and gestured and murmured incantations under their breath, invoking protections against the cursed. *Superstitious fools*, Bahl thought to himself, *only daemons are attracted by speaking their name.*

The old man cleared his throat again, regaining his audience's attention. "Maybe he's a daemon that wanders the Land. Nothing is known for sure, except that he appears without warning, often just before a battle. He commands his own fee and takes no argument. Do you remember the late Duke Helrect?"

"The one who killed his wife and became a monk?" asked one of the more vocal listeners.

The storyteller nodded gravely. "He did become a monk, but I heard from the Captain of the Guard there a darker tale. It was rumoured that his wife was a sorceress who consorted with daemons and wanted to enslave the city. The duke's mage tried to denounce her, but she struck him down before he could reach the palace."

Bahl grimaced at that. The woman had been ambitious, true enough, but hardly a creature of evil. The mage had been more than a match for her mean abilities, just not impervious to arrows. He said nothing. Stories had a life of their own. Sometimes in a land of magic there were forces that changed even truth. He turned his attention back to the old man, who was imbuing the story with high emotion now.

"Then she barricaded herself in her tower, and any man who neared it fell dead. The captain told me that he was taking counsel with the duke when, despite the locked doors, a daemon appeared in the chamber—to kill them all, or so they thought. The daemon named himself Aracnan and said he had been sent to their aid. He told the duke to enter the tower at first light—and then he was gone. The duke broke down the tower doors at dawn and found his wife, torn into a thousand pieces, and all of those pieces scattered over the room."

The storyteller paused with a theatrical shudder. "The duke went to offer thanks at the Temple of Death and was told by the priests that the price of their master's aid was that he must renounce his title and become a monk."

He turned back to the wagoner and addressed him directly: "You're

wrong. Aracnan doesn't work as an agent of Bahl; he is older and more powerful than even our Lord. It's said that he is a messenger of the Gods. You
should have sent the boy with him, rather than cross him."

The wagoner belched his opinion of the storyteller. "Perhaps, but I don't
believe that my son has any destiny except to cause me trouble and carry cloth
for the rest of his life. He's no good for anything else, that's for sure—can't
take orders that don't come with a whip, so not even the Swordmasters will
want him. At least the scroll your daemon wanted to give the boy will fetch a
few coins, though less than he has cost me over the years, more's the pity."

"I still say he wanted nothing good with that boy," a voice broke in. Bahl
turned to look towards the new speaker, but kept from meeting his gaze. The
man wore white on his collar and Bahl had no wish to be recognised yet.

"Carel, Nyphal is not watching over the boy, so keep your fool mouth
shut," replied the wagoner. Bahl assumed they were good friends for no one
spoke to a former guardsman like that, no matter how silver his hair might
be, unless they were close.

"What did the scroll say?" someone called out.

"Can't open the damn thing. Carel here reckons it's magical, that only
the boy can read it, but the lanky bastard won't touch it. There are some symbols on the outside, but what they mean, Death only knows." He belched
again and sat back as he felt the beer rising in his throat, then wiped his
cracked lips while looking expectantly at the crowd.

After a few moments Bahl signalled the bartender to give him another.
"And what price for the scroll?" he enquired. This way was worth trying first.

"To you? More than you could afford. I have enough trouble with my
son; the thought of having to deal with another white-eye makes me more
than thirsty." The man glanced over to his friend, the former Ghost, and Bahl
saw he was flanked by four armed men, no doubt wagon train guards.

A bulky mercenary sitting off to the left chuckled, and eyed Bahl's fine
armour with the smile of a thief. With a nod to his companions he stood. His
thick jaw marked him a half-breed: Farlan mixed with one of the nomadic
peoples, maybe. The Farlan were an elitist people, but even those regarded as
inferior stock could look down on a white-eye.

"Perhaps you should buy us all drinks, white-eye. Or donate those fine
gold rings at your waist. Very exclusive tavern this is; not just anyone drinks
here—not unless they're stupid, or willing to pay for us all."

Bahl looked down and realised his cloak was open enough to show the
dragon-belt at his waist. Four thick gold rings hung from it, worth far more

than their weight. The man couldn't take his eyes off them; his stubby fingers stroked the hilt of his dagger. Before anyone could blink, Bahl had drawn his broadsword and levelled it at the man's throat. Crackling threads of light danced up and down the five-foot-long blade before fading to nothing around Bahl's glove.

The mercenary looked deep into Bahl's colourless eyes and utter panic showed on his face. A bolt of lightning leapt from the blade and the mercenary spun in the air as it threw him backwards. He hit the edge of a table and crashed down on the floor. Sparks and tongues of flame danced around the room so ferociously that even the fires and lamps shrank back in fear.

No one else moved. They all averted their eyes, desperate not to be the next to attract Bahl's attention. Bahl's free hand bunched into a fist, and he sought to compose himself. Tonight more than ever, his rage was close to the surface; it felt like a red mist of violence lurking at the edges of his vision. He drove it back down, and as he calmed himself he noticed how the new odours of burnt flesh and urine cut through the air.

"I will take the scroll now."

The cowering wagoner scrabbled it out of his bag, dropped it, picked it up again, and gave it to Bahl, retreating hurriedly back to his seat. The giant looked at the scroll in silence, a puzzled expression on his face, and then passed his hand over it, muttering wordlessly.

"Lord Bahl," said a voice. Bahl turned to see the Ghost—Carel?—down on one knee, eyes on the ground.

"My Lord, I would swear on the name of the Palace Guard that Aracnan meant to kill the youth. It was the sight of Nyphal that held him back."

Bahl nodded, to himself more than anyone else. It was true only the youth would have been able to open the scroll, and probably fortunate that his instincts had stopped him, though it wasn't intended to kill. He tucked it into his belt. The College of Magic would no doubt enjoy prising its secrets apart.

"Bring the boy to the palace. I will take him off your hands." The offer surprised him as much as the wagoner. *What do I do with him?* he wondered in the privacy of his own mind. *Was Aracnan pursuing a mission of the Gods here, or some private enterprise of his own? Either was possible.*

Abruptly Bahl froze, like a dog catching a scent on the wind. The tavern and its occupants faded from his awareness and instead he felt the city around him, stone houses and damp streets and gutters clogged with rubbish, and a mind like his own. Aracnan.

He sheathed his broadsword and made for the door. As he pulled it open, the sensation grew stronger. Aracnan was on a rooftop ahead, masked by shadows. Somehow he'd been able to conceal himself from Bahl until now, perhaps just to prove he was more skilled in magic than Bahl would ever be.

The Duke of Tirah stepped out and pulled the door closed behind him. He took a moment to check for curious faces, then, when he was certain he was alone, he walked left to an alley until he was out of sight of the tavern. Then he waited.

"Surprised, my Lord?"

Bahl hadn't even seen the mercenary cross the rooftops to reach him. It was disconcerting that Aracnan could get around him so easily.

"Impressed. But also curious. You've never needed to hide yourself in Tirah before."

"Times, it seems, are changing. Someone doesn't want me in this city, so I shall be brief. It was hard enough to find you without inviting another attack."

"Attack?"

"That is my problem. Your beloved city is safe. What I came to tell you is that the boy is to be your Krann. I was told to bring him to the palace, but he would not come."

"My Krann . . . So that's what the Siblis had sensed; they were following the call of his gifts. And the tavern, did you encourage me to go there?"

"I did, but only gently. You'd have noticed if I'd had any ill intent towards you."

Bahl paused, about to speak, then shrugged and returned to more important matters. "The boy refused? How is that possible?"

"With this one there'll be no simple answers. The boy's trouble, but now he is *your* trouble. Take care, my Lord. The Land has not been so dangerous a place since the Great War."

Isak stumbled on down the street, stubbing his toe on the cobbles, but there was no chance of a rest. He'd been drifting off to sleep in the warmth of the stables, soothed by the comfortable sighing of horses, when the door had burst open and his father appeared, his face contorted into a mask of terror and rage.

"You've done it now," Horman screamed, "and you'll get what's coming to you, white-eye bastard! Soon I'll be rid of all your trouble at last. You're going to the palace, and I hope you rot there!"

Before Isak had been able to say a word, a mob of drunken men had set upon him with drink-fuelled passion, and with so many of them, there had been no chance of fighting back. Instead, Isak took a deep breath and forced his way out through them, then took to his heels and ran, not caring where he was headed. The cobbles were painful against his bare feet so he turned into the nearest alley and hopped the fence at the end, picking a direction at random. His mind was racing: *what had he done now?* There had been real intent in the punches he'd received; they were going to kill him if they caught him.

Isak had to escape—or find a patrol—so he headed for where most of the towers were situated, where the rich folk must live. There'd be guards there, surely. Soon he found himself on the long avenue leading up to the palace. The moons escaped the clouds for a moment and shone down onto the smooth walls and the Tower of Semar, which loomed out from behind them. They lit a path for Isak to follow, but instead he just stood and gaped at the sight; he was still standing there when the leaders of the pack caught up.

Before Isak had fully grasped what was happening a fist flew into his stomach and drove the wind from him. As he doubled over, that blow was followed by a knee to the groin. Thin hands gripped his shoulders, and Isak saw a man's ratlike features for a split second before they smashed into his face, then he crashed to the ground. A hot sharp burst flowered in his side as he was kicked and spun onto his back. Now the rest of the gang had caught them up, but they silently kept their distance from the fight.

As Isak blinked back the pain he saw the drizzling rain glint in the moonlight as it fell around him. With an effort, he forced himself to his knees, his eyes fixed on the hatred blazing out of the face of the man who'd hit him. The man drew a knife from his belt, ignoring a cry behind him, and as Isak struggled to stand, his attacker lunged forward, a hungry smile on his lips.

Isak heard someone—Carel, maybe?—shout out a warning, but his eyes were fixed on his attacker. He managed to bring his left hand up, grasping the hilt and stopping the dagger from sinking into his throat. Pain screamed up his arm and into his shoulder as the edge sliced his palm, but he kept his grip for long enough to be able to grab at the man's wrist with his other hand, then pulled his stunned assailant close and buried his teeth into the man's hand.

The assailant screamed and dropped the knife, which clattered onto the cobbles and was immediately forgotten. He swung desperately at Isak, who released his bite, gave the man a bloody grin, and threw him against the wall of a house behind him. The man was reaching for another weapon, but this time it didn't matter: Isak held back his blow until the man had just got a finger round the hilt of the second blade, and then he lashed forward with both palms to smash into the man's throat with a sickening crunch. As the man twitched and went limp, the only sound was Isak's breathing, ragged with pain and wrath.

The broken figure slid slowly down the wall and crumpled in a corner like a doll. Isak stared down at the man, then at his hands. The rain was running red trails down the fingers of his left hand; the other was washed clean as he watched. Then, a little belatedly, he remembered the rest of the gang behind him and took off down the street. As Isak started to run again, the pack stirred into action and followed after him, baying for blood.

Carts and stands that by day were overflowing with produce and wares of all kinds now stood empty and dripping: the Palace Walk Market was the largest in this part of the city, but tonight it was dead, offering the injured youth no hope of sanctuary. The only light came from the palace up ahead.

The richer parts of the city cowered in the shadow of the fortress walls that surrounded the peak of the hill. Guard towers dotted the length of the massive wall, but in a city famed for its spires it was the Tower of Semar that stood out. It rose up and up, impossibly high, a myth come to life, but myth or not, that was where Isak was headed.

"You're certain?"

"Yes, my Lord." The soldier remained on one knee, sounding anything but certain, as though scarcely able to believe what he was telling his lord. "My Lord, I'm quite sure it was Ilit. I was on the wall and I saw him appear as Chief Steward Lesarl was crossing from the barbican to the hall. They spoke, and then the Chief Steward showed him to the side door that leads to the tower stairs."

"What was he carrying?"

"How did—?" His voice trailed off. You didn't question the Master. "He had something in a sack, something bulky, and what looked like a sword."

Bahl sighed. There could be no doubt now. Isak really had been Chosen by Nartis as Krann, the God-appointed heir to Lord Bahl and future Lord of the Farlan. White-eyes could only have children with their own kind, and female white-eyes were incredibly rare, so their patron God chose a successor rather than wait for acceptable progeny. The Gods would send gifts to place their Chosen above the rest of humankind, bestowing priceless weapons or talismans, tools to keep the tribe strong and safe.

It wasn't unheard of for Ilit, the Messenger God, to bring the gifts, but it was far from common. It was a portent Bahl didn't care for, especially when that God had gone to the steward of the Palace rather than its lord. Bahl heard Aracnan's words echo in his mind: *This boy is trouble.*

They had headed towards the tower. Whatever the gifts were, it had obviously been deemed necessary to leave them in safer hands than his. The old lord sighed. He'd had enough surprises tonight, and the boy hadn't even arrived yet.

CHAPTER 3

THE JUTTING BARBICAN TOWERS loomed large as Isak rounded the fountain in Barbican Square. He slipped on the rain-slicked cobbles, flopping down like a sodden rag. The jolt drove the wind from his lungs and pain flared in his bruised ribs. He rolled on to his back and stared up at the gloom of the night sky, blinking away the fat raindrops that fell into his eyes. A groan escaped his lips as he forced his head up, but then he saw the pack behind him, closing fast.

Get up, you fool, fight the pain and run. The thought spurred him into action, forcing him up from the ground. He had only forty yards to go, so he lowered his head and sprinted for the drawbridge. Mercifully, it was down and he muttered a quick prayer of thanks to Nartis as he flew across. The light from the arrow-slit windows illuminated the rain that prickled the surface of the black moat water. In his desperation Isak had thought only to get into the protective lee of the gate towers; now he slammed into the iron-bound gates and rebounded, scrabbling fruitlessly for a way to get inside.

He brushed his sodden hair back from his forehead and wiped away the mixture of rain, blood, and dirt to clear his eyes. As the downpour worsened, Isak looked up to the heavens, not praying to Nartis this time, just with a look of beaten accusation as his pursuers arrived.

The youth curled into a ball, bloody hands shielding his head as the men laid into him. Triumphant grunts accompanied each blow. One kick rolled him on his back and he couldn't stop his eyes flickering open for a moment. He glimpsed the face above him, distorted and robbed of humanity and suddenly the face disappeared, thrown sideways as the beating abruptly ended. Isak twitched, tense in expectation of the next blow, but it never came. Carefully, he looked up to see his attackers standing sullen, red-eyed with unspent anger. One was picking himself up from the floor, unhurt, but obviously bewildered.

Now Isak could see that two palace guards had taken up position on either side of him, hands resting on the pommels of their long swords. Their black armour, over which was draped the stark white livery of their Lord, looked fearsome in the half-light. They were dressed for battle, with helms covering their faces. Isak looked to his left, at a door set into the wall. A shield was propped just inside the doorway, an eagle with outstretched wings, painted black on white. Lord Bahl's coat of arms.

A gust of wind rustled along the wall, spreading a shiver through the men huddled on the drawbridge. They were wavering, about to turn and run, but then Horman arrived and stiffly forced his way to the front of the group.

"That bastard white-eye just killed a man," he shouted. "He's my son and I know the law. Step aside."

One of the Ghosts stepped forward. He said nothing as he gestured for Horman to approach. He took his hand off his sword as he reached up to remove his helm. Isak felt a surge of panic. Before the age of eighteen summers, a child remained the property of his or her parents, unless they chose to let that child become an adult earlier. Most parents gave in to their children and declared them adult at sixteen or seventeen summers, but not Horman: he had needed to do nothing to keep Isak a slave, and in the eyes of the law he was still a child. Now Isak could be hung on his father's word for the man he'd just killed.

Unhurriedly, the guard standing with Horman bent his head to pull off his helm, so deliberately that Horman almost reached out to take the helm from his outstretched hands. A single soldier's plait unfurled. The guard looked up to meet Horman's gaze with eyes as white as Isak's. Horman still had his mouth open in surprise when the guard hit him.

The other guard stepped forward, his sword rasping from its sheath. Isak's pursuers shrank away, then scurried back across the drawbridge until only Carel remained. The guard walked up to him, sword lifted, until he spotted the white collar, whereupon he nodded and stepped back. Carel returned the nod and took Horman by the shoulders to pull him to his feet. Horman was unsteady; the white-eye Ghost was Isak's height, but much bulkier, and his punch had left Horman dazed and shaking.

Touching a finger to his lip, Horman held the bloody digit up to inspect it. He shrugged Carel off and scowled at Isak. "Fine. Don't come back, ever. You're dead to me."

The words hurt more than Isak could understand: he *hated* his father. He could think of nothing to say. Horman spat on the floor and turned away, slapping down the hand Carel raised to slow him. Carel looked at Isak and shrugged.

"Remember me when you're a general, Isak," he said, then Carel too turned and walked away. Isak opened his mouth to call after him, but the words wouldn't come. After a few heartbeats, he clamped it shut. He looked down and saw the mess of blood on his hand. He felt hands underneath his shoulders, lifting him to his feet. The white-eye guard was staring at him, but Isak was too numb to react.

"Can you walk?" asked the normal guard, frowning.

Isak nodded, gingerly touching the ground with his toes before trusting his weight to them.

"Was that really your father?"

Another nod.

"Do you know why you're here?"

A shrug this time. Isak didn't look at the guard; he kept eyes on his father, swiftly disappearing into the night.

"Who told you to come?"

"No one did. They chased me from the stable, I don't know why. I thought if I could find a patrol my father wouldn't beat me to death, and here must be the best place to find a patrol."

"Did you kill the man as he said?"

Isak held up his injured hand for the man to see. "I did, but he was trying to cut my throat at the time."

"And you're sure no one sent you?"

Isak gave him a wary look. "Of course. Why do you keep asking me that? Who would have sent me here?"

The man gave up. With an exasperated click of the tongue he turned back to the guardroom and motioned for Isak to follow. His comrade stayed for another moment, his expression disconcerting as he stared into Isak's eyes. When Isak straightened up and looked back at the white-eye, a spark of belligerence flared to life in his belly. Strangely, it was the guard who shivered and looked away.

The normal guard, the smallest of the two by a good five inches, motioned again for Isak to enter the guardroom and this time the boy followed the flicker of a fire and stepped inside towards the warmth. He picked his way past two short-handled glaives propped against the wall and placed himself as close as he could to the flames. There was a small table in the middle of the room on which was a pile of rags and an empty plate. Isak fingered through the oily rags, looking for the cleanest, which he wrapped as tightly as he could around his injured hand.

The white-eye guard stepped inside and pulled the outer door closed. It was a thick piece of oak with a massive iron lock, but the door was dwarfed by the slab of granite on a simple iron runner—presumably to be used in times of siege. Once the room was secured, the man turned and examined Isak again. Isak couldn't work out if the expression was hostile or puzzled, but he decided he was too hungry or cold to much care anymore.

The other guard moved to the far end of the room where the outline of another stone slab was visible. He pulled a chain hanging through a hole in the ceiling and gave a short whistle. The sound was repeated somewhere above, and it heralded a widening of the dark crack down one side. Isak could feel the grinding of stone through his bare toes.

The guard plucked a burning torch from a holder on the wall and ducked through the growing gap. "This way," he said tersely.

Thirty yards of narrow passage took them to an iron-bound wooden door set at an awkward angle to the wall. Pushing this open, the guard stepped back to allow Isak to squeeze past. Ducking through the doorway, Isak peered into a large noisy hall, then descended the handful of worn steps. A huge blazing fire was opposite him, above which hung spitting haunches of meat attended by two young girls. The room contained a score of long tables, and some of the men—Isak guessed they were guardsmen from their austere uniforms—turned to look at the new arrivals but quickly resumed their meal. The high beams of the chamber were hung with regimental flags and drapes covered the walls, interspersed with shields, swords, and broken standards, no doubt trophies from past battles. The scents of pipe smoke, burnt fat, fresh bread, and thick stew hung tantalising in the air.

Isak craned around, peering at the hall's ornaments, recognising a handful of the emblems from his travels. They'd probably been won in the battles recorded on the wall tapestries. Though the hangings were faded and soot-stained, he was still able to make out the lines of troops and enemy formations. He turned back to the guard, who pointed at one of the servants, then stepped back inside the passage and closed the door. Isak stared after him; clearly they didn't care that he'd killed a man. It didn't make a whole lot of sense—but nothing had this evening, and Isak wasn't about to cry over spilt blood.

The servant wore the traditional Farlan costume of wide loose trousers bound down at the feet and a thick paral shirt, neatly arranged and tied at the waist with a belt the thickness of a man's hand. It looked as if he were about to leave for the temple to take up some candlelit vigil, except the man's belt was decorated with Lord Bahl's eagle rather than any divine symbol.

The servant glowered at Isak; he too said nothing, but pointed at an empty table and left, returning shortly with a bowl of steaming venison stew, a flatbread draped over the top. Isak fell upon it ravenously, eating as fast as he could in case there'd been a mistake and it was removed before he'd finished. He'd barely started to mop up the last of the gravy when the empty bowl was replaced by a second, and accompanied this time by a flagon of beer. He ate this helping more slowly, but he was a growing boy already well over six feet tall and it took a third large bowlful to satisfy him.

Finally he settled back, wiped a smear of juice from his lips, and looked around at his surroundings. It was the first chance he'd had to properly inspect the room. The tapestries, he could now confirm, were indeed scenes from famous battles, with the names of the actions woven into each picture in a variety of ways: in one it was spelled out in the shading of the trees in the background; a second was embroidered on a general's banner. Isak remembered Carel's tales of these very engagements: most featured Lord Bahl at the forefront of the action, riding a dragon or a rearing stallion, always leaving great swathes of dead in his wake.

The tapestries were displayed around the room in chronological order, as far as Isak could see. The oldest, which happened more than two hundred summers ago, was positioned behind the top table at the right-hand end of the hall; the most recent engagement was sited by the grand main door—Isak knew Carel had taken part in that one shortly after joining the Ghosts. He spent an idle few minutes looking for a figure that could have been the white-haired old man in his youth, but most of the soldiers were just blank shapes rather than people. It gave him some comfort to think that some of those soldiers had been white-eyes: at this distance they all looked the same, and they had fought together, as a team.

He smiled, thinking of Carel as a young man like himself; unsure quite what he should be doing, keeping close to the veterans, trying to absorb everything he could see while also keeping himself alive. Now he had the luxury of time to think, Isak wondered again why Carel had walked away at the palace gates—how could he just assume that Isak would be accepted here? Even Isak knew this was not how men were recruited to the Guard. What in the name of Death was going on? For that matter, what had sent his father into such a rage? Isak knew his father was quick to anger, but he'd never seen him like that, or his friends. They had been like feral dogs, worked up into a frenzy; something must have happened to make them like that. Isak felt a shiver run down his spine. Somehow he knew it was to do with that strange mercenary, Aracnan.

Now he looked around at the other men in the hall, searching for a friendly face. They were a motley collection; the handful of Ghosts were clean and neat in their uniforms, but most of the diners were forest rangers, dressed raggedly in dark woodland colours. Though their hands were clean for eating, mud still stained their clothing, and he could see a couple of dressings that looked hastily wrapped. One ranger had blood dried into his mess of hair and stained down his tunic. The rangers were all lean, tanned by sun and wind; they lacked the obvious bulk of the palace guards because their battles were not fought with armour and pikes, but with stealth and camouflage and swift arrows flashing out from the trees.

Those who bothered to look back at Isak spared the boy only a moment's disinterested gaze. Perhaps they knew why he was here, perhaps not: the only thing Isak knew was that he had much to prove before he would be accepted. No one appeared to care about the colour of his eyes—that made a change, for it made most people keep their distance. He wasn't totally ignored, though, for now the dogs roaming the hall came to greet him, licking at the mud and blood on his bare toes and sniffing up to the empty plate, but once satisfied there was no food left for them, they returned to loiter by the great open fire where they panted and stared longingly at the spitted joints of meat that perfumed the hall.

High above, at the very top of the Tower of Semar, Lord Bahl paced in his quarters as the gifts destined for his new Krann called out through the lonely night. Whatever they were, they gnawed at his mind, but Bahl was a disciplined man, one who knew well the corrupting nature of magic. He had no intention of letting magic rule him as it had Atro, the previous Lord of the Farlan.

Lord Atro had ruled the tribe for four hundred years before Bahl killed him. An evil man even before he came to the palace, he had delighted in his newly found power and had murdered, tortured, and defiled as he pleased. Raiding tombs and desecrating temples had fed his addiction for magical artefacts, and the more he loved them, the more they called to him. By the time that Bahl fought his celebrated duel with Atro, the old Lord had been barely coherent, but even so, the battle had nearly cost Bahl his life.

"My Lord, please calm yourself. The boy is down below, but he can wait.

I need you to relax, or we will lose our new Krann in a matter of minutes." Lesarl, Bahl's Chief Steward, stood at a table to one side of the room. Bahl was not one for fine surroundings: the chamber, the smallest and loneliest room at the very top of the tower, was unimpressive by anyone's standards. Bahl was content with simple but sturdy furniture—a small oak table, a pair of overfilled bookshelves, and an oversized bed that took up much of the remaining room. It was a retreat from life as much as from the opulence in the palace's public rooms below. Apart from that, all that could be said for it was that it commanded the best view of the mountains—on those days when mist didn't obscure the city.

"Why today?" He looked at his steward.

"I have no idea. A test for you?"

This elicited only a grunt, but Lesarl hadn't expected much more. He poured a glass of wine from the jug on the table and held it out to his lord until Bahl sighed and took it. With Lord Bahl in this mood he was capable of anything. Getting a jug of wine down his throat might actually help matters.

"I was wondering whether you would return tonight. You've never spent so long in the forest before today."

"I always return."

"Is it worse?"

"Always worse."

Lesarl warmed his hands in front of the fire and looked up at the only painting in the room. What was most remarkable about the painting was not the artistic detail, nor the undeniable beauty of the woman who lay beside a stream, but the contented smile on her lips, for these were the lips of a white-eye. Lesarl had never—he thanked the Gods—actually met a female white-eye, but they were known to be as selfish and aggressive as their male counterparts. All white-eyes were born with violence in their blood, and no matter how lovely, how serene she looked in this picture, this woman would have been a real danger when roused.

"Lesarl, stop staring. Your place is not to remind me of the past," Bahl growled, his hand reaching for the ring hanging from a delicate chain around his neck. Ineh, the girl in the painting, was pictured wearing that very ring. The painting and the ring were the only things Bahl had kept.

"I'm sorry, my Lord," the Chief Steward said, turning back to face Bahl. "Her face always distracts me. I swear those eyes follow me down every corridor like a nursemaid."

"A nursemaid? She should have been mother to her own children." For a moment Bahl forgot the boy and the God's gifts below and was drawn into a happier time, but the call of the present—or maybe the future—brought his attention back to Lesarl. "So, are you going to tell me what you took down there with Lord Ilit? I can feel something unusual, nothing I am familiar with. There is . . ." His words tailed off.

"Are you sure?" began Lesarl.

"Yes damn you," roared Bahl, "I think I know my own weaknesses well enough! Your place is not to lecture me."

Lesarl shrugged, hands held out in a conciliatory gesture. He could not argue with that: it was Lord Bahl's ability to turn those very weaknesses into strengths that had rebuilt the Farlan nation. "It's a suit of armour and a blade."

"And?" demanded the white-eye. "I can tell there's something more—I feel it grating at my bones."

"My knowledge is limited, my Lord, but I don't believe there can be any mistaking them. Siulents and Eolis, the weapons of Aryn Bwr, are back."

Bahl inadvertently spat out his mouthful of wine and crushed the glass to powdered crystal. Aryn Bwr: the last king. His crimes had caused his true name to be expunged from history. Aryn Bwr, first among mortals, had united the entire elven people after centuries of conflict, and the Gods had showered him with gifts—but peace was not the elven king's true motive. Aryn Bwr had forged weapons powerful beyond imagination, powerful enough to slay even Gods of the Upper Circle, and he had led his people against their makers. The Great War lasted only seven years, but the taint of the horrors committed by both sides lingered, millennia on.

"Gods, no wonder Ilit didn't come to me . . ." His voice tailed off.

"I couldn't believe it, holding Eolis in my hands . . ." Lesarl's voice was shaking too.

"Is our new Krann fortunate or cursed?" Bahl wondered.

"Who knows? The most perfect armour ever made, a blade that killed Gods—I don't think I would want them at any price. But blessed or cursed, what does it mean?"

"They will make him the focus of every power broker and madman in the entire Land. That is something I would curse few with." Bahl frowned, brushing fragments of glass into the fire.

"How many prophecies mention them?"

"Neglecting your studies, Lesarl?"

He laughed. "I cannot deny it—but in my defence I have been running the nation, so the omission is hopefully forgivable. The whole subject is beyond me, in any case. I can work with the stupidity of people, but prophecies, no, my Lord."

"It is the most complicated of sciences; it can take a lifetime to understand the rambling mess they come out with."

"So what are we to believe?"

"Nothing." Bahl laughed humourlessly. "Live your life according to prophecy? That's only for the ignorant and the desperate. All you need to know is what others believe: the cult of Shalstik, the prophecy of the Devoted, of the Flower in the Waste, of the Saviour, of the Forsaken . . . Know your enemy and anticipate his attack. With the unexpected arrival of this new Krann, the eyes of the whole Land will be upon us. The longer we can keep his gifts a secret, the better."

"Will that be possible?" Lesarl looked dubious. "When the Krann is seen without gifts, half the wizards in the city will become curious. I don't know what their daemon guides will be able to tell them, but power attracts attention. Someone will work it out, surely. The Siblis—they could sense them from who knows how far away?"

"The Siblis used magic so powerful it was killing them, I doubt anyone else will be making so great an effort. But yes, you're right: at some point someone will work it out, but any delay helps us. If the mages get there first, at least they will probably come to you for confirmation. Flatter their intelligence and wisdom, then make it clear that people will die if it becomes common knowledge that Siulents and Eolis are back in play. We'll decide how to deal with anything the priests might say some other time. For now, let's go and see whether the boy is worth all the trouble he brings."

Isak dozed at the table, his head resting on his arms, despite the constant rumble of conversation that filled the room. The bitter scent of fat drifted over from the fire and in his soporific state he licked his lips, tasting again the venison stew with which he'd filled his belly. Meat was a rare pleasure in Isak's life, for hunting rights were exclusive to those folk who paid for permission. Nomads, travellers, the poor—they could only supplement their usually meagre diet with birds shot on the wing, and that was difficult enough without the clatter of a wagon train to scare them away. It was one of the few times that Isak's natural skill and keen eye served his people well: bringing down a goose or wild duck for the communal cooking pot was one of the rare times his father ever came close to praising him.

Slowly, through his reverie, he became aware of a change in the hall. The voices had stopped. The hairs on his neck rose and a tingle of anticipation ran down his spine. He looked up to see every man in the room standing. One ranger at the next table glared at him and after a moment of panic, Isak jumped up—and found himself face to face with a thin man several inches shorter than he was, and behind him, a giant, close to a foot taller than Isak, wearing a blank blue mask.

"So, you're the new arrival," said the smaller of the two. The man's smile widened as he looked Isak up and down. Isak, feeling like a cow in a cattle market, fought to keep his calm.

"Welcome to Tirah Palace. Does my Lord have a name?"

"Ah, my name is Isak. Sir." Isak's eyes darted from one face to the other. The masked giant hadn't moved even a fraction. It was as if he were a statue, thought Isak. A memory stirred in the depths of his mind, a shape just below the surface. *Oh Gods, this is Lord Bahl.* Still the man didn't move or speak, but his eyes stared deep into Isak's own, and Isak felt as if the man gazed on his soul itself, inspecting and assessing with cold dispassion.

Isak could feel all eyes on the old white-eye; Lord Bahl possessed an aura of command that demanded the attention of everyone. It was like a blazing fire in the centre of the room; even with his back turned Isak would have felt the heat prickle on his skin. Abruptly, the man held out his hand. Isak stared at the huge fingers before him, blinking as if he'd never seen a hand before, then, shakily, he took Bahl's wrist and felt the massive hand close about his own.

"Isak. Not a name I'd have given a son of mine, but a man must make his own name in the end. I imagine the Gods will not hold your father's crude humour against you. Welcome, Isak."

"Th—thank you my Lord," was all Isak could manage. He was used to his name; he scarcely even remembered these days that Horman had named him Isak—Kasi backwards—to mock the Gods who had taken his beloved wife from him. Now, as Bahl gripped his forearm, Isak felt a sudden pressure behind his eyes. He could feel the immense presence of the Land beneath his feet, and the thump of his heart booming through his head. Then the memory of his dreams flooded back, coursing in a torrent through the contact. Isak's knees buckled under the weight, stars bursting in his vision before everything faded to black.

CHAPTER 4

H E REMEMBERED THE ISLAND, the feel of the scorching sun and chill marble . . . and the numbing terror. He remembered the chamber, the ranks of pillars supporting a bloated dome set with sparkling clusters of stars, and the sound of ringing steel and death; the shocking scarlet of blood. He remembered the dead man whose face now rose out of the shadows.

When Isak opened his eyes that same face was staring down at him, blank but unmistakable. The rest of the room was a buzzing distraction, nothing more. Obeying the burn in his throat, Isak gasped for air.

"Wha—"

"Be still," said a calm voice beside him. Isak turned his head slightly to see a middle-aged man kneeling beside him. A green patchwork cloak and battered mail marked him as a ranger. Isak tried to raise his hand, but it felt like he was moving another person's limbs rather than his own. The ranger reached out to stay him a little longer, but Isak shrugged his hand off. With an effort, he forced himself to sit upright; he still felt undignified with his legs splayed out wide, but it was better than remaining flat on the floor like a fainting maid.

"You can stand?"

Isak nodded. He refused the offer of a hand from the ranger, pulling himself carefully upright. He was still shaking a little and tried to hide it by brushing the mud from his shirt. The man with Lord Bahl had a curl of a smile on his lips. Once he judged that Isak had regained his equilibrium he stepped forward, hands held out with palms up in greeting. "I am Lesarl. I place myself at your service."

Isak hardly heard the words; he was taking a better look at Lord Bahl, the man in his dreams. Under a snowy cape the gigantic white-eye wore a misty-grey suit of armour and a broadsword strapped to his back. It was all Isak could do not to faint away again: his dreams had always been vague, obscure—perhaps for his own sanity—but he knew with terrible certainty that this was the face he'd always seen as blank and inhuman: now he knew why. Bahl's hood echoed the smooth expressionless features of statues of Nartis.

Shaking the feeling of strangeness from his head, he turned his attention to Lesarl. "Are you useful for anything?"

Despite the snorts of laughter that crept from the corners of the room, Lesarl showed not a flicker of reaction. He had dealt with wits sharper than a white-eye's before. "Your master finds tasks for me to perform from time to time. I am the Chief Steward."

His words had the desired effect. Even as cut off as the wagoners were, they all knew perfectly well that the Chief Steward ruled the Farlan nation; if Isak had not been so dazed, he might have recognised Lesarl's name in time. The Chief Steward wielded complete authority, as he saw fit, in Lord Bahl's name, but this was balanced against an untidy death if Lord Bahl ever became displeased with his conduct. He was not a man to casually insult.

Isak nodded dumbly, not knowing how to apologise for his rudeness, but Lord Bahl passed over it. "We can deal with who's who tomorrow. For now, you need sleep. You will have a room in the tower. Come." The Lord of Storms didn't wait for a response, but turned to lead the way.

Isak tried to collect his wits. The aura that surrounded the huge man was almost tangible and his physical presence was breathtaking. Isak felt as if Bahl's powers, both temporal and physical, were radiating out, enveloping all those around him. Bahl stood over seven feet tall and was bulky for a Farlan, but every step was graceful; he moved with purpose and efficiency. As Isak's head cleared, he remembered that Bahl's armour was magical—though he couldn't see any runes inscribed on its surface, he knew they would be there somewhere. Merely focusing on the misty surface of Bahl's cuirass seemed to thicken the air in his throat. Something deep inside Isak recognised that metallic taste and craved more.

Then his mind snapped back to what Lord Bahl had said. "A room in the tower? I don't understand, my Lord."

Bahl stopped in his tracks. He turned back, shoulder shifting up: an instinctive movement. Thanks to Carel's training, Isak recognised that Bahl was ready to draw and strike if need be. Isak could almost see the massive broadsword appear in front of him and for a moment he wondered if he really had, but then the image faded.

"You don't know?"

"No, my Lord. My father said nothing. I thought I was going to be hanged."

"Well then, allow me to explain," Lesarl said with sardonic smile. "We have a tradition here not to hang the new Krann when he joins the Chosen."

Isak couldn't help himself as a string of expletives poured from his mouth, provoking peals of laughter from the Ghosts and breaking the tension in the room. Bahl narrowed his eyes and Isak hurriedly composed himself, though his head was spinning in confusion. This all felt more like a practical joke than divine edict. He was cold, tired, hurting, and more than a little aware that he was making a fool of himself. He had no idea what would happen next.

"Are you an adult?" Lord Bahl asked him suddenly.

Isak shook his head mutely, suddenly afraid that whatever was going on, his father could still ruin it. Horman could have declared his son an adult at fourteen and thrown him out, but instead he had insisted Isak was still a child and condemned him to another four years of near-slavery.

"Very well. Lesarl will have your father persuaded to make you my ward. That life is behind you now. Now you are Krann of the Farlan and Suzerain Anvee. There is little to come with that title other than Anvee itself and the estate of Malaoristen, but you do hold court rank. The rest can wait. I'm sure Lesarl will have papers for you to sign, but none of that matters for now."

Isak stayed quiet, concentrating on not gawping like a dying fish as he worked the words through his head. Krann? Suzerain? That was only one step below a duke. Now he was too scared to comment, and torn between laughing at the absurdity and sinking back to the floor until life made sense again.

Everyone knew there had not been a Krann of the Farlan for two hundred years, not since Bahl himself was named heir to Lord Atro. It was something other tribes did; the Farlan had no need. His limbs trembled, as though the ground beneath him was shaking with indignation, or perhaps trepidation. Was there now a need? He'd never doubted that there was more to life than bales of cloth, but a suzerainty? A court title? And money? Dukes and suzerains were men of wealth and ancient family, people who held glittering balls for the equally wealthy and splendid—though it was true that Bahl, a white-eye and as remote as the Gods, was Duke of Tirah and foremost in all of the Farlan lands.

Now the eyes of the Ghosts grew sharper. Isak saw men who'd bled for their tribe, who'd stepped over the corpses of their friends to fight on, with no time to stop and mourn: men who must now answer to an untested youth. They could hardly be impressed with their new Krann thus far. He shuddered: he, who had never even been in a real fight, might soon be called upon to lead these battle-hardened men to war.

Bahl led Isak back down the hall to a doorway which opened into a dim corridor. It was silent apart from a brief scuffle of feet somewhere off in the distance. As the door shut behind them, the welcoming aromas of the Great Hall—food, burning logs—were replaced by scents of dust and age. Brands ran down either side of the corridor, and the flames made strange dancing shadows on the walls. Flags and drapes covered the walls, the colours muted in the flickering light.

Isak hesitated: he could almost feel the millennia radiating from the stone underneath. The place was more like a tomb than a palace. Lord Bahl moved on, ghosting along without sound, followed by his Chief Steward, who stepped carefully and quietly. Isak, watching them, thought irreverently that serving Lord Bahl so long had caused the Chief Steward to adopt some of his Lord's ways.

A stairway carved with images of the Upper Circle led up off to the left; the stretch of right-hand wall was broken by four plain doors, but Isak's eyes were drawn to a pair of ornate double doors at the far end of the corridor and he began to feel a pull, both foreboding and enticing at the same time. As he drew closer he could see the double doors were framed by a dragon made of wrought iron. Ribbed wings swept down each side almost to the floor, while its glaring beak jutted out from the wall, glaring at anyone approaching. Bahl went straight up to the door and opened it. The click of the latch broke the silence and stirred Isak into movement.

Beyond was a large circular room, a dozen yards in diameter and high enough to accommodate even the largest of white-eyes. On the walls were faintly scrawled geometric chalk markings, but a taste of magic in the air made it clear they were not simply idle scribbling.

Isak stepped towards the nearest one, narrowing his eyes to try to focus on the complex shapes and patterns of runes. A rumble from Bahl warned him against getting too close: obviously he didn't want curious fingers within reach of the writing.

As he turned away from the walls, Isak realised there was another person already in the room; a maid kneeling at Lord Bahl's feet. She stood up as Bahl passed her, heading for the centre of the room, and Isak caught a glimpse of pronounced features betraying more than a little apprehension. Then she saw Isak and dropped her head down low, apparently hiding her fear behind a fall of long, thick hair. She followed Lesarl into the black circle marked on the floor, standing as far from Bahl as she could. Holding a bundle of what looked like bedding tight to her chest, the girl stood with hunched shoulders, her eyes fixed on the floor before her. She looked as if she were braced to go out in a gale.

Isak stepped into the circle and pushed down with his foot: it wasn't stone, but something smoother and more yielding. As he focused on it, Isak suddenly found himself dizzy, and a sensation of falling rushed over his body. The more he stared, the more insubstantial the floor seemed.

"How do I go down?" he asked.

Bahl had raised a hand towards the wall where a birdlike shape was drawn. He gave a dry laugh. "Patience, young man. You're not ready for that. Down is a greater step than you might think."

"What's down there?"

"I said patience. Explanations are for the morrow."

Isak nodded this time and kept quiet.

Returning his attention to the image on the wall, Bahl began to mouth words and make gestures. A ghost of colour lingered momentarily after his hand had passed through the air, then melted away. Before Isak had time to ask another question a silent wind began to whip up from all around, tugging at clothes and the bundle carried by the maid.

Strange, shadowy shapes danced around their bodies, wings without substance tearing past Isak's face with ever-increasing speed. He flinched, but Lord Bahl stood still, as solid as a mountain. The flight of wings turned into a storm, nipping and dragging at their clothes as the platform under their feet started rising suddenly. While the girl was clearly terrified, Isak was too astonished to feel anything else. He had never shown much of the natural tendency towards magic that white-eyes were supposed to have. The handful of times when something unexplained had happened had been when he was getting a beating or having a nightmare. It was never in a form that could be controlled or predicted, and it was too rare to make his father think twice about giving him a thrashing. For the first time in Isak's life it suddenly felt as if magic might be easy and accessible.

The journey itself lasted just a few heartbeats, then the wind suddenly fell away to reveal a room six yards across. The walls of the room were only gently sloped, and Isak realised that since this room was half the diameter of the one below, they must have travelled further than it had felt. The maid, a relieved look on her face, darted on to the solid floor and went to make up the low bed.

Isak looked around the room, then followed the girl off the dark platform and onto solid flagstones. The room was unremarkable; even Isak, a wagon-brat, felt mildly disappointed at the musty air and plain furnishings. There was a battered desk with a worn leather-backed chair before it and a clothes trunk next to the bed. The fireplace was very plain. It didn't fit the decadent image he had of palace life.

"My Lord, I am reminded of another matter that you will wish to attend to immediately," announced Lesarl. "Might I suggest we retire to the top room?" Bahl turned enquiringly. The blank look on his steward's face seemed to answer his question.

He turned back to his new Krann and said, "Isak, you need to sleep more than you realise. Any questions you have can wait for later. I will wake you when it is time."

Without waiting for a reply, Bahl repeated his motions and the pair disappeared upwards in a sudden flurry. Isak found the chair behind him and sank down thankfully. The weight on his mind had drained his limbs of strength and he suddenly felt desperately tired. This wasn't what he'd imagined, but the presence of a bed was enough; anything more than a rug on the ground was luxury.

He turned to the desk, where he found a razor lying snug in a bone sheath, beside it a copper bowl, a water jug, and a polished copper and glass mirror. Leaning forward, he caught his face in the mirror, a perfect reflection that sent a shiver of excitement through his body. It had been made with magic: there was no other way to produce such a smooth surface. It might have been a paltry extravagance for a palace, but it still cheered Isak's spirits.

His eyes drifted up to the single shelf above the desk. A few dusty books lay on it, all of them looking older than he was. Carel had taught him to read, but it had always been a chore rather than a pleasure. Scanning the titles—*From across the Sea*, *The Campaigns of Manayaz Vukotic*, *Duels of Words: The Founding of the College of Magic*—Isak decided he was too tired to face any of them tonight, although the second one made him linger a moment, wondering why it was here in the first place. Manayaz Vukotic had died as the worst of traitors, for he had led his tribe against their patron God during the Great War. This act of heresy had condemned Vukotic himself to an eternity in the Dark Place, and his five children to be cursed with vampirism. Odd to have an account of his successes in the new Krann's quarters, no matter what lessons could be learned from them. Isak hadn't expected that sort of book to be readily available, even here. Perhaps it was a test of some kind, though to what end he couldn't fathom. With a sigh he looked back at the maid, this time seeing her properly. She was pretty, taller than he'd first thought, and with what looked to be a fine bosom under her thick robe.

"What's your name?" he started.

The girl gave a small shriek at the unexpected break in the silence. She stared round, looking horrified that Isak was capable of speech. Isak wondered if some of Bahl's guests were a little less than friendly to the maids when left alone with them.

The girl steadied herself, reassured perhaps by Isak's equally startled expression. She looked him over quickly, then said, "Tila, my Lord, my name is Tila Introl. I am to be your personal maid."

Isak had no idea why he needed a personal maid, but she was pretty so he had no complaints. He looked around the room for a way to open conversation, prodding absentmindedly at the bloodstained bandage around his left hand. Then the books caught his eye once more.

"Can you read?" he asked, nodding his head encouragingly towards the dusty tomes.

"Of course, my Lord. My father has an extensive library." She sounded a little surprised.

"Your family has money?" he asked, bemused at the idea that his maid was highborn. No one else could afford any sort of library.

"Yes, my Lord. My father is Anad Introl. He is Gatekeeper of the City, and a member of the city council."

"Does that mean I should have heard of him?" Isak asked.

"No, my Lord," she said with a worried expression. Isak forced a smile at her; he'd snapped because he was tired. Tila looked a little uncertain, but she returned it; Isak had always been able to elicit a smile from people, even his father sometimes, despite his unwillingness to like anything about his son. Carel said it was part of being a white-eye: after all, men had been willing to rush to their deaths at Lord Atro's command; Lord Bahl was considered withdrawn, practically a hermit, yet his presence was enough to command complete attention and obedience. Carel had told him that every white-eye he'd ever met, no matter how brutal, possessed some remarkable redeeming quality.

Isak was pretty sure he could start to put people at ease by making them laugh, so Tila's hesitant smile gave him hope. The last thing he wanted was a maid who hated white-eyes.

"It's traditional for the palace maids to come from the noble families," Tila began hesitantly. "Lord Atro initiated it as a hostage system so he could keep control of the nobility, but the tradition has continued. The rest of the palace has proper servants; we're only here in the main wing. Sometimes it feels more like a finishing school. Readying us for being married off." She looked down at the bed. "I'm sorry, my Lord. I've been chattering away; I'll finish here and get out of your way. We were all instructed to keep from wasting your time—"

"You aren't in my way," he replied quickly, "and as for wasting my time, you probably have far more idea than I do about what I'm meant to do with it. I know what a Krann is, but not what will be expected of me. Can you tell me anything?"

"No, my Lord, I'm sorry." The girl shook her head. "I was just woken to make your room ready; we weren't even told to expect you. I'm sorry it's dusty and bare in here, but Lord Bahl is the only one who can bring us up and he's been in the forest for weeks. There is a library, on the second floor; I could try to find you some lore books, I suppose. The Chief Steward will know but . . . well you don't want him to think you're in his pocket. The only other person is Lord Bahl; he was once Krann, but I wouldn't dare ask him."

"Why not—does he beat the servants?" Isak asked, on more familiar ground now.

"No, my Lord," Tila replied quickly, "Lord Bahl is good to us; he doesn't even notice us most of the time, which suits me fine. But you do hear stories—"

"What sort of stories?" he said, annoyed at his own ignorance—even the maids knew more than he did.

"Well—" she sounded a little dubious, as if unsure of how much she should say. Spreading gossip was dangerous, but if the new Krann was going to survive in the palace, he had to know.

She took a breath and started, "Stories about what he did to the last lord, to Lord Atro. I suppose it's romantic, to avenge the death of one's lover, but—"

"But?"

She looked disinclined to go further, wondering if she should even have started this conversation.

"What sort of stories?" Isak pressed her. "What happened? When?" Horman had banned all talk of white-eyes around Isak; though tales of blood and violence were a staple diet at the fireside, Isak had never been welcome. All this was completely new to him.

"Surely you must know?" she started, but as she saw him stiffen, she quickly continued, "They say that three entire streets were destroyed in the battle. It ended in Cornerstone Market and *bits* were found as far away as Myrenn Avenue. Atro was hacked apart, and they say that when they tried to gather all the pieces together to bury them, half of them were burnt."

"Is Myrenn Avenue far from the market?"

Tila gaped. "Far? It's more than two hundred paces! Two hundred paces—for pieces to fly through the air!"

"Oh that's easy, I can do that."

A look of panic flashed over her face, but Isak smiled as she started back and she realised that he had been joking. Tila gave a hiss of exasperation at her own gullibility and opened her mouth to retort when the words died. Isak's own smile faltered as he realised she had checked herself, remembering her position in relation to his: she was a maid, noble-born or not, gossiping to the new Krann rather than attending to her duties. She pushed errant strands of hair back behind her ears as she turned back to the bed and tugged the sheet flat with a practised hand.

Her tasks finished, Tila straightened her dress and then sat down on the floor facing into the dark circle there. She didn't seem to trust the magic that held it, though the platform was solid and secure. Isak looked at her, but now she kept her eyes lowered.

"Do you want to go back down again?"

She twitched at the sound of his voice, then forced herself to look at him. "How, my Lord? Lord Bahl is the only one who can take us. The Chief Steward is still up there, so no doubt he will be down soon."

"I can take you down," Isak said brightly. "I'm pretty sure I can do what he did. It didn't look that hard."

"Didn't look that hard?" Tila looked shocked. "It's magic, so what's so simple about that?"

Isak paused. When he'd entered the circle below and watched Bahl trigger the magic, it had looked simple; it had felt to him as if the tower had welcomed him with its secrets. How did you explain that without sounding like a madman? She would think he meant that the tower had spoken to him, but it wasn't that it was alive, not at all, just that he thought it was able to recognise someone like him. Isak hadn't felt as though he had been Chosen until the magic of the tower had treated him as such. He'd bluster the rest for a pretty face.

"If you don't know anything about magic, then I can't really explain it to you."

"Well, I suppose you are a white-eye. 'Pretty sure'—what exactly does that mean?" She still sounded unconvinced.

"Well, if it doesn't work we'll fall hundreds of feet and die—but I really think I know how to do it. Don't worry," he added, with what sounded like entirely too much enthusiasm for her liking. Grabbing her arm he pulled her up and into the centre of the room. Tila yelped and tugged away, but Isak was so intent on what he was doing he didn't even notice her efforts.

Closing his eyes, Isak visualised himself standing alone in the tower. As the dry scent of the air receded from his awareness, he felt only the warm presence of Tila's arm under his fingers. As he tried to focus, the warmth slid down his fingers until the tips became hot. Tila flinched slightly as he let go of her arm, but she had the sense to keep quiet rather than break his concentration. Then her presence faded from his awareness and he was left disembodied and alone.

An image of the symbol drawn in the room below appeared in his mind. He felt the cylindrical tower, so still and strong about him, the air motionless on his skin while the wind outside tore upwards past windows and beyond the conical peak that pierced the clouds. The symbol flexed gently as he focused on it, the outstretched wings flickering as the wind felt its call.

Isak chanced a breath. Now he could see how to release the wind, to channel it through the symbol and into the chimney. He was sure he could control it, but he wanted to enjoy the sensation for a while first. The magic he'd sensed vaguely over the last few years was suddenly within reach and under his control; it set every nerve ending aflame and made him want to laugh with delight. Finally he reached out to the symbol and gently took hold of it. At his touch, the symbol quivered, trembling as it held back the eager wind. He clasped it for a moment as an understanding of the magic in it poured into him, then he opened it, and a broad grin appeared on his lips as the first feathers flashed around his chest and down his spine.

Then the air burst into life. Even with his eyes closed, Isak could feel the shadows dancing past, running questing fingers over his face and head. Tila moved closer to him, hiding in the lee of his large frame as the wind played through her hair and tugged at her clothes. The air grew dense, pressing the two of them together as the wind rushed and raged.

With his eyes closed, Isak could feel their swift movement down until, with a jolt, they arrived at the bottom and the wind melted away to nothing. When Tila dared to look up, there was only the gloom of the lower chamber and the now-still chalk markings on the wall.

Isak turned to look at her—suddenly aware of the closeness of her body from when she'd instinctively leaned towards him—but as he did so Tila took a smart step away and busied herself tidying her hair. Bobbing low in a curtsey she backed towards the door. "Thank you, my Lord."

"Will you come to see me again?" As the words left his mouth Isak cursed himself for sounding stupid. There was something about her he found comforting—even when her pretty face was clenched in a mask of fear, it felt more welcoming than the blank looks that had greeted him in the dining hall.

"Of course, my Lord. I am *your* personal maid," she said. "Your chambers and meals will be my responsibility." At last she met his eyes, and this time she looked at him as if he were human, not just some damn white-eye, which pleased him.

"Oh. Well, good," he said, finding his voice again. "But that's not what I meant. I meant to talk. I don't know anyone here, or what in Nartis's name I should be doing. Put me in the middle of a forest and I can survive, but this place is beyond me. I was never taught much in the way of history, or etiquette."

"Of course, my Lord," Tila repeated, this time with sympathy on her face. "I shall await you here tomorrow morning to fetch you to your breakfast. Lord Bahl would probably prefer you to eat in the Great Hall, with the Ghosts, but if you need me before, just send someone to find me, Tila Introl, as I'm sure my Lord remembers."

"Yes, of course, Tila Introl, daughter of the Gatekeeper. I, of course, am Isak—just Isak. My family name is Fershin, but like Lord Bahl I was never considered worthy of it."

Tila opened her mouth, no doubt to apologise, as most people instinctively did at hearing that, before closing it again—much to Isak's relief. The last thing he wanted was her pity.

"But if what Lord Bahl told me is really true, I suppose my name is Suzerain Anvee now—but let's stick with Isak, shall we?" He smiled at the notion and saw relief on her face as she curtsied and scurried away back to her bed.

As soon as the door shut behind her, whatever he could sense under his feet forced itself into his thoughts and drove all else away. His gaze drifted down to the circle he was standing on. The urge to let his eyelids drift shut grew overpowering as the winged symbol appeared in his mind. As he reached for it, Isak felt a presence beside him. Alarmed, he opened his eyes, but saw nothing until he looked up and realisation dawned at last. He closed his eyes and felt himself in the still tower with the wind rushing all about, but this time he was not alone: there was another with him, one who drew the wind to himself.

Don't you think you've gone far enough tonight? Bahl's voice in his head felt strangely natural, and Isak smiled and nodded, as if the Lord could see him. Maybe he could. There was an edge to the voice which urged caution: down was obviously as large a step as Bahl had said it was. Whatever was calling him from down there wasn't alone.

Isak's curiosity was piqued, but he could tell there was no hurry. There was a taste of envy in the tower now—whatever was waiting for Isak would not accept Lord Bahl, and the man knew it.

Sleep now. Tomorrow will bring challenges enough without the need for you to chase more.

CHAPTER 5

BAHL GAVE A GRUNT OF APPROVAL, satisfied that this time Isak would do as he was told. He withdrew his hand from the central chimney and turned back to Lesarl, who wore a questioning look.

"He has some skills; the tower accepted his command immediately."

"That's to be expected, no?"

"I'm not sure. This boy is odd; he reacts to magic as if it is the first time he's seeing it—much like I did when I first came here. But he worked the tower with a practised hand."

"Well, he is younger. You were a member of the Guard for how many years before you were Chosen, twelve? Perhaps your skills developed over that time because you were here, but the Krann's remained latent because he grew up on a wagon train?"

Bahl didn't reply. From the mantelpiece he picked up a plain wooden pipe, black and scarred from years of use, lit it, and settled into a solid armchair by the fire.

"What do you make of him?"

Lesarl sighed. "By himself, a country boy who'd be a good guardsman and has enough brains to become an officer. He's quiet, which is good; more often than not the loud ones turn out to be maniacs. With those gifts, I have to assume there is more, but I simply cannot read the boy."

"There *is* more to him, I'm certain. There's a wildness in his eyes that I find rather worrying, and yet . . ." Bahl's voice drifted away, to be replaced by the crackle of the fire. His stared into the flames, like a man looking for signs and portents, and said quietly, "I saw Aracnan tonight."

Lesarl gave a start. He had not been expecting that. "Aracnan? The walker-in-shadows? Was he after the boy?"

"No. Aracnan does more than just kill. He had been sent to bring Isak here and present him, like the Tyrant of Mustet did for me."

"I thought such missions were only given to mortals, expendable ones too, considering what happened to the Tyrant afterwards." Lesarl frowned in frustration. Without any unnatural skills himself, the Chief Steward would never fully understand that side of the Land.

"More commonly, but not always. Aracnan has frequently been asked to perform tasks by the Gods. It's said that he can hear Death's call wherever he is, that there's some connection between them."

"And no one has ever tried to find out what? Or have none survived to tell the truth?"

"That's not for me to say. I doubt even a mage's daemon companion would dare tell. A powerful mage might live as long as I do, but Aracnan is immortal, and thus of greater consequence. He is not a good enemy to make, and he likes his secrets."

"Ah, daemon companions, what I could do with one of those—" Bahl's expression cut that sentence off, but the wistful look on Lesarl's face remained as he continued, "Oh I know it would be heretical, but mages claim necessity and the priests turn a blind eye. Just think of what my spies could do with—"

"Enough. You've already asked the Archmage about special training for some of his students. Yes, he came to me with that one, outraged at your lack of ethics."

"That treacherous old goat, I'll—"

"You'll take the warning like the good servant that you are," Bahl snapped. "I don't remember you suggesting it to me, so let the matter slide. I want the College of Magic close to me and back under our complete control. Now, didn't you have some news for me?"

Lesarl's face brightened as he remembered and he pulled a battered sheaf of parchment from inside his jacket. "The reason I actually went to see the Archmage was that he wanted to give me the deciphered copy of Malich's journals at long last. He wasn't happy about it at all. He still thinks that all magic-related research should remain in the restricted libraries until he and his colleagues see fit. He insisted I collect this in person."

"So they did contain Malich's research? How did you convince him to release them?" Bahl sounded a little impressed at his Chief Steward's powers of persuasion.

"Because they did indeed contain the research; and because it was principally necromancy, your religious status has legal primacy." Lesarl gave a satisfied grin. "I'm sure that with a little prodding I could also have extracted a message of thanks to you for letting them do the translation in the first place."

"Despite the fact it would have taken much longer to find anyone else capable?"

"Well, yes, but he appreciated my point all the same. Anyway, in between bouts of paranoid ranting that greatly flattered the abilities of my spies, Malich focused mainly on one of Verliq's conjectures to develop his rituals that followed a progression of—"

"What was the conjecture?" The burr of Eolis and Siulents down below was wearing Bahl's patience thin.

Lesarl thumbed through the pages of parchment hurriedly. "Here we are: this is what the Archmage wrote as a quick explanation for me: "A Crystal Skull—being created specifically to counteract the magic of the Gods in general, and Death in particular—cannot return a soul from the land of no time. Experiments have proved that souls do not retain sufficient integrity when removed from the physical world. However, in the state in between the realms, ghosts and wraiths should preserve enough of their self to be returned to life if a suitable vessel is found."

"Malich did not record the actual ritual he claimed to have devised, but the College council believe they could recreate it from his various allusions; not that they would dare do so, of course. There were a number of additional factors: performing the ritual when the Gods stepped back from the Land, during twilight or on Silvernight, as well as the sacrifice of life according to some sort of covenant—"

"The Law of Covenant," supplied Bahl absentmindedly, "the most fundamental principle in magic."

"Yes, that's it. Anyway, this all requires the channelling of vast amounts of energies through the Skull."

"Strange that he would devote his life to something he could never expect to test."

"That is why I doubt much of what was written. Advancing the theory of necromancy is an odd obsession for a man wanting to achieve immortality. What use this would be to him I have no idea; neither he nor that Menin apprentice could have helped their cause by it. This concerns long-departed souls, not the recently dead that he used as soldiers, and who of note could they return to life? Malich does claim that he returned a childhood friend once; that he managed to obtain a Skull for a brief while—"

"Hah!" said Bahl, with a snort of derision. "I think we might have noticed that when we took the castle. "I doubt I would have survived a fight against a necromancer of his skill if he held a Crystal Skull. Did he enlighten us as to which Skull?"

"Surprisingly, yes; he claimed it was the Skull known as Knowledge."

Bahl laughed. "Not only was the man a liar, he was a bad one at that. Knowledge was destroyed almost seven thousand years ago. Malich's mind must have been more rotted that we thought; the owner destroyed Knowledge in his madness after the Last Battle. If he hadn't, it would have resurfaced constantly over the years since, as those that did survive have done."

"Exactly, my Lord. It makes Malich's claims as ridiculous as his influence is dangerous. He's caused us enough problems; the Azaer daemon-cult he championed has spread heresy throughout the tribe. Now that he's dead, can we not just erase any possible legacy?"

"Bring me everything the mages have first. I want to read these theories of his in greater detail."

"My Lord?" The Chief Steward looked surprised. "I wrote the summary myself so no one else would read this material. The evil Malich wrought has been corrosive enough. Even the wizards themselves took no chances; that's why they divided the work between twenty of them. Necromancy will bring damnation to anyone, even to you, my Lord. And Nartis has every reason to hate the Skulls after the death of his brother Veren—"

Bahl half-rose from his seat, sparks of anger flashing from his white eyes. "Do not presume to lecture me on theology! The prattling of priests and the chatter of old wives do not concern me."

Lesarl froze for a moment, then dropped to one knee. Grim-faced, he bowed his head in apology. "Forgive me, my Lord, I forgot my place. Of course you know better than I do." After all these years he should be used to Bahl's outbursts, but they were unpredictable and alarming and could still sometimes catch him off-guard.

Bahl felt a second surge of anger at Lesarl's accusatory expression, but he made it subside. His Chief Steward was correct. *Damn you, Lesarl; I do know how dangerous a course I'm taking. I don't need you to remind me of that, but you aren't the one tormented by dreams of the dead.* Uncomfortable silence reigned for a dozen heartbeats before Bahl eased back into his seat.

Lesarl took that as his cue to rise again. He had served Bahl for most of his life and had long since learned to bear the old lord's fluctuating mood. There was a longer pause until he spoke again.

"There was, my Lord, one other point of interest. Malich's Menin apprentice added a footnote which stated that his master had mentioned a Skull being located in the palace on the White Isle. It had been during one of the many fits that the man must have been suffering by then. Malich would not have been capable of writing for long periods, according to the Archmage;

the journals are frequently in his apprentice's handwriting. He mentions preparations for a journey, but no destination, so we cannot be sure. My opinion would be that it is merely babble; a madman's raving, but—"

"But it's hard to be sure," Bahl finished. "There are ways to find out such information if you're willing to pay the price. He was in league with several daemon-princes, after all. The elves of the forest? Perhaps they hoped Malich could be made to get it for them. The White Isle is certainly somewhere no elf would dare venture, but a man might survive, and Malich's ascendance did their position no damage at all."

"Lord, would it be presumptive to ask what you propose to use the Skull for?" asked Lesarl, his voice wavering a little.

"Yes, it would. Be content that it is my will. Do whatever you must." Bahl's face softened a little. "Lesarl, I know you must ask those questions that no one else would dare, but do not press me any further on this."

Bahl thought back to Cordein Malich's beginning: he had been a student of astonishing promise when he arrived at the gates of the College of Magic; talented enough that the conceited mages in Tirah had not questioned why he had travelled all the way from Embere to enrol. After Malich's second summer there, his behaviour had grown increasingly erratic. A number of bizarre accidents befell several people on his growing list of enemies. The Archmage of the day had been on the point of throwing Malich out—despite his remarkable talent—because of the unhealthy influence he held over the other students, when Malich suddenly disappeared, together with a number of forbidden works from the restricted library.

Some decades later, Bahl only just managed to prevent all-out civil war when, during a preemptive attack on Malich's fortress deep in the forest, he had succeeded in killing the necromancer.

What they found there had sickened even the white-eyes of the Guard, and resulted in more than a hundred Farlan nobles and mages being condemned to death for treason and heresy. Before the castle was burnt to the ground, Bahl had removed Malich's entire library. Some of the works were carefully and totally destroyed; some were spirited away to be studied secretly, and at length.

He'd waited a long time for these journals to be translated. He pressed Lesarl again. "And there's no clue in Malich's journal about where on the White Isle the Skull is kept? I hate to think how long it would take to walk every corridor of the palace there."

Lesarl scratched his chin, clearly unwilling to encourage Bahl in any way, but he knew better than to lie. "It does say that the Skull is watched over by the first among men. It's a reasonable assumption that this means Kasi Farlan, but there is no guarantee. How much help that is, I don't know. The palace covers much of the entire island, doesn't it?"

Bahl nodded. He drew on his pipe, frowning when he realised it had gone out, then discarded it on a table. In that moment he looked suddenly old. With his shoulders hunched and his gaze distant, Lesarl thought his Lord resembled his own father who, in his later years, had been haunted by all he'd seen in Bahl's service.

The Chief Steward shivered at the image and cleared his throat noisily to dispel it. "I do have one last piece of news, something I had not intended to bother you with until, well—" He coughed nervously. "It seems that Duke Nemarse, the ruler of Raland, has been doing a little plundering on the quiet. He discovered some tombs near his southern border. My agent discovered a soldier who had been involved in the excavation; apparently he believed he was not sufficiently compensated for committing sacrilege, and declared as much to the whole tavern. One of the things he mentioned was a skull as clear as glass—not much to look at, he said, but the duke made a point of personally collecting it from the man who'd brought it out."

"And where is this man now?"

"He seems to have disappeared, my Lord. My agent is looking for him now. But, there remains the possibility that Duke Nemarse actually possesses a Crystal Skull. Raland would be easier to search than the White Isle, and certainly safer."

Bahl nodded. The Palace of the White Isle was vast and otherworldly; Raland was indeed a far easier target. Duke Nemarse was a fool and a coward; every mercenary captain he'd employed had either left within the year or attempted a coup. The only thing that kept the duke in power was a series of expensive commissions to the city's assassins.

"Send one of your more direct agents to track this soldier down and do whatever is necessary. I want to know every detail of the duke's activities, and stop this rumour going any further."

"The agent in question should be eminently suitable: she has the mouth and manners of a cavalryman, according to the temple-mistress, but her 'special talents' are described as 'proficient.' Her standing orders mean she should already be on her way home with the deed done."

"Ah, one of those." Bahl smiled.

In the city of Helrect, halfway between Tirah and Raland, Chief Steward Lesarl's agent squinted down at the cup before her. It was a public holiday there; anyone not inebriated at this hour was either well on the way towards it or, quite possibly, dead because of it. Legana had seen examples of all of those when she had travelled through the city streets a few hours earlier, hurrying through the twilight to reach the inn before the day faded completely. Even for a woman of her skills, Helrect's streets under cover of darkness were a dangerous place to be and the general drunkenness only exacerbated the problem.

She looked past her drinking companions to the bonfires that set the boundaries of what was visible. She didn't have to worry about her safety, not now she was sat in the midst of a company of Chetse mercenaries whose commander was extremely fond of her, but the instinct to constantly check her surroundings was too ingrained to change. She soon regretted the move; focusing was proving rather difficult and even when she did manage to see clearly, she still saw nothing more than the dilapidated sight of Helrect.

"Oh Gods, I hate this city," Legana muttered, raising her cup once more. The man beside her snorted with amusement and reached out to give her a pat on the shoulder. His palm felt like a large ham thumping down.

"Hah, you're drunk, woman! You always get depressed when you're drunk." Destech, the commander's lieutenant, considered Legana his friend for a reason only a Chetse soldier would ever consider. He cocked his head to one side and took a good look at her. "You're not so pretty when you're drunk either, which is odd, because I'm drunk too, and most women'll do once I've got a few jars inside me."

"Get your bastard hand off me or I'll break your nose back the way it was," Legana growled. "Even drunk, you still look like the arse end of a pig." She tossed back her copper-tinted hair to look Destech in the eye. He withdrew his hand, chuckling.

The Farlan agent's dyed hair shone disturbingly in the firelight, a reminder that she was a devotee of the Lady. Some of the Lady's followers were gentle people who spent their lives doing works of charity, but Fate was not a patron who attracted the rich. Her temple communities were self-supporting, rather than relying on endowments from dying aristocrats. The disciplines taught in the temples had a range of uses in the outside world and

Chief Steward Lesarl was one of those men delighted to employ every one of those disciplines. Destech was a soldier, a hardened veteran, and he had sense enough to know how far to push her, and when to withdraw.

"Ah my dear, the city's not so bad," commented the man on Legana's other side. He was middle-aged and powerfully built, even by the standards of Chetse soldiers, but he wore a sour expression that belied his words. Commander Tochet had once been first among the generals of the Chetse Army; Commander of the Eastern Tunnels, the most vicious battleground of their long-running war with the Siblis. His fall from grace had carried him from minor conflict to minor conflict and now he travelled to Raland to be Duke Nemarse's bodyguard.

Legana laughed. "You're only saying that because you're trying to get used to the idea of living in Raland; I've just come from there and it's a bigger shithole than this dump."

"So you say," Tochet replied, "but you won't say why you were there and that's rather more interesting to me."

Legana shifted in her seat. "One of the Chief Steward's little projects, that's all—nothing to concern you." Tochet was her friend, but she could say nothing of why she'd been there. The man she'd been sent to find had died in a bar fight, presumably arranged by Duke Nemarse, and she could guess what Lesarl's next move would be. She didn't want her friend protecting the duke when that happened. "Why don't you come with me instead?"

Tochet broke into a smile and put his hand on hers. "Do you mean all these years of wooing have finally paid off?"

"Hah, not unless there's something you've been hiding from your men all these years." She delicately removed the Chetse's hand from hers and gave him her best smile. Legana knew Tochet couldn't resist that; he was a fool for any pretty face. "You know perfectly well that I meant to command the forces in Lomin; Scion Lomin won't accept a Farlan's authority and you're the perfect alternative. He could hardly refuse a man of your experience."

"Well now, I've given my word and a mercenary has nothing if he breaks that. I have accepted the commission from Duke Nemarse and that's where we'll go. It will be a good rest for us after Tor Milist; I'm buggered if I'm doing that all winter again. I said as much to Duke Vrerr, so I don't think I'm his favourite mercenary any longer."

Destech snorted in amusement. "You'll be even less popular when his wife gives birth."

"And without you to support the duke?"

"With me, without me. Lords stand on their own feet or they fall on their own. Vrerr is an idiot; he turns his own people against him. No one likes the White Circle, but he's doing grand work in bringing over the neutrals. If it wasn't for the men from Narkang he'd have died a handful of times already."

"Men from Narkang?"

"I think so. They're not a friendly bunch, and I must have seen five different agents over my time there, but my orders were always more intelligent when one of them was around. They're hard men. I've seen the type at home; good soldiers, too good to waste on the line. They're the bloody hands that drive history."

"Why would the King of Narkang get involved? He knows meddling in Tor Milist might bring him in conflict with the Farlan."

"From what I've heard, that man's not afraid of anything, but it would be an inconvenience to him if Tor Milist fell. This fair city of Helrect is run by the White Circle and rumour has it they pull the strings in Scree too. If Vrerr is overthrown, King Emin suddenly has a nation to rival his own just over the border; one full of experienced soldiers and mercenary companies. As long as King Emin's not obvious about it, your masters will turn a blind eye because they don't want the White Circle there either."

Legana glowered: the White Circle was a sisterhood of noble-born women, one so close-ranked that even Lesarl hadn't been able to penetrate far enough in to discover who was really in charge—or, more importantly, what their real ambitions were. Publicly they claimed no agenda beyond a fairer, less corrupt system of governance, but they were active recruiters and Lesarl considered altruism and power rare companions. Legana expected to be assigned to infiltrate the Circle one day soon; even she, a trained killer of both talent and experience, was willing to admit a slight unease at the prospect.

"And is there any way I could persuade you to come north?" Legana knew Tochet was a man of his word and would not be swayed, but as a friend she had to try again. "Land? A title? To go home?"

"Farlan land? Hah! Too cold and too wet. Don't care about titles; the only words that count are those carved above the entrance of your stonedun. Going home? That I could hope for, and nothing more than that. Lord Bahl might hold better sway with Chalat than any other man, but what I called him, no Chetse would forgive. I lost my head, I know, but there's no taking some words back." He drained his cup and was about to reach for more wine when his hand sagged. Legana saw the fatigue and sadness on his face, the look of a man who was getting too old to be a mercenary.

"But if a truce could be arranged somehow? Living your life out in Cholos or Lenei would be home enough, wouldn't it?"

Tochet scowled. "If he forgot himself and did welcome me with open arms, I'd push a blade under his ribs and plant a fat kiss on his lips as the life ran out of him. He had my wife killed, my children, my cousins . . ." Tochet's voice trailed off and men round the table fell silent. Legna saw anger on their faces, not sadness, and raw murder in their eyes. "There's no taking back there. No forgiveness. And now I'm for my bed; the fun's gone from the evening and we're marching out tomorrow."

Tochet rose and looked around at the tables of Chetse soldiers. His men had not risen at his departure, but they watched his every movement with sober eyes. Taking a leather purse from his belt, Tochet tossed it onto the table where it fell with a heavy clink.

"There you go; you've all toasted my boys before and you'll do it again tonight. Make sure you can walk in the morning." Touching Legna on the arm to say goodbye, he made for the door of the inn. After a moment, she caught him up and slipped an arm under his. She knew she couldn't ease the pain in his eyes, but a friend had to try.

CHAPTER 6

GRADUALLY THE DARKNESS GAVE WAY to leaden shades of grey and a seeping chill that drained the warmth from Isak's blood. All alone in the void, he felt his body grow numb and fade until he could hardly sense any part of him.

Then there was pain; a cold discomfort that grew to become a hungry licking flame. The swirls of grey began to thicken and press down on him, swamping his eyes and mouth, causing him to choke in the silence. He tried to struggle free, to fight his way clear, but the cold had sapped his strength and the pressure was all around. There was nowhere to escape to and soon he fell into helpless exhaustion, surrendering to the tug of icy depths that dragged him further down to a place of no light and no memory, only the chill cradle of the grave.

And a voice.

"Isak.

"Raise your head, Isak.

"Raise your head and see me."

He had scarcely enough strength to obey, but somehow, he did lift his head. He could see nothing, but an image of a figure was imprinted on his mind: a man, tall and powerful, terrifying, and yet almost featureless, with blank eyes, smooth, midnight-blue skin, and only the impression of a mouth. The only shape that had any definition was the ornate bow that rested at the man's side. The pitch-black frame was flecked with gold and silver, and set with spirals of jewels.

"I am your master now. You are the blade I wield; the arrow I send high into the night. You are my Chosen, you share in my majesty, and the Land will see my glory echo in your deeds."

Isak tried to flee the voice, to hide from the words crashing through his head. He could sense others all around now, the faint touch of their movements and the melodious echoes of their voices, but the figure swept them all aside—except for one, the softest touch of them all, one that was scarcely noticeable until the others were gone and then it was a thread of pure light, distinct against the dark background and impervious to the figure's palpable fury.

It began to move, caressing the curve of his hip and moving up over his belly towards his heart. Isak relaxed under its soothing touch, then curled tightly as the stench of burning flesh filled his nostrils. Pain blossomed on his chest, then drove so deep the light burst through his body and burned a path through the darkness. In a heartbeat it had dissipated and all that remained was a faint voice: the sound of a girl calling a name, but so distant her cry was lost on the wind.

Isak woke with a scream, feeling as if the walls lurched and shuddered around him before reality reasserted itself. He took great gulps of air and tried to open his eyes, but the light streaming through the window made him gasp. Grasping at the unfamiliar sheets Isak battled to regain his wits. A shiver ran down his spine and into his legs; it felt like his soul returning. Every part of him ached, his throat burned, and his limbs throbbed, but it was the smell of burnt flesh that scared him most.

He sat up and grabbed the copper mirror from the desk to inspect his reflection, but he had to squint down to see it: a runic shape in stinging scar tissue on his sternum. It wasn't anything he recognised—not that he'd really expected to—but it wasn't even something from his dreams of the island palace.

In the looking-glass he could see it more clearly: a circle of scar tissue with a horizontal bar across its centre, no more than two inches across. The bar did not quite span the width of the circle, but a vertical line at either end made that connection, with one going straight down, the other up.

Suddenly his thoughts were interrupted by the taste of magic emanating from the chimney at the centre of the room: Lord Bahl. He grabbed his ragged shirt and quickly pulled it on, making sure the bone thongs were fastened and the scar covered. As Lord Bahl appeared, the scar was covered, but Isak could not hide the haggard look on his face.

"You slept badly. Dreamed badly."

It was not a question. Isak looked up at his new master with incomprehension. As he struggled up and propped his body against the wall, he realised he was shivering uncontrollably. Bahl noticed the cold as well and threw several logs onto the dead fire, then made a flicking motion with his wrist. Flames at once sprang up in the fireplace, hungrily devouring the dry wood. Isak stared in wonder at the fire, but Bahl just waved it off and drew up a chair for himself.

"That's nothing. I'm surprised that you can't do that already, considering how the tower responded to you. But that can wait. Right now, we should speak of what you are."

Isak struggled to answer, his head still fogged from the dream. "What I am?" he muttered. "What else is there? Carel said white-eyes are born to be warriors, to fight for the tribe."

"Carel?"

Isak opened his mouth to reply, but stopped when he realised Bahl's face was uncovered. The reclusive Lord of the Farlan rarely went out in public without the blue silk hood tight around his face, and Isak had never before seen Lord Bahl's actual features. He wondered how it could have taken him this long to notice, but after a moment he shook the question from his mind—considering what had happened to him, such a small detail was easily overlooked. Now he saw a powerful man with a harsh face, solid features all sharp lines and blunt corners. His brow was thick and strong, and his nose, but his features had an *abrupt* look, as if a craftsman had been interrupted in his work. The shape was there, the basic lines hewn with skill, but there had been no time to smooth the edges.

That in turn reminded Isak of the palace in his dreams and its unfinished statues, but before that could distract him further he forced the memory away. This was not a face used to patience.

"Carel is my friend, a friend of my father's. He was in the Palace Guard before he joined the wagon train. Sergeant Betyn Carelfolden, Third Squad, Vanguard Company, Eighth Regiment. He was the only one who didn't care that I was a white-eye. He taught me to fight so I could come and take the trials for the Guard."

"A squad sergeant, that's good news. He'll have bawled you into the right habits then, so I won't have Kerin whining that he has to teach you the different ends of a sword. But that's not going to be enough now; if you out-live me, you'll be Lord of the Farlan one day. Before anything else, remember that nothing Sergeant Carelfolden—or anyone else—has taught you can pre-pare you for the life you will now lead. There are dangers that ignore all of your strength, all of your skill. You are but a child among wolves, blessed by the Gods for the whole Land to resent and envy. You have no friends now; no one you can trust with your innermost thoughts. Over the months to come you will realise that you now stand apart from the rest of the Land, between mortals and the Gods, but kin to neither."

Isak, following this with some difficulty, broke in and asked, "But you had someone once. Couldn't you trust her completely?"

Bahl stood silent for a few moments, then a deep breath signalled a victory for control. He answered, as if nothing had happened, "Her I could trust, yes. She was the only person I *could* trust completely, and because of that she was used as a weapon against me. Don't speak of her again, unless you want bad blood to come between us."

Bahl stopped again, but this time it was to gesture towards Isak's trembling hands. "You're tired, I know; let me explain why. It was Nartis who spoke to you in your dream. Now that you're one of the Chosen, you are his property—whether you want it or not. White-eyes were created to signal the end of the Age of Darkness; to show that the Gods were once again with us. We are born to rule, to lead the armies of the Seven Tribes of Man. By choosing one of us to lead, the Gods broke the dynasties and the traditions of blood ties and birthright that had contributed to the Great War. I know the dreams are difficult to endure, but through them Nartis will give you the strength you need to survive. You'll be as big as I am, able to endure pain that would kill any normal man, and still have the strength to fight back afterwards. You'll feel the storm running through your veins—"

"What about the thread of light?" Isak interrupted again.

Bahl frowned, leaning closer to Isak to stare deep into his eyes, a mesmerising, unremitting glare like a cobra staring down a rabbit. "I don't know about a thread of light. You should have been alone with Nartis, becoming part of him."

Isak shook his head. "No, we weren't alone, I felt others all around us, other minds. There were whispers I couldn't make out before Nartis drove them away."

"That's all they are," Bahl said firmly.

Isak blinked. "What?"

"The whispers; that's all they are, just voices. Spirits holding onto a few memories; they're attracted by life, by strength, by magic. They're distractions, nothing more. You'll learn to ignore them easily enough. As for the light, it's the same: another entity—stronger perhaps, but not what you were born for. Stay true to your nature and your God."

This time Isak nodded. Carel had spent many an evening entertaining them all with tales of mythology: the Land's pantheon of Gods were eternally plotting and feuding. Larat, God of Magic and Manipulation, was particularly famed for stealing the followers of other Gods, and for making reviled traitors out of devoted servants. The pain Isak had felt during the dream must have been a taste of the price of betrayal, and if that was the case, he knew it was not something he ever wanted to experience in full. "Could it have been another God like Larat? Trying to cause trouble?" he asked.

"That's possible—Larat lives for discord," Bahl said, although he sounded uninterested in pursuing Isak's theory much further. "But don't think too hard about it, just stay true to what you are. Only Death is stronger than our patron, Nartis. No other God can offer you more than Nartis has promised you by making you my Krann."

Isak nodded, his eyes dropping as the sting of his chest intruded on his thoughts. His hand instinctively rose to touch the sore area before he forced it back down, unwilling to draw Bahl's attention there. He wasn't quite sure why, but he didn't want to show the scar to anyone yet.

"Try not to worry about it now," Bahl began, interpreting the movement as nervousness. "We can talk again when you're feeling more yourself. Right now you should compose yourself and report to Swordmaster Kerin; he will need an idea of your abilities before he begins your training. Once that is done, the day is yours. I don't have time for you today. I have told Kerin to give you a sword that befits your new rank, but I suggest you don't leave the palace; let Lesarl introduce you to useful men like Suzerain Tebran and the colonel of the Ghosts instead. At some point you should go to the temple and sacrifice to Nartis, but there's no rush. We'll send some men with you to give you some space from the curious.

"Beyond that, your first priority is your weapons training. In a few days Lesarl should have time to formally draw up your ownership of estates, incomes, and the like; just remember he is in my service to bully the nobility, so don't let him do the same to you."

Isak sat and stared up at Bahl. He hardly knew what to make of the situation—everything was flying at him so fast. Even after Bahl's words in the hall the previous night, it didn't feel real. Estates, a suzerainty, a court rank? Yesterday Isak could have been whipped for looking a knight directly in the eye.

"What are people supposed to call me now?" he asked, a little diffidently.

Bahl gave a laugh. Considering the full import of Isak's elevation, it was an inane question, but he could see why it was important. The boy had been the lowest of the low; now he was at least determined to know what respect he could demand from others. He understood why that would be important to a wagon-brat.

"They have a few choices. 'My Lord Suzerain' or 'Lord Isak' is the formal way to address you, but since your court rank is technically that of a duke rather than a suzerain, 'Your Grace' would also be perfectly acceptable. No doubt you'll hear it from someone wanting to flatter you. Just remember your rank is below the other dukes, so you'll still have to bow to them. Krann Isak would be a little direct, but also acceptable. Otherwise, you are Isak, Suzerain Anvee, Krann to Lord Bahl, and Chosen of Nartis. Ah, but some might call that impious. It would be better to say: Chosen of Nartis and Krann to Lord Bahl."

"So I have a family name now."

"I suppose so, but don't grow too fond of it. As one of the Chosen, tradition says you should be addressed as Lord Isak, and you lose it when you become Lord of the Farlan anyway, though I hope that will be a long-distant day." Bahl smiled, rather uneasily, as though the expression was unfamiliar. "Anvee is dull and overgrown in any case. There's not much of interest there, only a handful of towns and villages populated by shepherds."

Isak opened his mouth to ask another question, but Bahl had already turned and entered the central chimney. He shut up and watched the giant disappear, enveloped in a grey blur.

Left alone again, Isak clambered to his feet, draped a woollen blanket from the bed around his shoulders, and made for the fire. He nudged the chair Bahl had sat in out of the way and squatted on the floor to stare into the flames. The fire looked just like any other, with no sign of its unnatural birth. Isak smiled; maybe, after today, he wouldn't envy it that. After a while he realised his head was clear and the dull ache in his muscles was receding. He stood and stretched. Perhaps he could face the day after all.

He removed his shirt again and took another look at the scar on his chest. The rune was no more than two inches wide; a minor thing for all the trepidation it had provoked in him. Despite the fact that he could only just see it, when he put the shirt back on the throb of its presence remained. The pain was nothing compared to the nag of its unknown significance.

Investigating the clothes trunk, Isak found a better pair of breeches than his own, and some sort of shapeless shirt with sleeves so short and fat it looked as if it had been made for a Chetse rather than someone of Isak's build. He guessed he looked a little foolish in it, but the shirt was warm so it would do for the meantime.

There were no boots in the trunk, so Isak closed the lid, looked around the room once more in case he'd missed anything, and stepped onto the murky platform. This time he savoured the taste of magic it contained, an almost metallic flavour that drove the last vestiges of sleep from his mind. He took a deep breath and focused his mind on the bird symbol down below. A momentary rush of giddiness passed away and when the lower chamber and Tila's slightly alarmed face were revealed, Isak looked calm and controlled.

"Ah, there you are." As he stepped forward the girl curtsied.

"Oh, please don't do that every time I see you," Isak begged. "It makes me feel stupid."

"I—yes, my Lord." They stared at each other in silence until Isak gave an enquiring nod at a pair of boots Tila carried.

"Oh yes, I borrowed these from one of the guardsmen. I hope they're big enough for you. I've sent for tailors and a cobbler to attend you this afternoon—if these will suffice for the morning, that is."

Isak took the boots from her and pulled them on. They were simple, but well made—and certainly better and newer than any he'd ever worn before. The fit was snug, and his toes were crammed together especially tightly in the left, but it was far better than bare feet on cobbled or flagged stone. He beamed at the improvement. Tila gave him a relieved smile.

"Should I ask Lesarl for the money to pay the tailors then?" he asked, recalling Bahl's earlier instructions.

"Not at all, my Lord."

"Why not?" he asked, wondering if he had missed something. "They're hardly going to dress me for nothing."

She smiled again, and this time Isak thought she was being a little condescending.

"I think in fact they would dress you for free, my Lord," she explained. "You are a suzerain, and if their work pleases you, you would be expected to have much more work for them in the future. My grandfather always said that a good tailor was the first requirement of a gentleman."

"I'm far from that."

"On the contrary, my Lord, as Suzerain Anvee, you outrank almost every gentleman in the nation. My Lord, may I be bold and speak freely?"

Isak shrugged, lips pursed as he anticipated a comment on the shirt he'd just put on.

"The talk of the palace is that before your elevation to Krann, you lived on a wagon train." She paused, wary of looking foolish or giving offence, but Isak nodded without further comment. "If that is the case, I would venture to guess that you find yourself in a life about which you know nothing. Perhaps I might be so free as to offer what advice I can? This is the society I have grown up in. It might be asking you to trust me excessively, but I assure you that any disgrace or humiliation visited upon you would reflect upon me. I am not unattractive, I know that, but I am unmarried at seventeen because my father has no money for a dowry, despite his position. Proving myself an able counsellor to you could compensate for that—it could demonstrate my usefulness to any man beyond the first duty of bearing an heir. I have as much to lose as you do, and as much to gain."

Isak considered her words. He wasn't quite ready to trust her, but she had acknowledged that already. At least he knew to be wary, and what more could he ask for?

"Go on then," he said grudgingly.

"Yes, my Lord. You are now a man of court rank—how society regards you will be determined, first and foremost, by the way you present yourself."

"I've no intention of presenting myself to anyone. If I'm Krann, then surely people should be coming to me."

"And I'm sure they will, that's the way of politics. However, to wield power successfully, one must cultivate friendships as well as receive them. Isolation is no way to achieve victory in any arena."

"Lord Bahl seems to manage."

Tila paused. "My Lord, to the other nobles you are just a youth—albeit one with potential as a soldier. The divine edicts are clear; the Chosen are just that: made fit by the gifts of the Gods, but they must prove themselves worthy of those gifts, and they must hold on to power by themselves.

"Lord Bahl is one of the greatest warriors in the Land. In combat, he is matchless. Quite aside from the fact that our finest regiment is loyal to him to a man, no Farlan alive could beat him in a duel. In the political arena, he's well protected by his Chief Steward. You, on the other hand, are untested in any form of battle, and you're a stranger to the viciousness of polite society."

"So, as my advisor, what would you have me do?" Isak shifted his weight from one foot to the other. As he grew irritated, so he felt the squeeze on his toes become more noticeable.

"Show yourself to be their equal. Dress and act as befitting a man of your station and they will soon be flocking to court your attention. If you are quiet and considered, welcoming but never overly so, then you will have the time you need to learn how to deal with the men of court rank: the dukes, suzerains, and counts. They are men of guile who will use the law, force, influence, and rumour to gain what they want. To play their game, you must first understand its rules."

"And then what?"

"And then men will align themselves to you. They won't all be trust-worthy, of course, but that will be how you can develop your powerbase grounded in something more than military might. Lord Bahl's intentional rejection of high society has caused him more than a few problems in the past."

"That sounds like a dangerous opinion to me."

Tila stared at Isak in alarm before realising he had not meant it as a threat.

"I—I don't believe so, my Lord. It is well known that Lord Bahl takes little interest in politics or the cult of Nartis, and that this has caused prob-lems in the past."

Isak stayed silent while Tila's words churned through his head. Yet more change, more confusion in his life; more playing the games of other men, something he had yearned to be free of. *Damn them*, he thought all of a sudden, *I'm a man of power now and that means I should be able to live my life how I want. Why should I bend to another man's will? Let the Land now bend to mine.* He opened his mouth to say exactly that to Tila, then the words faltered in his throat. She was trying to help, to be a friend. Right now she was the only one he had here; no need to reject everything she'd said.

"You might be right. I'll have to think about it all," Isak said. "In the meantime, Lord Bahl told me to find Swordmaster Kerin."

Tila gave a half-curtsey, bowing her head a fraction too slowly to avoid showing the rush of relief that flowed over her face. "He will be on the training ground, my Lord. This way."

She led him down the empty corridor towards the Great Hall, where the wide stone stairway brought noises from the rest of Tirah Palace. Isak resolved to investigate the place at a later time. He smiled. The high roofs and hidden eaves of this ancient place would soon welcome him and share their secrets; with no father to curse his absence, Isak had only his own fancy to obey.

Tila pushed open the door to the Great Hall, walked in, and cast a pointed look at those within. Then she stepped aside and drew herself up by the door, holding it open for Isak.

"Today I will have your personal chambers prepared. Lord Bahl has given explicit instructions that you sleep in the tower for a few weeks, but chambers in the main wing above us are also to be yours."

Isak nodded and walked past her into the hall. Only four people were inside, two servants tending to the fire, now standing to attention, and a pair of guardsmen. The younger was still sitting, his bloody leg stretched out on the bench, while the other, a grizzled man of a similar age to Carel, had risen to his feet. A length of bandage trailed from his hand.

Isak, not sure what to do, gestured at them to continue what they'd been doing as he strode past them and to the tall double doors that led outside. One was slightly ajar, enough to see daylight, and when he opened it fully, he found himself at the top of a wide stone stairway with no rail that led down to what was obviously a training ground. To either side was a drop of almost ten feet; unsurprisingly, the steps were badly worn in the centre. A mass of grey cloud hung in the sky, resisting the wind's listless attempts to drive it away. Isak could hardly tell where the sun was, so quickly gave up gauging the hour, but guessed he had slept far later than usual.

Off to the left stood the barbican, flanked by two sharp towers. The dark maw of the keep tunnel rose up from the ground, its length sufficient to prevent any light from the other side from showing. Isak turned and looked up at the great bulk of the main wing. The Tower of Semar rose behind it. He felt himself start to topple backwards as he strained to see to the very top. Against the diffused morning light the huge tower that reached up into the heavens looked elusive and shadowy. Now Isak was inside the palace, he realised just how large the fortress was—and still the tower looked impossibly tall.

The high stone walls encircled a vast tract of land. They were dotted with defensive towers, and there were stables and barracks nestling up close in several places. Various plots within the wall were fenced off for livestock and for huge kitchen gardens, but the majority held soldiers. A line of archery butts were taking a beating at the far end, while the wide stretch of ground in between contained drilling foot soldiers and cavalry.

The palace was not built for defence. It had grown over the years, and the ancient wall surrounding the training ground was now a patchwork, first enlarged after an original section around the tower had been destroyed by magic. These days it was so long that it would take thousands to man it. But no one had ever succeeded in laying siege to Tirah Palace because the Farlan Army was a mobile one, manoeuvrable and superbly trained. The horses were drilled as hard as the soldiers, and their rapid response, tight formations, and excellent logistical management meant that few enemies ever got the choice of battleground. Organisation of supplies was so crucial for the Farlan Army that the Quartermaster-General outranked even suzerains, in peace time as well as at war.

Isak trotted down the steps and made his way to a nearby groom who was attending to a tall chestnut hunter. The magnificent animal remained patient and still as the groom inspected a foreleg hoof.

Isak took a moment to admire the warhorse, a finer creature than any he'd seen before, before asking, "Can you tell me where I can find Swordmaster Kerin?"

"The Swordmaster?" replied the groom without looking up. "He's busy with the rich boys of the Guard. Wait till he's finished; some of them are knights and they don't like commoners interrupting."

Isak smiled. Only a day back he'd have obeyed that advice. "Tell me which one he is anyway. I think I outrank a knight, so they won't complain for long."

The man looked up, and dropped the hoof in shock. He quickly recovered himself and dropped to one knee, muttering apologies. "My Lord, forgive—"

"Don't worry, just tell me which one is the Swordmaster."

The man hopped to his feet and pointed to a group of men gathered in a circle thirty yards away. "Of course, my Lord. He's over there, training the highborn men. The, ah, the man in blue, with a quarter-staff."

Isak turned to follow the man's hand. The group was assembled in a half circle, centred on the man in blue and a mailed figure frozen in midlunge. The Swordmaster was pointing with his staff at the position of the other man's leg. He could see why the groom had been dismissive; it was a fencing class, teaching nobles how to fight with a rapier. The weapons were next to useless on a battlefield, but duels were common enough among the upper classes and skill with the narrow blade had brought many men fame.

As Isak approached, the assembled men stopped paying attention and stared instead at their new Krann. He smiled inwardly, wondering what rumours were flying around the palace. A commoner arriving in the dead of night and soaked in blood, declared as Krann to Lord Bahl and future Lord of the Farlan—no doubt there were many assuming, as some part of Isak still did, that this was all a joke.

To the Swordmaster's credit, he hardly hesitated as he felt his audience's attention stray. Turning smartly, the slim-built, greying man hefted his staff, took a step towards Isak, and then dropped to one knee.

"My Lord Isak, you honour us with your presence." As he spoke, Kerin looked up, assessing Isak with an unwavering gaze that betrayed no trace of apprehension.

"You're Swordmaster Kerin?"

"I am, my Lord." Kerin didn't blink or shift his attention for an instant. For a man kneeling, the Swordmaster showed no intention of being impressed yet.

"Well then, Lord Bahl told me to report to you."

Kerin rose, leaning heavily on his staff, but Isak wasn't fooled. From the rapt attention the others had been giving him, he guessed Kerin was worthy of his title.

"That he did, my Lord, and now you're out here, you're under my command. There's no room for titles here; no room for more than one commander. If you don't like doing what I say, tough shit. You'll do it or you'll not walk this field."

Isak blinked in surprise; that hadn't been how he'd expected things to start out—but then he remembered Carel repeating to him, again and again, whenever the subject of joining the Guard came up: *Keep your damn temper under control and your mouth shut. Either you'll learn to take orders, or they'll chew you up and spit you out. There's nothing that the Swordmasters haven't seen before; make sure you show yourself to be more than just a white-eye.*

Isak gave a small smile; if he was now the Krann, none of these men had seen one of those before, but he still had something to prove to them. Better he showed them the man he could become, rather than the animal they all expected.

"Think I'm joking, boy?" The Swordmaster broke in on his reverie. "There's near enough a thousand men on this ground; defy me and you'll find out whether their loyalties lie with me or some wet-behind-the-ears suzerain of a place no one's ever been."

Isak held up his hands in submission. "I've not yet had a chance to get used to my title; I think I can put it aside for the moment." He looked around at the men assembled. Disappointed at what he saw, Isak craned his head past them at the nearest troops. "I thought there were other white-eyes in the Ghosts?" he asked finally.

Kerin snorted. "That there are—seventy-six of the vicious bastards at the last count."

"You don't like white-eyes?"

"Hah! Boy, to me you're just a soldier—and right now, *you're* not even that. The best way to piss me off is to be touchy about what you are. You want to know why I call them vicious bastards? It's because they are. I could count on my fingers those white-eyes in the Guard who've spoken more words to me than you just have. General Lahk is the only one that's properly civilised, saving yourself perhaps, and the general broke another white-eye's neck with his bare hands a few years back." There was a hint of a smile of Kerin's face as he spoke, the confidence of a man in his element. Isak suspected even the white-eyes of the Guard, bastards or not, would follow the Swordmaster's orders without question.

"I'm keeping the others away from you because they'll want to get into it first chance there is. Like their pecking order, do our white-eyes, and none of you can control your temper. If it starts, someone will die; that's why they'll be flogged if they even walk past you. Now, enough talk. Can you fight?"

Isak nodded, biting back his frustration. Kerin seemed to be suggesting Isak didn't even have much in common with other white-eyes—even amongst his own, would he still be an outsider?

"Good. Give him a staff, Swordmaster Cosep," Kerin ordered a stout officer in Bahl's livery. The eagle on his chest was gold rather than the usual white, and Isak guessed that was the mark of a Swordmaster, the most skilled of all Farlan soldiers. Kerin acted as if he were the highest-ranked among them; he must be high enough that he had no need of markings or livery.

Isak had not even managed to gauge the weight of the staff when a loud crack broke the air and a burst of pain flared in the side of his head. He stumbled forward, almost dropping his staff in the process. Cosep stepped smartly back as Isak staggered and winced. His vision went black for an instant, then he saw Cosep smiling, the Swordmaster's eyes angled to Kerin rather than Isak. Instinctively, Isak threw himself to the right as Kerin's staff flashed towards him again—this time it would have done more damage than just a clip round the ear.

"Come on, boy, at least *try* to defend yourself," the Swordmaster called, sounding bored.

Isak took a step back to collect his wits, but Kerin was on him again, swinging a sloppy stroke at Isak's head, perhaps hoping to tease a reaction out of him. Instead, he almost lost his staff as Isak lashed out angrily at the oncoming weapon and smashed it away. That gave him the moment he needed and now he was on the attack. He struck out, again and again, and as Kerin stepped smoothly over a long swipe at his shins, he grinned at Isak's unexpected speed.

Now Isak held the staff like an axe, hands apart until he slid them together for a stroke, aware that his height and reach gave him the advantage.

Kerin was chancing the odd blow, but was too sensible to go toe-to-toe with a white-eye. Isak felt the man watching his every step and movement, drinking in the details while watching for a flaw to exploit.

For a man approaching fifty summers, Kerin moved with the speed of one of his pupils, diverting one strike over his head with apparent ease, then turning in behind a straight thrust with a delicate pirouette and jabbing backwards at Isak. Years of experience meant Kerin immediately dived away when he felt his blow meet nothing but air, but the pleased astonishment was plain on his face as he rolled and jumped up, staff ready to defend himself.

No blow came. Isak had stayed back, his staff loose in his hands and a smirk on his lips.

"You underestimate me, old man."

"Hah, maybe you do have a sense of humour after all," Kerin laughed. "Let's see, shall we?"

Kerin darted forward, launching three quick strikes before retreating a step. Isak obliged by moving up to attack, suddenly under assault from both sides as a staff from the crowd flicked out and slammed into the back of his knee. Isak gave a yelp as his leg buckled and stabbed down with his staff to avoid falling completely. Lunging forward as if he had a spear in his hands, Kerin caught Isak hard on the shoulder and knocked him backwards on to the muddy ground. Isak collapsed flat on his back, to the sound of chortling from the onlookers. He found himself blinking up at the grey clouds above.

The packed earth was cold and damp against his back and for a moment he felt like he was back in the street, surrounded by his father's cronies. As Isak collected his wits, a cold fury gripped him. He pulled himself up and found the staff lying at his side. Without thinking, he snatched it up and swung round savagely, taking his unknown assailant off his feet. There was a sickening snap as the ash staff connected, and then Isak tackled Kerin with short, controlled blows. The Swordmaster fell back, step by step, parrying each thrust. Then a stinging blow jarred the staff from his fingers.

Knowing he was beaten, Kerin ducked his head to take the final blow on his shoulder. He fell heavily and a shout went up from the watching men. They stepped forward protectively. Isak drew his staff back and readied himself to strike the first man who stepped within range. Seeing the look of murder on Isak's face, the men went for their swords.

"Stop! Get back." Even from the ground, Kerin's voice commanded complete obedience among his men. "You too, Krann, put up your weapon now."

Isak spun around, staff raised, but faltered when he saw Kerin kneeling on the ground, a trickle of blood running from his eyebrow. The Swordmaster's staff lay forgotten on the floor as he clutched his shoulder.

"All of you, put up your weapons." Kerin dragged himself to his feet, wincing, and looked for Swordmaster Cosep and the third man, another Swordmaster, who rolled on to his side and swore though gritted teeth, hands clamped around his right leg.

"Damn. You two—get him to the surgeons." The men nodded and bent down to pick up the unfortunate Swordmaster. Putting an arm around each of their necks, they gently slid their hands under the man's back and thighs, lifting him with as much care as they could. Isak watched them go and his anger fled. He let his quarterstaff fall to the floor.

"I should have seen that coming. Well, I think we can assume you've been trained in weapons. Can you use a sword?" Kerin asked.

Isak nodded. "I was taught by a sergeant of the Guard; he made me learn the forms—said I'd have to one day anyway."

"And he was right. You were going to come and take the trials?" He gave a grim laugh that ended in a wince. "Well, I think it's clear you would have passed. Now, Lord Bahl said to give you a sword until you get your own. A man of your rank should always wear one." Kerin paused, as if considering something, then walked over to a bundle lying unminded on the ground. He retrieved it and unwrapped from a cloak the finest sword Isak had ever seen. It was a slender blade, an inch wide, with an ornate golden guard. The leather scabbard was a rich scarlet, bound with gold thread and lined with red-dyed raw wool.

"Here, take this for the moment. It's rather more fitting to your station than a cavalry blade from the armoury."

Isak took the sword, drawing it halfway from the scabbard to inspect the blade. It looked old and worn, but it was still in fine condition. The metal was black iron, ensorcelled steel that was both lighter and stronger that any other metal. The symbol of an eagle had been engraved near the hilt, outstretched in flight as on Bahl's personal crest.

"Thank—" Isak's reply was cut short as one of the men watching gave a strangled cry of outrage. The Krann turned to look at him, a man of about thirty summers, obviously wealthy, with a scarlet sash draped over his shoulder and across his body; Isak saw that echoed in the dress of three or four others there.

"You have something to say, Sir Dirass?"

"Master Kerin," the nobleman began angrily, "he's little more than a boy.

Whatever his rank, he's certainly not worthy of carrying any Eagle-blade, let alone yours. Just because he bested you with a staff? It's an insult to those of us who've dedicated our lives to earning an Eagle. If my father were to hear of this—"

"If your father were to hear of this," Kerin interjected quietly, "he would remember the oath he swore when he received his Eagle-blade, and he would also remember that I am the one who commands the Swordmasters. Suzerain Certinse's rank does not give him authority over me, as you well know."

"So because this boy can best you with a farmer's stick he deserves one of our highest honours?" The knight's voice was thick with contempt as he moved forward to Kerin. Cosep stepped in between the two.

"That's too far, Certinse. You will apologise now and remember your place." Swordmaster Cosep reached out to rest a hand on Sir Dirass's shoulder, but the man shrugged him off angrily.

"Apologise? My family is not in the habit of apologising to inferiors. I don't intend to set the precedent."

"Your family," retorted Kerin, "seems to be more in the habit of running away with tails between legs, if recent history is anything to go on."

Sir Dirass made a grab for his sword, but Cosep saw it coming and slammed his fist into the knight's shoulder. Dirass stumbled back with the point of Cosep's blade at his throat.

"Do you think you're ready for an Eagle then?" Kerin asked the enraged nobleman.

Sir Dirass blinked at the question. With a slow, wary movement, he nodded.

"Do you think the Krann to be unworthy of one?"

Another nod.

"Well then; if you can take it off him, the sword is yours. I don't deserve it myself if my judgement is so wrong."

"Kerin," roared Cosep before Sir Dirass could accept the challenge, "this goes too far!"

"Keep out of this. This is my blade, and my decision." Kerin rounded on his colleague, pointing a warning finger at the Swordmaster who, after staring at Kerin for a moment, threw his hands up in disgust and withdrew.

"Sir Dirass Certinse," the Swordmaster said formally, "if you accept this test and fail, you will never receive an Eagle. If you accept, you must disarm the Krann to take your prize. Make no mistake, this is not a duel; we've had enough blood spilled already today. If you agree, fetch a shield and make ready."

Kerin took a teardrop-shaped shield from one of the onlookers and walked over to Isak, who was not quite sure what was happening—other than what Kerin had said about the knight's family had upset him enough to make him draw on his unarmed superior. Kerin held out the shield.

"You want me to fight a duel for you?" Isak asked.

"It's not a duel; I think you're fast enough to avoid getting anything more than a nick if you pay attention."

"With the mood he's in? And anyway, I've not been taught to use a sword like this—this is a nobleman's blade."

"Dirass knows the rules well enough, he's sparred like this a hundred times. If he goes too far, I'll stop the fight and have him thrown in a cell, no matter who his father is."

"And who is his father?"

"Suzerain Certinse of Tildek, but technically you outrank the man now."

Isak stepped back and frowned. This wasn't his battle, but the faces around him made it clear he had no choice. "Fine, give me the shield," he said.

He took the curved wooden shield Kerin handed him and watched as his opponent slid his on so the point was up by his shoulder. He did the same, gripping the leather handle at the wide end tightly, and twisted his arm back and forward to get the feel of it. Reaching his left arm out as far as he could, he looked over his shoulder to check that the tip could not catch him, no matter how far he stretched out. The edge of the shield was bound in steel, roughly hammered into shape with the tip bent outward so it would be a danger only to his opponent.

Now Isak tugged Kerin's beautiful blade clear of the sheath. It was perfectly balanced, that much he recognised, but he knew nothing of duelling. He needed to see how this man moved. The knight had a light and quick step that belied his bulky frame. He didn't enjoy Isak's height or reach, but he did have years of experience instead.

Something deep inside Isak wanted to charge the knight immediately, but Carel had sliced and battered the young man often enough to curb that instinct. Not all of the scars on Isak's body were punishment from his father; some were down to Carel's incessant drilling.

Isak walked briskly up to Sir Dirass, wasting no time, and swung a clumsy overhand swipe at the knight. It was parried easily, but the knight wasn't going to be fooled into thinking Isak was a complete novice, no matter what he claimed. The Krann's second strike was a thrust at the nobleman's leg; Sir Dirass struck back with two neat blows, which Isak just stepped back from.

Now the knight moved into his stride, giving Isak no time to get a feel for the delicate weapon. Sir Dirass cut right and left, fast and accurate, and turned aside every one of Isak's blows with practised ease, stepping with the grace of a dancer. He used his shield as skilfully as his sword. Now he almost clubbed the sword from Isak's hand with his shield, now he delicately flicked his own blade out to catch Isak off-guard, the in-drawn breaths of the onlookers testament to his skill. His eyes were red, bloodshot with rage, but his experience meant his anger added purpose to his movements rather than recklessness.

The knight stabbed forward, the edge of his sword running along the rim of Isak's shield, then stepped to one side and slashed at Isak's hamstring. His shield, held high, caught the downstroke of Isak's weapon as his own failed to reach.

Isak pulled his weapon back, then thrust fiercely, uncontrollably, and to everyone's surprise caught the knight's sword, twisting so for a moment the blades locked. Sir Dirass disengaged with a savage flick, then smashed his shield into Isak's shoulder. Falling backwards, Isak slammed his heels into the dirt and brought his own shield down as fast as he could. It wasn't fast enough to stop the sword flashing up past his groin, but the stroke missed.

A bellow from Kerin prevented a second: "Certinse! I said disarm, not mortally wound him!"

Isak crouched on the ground, the knuckles of his right hand ground into the packed earth and his shield covering his body. He had managed to get his foot underneath his body in time to stop him falling flat on his back. Now he forced himself upright again.

Sir Dirass looked unashamed. He kept his sword low. His eyes never left Isak's.

"That was a coward's chance," growled Isak. "Does that run in the family too?" A snort from the assembled men and Sir Dirass's furious glare told him the jibe had hit home. His opponent had a weakness.

"Watch your mouth, white-eye."

"Or what? You'll run away? Hide behind your bitch-mother's skirt?"

"Enough! This is over!" But Kerin's shout went ignored this time. Isak grinned as he felt a familiar growl of anger stir in his belly. The animal inside him was just warming up. This man needed a lesson.

"Come on then. If you want it, come and get it. Or are you just another example of your worthless family?"

With a howl, the knight threw himself forward, hacking savagely with his slender blade, any pretence of form now gone. The white-eye again suppressed the almost overwhelming urge to charge, instead contenting himself with warding off the blows while waiting for the opening he knew would come. The crowd moved to keep up with Isak's steady retreat.

The knight was beginning to tire now, and finally Isak launched his own attack. He might not have been trained to the rapier, but Isak was young, and immensely strong, and extremely fast. Now he used all that roaring power to direct a flurry of blows at Sir Dirass that stopped the knight in his tracks. His thrusts were clumsy, but they were fierce. Carel had been trained on the battlefield, and that was the way he'd taught Isak: momentum was crucial; the advancing infantry, the charging cavalry—theirs was the victory to take.

For the first time, the knight looked a little uneasy, but then Isak moved forward and suddenly realised he was closer than he had intended. He jumped back quickly, but Sir Dirass had seen it too and lunged as hard as he could. Isak just escaped, arms splayed out wide as he fought for balance, then swung out hard at the knight's neck. Sir Dirass had almost lost his footing in the lunge but he got his shield up in time. Both stepped back unscathed.

There was a smile on Isak's face now. He had the measure of his enemy; now to irritate the knight into foolishness. His darting steps became more pronounced; his shield dropped a little lower and his grin broadened. Sir Dirass's face tightened. A pace forward closed the ground between them. The knight's sword was ready as he waited for Isak to retreat to where a second step would bring the knight close enough to run Isak through. That second step never came.

With an astonished gasp, Sir Dirass looked deep into the cold eyes of his killer as Isak stepped into the feint. No emotion showed on Isak's face as his sword tip slid between the knight's ribs.

Sir Dirass shuddered and went completely still, his fury turned to disbelief. He took an involuntary breath, and the onlookers gasped with him. Isak's movement had been so smooth that it took them a moment to realise he'd run Sir Dirass through. The knight's arms wavered, then dropped. He fell to his knees. With a quick jerk, Isak withdrew the blade. A spurt of blood followed it, splashing onto his borrowed boots. The corpse sagged and crumpled to the ground.

No one spoke. Isak stared down at the body with the rest of them. Now his stomach felt empty. The addictive rush of violence had been replaced by a palpable absence, a cold ball aching inside. He couldn't regret what he'd done; the man had meant to kill him—even an inexperienced swordsman like Isak recognised that. The breeze brought a taste of bread on the wind, a tantalising smell. He was starving. He wiped the blade clean on his shirt, turned, without a word, and headed back to the Great Hall.

Tila watched him go, sickness and fear welling inside. The bitter taste of bile sat at the back of her throat.

What sort of a man are you? She wanted to scream out the words. *How can you be so meek and unsure one moment, then so brutal the next? Are you no different to the rest of your kind after all?*

She had once watched her uncle killed in a duel, but that fight had been wild and ragged. Here, Isak had moved like a Harlequin dancing the steps to an epic poem, but he had been so dismissive when he ran the man through. For certain Sir Dirass had tried to kill Isak, but the vacant expression on Isak's face chilled her. Tila stood and stared with the soldiers until Isak had disappeared through the tall doors of the Great Hall, then the spell was broken and Swordmaster Kerin barked an order—angry sounds that Tila could not form into words. She drifted forward, hardly noticing that she had picked up the scabbard, and went after Isak. She was terrified to face him, but still she followed.

"Well, Kerin, please explain yourself." Lesarl's voice sounded cold, but his eyes laughed and danced. "Our new Krann was in mortal danger, was he not?"

"Yes, Chief Steward." Eyes downcast, Kerin felt the weight of the day's events grow darker and heavier with every passing moment. "I did not foresee Sir Dirass acting that way—we were far from friendly, but I didn't think he would disobey a direct order. Sir Dirass went for a cut to the groin, then Lord Isak began to bait him, insulting his family to get him angry. I think the Krann decided to kill him after that."

"And you're surprised?" Bahl's voice was quiet, restrained. Kerin had expected fury, but this disturbed him even more. "The knight went for a killing blow; Lord Isak's a white-eye, you do remember that? What were you thinking to put him in a duel? You'd not have done that with any of the other white-eyes under your command."

"I—" Kerin looked helpless, hardly able to explain a decision he himself didn't understand. His memory was dreamlike, as though he was not completely sure he had even given the order. "I thought Isak would keep his temper, I thought Sir Dirass would obey my orders—"

"I think the Swordmaster is showing his age," Lesarl interrupted. "Perhaps it is time I organised a quiet pension somewhere; some rich widow out in the country, maybe?"

"My mind is as sound as ever," snapped Kerin. "Dirass Certinse was always an impetuous man. Yes, he was desperate for his Eagle, but killing the Krann? He has—*had*—more sense than that."

"Then why, my Swordmaster, is that exactly what he tried to do?" Still Bahl was not angry.

"I cannot say. He looked like a man possessed, but—"

"That," said Lesarl firmly, "is a theory you will refrain from advancing in any other company, unless you want to find yourself closeted away in a monastery for the rest of your life."

Kerin was taken aback at the strength of Lesarl's reaction. "I didn't mean—"

"I don't care what you meant, or what you think. If I hear the slightest mention of malign influences affecting the decisions made out there today, I will hold you responsible for them."

"Yes," rumbled Bahl in a thoughtful way. "That idea is a disturbing notion. It will be dissuaded. Let them dwell instead on the fact that he is a natural soldier. By the time he leads troops into battle, he will be able to match more than just one potential Swordmaster." The old lord gestured towards the door. "Thank you, Swordmaster. That is all."

Unable to voice any of his many questions, Kerin bowed his head in acknowledgement, still a little stunned that the matter had been dealt with so swiftly. By the time he collected himself and made for the door, Bahl had already turned his attention back to the papers on his desk.

Bahl waited until he heard the door close behind Kerin, then pushed the papers away and looked over to his Chief Steward's expectant face.

"I will speak to the boy, remind him of the importance of retaining his composure, and not destroying valuable soldiers."

"And what of Certinse's parents? When they hear of it, the suzerain will lodge a suit against Isak and the Swordmaster. Damn the boy, why couldn't he have killed someone rather less important? If he's desperate for blood there are plenty of criminals in the gaol."

"Enough, Lesarl; his blood was up and the man tried to kill him. You can't expect less from a white-eye; I would have done the same. I'm more interested in why this happened at all. Kerin's too sensible to start this duel, and Sir Dirass was a grown man. Quite aside from the fact that he's fought with white-eyes before and must know their temper, the political problems it would bring alone would have stopped his hand."

Bahl stared over his desk at the blank wall, deep in thought. Then he looked at Lesarl. "Aracnan said there had been something wrong when he met the boy; you say the father demanded Isak be hanged last night, and now a intelligent man takes it upon himself to defy orders and attempt to kill him," he said softly.

Aracnan's words the previous night came back to him. *The boy's trouble, but now he is your trouble.* He expected those words to come up rather often now.

"Well, speaking of problems," Lesarl broke in, "Cardinal Certinse has demanded an explanation. The arrogant bastard's already acting as though he were High Cardinal of Nartis. He informs me that he has written to both of his brothers to let them know about 'this latest outrage.' I don't know whether the man still thinks he can intimidate me, but I had hoped to put this problem with the Knights of the Temples behind us. Knight-Cardinal Certinse might use this as an excuse to come home, and perhaps bring a few of his men along for protection. If that looks likely, I'd sooner have him killed before he crosses our border."

"I think you're getting ahead of yourself there."

"Well, you must admit it is a possibility. The cardinal and Suzerain Certinse I can probably shut up; the Knight-Cardinal is a different matter. What would you have me do there?"

Bahl sighed. "Let's deal with Isak first. The Devoted are a problem for another day."

CHAPTER 7

QUITIN AMANAS WAS A STRANGE MAN. His family and friends all knew it, and it looked like the palace guardsman standing stiffly before his desk was well on the way to forming that same opinion. No doubt his reaction to Lord Bahl's summons was not quite what the man had expected, because Amanas was relieved rather than apprehensive. Though the new Krann had been in the palace barely a week and the city was still aflame with gossip about him, Amanas had been expecting this summons for a lot longer; he would be glad to finally meet the one at the root of all this excitement.

"Tell me, young man, what's the Krann like?"

The soldier blinked in surprise. "He's—well, he's a white-eye. They're all pretty much the same, aren't they, sir?"

"But he's one of the Chosen, and that will make him different."

"Still a white-eye, sir—quiet till you piss him off—ah, if you'll pardon the expression, sir. Killed a man on his first day; they say he did it like it was an everyday occurrence."

"I'm sure there was more to it than that."

"Oh, probably, sir," the guardsman agreed quickly, rather patronisingly in Amanas's opinion, "but that's all I've heard."

"Tell me, do you know what I do?"

"You, sir? Well the library is where all the family trees are kept. I suppose you're needed to sort out his estates, now that he's a suzerain."

Amanas wrinkled his nose, the guardsman smelled how soldiers always smelled: a damp scent of metal and ripe sweat-stained leather that the pristine white livery covering it could do nothing about. The longer the guardsman stood there, the more palpable it became—hardly his fault, of course, but still it made Amanas uncomfortable. Men of violence were unpredictable. He imagined it would be a small thing for the guardsman to draw the sword at his side and run him through. No doubt as a soldier he had done it many times before. Once more would probably matter little at his day of judgement. It troubled Amanas to be confronted by such a person.

"I do keep the library, but I also produce the crests and colours for newly ennobled men, as well as personal emblems for men of good family when they come of age. No doubt you thought that was just a case of drawing a suitable creature to carry on your shield?"

The soldier shrugged, plainly confused by the whole situation. "I won't deny that I've dreamed of a knighthood, like every man in the Guard, but I've never really thought about that part of it, how the crest would be drawn up."

"Actually, it is a little more complicated than just 'drawing something up.' It requires a blend of magic and artistry. If you like, I could show you how. Give me your hand."

At the mere mention of magic the guardsman recoiled from Amanas's outstretched hand.

"No? Oh well, perhaps it would be tempting Fate—her sense of humour is somewhat notorious, after all. In any case, my powers are very weak and specialised. When I touch a man I can visualise something of his spirit, and what he could become. The interpretation is, of course, a vastly different matter, and much depends on context. Karlat Lomin is a good example of that; you know of him, Scion Lomin?"

The guard nodded. "Of course, sir. Everyone's saying how his father the duke has taken a turn for the worse; that he won't last through winter. It won't be long until the scion becomes the fourth-most powerful man in the country. And last week," he added in a concerned voice, "the Krann killed Scion Lomin's cousin in weapons training—ran him right through, sir."

"So I heard, most unfortunate. The scion's crest is that of a snarling wolf's head. The obvious implications are borne out by his noted prowess at arms, but if you take his family crest into consideration—a castle keep—then it could just as easily refer to how men see wolves, as savage and violent creatures."

The guardsman took a step back. "I wouldn't know about that, sir, but I'd advise you to be more careful with your opinions of the scion; you'd have to be mad to get on the wrong side of him."

"Oh, I'm not important enough to bother the great house of Lomin. In any case, my talents are very useful to the nobility in general. You need to have a tendency towards prophecy to do what I do and that's rare enough to protect me."

The guard took another step back, his expression showing that he really did think Amanas was mad now.

"Oh now, don't look like that. There are clear signs of becoming a true prophet. You're quite safe from me." Amanas chuckled. It was nice to have the man of violence worried. The poor souls who went beyond foresight and became prophets were left utterly insane by the things they saw; most had to be chained up for the safety of everyone concerned.

"My point was that this is something I can do when I'm in the presence of the man, in contact with him," he explained. "But this Krann . . . I've never met the man, but for months I've been dreaming of a crest. I'd had it made up it into a shield even before the Krann was Chosen. He must be more than just a white-eye to have that effect."

The guardsman didn't seem to know how to respond to that. He was disquieted by the whole conversation. After a long pause, he said gruffly, "Well, we'd better not keep Lord Bahl waiting."

Amanas nodded and rose to lead his guest to the library, a dark room panelled in old oak, with scroll-holes down the left-hand side and two rows of reading shelves on the right. A number of lecterns stood in the centre. Some huge books, obviously valuable, were chained to the reading shelves, but the Keymaster ignored these and instead shuffled along to the door at the far end which opened into something that looked like a jeweller's strong room.

Once Amanas had unlocked it and retrieved a lamp from one of the lecterns, the guardsman could see neat piles of paper on the narrow shelves that lined the cubby—and on one shelf, something large, wrapped in some sort of dark cloth.

Amanas moved some of the papers out of the way and reverentially withdrew the object. He looked over his shoulder and glared at the guardsman. "Do you know why two of your comrades stand guard outside my office door?"

"No, sir, only that Chief Steward Lesarl ordered it."

"Ah yes, the Chief Steward; a man of remarkable insight. This library is more precious than most people realise. It was all I could do to keep it from being moved to the palace or Cold Halls once Lesarl realised that. Our nobility is a faithless breed that sires bastards as though they were in competition. My records are meticulous—they must be so—and my skills allow me to see through the lies. I suspect only the Chief Steward, one of his agents, and I know the full extent of a certain count's escapades, but since some of those sired are at marrying age now, a watchful eye must be kept on negotiations.

"Even the Dukes of Perlir and Merlat travel to Tirah to present their heirs to me; they all understand the need for such a tradition, and it has become a rite of passage nowadays. I suspect white-eyes have less of a care for such things though, hence my summons."

Gathering up the corners of the material, Amanas balanced it precariously in the crook of his arm while he wrestled with the lock. When the guardsman offered to help he gave the man a grim look in reply and struggled on by himself, careful not to expose any part of the object to the man's view.

He hugged it protectively to himself as they walked down the street side by side. The Heraldic Library was in the oldest district of the city, surrounded by the tall, ancient buildings where the oldest families lived and the richer dukes and suzerains had their—now much-neglected—court residences.

Cutting through the merchants' quarter took the pair on to Hunter's Ride, the road that ran from the river to intersect Palace Walk where it began its gentle climb towards Tirah Palace. The day was wet and dull; a scattering of early snow had briefly clothed the city in white, but it was too warm for the flakes to settle. Many of the innumerable statues that lined the city streets were crying tears of melted snow, which struck the Keymaster as a poor omen.

It was market day in Irienn Square up ahead so the guard nudged Amanas right, down Hunter's Ride, and the noise and bustle of the docks fell away behind them. Folk kept a respectful distance, standing aside to let them past, and one woman with a basketful of eels afforded Amanas a sympathetic look, assuming the worst.

Everyone was out today, going about the ten thousand different tasks that keep any city running smoothly. A portly man stamped heavily down the other side of the street from them; the thick gold chain around the man's neck and clerks scuttling in his wake marked him as a successful merchant.

Then Amanas caught sight of a gutter-runner moving along the edge of the tiled roof high above the merchant's head. Like all those who lived above ground, he was dressed only in rags and had little meat on his bones. They were scavengers who used the network of rooftops to travel quickly across the city. People often used them as the quickest way to get important information to its destination. The gutter-runners had a fierce code of honesty that ensured they were tolerated—even somewhat fondly—by Tirah's citizens. It was perfectly possible that the merchant was the child's employer that morning.

Amanas and his escort were waved through the barbican gate by the pikemen flanking it. When they emerged back into the daylight, Amanas hissed in irritation at the mud caking his boots. He insisted on stopping to scrape off the worst of it before he was ready to labour his way up the open stairs to the Great Hall.

Finally he stepped over the threshold, squinting, and for a brief moment he felt like a fish out of water; foolish and delicate in a world that was not his own. He could hear the laughter of men ringing in his ears. He had dreamed of this scene several weeks past, and though dreams themselves usually meant nothing, dreams of the Chosen before they come to power were different: they spoke of the Gods. He remembered her emerald gaze—eyes that could pierce the darkest recesses of the soul. He knew of only one Goddess whose eyes were green, and Fate was not a patient mistress.

The Keymaster tightened his grip and entered the hall. It was years since Amanas had last come here, and in the intervening period it had hardly changed: it was still a dark and smelly army mess, lacking even the meagre dignity one might hope for in an elite legion. Groups of men were clumped around the two rows of tables that led up to the high table at the far end. Even that was hardly grander than the others, just a little longer and set on a raised platform.

Amanas moved into the centre of the room and paused briefly to look around at the fading heraldry and flags that hung from the roof beams. Then he advanced a little further until Lord Bahl looked up. He stopped and waited to be addressed, but the old white-eye did nothing more than tap the young man beside him and return to his conversation with Chief Steward Lesarl.

The youth was clearly the new suzerain, a white-eye who towered over Amanas when he stood, but still conceded both height and weight to the Duke of Tirah. The Krann stared at the Keymaster for a few moments, then stabbed his eating dagger into the table top and walked around the table to reach the man, licking his fingers as he did. Amanas gave a short bow, cut short as his eyes reached the sword at Isak's hip. When he saw that he gave a slight squawk, prompting a smile to appear on the Krann's face.

"Something wrong?"

"Certainly, my Lord Suzerain; that sword that you are wearing is not *your* sword."

"So?"

"So it belongs to the Knight-Defender of Tirah and should only be worn by him."

The Krann looked back towards the high table in confusion. "I thought it belonged to Kerin? He's the one who lent it to me."

Amanas winced at the informality. "Swordmaster Kerin is the Knight-Defender of Tirah—that is the full title of the man who commands the Swordmasters."

"I still don't understand."

The question in Lord Isak's voice attracted Lesarl's attention. The Chief Steward spoke up before Amanas could reply. "He means, my Lord, that it's a gross breach of protocol to wear a ceremonial weapon belonging to another man."

"Kerin didn't seem to mind," Isak countered sharply.

"Unlike some present," replied the Chief Steward, gesturing to the newcomer.

"Enough. Argue when you're elsewhere." Bahl didn't look up, but gestured for Lesarl to continue their conversation.

"Well," continued Isak after a careful pause, "if you have nothing more to criticise about my attire, Lord Bahl said you needed to speak to me about my crest."

"Normally, yes, my Lord Suzerain. In this case, however, it will not be necessary." With a flourish, Amanas slipped the covering from the shield and held it up to the light.

A gasp ran around the room as the Keymaster held up a polished silver teardrop shield and turned almost a full circle to show everyone present Isak's crest embossed in gold.

Isak gaped at the shield. It was the work of a jeweller rather than a blacksmith. Even in the faint light, the glitter of the gold momentarily dazzled him. It took him a while to properly take in the image on the shield itself, the crest that he would wear on his clothes for the rest of his life and would fly from his banners when he rode to war.

Rearing high on its hind legs, claws ready to tear and rend, was a dragon of purest gold. Isak could see the fangs curving down from its mouth and a set of horns curling back past its head. He could feel the anger in the set of its shoulders, the sweep of its wings, something he recognised only too well. This was the taste of his own familiar rage given form.

Then his hand started to tremble as something else drew his eye. He reached out to take the shield from Amanas. A crown hovered above the dragon's head and as he saw that, foreboding sank into Isak's stomach, as heavy as gold.

"Careful, my Lord, the silver is still quite delicate," Amanas warned.

"That's solid silver? Then why—?"

The Keymaster held up a hand to suppress the question, then bent down and placed the green velvet in which the shield had been wrapped on the floor. He placed the shield face-up on the material, then stepped back.

Isak opened his mouth to speak, but before he could think of anything to say he felt a pulse of warmth come from the pile: magic . . . He turned to Bahl. The old Lord had also noticed; he fixed his stern gaze on the shield.

Without warning, the cloth underneath burst into flames. Isak flinched back in surprise, then stepped forward again as he felt no heat coming from the fire. The orange flames turned to green, all the while lasciviously caressing the lines of the shield. A furious cloud of magic grew up around the shield, swirling tighter and tighter as the green flames burned the velvet away to nothing. Isak suddenly realised that the magic was being drawn into the silver of the shield while a finger of energy wormed through the cracks in the flagstones and disappeared into the floor. And then it was over. Amanas was gone, the fire spent; only the shield, astonished faces, and confusion remained.

"Pick it up," Bahl commanded in a distant voice.

"What? But—"

"Do it."

The Krann shrugged and touched his finger to the silver. An expression of wonder ran over his face as he stroked the mirror surface with the palm of his hand, then picked up the shield to show the room.

"It's cool, perfectly cool," he marvelled. Turning the shield over in his hands, Isak suddenly stopped and rapped his knuckles against the surface. "This can't be silver, it's too strong." He took each side of the shield in his hands and pushed together, gently at first, but then with all the enormous strength he could muster.

"It's far too strong to be silver," he repeated.

"It's silver." Bahl's confirmation brought a frown from Isak. "Silver absorbs magic better than any other substance. That's a gift from the Gods for you, and emerald is the colour of the Lady, Fate herself."

Amanas had slipped out of the room long before anyone remembered to look for him. He was pleased, and returned to his wife with a satisfied smile on his face and a refusal to discuss what had happened earlier that evening. It was only when the Duke of Tirah paid them a visit the next day that she discovered why.

CHAPTER 8

"**I** CAN'T DO IT. I can feel it there, but nothing's happening."

"Nothing?"

"Nothing. Can't you tell?" Isak struggled to control his boredom. Running through the drills Kerin had devised for the last fortnight was dull enough; standing and staring at a wooden post for a whole hour was infinitely worse.

"To me, it feels like you simply won't relax and let go." Bahl's voice was irritatingly calm and steady, as if the man was used to spending his days like this. They were out on the training ground. Nearby, a cavalry squadron was perfecting a variety of complicated formations. This one involved a wedge of soldiers of the Palace Guard who stood in the centre, flanked on either side by wheeling lines of light cavalry. The cavalry might not have been professional soldiers like the Ghosts but they were made to work hard for their annual stipend.

"Why would I not let go? This isn't exactly entertaining."

Bahl's eyes flashed. "Watch your tone, boy. Even if you did manage to use the magic inside you, I could still cut you down like a child. Do you think I'm trying to teach you conjuring tricks? Magic can turn the tide of the battle; you *must* be able to command it at will, or you'll be as dead as your men on the field."

Isak looked up at Bahl's tone of voice and saw his hand tighten slightly. This was the first time it had contained even a trace of anger. He turned and bowed his head. "I'm sorry, my Lord, I didn't mean to be rude. It's just that I don't understand what I'm not doing."

Bahl didn't reply immediately and an awkward silence descended. When Bahl spoke again, his irritation was entirely absent. Isak knew he was in sore need of learning that particular skill.

"Then we will have to get around the problem. I will ask the High Priest of Larat to come and see whether he can shed any light on the matter."

"Larat? No, not a chance—"

"There will be no arguments about this," said Bahl firmly.

"But what about the light in my dream?"

"I said no arguments. The High Priest is a good man and understands the nature of magic as well as any. If I ask the College of Magic, they will try to turn it to their advantage; the Temple of Larat is poor, so they will be glad to receive our favour."

"But—"

"*Enough*. It's lucky for you I am not Atro. He was not so forgiving when questioned."

"Luck? I don't know whether I believe in that anymore." Isak looked up and stretched his shoulders, flexing muscles that were aching from uncomfortable nights and daily weapons practise. He caught Tila's eye and smiled. She was sitting off to one side, so bundled up against the chill of the wind that only her eyes were visible.

The girl had been reserved around him for the first week, jumping at any sudden movement, but the familiarity of Isak's company soon began to wear away at her resolve not to forget the death of Sir Dirass. Isak had even made her laugh—the first time it had happened he was not sure who had been more surprised, but it was not the only time he had brought a smile to her lips.

"How did you manage?"

"Hmm?"

"With Atro—how did you manage to live around such a bastard?"

"I kept quiet and ignored what he did. I wasn't like you when I came to the palace; I had joined the Guard as a child, as soon as my family could get rid of me. I was twenty-four when the Tyrant of Mustet appeared at the barbican gate and announced I was Chosen of Nartis. While I had no interest in being Atro's tool, I didn't care that he was destroying our tribe either. I was more like General Lahk than you."

Isak nodded. He'd seen the stern-faced white-eye stamping around the palace, but the general had offered neither friendship nor conversation. The guards said Lahk had been taken to the Temple of Nartis by Bahl twenty years back. Lahk was the only white-eye other than Bahl to have reached a position of some power, but Nartis had rejected him as Krann. His body had been scarred with lightning, and it was whispered in the barracks that his soul had been burnt out too, for the general cared for nothing but serving his lord.

"Until you met Ineh?"

A flicker of pain ran across Bahl's brow, but he just nodded sadly. "Ineh."

He savoured the name as he said it, as though it left a sweet taste on his lips. Isak was desperate to ask more, but he was nervous of going too far.

"Are they right in what they say?"

"Which is?"

"That it's better to have loved and lost?"

Bahl gave a short, bitter laugh. There was no humour in his eyes when he answered, "You really are a strange one. I can't think of that occurring to any other white-eye. No, it doesn't matter; just be careful not to pry too far. Is it better? Perhaps, I felt more alive then; she gave me a reason to be more human. Atro was a tumour in the belly of this tribe, but it was only when I met Ineh that I cared. Only then did I bother to notice the hurt he was causing. To live with such loss I would not wish on any man, but to live without the joy that came before . . . if a man can stand before the Gods and choose not to have known the one he has lost, he never truly loved her."

"I'm sorry." The words sounded absurd, worthless, and Isak almost winced as he said them. Bahl didn't reply, other than for a tired sigh. For a minute he looked like a sad old man, then the blank visage reasserted itself, burying all emotion deep inside once more.

"Don't be sorry. Regrets are no use to a Lord of the Farlan—which reminds me, Lesarl tells me you have a problem with keeping your own counsel during meetings. That's another skill you could happily study."

"What do you mean?"

"I mean what you called the Marshal of Quetek. However apparent it was, that observation cost Lesarl severely."

"Well, the man was being paid enough already, *and* he was demanding that Lesarl help him arrange a marriage. He was practically drooling at the thought."

"The girl's a maid in the palace, no? I've seen her. You'd probably drool yourself."

"The girl's fourteen summers! The Marshal of Quetek is over sixty, with a grown heir already. He's in no need of another wife."

"But he will have one, whether you like it or not. And if you did somehow manage to stop him, he would no doubt force his maids into his bed and turn them out of the house when he tires of them. If he marries, there is some constraint on his behaviour—and the girl is going to be married anyway. To wed an old marshal means she'll soon be a widow of property. Next time, think before you start to moralise to your elders."

"I wasn't moralising. I just didn't like the man. Why should I hold my tongue?"

"And that's what you should learn."

Isak frowned. "Perhaps I should, but I've no desire to. I've spent my whole life biting things back, keeping quiet when I'm in the right and taking every insult I get from men I could break in half. People might still hate me, but at least now they're going to have to be careful about it."

For a moment Bahl looked concerned, as though he had just been reminded of a deeply troubling conversation, then he muttered, "Fine, just don't try to make any more enemies—those will come fast enough without you adding to them. Now go and clear your mind for when the priest comes. The calmer you are, the easier it will be for both of you."

"Isak, it's time."

Isak didn't reply, but raised a hand to acknowledge Tila's words. He was sat on a cushion in the palace shrine, high under the eaves of the palace. There were scenes of Nartis hunting on every wall, and the ceiling represented a night sky. The many pillars in the room were painted like trees, each one reaching up and spreading branches into the ceiling to meet the sky.

This room was an oasis of solitude, far from the bustle of the palace, and one that only the rich could afford. Even in Isak's formal chambers, luxurious open rooms on the second floor, there was always noise: the tramp of servants, guards, and palace residents shook the corridors, while from outside came the pounding of hooves and constant shouted orders from the training ground.

Up here, where few were permitted to go, Isak could enjoy his own company in what little free time he had. When not training or shadowing Lesarl through innumerable meetings, he was struggling through a library of dusty texts, learning to be both politician and religious figure. He was floundering under the sheer weight of both.

His thoughts turned to the man who would be waiting for him downstairs. Lesarl had taught him never to rush to meet anyone but an old friend. Even for Lord Bahl, Lesarl would calmly find a break in his work and walk to where he was required, retaining his composure at all times. When it was urgent, Bahl didn't have the patience to send a servant.

Even though it had been only two weeks, Isak could already appreciate the advantages. He couldn't claim to like Lesarl, but his respect for the Chief

Steward was growing daily. The man could infuriate with a smile and a gentle handshake. Isak had learned to his cost the price of becoming annoyed and leaving himself open to goading. Lesarl now owned a valuable manor in Anvee: an object lesson, Lord Bahl said, in agreeing to anything—particularly a wager—while angry.

Lesarl strode around with an aura of almost palpable confidence that made men defer to him almost as much as they did Lord Bahl. Isak recognised that regal presence was something else he should cultivate.

"Tila, did you learn the story of Amavoq's Cup when you were younger?" he asked.

"Of course," she said. "Why?"

"Because I didn't. I hardly know any of the old tales. There's a picture of it over there on the wall—I'd seen it on a temple wall before, but never thought to ask. Earlier today I saw Lesarl send off a carriage loaded with as much gold as it could carry, to be sent all the way to Merlat, all because of that bloody cup."

"Well, Amavoq's Cup was only the origin of the dispute with the Yee-tatchen. Quite a lot more has happened in the meantime."

"But the point is I didn't have a clue, and when I asked I looked like a fucking idiot—"

"Isak!"

He turned at her shocked voice, then realised what was wrong. "Oh don't worry, Nartis isn't listening."

Tila was blushing furiously at his words. "Isak, you can't say such things, especially in a temple! What if anyone heard? Even a Krann can be charged with impiety, and the Gods—"

"Stop worrying; you're the only one to hear. I think I'm bound closely enough to Nartis to feel his presence in one of his shrines. As for impiety, how would they enforce it? I'm apparently a senior figure in the Cult of Nartis, and Lord Bahl is the official head. I would assume a charge of impiety against me would require, at the very least, his signature. Even if it doesn't, am I going to be dragged by a few elderly priests to the courts?"

"What about the dark monks?"

"The who? Something else I'm supposed to know? Is there anything else?"

"I . . . I don't really know, but there's not much I can tell you about the dark monks; no one really knows a lot, other than that they're called the Brethren of the Sacred Teachings and people say that they seek out and assassinate heretics throughout the Land."

"Wonderful! Religious fanatics and assassins; what a sensible combination. Still, there are none in earshot, so I'm still safe." He eased himself up off the cushion, wondering idly what myth was behind the lack of seats in any temple dedicated to Nartis. No explanations came to mind and he dismissed it quickly. He had kept Lord Bahl waiting quite long enough.

He adjusted his long robe, dark blue like those worn by all monks of Nartis. His was distinguished by the dragon brooch pinned on his chest. Nobles were expected to wear their crest in some form at all times, and now he knew that, Isak had begun to notice the subtle embroidered patches and jewellery men in the palace wore. Tila was getting more made for him, a number fitting to his high station. He wouldn't have bothered, except for the way Tila said "your high station" had made it impossible for the wagon-brat in him to refuse.

He ran a hand over his shorn head and smiled at the thought of what Carel would say if he could see him now. He loved being able to walk into any shop he liked and be fussed over like a prince, although Tila's efforts to convert him to fashion were floundering. Every day another outfit arrived for his consideration, though he preferred the simplicity of the formal robes that were spurned by most of the nobility of his age. They preferred a gaudier look bedecked with ornamentation. But in all of this, he had managed to keep his scar hidden. He still wasn't quite sure why it mattered, but now he was shadowed by servants and guards he felt he wanted to keep some things secret from the rest of the palace.

As Isak descended the main staircase, he felt a flicker of trepidation in his stomach. Beside him, Tila's shoes scuffed on the stone steps as she kept up with him. In deference to the High Priest, she wore a white scarf over her head, wrapping it around the single plait that ran down her back. As they reached the bottom of the stairs, Tila asked whether any of the charms in her hair were showing.

Isak suspected that he didn't know the reason for that tradition either, but at least he understood that she didn't want to wear another God's rune so obviously in front of a High Priest, even though adults could wear as many charms as they wanted. Tila had inherited four antique pieces from her grandmother that she loved.

"Lord Isak," called the guardsman at the foot of the stairs, "you're expected. This way." He pointed to his left towards the Great Hall where the last door before the entrance to the hall was open. Swordmaster Kerin stood in the doorway looking uncomfortable in his formal uniform, a dress version of the Palace Guard's black and white livery. The Swordmaster bowed as Isak approached, which made Isak frown in surprise—only that morning Kerin had been screaming curses at him out on the training field.

"Inside," he muttered. "Relax and do what you're told, even if you don't feel like it. The man's going to look inside your mind; it's dangerous, so don't fight him or decide to 'try something' yourself, understand?"

Isak nodded and Kerin backed away through the door to let the Krann pass into the ducal audience chamber, a room fifteen yards long and empty of furniture except for the Lord of the Farlan's ceremonial seat. The room was seldom used these days as most suits and requests went through Lesarl. The Chief Steward maintained offices at both Tirah Palace and Cold Halls, once a palace, now the city administrators' offices, on the north side of Irienn Square. He had been known to make people queue outside in bad weather, just to ensure their business was sufficiently important. His personal suite of offices commanded a fine view of the square below.

Inside, the cluster of men stopped talking and turned. Lord Bahl, in formal attire and wearing a silver circlet on his hooded head, was seated on the massive ducal throne. Beside him, on a more temporary seat, was the High Priest. The flashes of purple and yellow on his dark blue robe marked him as a follower of Larat. There was another priest in similar robes standing beside the High Priest's chair.

Despite Isak's misgivings, the man—Afger Wetlen, so Tila had told him—looked a far cry from the conniving devotee of Larat he'd been expecting. The High Priest was a bony old man with a sickly complexion and rheumy eyes. He seemed to be having difficulty enough remaining upright in his seat, let alone pursuing the schemes of a duplicitous God. The sharp-eyed priest supporting his master's elbow was a different matter, but Isak reminded himself that most people looked that way at a white-eye, so there was no point reading anything into it.

Four novices who had accompanied them were huddled in a far corner, no doubt terrified by the presence of Lord Bahl. They'd probably been brought along because they were showing some tendency towards magic—it usually started to manifest at puberty. If they could sense power on even the most basic level, they would find Lord Bahl's presence extremely disturbing. Isak grinned widely at them, which made them shrink back even further, and walked over to the seated men.

Lord Bahl introduced Isak, saying formally, "High Priest Wetlen, may I present to you my Krann, the Chosen of Nartis, Lord Isak."

"My Lord." The old man struggled to his feet, helped by the young priest at his elbow. "I presume Lord Bahl has told you something of what I intend."

"Not really, not in detail," Isak admitted, trying not to feel any fear.

"It is rather difficult to explain. No doubt he thought it best to leave that to me, so I will do so while we get settled." The old man gestured at a door in the wall of the main chamber that Isak hadn't noticed. "Lord Bahl has been kind enough to allow me the use of an antechamber as we will need to be alone."

"Your Eminence?" The young priest at his side looked rather alarmed, but High Priest Wetlen just waved him away.

"I will be fine. Your presence will just complicate matters," he said sternly. "I'm not so old I can't sit still without your help." He swatted at his assistant, but his effort ended abruptly with a sharp hiss of pain and he capitulated. "Very well, help me in there, and then leave us."

Isak could hear the old man's frustration at the failings of his body. The attendant priest made no comment, but waved at one of the novices to bring the chair. The boy scuttled about his task, his eyes darting from one white-eye to the other as the four of them passed Bahl and went through the door on his right.

"Come on boy, put it down there—no, facing the table. Fetch that cushion and place it before the chair. Lord Isak, I suggest you sit on the cushion and focus your attention on the painting above the table. It will help things go smoothly if you have something to concentrate on." The High Priest eased himself into the seat and gave a quiet sigh of satisfaction before patting at the various charms at his belt.

"Now then, my Lord—yes, Unmen, you can go, and shut the door behind you—now then, Lord Isak, Lord Bahl has requested that my Aspect guide is not present during these sessions. If you would sprinkle this powder in a circle around us, it will ensure that is the case."

Isak took the brass vial the old man had proffered, but he made no move to remove the stopper. Instead, he asked, "Aspect guide?"

"Yes—oh, but of course, you wouldn't have one; limiting, if you ask me, but perhaps it is for the best. Do you not know about them at all?"

"I know what an Aspect is."

High Priest Wetlen gave a phlegmy chuckle. "I assumed you would know *that*, at least. What I meant was whether you knew about magical guides, but I presume not. The mages understandably don't want it to become public knowledge, but this is how it works: to aid their researches, an apprentice mage of sufficient promise will find a guide to bind to him, and to use to build his grimoire.

"These guides are creatures of magic, very minor daemons, too weak to exert any control over their mage, but knowledgeable enough to substantially build on what is taught at the colleges. Crucially, they are also intelligent enough to know that their own power will increase proportionally if they do cooperate, and as creatures of magic, their perspective is most valuable.

"Theologically this is difficult ground, so priests with similar promise take an Aspect of their chosen God instead—a weaker choice, but more acceptable for a religious figure. Ducohs, my own guide, has been with me for more than sixty years."

"It has a name?"

"But of course." Isak's comment seemed to amuse the old man. "I have been High Priest for more than twenty years now, and as my strength and ability have increased, so have Ducohs's. Now, make a circle with the powder."

This time Isak did as he was told. His curiosity about this withered old man was mounting: he talked about an Aspect of Larat as he would an old friend. When he had finished, Isak replaced the stopper and handed the bottle back. The priest fumbled as he attempted to reattach it to one of the chains that hung from his waist, but the determined set to his mouth made it clear enough that he wanted no help.

"Right, now we are ready. Sit in front of me and concentrate on the picture. This will be disconcerting, so it is better to keep your eyes open and focused on something."

Isak sat and stared intently at the painting while High Priest Wetlen wheezed and muttered unintelligibly. The painting, a classical image of Nartis hunting, was old and ugly. Isak scowled. Whoever the artist was, he was an idiot who had no idea how living creatures moved or stood. Nartis himself was grossly parodied: shown almost naked, with deep blue skin and an excessively muscular body. The figure looked brutal, like a daemon, not a God, with no grace or subtlety about it.

Isak kept his eyes on the painting as the High Priest reached out and touched his head, gently drawing magic from the air around them so Isak's ears began to buzz and ring at the sensation of energies rushing through him. It felt like cool, ghostly fingers dipping into his mind. Then he felt the powers pause and hold, and he himself relaxed and unclenched his fists.

He smothered the alarm he felt in the back of his mind and took a deep breath, waiting for the High Priest to continue. He trembled as the smooth but relentless fingers traced the shape of his soul, and closed his eyes.

Swordmaster Kerin watched Lord Bahl as they waited outside in silence. The white-eye had his eyes closed and his head rested heavily on one hand. It was an unnerving sight: a tired king on his throne. To the Swordmaster, Bahl had always been a man of boundless strength and energy, impervious to the burdens imposed by power.

Bahl's eyes jerked wide open and he was already upright as a blinding crash of light and noise burst through the antechamber door. Kerin flinched away from the explosion, arms held protectively over his face as pieces of shattered door flew across the room.

In the silence that followed, they saw the broken corpse of High Priest Wetlen, and Isak, still sitting on the cushion, his face a rictus of terror as a golden nimbus glittered and surged above his shorn head.

CHAPTER 9

"**W**ELL, WILL IT WORK?"

The engineer mopped his heavy brow with an oil-stained cloth and chanced a look at his lord. The huge white-eye was standing perfectly still, looking out through the cloud to the city walls beyond. Either Lord Styrax was moving swiftly, albeit with economical purpose, or he was as motionless as the many statues of Karkarn, God of War and patron of the Menin tribe, that adorned their home city; there was no middle ground, and it was disconcerting to behold. There was no wasted effort on personal quirks: it was as if the Gods had perfected their design for the white-eye, and Kastan Styrax was the fruit of their efforts. Since their first meeting two months back, the engineer had remained in utter awe, and even now, as he looked at Lord Styrax's emotionless face, he found it hard to imagine the man was a mere mortal, made of flesh and blood.

"I believe so, my Lord," he said after taking a moment to smother the nervous hiccoughs that threatened to interrupt. "The wood is sound and my men have done a good job; I could expect nothing better, given the circumstances. I would prefer to test-fire it first, but without that option, all I can say is that I believe it will serve as you asked. If you were using a cut stone I could estimate—" His voice broke off as Styrax raised his hand. Apart from his head, it was the only part of the white-eye's body not encased in forbidding black armour, but the hand, like the armour, was the result of his greatest victory. Bone-white from wrist to fingertip, it had twisting swirls of scar tissue covering the skin and deep bloody stains forever caught under the fingernails. Rumour said Kastan Styrax had allowed it to be burned to achieve this great triumph: cutting down Koezh Vukotic in battle. No lone warrior had managed such a feat since the vampire had risen from the grave for the first time; he considered the price minor.

"The sinew is still strong?" asked a rasping voice from behind them. The engineer turned as General Gaur advanced on them, his lord's helm clasped reverentially in his black-furred hands. Few would interrupt Lord Styrax's conversations, but despite his monstrous appearance and hybrid nature, General Gaur was the closest thing to a friend the white-eye had.

"We brought two sets just in case, and one survived completely intact," confirmed the engineer. "I've checked the catapult and it's still in firing order."

"Excellent. You have done everything I need you for." The engineer paled as his eyes were drawn to Lord Styrax's huge broadsword.

"Gaur, accompany our skilled friend to the horses and get them ready to move. And send Kohrad to me."

The engineer sagged with relief as General Gaur began to walk away, pausing for a moment to allow him to pick up his tools and catch up. Clearly they weren't going to kill him now his task was over, as he had begun to fear. As the tension flooded away, he began to hiccough again, trying desperately to smother them with his hands, but the general prodded his shoulder with one taloned finger and beckoned him on.

Lord Styrax hadn't moved an inch, despite the odd noises, and the trails of unnatural cloud made him appear almost ethereal in the morning light. The engineer shivered at the sight and scuttled away, hiccoughing madly, as fast as he could. He was careful not to look back again.

Styrax tasted the air. The bittersweet flavour of magic hung thick around him. The fog that surrounded his small army made it difficult to see anything more of the city than an outline of stone against the morning sky. Out of the corner of his eye, he could see Larim, one of Larat's Chosen, currently engaged in making them invisible from the city walls. The strain was only just beginning to show on the young white-eye's face.

"Father, Larim seems to be a match for the test you set him. I think that old crow Lord Salen will have to be more careful of his position in future. There's quite a gleam of ambition in Larim's eye."

"I think you're right, Kohrad," Styrax replied, not taking his eyes off the wall. He raised his arm straight out for his son to duck underneath; steel clanked against steel. "Don't underestimate the cunning of crows though. Lord Salen has been busy himself recently, I think the contest will be most entertaining to watch." Styrax paused. "Kohrad, my arm feels unseasonably warm."

"That's because it's on fire, Father."

"Stop it then."

"Yes, Father—I was just frightening away Gaur's fleas."

"Don't. You shouldn't make fun of him when there are nobles around. General Gaur has no allies among them, only enemies, and he's as devoted to you as he is to me."

"I hardly think that's possible."

Kohrad looked around for his father's friend. The bulky general was on his way over, his massive jaw working away as it always did when he was thinking. His fangs moved up and down through the rough bristles of his face.

"And still it is true, whether you let yourself see it or not." Styrax turned to face his son, letting none of his sadness at Kohrad's glazed expression show on his face. Small flames still ghosted over the red-stained steel of his son's armour. Kohrad enjoyed wielding flame and destruction rather more than his father was comfortable with; Styrax thought it was beginning to cloud the young man's mind. However he'd found that armour, the only secret he kept from his father, it hadn't been the blessing Kohrad considered it.

"Despite his looks, I still don't think Gaur really suits being a soldier," Kohrad said, in a rare moment of reflection. "He's too serene, too at peace with the Land. He never lost his temper with me when I was growing up. Now I realise that must have been hard." Styrax gave a snort of amusement but didn't interrupt. "I suppose that makes him the best man to trust your army to, but it still seems perverse."

"As is much in life," the white-eye Lord agreed. "Battle is all he's ever known, and you would wound him gravely if you suggested he gave up furthering my cause."

Kohrad gestured towards the walls of Raland up ahead. "Speaking of your cause and the perversity of life; all those years of research to find the damn thing and this fat fool digs it up just a few months before we arrive . . ."

"I know," Styrax said with an ironic smile, "but I cannot decide whether it is merely a lesson in the unpredictability of life, or a dire portent for this Age. However, whatever the reason, I think it is time we showed these people how easily we can take what is theirs. Are you ready?"

"Of course—but I'm curious to know why you are certain there will be a soft landing waiting for me."

"The first rule of warfare." He waited for his son to fill in the words.

"Know your enemy," Kohrad confirmed, "although some might say that knowing yourself is the first rule."

"That is necessary long before a man leads an army to battle." Styrax could sense his son's reluctance to cede the point, but the boy was a white-eye too, and filial loyalty could only go so far, after all.

"I still think that having a vastly larger army would be a better rule to start with."

Styrax gave his son an affectionate thump on the shoulder. "Perhaps, but it lacks elegance, and there is not much to take from that into the rest of life. If there is a lesson to be learned, no man should ignore the opportunity. If there isn't, open a jar of wine and find wisdom there."

"For someone with such insight, you're still taking a gamble, however educated your guess might be. You can't know everything about a man's character. For instance, this duke could enjoy waking up to the dawn just as I do now—remember our hunting trips? Since then I've always preferred a west-facing window. The duke might also, despite the impressive view from this window."

"True enough," Styrax agreed, "but do not *over*estimate men either: most remain slaves to their weaknesses, and our friend the duke is one. He is so weak he'll need to feel his power the moment he wakes. However, another rule of life is not to gamble with what you hold most dear, and I never do. Our agent in the city made sure."

"Your men would have accepted your guesswork without a word. Gaur would have."

"That's because I have the best army in the Land, and to be victorious, an army needs faith in its leader. You questioned me because you were not born to follow orders."

"You're very sure of that. Gaur himself is evidence that breeding counts for nothing."

"The chances were always good," Styrax said quietly. "For a good litter, you make sure you have the finest bitch. I abide the company of few enough to risk keeping a fool of a son around to disappoint me. You have two positions to inherit in your life, General Gaur's and my own, and I am certain you will prove worthy of both. Enough of doubts—you have a task I can entrust to no other, so get yourself ready."

Kohrad stared back at his father, a mix of gratitude and suspicion on his face. There was no need to add that Styrax could do it himself. What they intended would be an outrageous gesture, one to make the whole of the West take notice. It was also a test for Kohrad. He would not return if he failed.

"Why aren't you doing something about it?"

Tochet opened his mouth to reply to Duke Nemarse's demand, then bit his tongue against saying something he would regret. The duke had been pacing around for half an hour now, all the while tapping his fingers against a small velvet purse that hung from his belt. These mannerisms annoyed Tochet, and the effect was exacerbated by the duke's high girlish voice.

"What would you like me to do? That noise is driving the horses mad, and I'm not sending my infantry out there."

"Well, do something; I'm not paying you to stand up here and gawp over the walls."

Tochet sighed. He'd tried to send some cavalry out, but they had gone only a few dozen yards before guttural animal calls had sent them into a panic. Whatever creatures were out there, they liked the smell of horsemeat.

"Destech," the mercenary commander called, and his lieutenant stepped closer, baring his filed teeth at the duke to make him back out of earshot. It was quite unnecessary; the duke couldn't understand a word of Chetse, but they had found little else in the way of entertainment in Raland.

"General?" Tochet no longer held that rank, but his men could think of him no other way. They would always respect him above all others.

"What do you think?"

"Same as you, sir." Destech had been with his commander for twenty years, and in that time they had fought many creatures from the Waste. They knew well not to underestimate the unknown.

"Damn. I don't know whether it's trolls or minotaurs, or something even worse, but I'm buggered if I'm leading the men out to find out what. The sentries said they heard something dragging, and something heavy falling, but maybe it wasn't a battering ram after all. What I don't understand is why the catapults and ballistae are still not firing, and where in the name of the dark place that mage is."

"I'll go and hurt someone."

"Thank you."

Destech turned and dropped down through the hatch in the centre of the tower platform at the highest point on the wall. Tochet looked down from the duke's Gate Palace towards the vastness of the Elven Waste. It was well fortified, but it was home to the duke's family too; when the tip of his long-axe had punched a hole in a tall vase, it sent the duchess into an apoplectic fit.

Tochet continued his vigil, looking out at the strange cloud that ignored the northerly breeze and instead sat in front of him. It looked even less natural now that dawn had fully broken. The men on watch had woken him just before dawn, when they'd first noticed something strange. Making his way up here, still shrouded in sleep, he'd been struck by the desolate splendour of the miles of silent, empty land he could see. Destech was back within a few minutes, grimly ignoring the kicking man he had by the scruff of his neck. The lieutenant was even bigger than his commander and had no difficulty pulling the soldier up through the hatch with one hand and depositing him at Tochet's feet.

"Think the mage has done a runner, General—which isn't a good sign if you ask me—but this scrawny little bugger was sat in a corner with a jar of wine."

"Ah, thank you, Destech. Now, Lieutenant, why have you not yet fired, as you were ordered?"

"Fire at what?" Even as he struggled up from a heap on the floor, the man managed to maintain the haughty arrogance that everyone in this city of goldsmiths appeared to possess.

"Destech, take him and hang him over the battlements."

A gasp ran around the other soldiers on the platform and the duke stepped forward, but Tochet silenced them all with a glance as Destech took the red-liveried solider by the throat and dragged him over to the edge.

He followed his commander's orders, throwing the man over the edge of the battlemented wall, and held him firmly by the ankle as Tochet leaned out to speak to him. The commander's words were drowned out as the soldier shrieked like a seabird and Destech had to give the man a violent shake before he finally fell silent.

Tochet resumed his speech. "Now, do you see the difference? I give an order; it is obeyed. This is a vital requirement of leadership. In this case, I don't care whether you have a target or not; those ballistae should be firing on that cloud. Disobey an order again and I'll throw you off the wall myself."

"You don't want me to—?" There was a look of surprise on Destech's face. Back home Tochet would certainly have ordered him to drop the man; a disobeyed order was not something any new commander could allow unpunished.

Tochet shook his head. "Not this time, no—that would mean you'd have to go back down and get those weapons firing one by one. Bring him up."

Destech gave the dangling figure one last shake, then hauled him back up over the side. The mercenary wrinkled his nose as he realised the sobbing wretch had soiled himself. He spoke in Chetse to his commander, though his scornful tone made the words clear enough. "A legion army; that's all I ask: we'd take this city in a day."

Tochet grinned and bent down to the trembling soldier's ear. "Now, go and follow my orders."

The soldier stayed frozen until Tochet stood up straight again, then ran for the open hole in the floor. His frantic voice sounded from down below, relaying the order to fire. One velvet glove remained on the floor at Tochet's feet. He kicked it into a puddle and turned back to the cloud.

"Catapult!" bellowed Destech suddenly, and Tochet angled his head up to see a flaming object high in the air, already falling towards them. The mercenaries dived for the small cover of the battlements, hands over their eyes in anticipation of the fireball. When it hit a few heartbeats later, Tochet was surprised not to feel the impact reverberate through the stone under his feet. Instead, all he heard was the crash of wood and glass.

Both Chetse jumped up and leaned out over the wall. A finger of flame spat out from the ruin of the massive window below and a rush of warm air rose up to meet them.

"Get down there, put those fires out," roared Tochet. Destech was already moving, pushing past the duke, who was still summoning up the courage to look out himself.

"What was that?"

"That was a missile, you damn fool. A missile that scored a perfect hit on your bedchamber. That cloud's covering a battery of catapults."

"But only one's fired."

Tochet looked up. The air was indeed empty: there were no more missiles in the sky, no sound of firing, or even reloading of the one that had fired. The cloud had closed up and sat there placidly again.

"Why would you use only one catapult to attack a city?" the mercenary muttered to himself. It sounded like a bad joke.

"What?" the duke asked him. Tochet ignored the man and answered his own question.

"When one's enough. Oh Gods." He looked out over the edge and was rewarded with another blast of hot air. It was enough to make him draw back hurriedly, though not before he saw the flickering fires already spreading.

"Tsatach protect us. Duke Nemarse, it's time we made for safer ground. I think that fire's going to spread faster than you'd believe possible."

The air had been driven from the room and the only sound was the slow tinkle of broken glass falling on cold stone. Enveloped in the warm caress of a ruined mattress, Kohrad held his breath and waited, savouring the eager desire of the flame that was held in check, aching for the precious kiss of air. Then he let it go, and a deep crimson light swept around the walls of the chamber and yellow garlands danced up the shattered bedposts.

He rose from the wreckage of the huge bed, the remains already black and charred. The early morning sunlight coming through the window was a weak and feeble thing in comparison, wavering from the tendrils of heat snaking through the room. His mailed hands stroked a delicately painted frieze above the fireplace; under his touch, the colours blistered and writhed to nothing. Fiery fingers dribbled across the stone floor, sucking life from the rushes before pouncing on the drapes and furniture. In seconds, the entire room was clothed in flame.

He heard the door crash open and drew his sword as he turned. For a moment, he saw only more wood to feed to his voracious flames, then movement caught his eye as someone fell back from the heat, his arms over his head, protecting his face. Kohrad strode out and hacked off the soldier's head with one two-handed stroke. Out of the corner of his eye, he caught the glint of a pike-head. He spun round and used his sword to turn it aside, then, grasping the shaft, he pulled hard and brought the pikeman close enough to smash his armoured elbow into the man's face.

Lunging forward, he stopped the next man in his tracks with his sword, swatted aside an axe, and, with a burst of fire, he drove his enemy back. The man, a Chetse, he suddenly realised, was brave: ignoring the overwhelming heat, he charged forward to drive his shoulder into Kohrad's chest. The impact knocked the white-eye back a little, but the victory was short-lived as Kohrad smashed his fist down on to the Chetse's helm and hacked at the man's ribs. The man collapsed, flames already licking at his axe-shaft and clothes. The room was his.

Kohrad started off down the corridor, then came to an abrupt halt as he felt a cold mind cut through the heat to touch his own. His father felt as if he were impervious to the power of the flames he wielded, and that reminded him of his mission. The object was somewhere above, nagging at his mind.

Reaching up, Kohrad touched the beam running across the ceiling of the corridor. That he could burn, and he used it to spread himself out around the building, cutting off the routes of escape. Once that was done, Kohrad began to consume the long drapes and polished furniture, filling rooms with magnificent sculptures of heat and light. He found a stairway and moved up floor by floor, like a wolf pack driving its prey. He cut down some of the panicked occupants as he found them and left others cowering in corners or hiding in wardrobes. Some were on their knees, praying with shouts and fearful cries, but their frantic appeals couldn't touch him. Kohrad was born of white-eyes, untouched by the Gods and subject only to the laws of fire and light.

Reaching the top, he came to a closed hatch-door; he forced his fist up through it, but something held it closed, despite the damage. A second blow smashed the frame to pieces which fell at his feet to join the pyre. The wooden steps were burning even as he ascended into the light of day. Another Chetse struck out with his long battle-axe, before Kohrad had time to escape the confines of the hatchway, but the burning white-eye swatted the curved steel aside, jumping up onto the level floor in the next movement and hacking into the man's spine with astonishing speed.

The soldier fell screaming, but as his cries faded into the reaching flames, Kohrad had already turned his attention to the others on the platform. No one else stepped forward to attack him, so Kohrad ignored the soldiers and focused his attention on the quivering shape of the duke.

The taste of blistered and burning fat rose up in his mind as he held out his hand to the duke. The man gibbered with terror, fingers tightening around the Skull even as his skin blistered and charred. Kohrad snapped the bones with ease, and as he prised the Skull away, he felt it cry out for his touch. With a sigh of satisfaction, Kohrad pressed the Crystal Skull to his breast, where it fused with the armour, turning the deep colour of blood.

The flames around him danced with renewed strength as he caressed the Skull. "So you're Destruction," he whispered. "I'd hoped it was you. One day you'll be mine, when we are Gods and Father has no more need for you, you'll become part of me forever."

He left the towering pyre without haste, leaving only the crackle of licking flames and the stench of burning flesh in his wake.

CHAPTER 10

THE KNIVES OF WINTER, honed on the jagged cliffs of the north, lashed at the great forest of the Spiderweb Mountains. Whispers in the night carried a restless memory of long-abandoned places, as the profane words of another Age burned once more in the hearts of the elves, the twisted descendants of those cursed by the Gods for their rebellion. Dark bargains were made, even before the seers announced a silver light shining out from the west. The first furtive figures returned to settlements that the Farlan had driven them from decades ago.

The Festival of Swords had slowly replaced the ruthless hunting parties of fifty years past as the elves retreated away from their tormentors: pageantry in place of savagery. Now the elves returned to find the Farlan watchtowers and forts in disrepair or empty, replaced by farms and villages now closer than ever to the cold depths of the forest, and exposed in the harsh autumn light.

When their first attacks met only feeble resistance, they grew bolder and more savage. The wind tore through ruined homes and carried the smoke from the pyres for miles. Even in the towns, where people hid behind the relative safety of stone walls, they could hear the drums hammering out through the night air, and guttural voices singing of pain and prophecy, of their time come again. The taste of revenge carried far on the wind.

"What do you mean by punished? General Elierl is not a child to be disciplined!" The walls shook as Bahl roared at the man sitting placidly in the centre of the room. Isak found himself leaning back from the sheer force of Bahl's anger, but the focus of that ire didn't even twitch. Perched on a low stool, the mage mouthed the words in echo of his Lord, his hairless head dipping back and forward as though following some sort of tune in his head. The movement continued after the mage fell silent, as he cocked his head and rocked back and forth, waiting for the reply.

"General Elierl has been removed from command of Lomin's forces," intoned the mage again after a long pause. His voice was distant, an echo from afar. Isak sat forward to take a closer look at the man, watching his movements in fascination, trying to fathom their part in the ritual. The mage continued, oblivious to the people around him.

Lesarl, when pushed for information, had told Isak the movement helped the twin mages to keep in touch with each other, but the Chief Steward had given up when his explanation provoked even more questions than it had answered. Isak had never even heard of anything like this, let alone seen it in action, and it made him wonder just what else lay within the forbidding walls of the College of Magic, hidden from the eyes of all but a few and hired out to only those who could afford such wonders.

"He has been punished for his failings," came Scion Lomin's distant reply. Every sentence was stilted, broken into pieces as one mage whispered the words to his sibling. Isak could imagine a face just like this one, pale and hairless, sitting in a high tower in Lomin, silently forming the words as he heard them. Perhaps they were even dressed in exactly the same way: an open-necked tunic showing a hairless chest, and the red and gold sash of the College of Magic around his waist.

"You had one of the tribe's oldest and most respected generals executed?"

The delay in the reply only infuriated Bahl longer. It was scarcely believable the young man in Lomin—not yet duke, however ill his father might be—would have dared do what he had just implied. Bahl began to pace around the oblivious mage until Lesarl reached out a hand to interrupt him.

"My Lord, the link will not last much longer; we need information now. Whatever the boy has done can wait until you are there."

"I did no such thing," interrupted the mage in his slow monotone. "The general was removed from his position and committed suicide in his chambers that evening. We mourn his loss as you do."

Bahl opened his mouth to bellow a reply, but stopped when Lesarl caught his arm. He turned to the mage's escort, a richly dressed man who, though of middle age, looked older in certain ways, like most mages. Isak noted his sunken face, perhaps the first step towards becoming a withered wreck like High Priest Wetlen had been. The mage nodded his agreement with Lesarl, looking anxious for his charge as he anticipated the failure of the link.

"Scion Lomin, what forces do you have left?"

"Four spear legions and one of archers with Lomin. Divisions of each are apparently under siege in Kohm, Castle Shaidec, Vitil, and Peak's Gate. We have not had news from Peak's Gate in three weeks now."

"Where are the enemy?"

"The majority remain here, from what we can tell. They cannot have had time to crush those garrisons yet, not the way they have been moving. Peasants arriving to seek sanctuary have reported a battle at Broken River a week ago, our cavalry must have been ambushed there. We have heard nothing from them."

Bahl gave a sombre shake of the head; a Farlan army without cavalry was lacking its greatest weapon. If the elves had destroyed Lomin's horsemen, they wouldn't worry too much about leaving smaller garrisons of infantry behind their lines.

"Can you hold the walls?"

"I supervise the defence personally."

"That is not what I asked."

The pause was longer this time.

"Yes, I can. They are preparing siege weapons, but at this time they are keeping the trolls well away. Our battle mages say they have the measure of the enemy and can keep the walls standing."

"Good. The army rides under Suzerain Anvee's command in two days. Do not do anything else foolish until they arrive."

As the mage mouthed those words, his eyes suddenly flew open and he gasped, then wilted backwards into the waiting arms of his escort. Two guards came in with a litter and carried the mage away, closely followed by his colleague. It looked to Isak like the dead faint was something expected. A strange life's calling, this: to fall into a trance until you faint—yet invaluable for a dispersed people.

Only when the door had closed behind them did Bahl sit and look at the other men in the room.

The Suzerains Tebran and Fordan had been summoned to attend this meeting. Kehed Tebran was a regular guest at the palace, for his domain surrounded Tirah's lands. He divided his time between his family residence and apartments kept for him at the palace; the best doctors were to be found in the city, and Lord Bahl had made it quite clear that one of his most loyal supporters could always rely on his hospitality.

Beside Tebran was his closest friend, Fordan, a belligerent old soldier who sat bolt upright in his chair, bristling with restrained fury. In a corner, perched uncomfortably on hard chairs, were his eldest son and Suzerain Volah's heir, both seventeen summers, who were watching the proceedings with keen interest.

"Scion Tebran, did you meet Karlat Lomin last year at the Festival of Swords?" Lesarl's voice broke the heavy silence and made the young man flinch in surprise. He'd been invited to sit in, and it was a carefully calculated honour. It had been made clear enough by his father that he and Scion Volah, his best friend, were to sit quietly and say nothing.

"I ah, I did briefly, sir," he said, trying to speak succinctly and fluently. "He spoke to Sohn—ah, Scion Volah, I mean—for longer; he was too suspicious of me, of course." The young man tried not to squirm under Bahl's relentless gaze. He looked relieved when it switched to his friend.

"Scion Volah?"

"I went to his celebration feast, yes, Chief Steward. He threw a ball when his father officially handed over Lomin's Torch to him."

"A good party?" Isak knew Lesarl well enough now to recognise the edge to that innocent question. He leaned forward and continued to glare at the scion to distract him further. The Krann and Chief Steward might have been far from friends, but neither had any time for the foppish young aristocrats of high society.

"It was excellent, yes; the best of the festival."

"I'm glad you enjoyed Duke Lomin's acknowledgement of his terminal illness; I am quite sure he does not. Tell me, at the festival, did you actually do anything other than drink and whore?"

"I . . . we joined in the hunt, sir, like everyone else."

"So you sat on a horse talking to pretty young girls and drinking brandy. Did you even enter the forest?"

"Lesarl, now is not the time," Bahl broke in. He could see Lesarl's questions running for ages, to no useful end. Isak didn't miss the look of relief on Scion Volah's face. "I'm rather more interested in the death of General Elierl."

"That witch of a duchess must be behind it!" spluttered Suzerain Fordan. "I've known Elierl for thirty years; he wouldn't have killed himself. That little bastard probably had him murdered so he could—"

"Enough, Fordan. I don't think the scion would be stupid enough to have him killed, but you are right: driving the general to suicide would take the duchess's hand. However, we are not going to do anything about it."

"What?"

"There are other matters to consider. Please trust me. Scion Volah, if you find an opportunity to reacquaint yourself with Scion Lomin, you will do so. No doubt he will be keen to host another party once the army arrives—after all, it is not often so many nobles go that far east.

"Isak, you will keep your distance from Lomin. I don't want a duel between the two of you, and frankly, I don't know which of you has the hotter temper."

It was meant, in part, as a joke, but Isak just scowled and stared at the floor. Since he'd accidentally killed the High Priest a few weeks back, life had been very different. People now stepped around him even more warily, wondering—as Isak himself did—just how dangerous he really was. What had actually happened remained a mystery to all of them, not least Isak himself, who had no memory of the incident. He recalled the presence of the old man, a dry, calm voice in his head, and then nothing but pain and light, and in the blur that followed, the High Priest had died.

For now, there was no sign that the question would be resolved, but the city was buzzing with rumours of the strange and terrible powers their Krann wielded. The original goal, to gain some measure of control over his magic, had failed completely, and now his frustration and anger had another point of focus. Secretive research in the palace library had revealed that the figure on his chest was an elven rune. Elvish, though the basis and common root of all languages in the Land, was unintelligible to anyone other than scholars. Elvish was built around one hundred and twenty-one core runes, each with a variety of meanings, depending on context. By themselves they were simple angular shapes, set in a circle, if they were single words. The scroll Isak had understood the most said they provided a general concept or idea, in the case of *his* rune, "heart"—although Isak had glumly realised that meanings could range from the stone in a peach to the crux of an argument, or the spirit of a nation.

Nowhere did he find a reason why the rune had been burnt into his chest, and until he could work that out, Isak had no intention of sharing the matter with anyone else. Instead, he'd taken himself off to the palace forge, where the master smith had been delighted to teach the Krann how to forge a sword, one in the elven style, which was far too complex and time consuming to equip an army, but ideal to keep the Krann busy and out of the way of nervous soldiers and palace staff. The result was a long single-edged blade, balanced in a very different way to a rapier. Kerin had claimed it immediately and set about mastering the weapon: he was like a child with a new toy.

Isak shook himself out of his reverie and started paying attention again as Bahl said, "Lesarl, make sure the army is ready to march in two days; everything we can put together in that time, and send riders out to every suzerain able to catch up."

"You're not riding with us?" asked Suzerain Fordan. He was a grandfather, and well past the age that any would expect him to fight a battle, let alone join a forced march in winter, but there was no man in Tirah who would dare to suggest he didn't come.

"There is a vampire in the city. I don't intend this one to be given the chance to fly before we catch it."

The news startled both Isak and the young scions, but the older men had seen it all before. Their expressions turned to sharp interest; they knew well the cat-and-mouse games it would take to catch a vampire.

As unofficial Commander of the Guard, Kerin stood to brief them all. The Swordmaster coughed to clear his throat and tugged the sword at his hip into a more comfortable position. "We've had killings on and off for several years," he began, "but there is no real pattern or regularity, which is why it went unnoticed for so long. The Guard isn't set up for efficient policing of the entire city." He paused for a fraction, giving Lesarl a look that was totally ignored before continuing, "It isn't the same creature we had last time, the one that, unfortunately, escaped us."

Tebran nodded. "Ah well, what can I say? The man was a drunken fool," he muttered, raising his mug in toast to his father, the man who had let the news slip in a tavern one night and caused the beast to flee.

The Swordmaster smiled and continued, "Most assuredly, but the vampire this time is cunning. That is why you were not told of it earlier, Lord Isak. The last one would have been a good challenge for your growing skills, but we fear this one is greater. Lord Bahl is the only mage we have capable of hunting one down alone."

Isak nodded, grateful that Kerin had passed over Isak's own inadequacies in front of men he would be leading into battle.

"I will stay for as long as needed, then catch you up," Bahl declared, then, looking pointedly at Isak. "Do *not* get it into your head to look for the creature; you've danger enough waiting for you outside Lomin. In the meantime, you're not to leave the palace without a detachment of Ghosts. I don't want you involved."

Two days later, Bahl sat in his personal chambers, trying to force the muzzy confusion of sleep from his mind. The effort of eating a bowl of honeyed oats defeated him and he sank back into his chair, looking down at the bustle below. The wind rushing in through the wide-open windows helped somewhat, but his fatigue was unnatural in origin: he had spent much of the previous night letting his soul soar high in the heavens. A storm had raged over Lomin, and Bahl had gone with it, directing as much of its strength as he could against the besiegers. The old Lord shivered at the memory of the intoxicating blend of pleasure and fear he felt as his own considerable magic entwined with that vast elemental power.

The effort required to master the storm was massive, and he couldn't even tell whether it had worked—the distance and the strength of the storm were too great to gain much more than an impression of what was happening—but it was a useful ability. Bahl suspected that Isak would be even better at it than he was; there was a savagery about the youth that would suit riding with the storm.

Bahl had played with this storm out of a sense of guilt: the real reason he was not marching with the army had less to do with the suspected vampire— although that was true—and more to do with the death of a friend, as Lesarl's knowing eyes had recognised. A white-eye's longevity meant that generally they had few friends, but those he had, Bahl treasured. He had been absent at the death of the one he loved most, so he had resolved to never let those who meant most to him die alone. The abbot of a nearby monastery was one.

"And yet it interferes with my duty to my people," Bahl murmured to himself. "Times are still so precarious; what will they think if I'm not there for the battle?" As if in answer to his question, the writings of a warrior-monk centuries dead surfaced in his mind: *Doubts cloud purpose, in battle as in life. No swordsman is complete without resolve and purpose of movement.* Bahl nodded wearily; his mind would not be swayed on the point, so he must cast off the guilt. It would do him no good to doubt his own actions, there were plenty of others to do that.

What did worry him was the elven army's strange behaviour. That they were attacking at the onset of winter was illogical; their rush to besiege Lomin deepened the mystery even more. Was there something in Lomin they wanted, or was the object of their attack more obscure than that? Was this siege the product of some minor prophecy, a feud between elven noble houses or something even more troubling?

"Damn you, Isak, why have these elves come? Have you brought this down on us?" Now he felt guilty for his thoughts: this was the first time he had voiced out loud the words he knew Lesarl was also thinking. It was an unfair accusation, perhaps, but a very real possibility.

Bahl hauled himself to his feet and walked to the long table in the centre of the room. Sleep would have to wait. On the table, neatly folded and pressed, were two leather undersuits, one tailored to Isak's current measurements and the second to an estimate of how big the Krann might be in a few weeks, somewhere between Bahl's size and Isak's current build.

The tailor had been overwhelmed when Lord Bahl himself had appeared in his shop late one evening, but it had been necessary. Isak was growing at a prodigious rate; he was already significantly taller and heavier than he had been when he arrived, and the growth spurt wasn't slowing down. Growing pains were doing little for the young man's mood, but the benefits were clear.

As for the armour on top of the leather, Bahl suspected that would find its own accommodation. The elves of old had been taken with Kasi Farlan, the man who'd been the model for all white-eyes, because he had matched them in size as well as skill.

Bahl picked the bundles up and tucked them under his arm. He started for the door, then hesitated and retrieved his massive broadsword from the stand beside the fireplace. Looking at the weapon, named by its maker White Lightning, he had to wonder whether even Eolis would tempt him away from this brutal and inelegant sword. Its fat double-edged blade curved out into spikes at the hilt which should have made it too heavy but for the magic it contained—yet he'd owned it for so long he couldn't imagine himself going into battle with any other weapon.

He made his way down to Isak's chambers, where he let the guard in the corridor knock once to announce him before striding in. Isak was rising from the desk as Bahl entered, a sprawl of open books before him. Lady Tila sat to one side and jumped up a fraction after Isak had. Bahl caught her expression and sighed inwardly; it looked like she was becoming fast friends with the Krann—perhaps more, judging by the closeness of their seats. He noticed her fingers closed tightly around the enamel crest that pinned the sash at her waist; it appeared that the girl's affection did not extend to all white-eyes.

Bahl tossed the bundle to Isak, who snatched it from the air like a dog catching a bone. The weeks together had given the two of them some sort of uneasy familiarity; both were cautious of intruding on the other, but there was an unspoken sympathy between them.

Isak, his books forgotten, set the bundle down on the desk and, with a gleam in his eye, he ripped open the linen packaging. He held the undersuit up to inspect it.

"It is time for you to take possession of your gifts." Lord Bahl's voice sounded unusually sonorous, and Isak looked up quickly.

"It's a suit of armour then?" He looked as though he wanted to ask more, but controlled himself.

"A suit of armour," Bahl confirmed. "And whilst I assume you would like to know why you're only just getting your gifts now, the only answer I will give you is 'because.'" He smiled a little at Isak's expression. "Not the answer you were hoping for, I see, but something you will have to get used to one of these days. The actions of the Gods are not there to be questioned. Sometimes it is simply a question of faith."

He saw no reason to tell the boy that he and Lesarl had wanted time to better prepare him for his gifts.

"There are two undersuits; the other is larger so you have one to grow into; no doubt you'll need more by the time you return. You lead the army out of the city in one hour, so come quickly now."

Without a word, Isak rolled the undersuit up again and handed the other to Tila. "Can you put that with my baggage and make sure everything is waiting for me?"

Bahl saw her rouged lips part fractionally. She obviously wanted to argue, but dared not in his presence. Had they been alone, Bahl could see she would have asked to go with Isak. A bad sign, that; the youth's infectious humour had drawn the girl closer to him than was good for either.

After the briefest of pauses, Tila ducked her head in acknowledgement, managed a quick curtsey, and fled the room. It was clear she feared for Isak in his first battle, as well she might. The boy was reckless and inexperienced, but every soldier had to muddle through a first battle, and it would be no different for Isak. He, like every other soldier, would return a changed man, but Bahl felt a flicker of concern at what those changes might be.

"Are we going underground?"

"We are; leave Kerin's Eagle-blade here. I think we'll be able to find something better for you."

Isak grinned. He looked uneasy as well as excited, and with good reason, for the changes Nartis had wrought over the past few weeks had made him taller and stronger. He was now of a size with General Lahk, already twenty stone in weight and strong enough to kill a grown man with his bare hands. His gifts would elevate him to a level no normal soldier could hope to reach: speed and strength accentuated beyond even a normal white-eye's power—and that took no account of what spells might be imbued into the metal.

"Your shield?"

Isak leaned over the desk and drew the shield out from the footwell. Bahl frowned when he saw it, once again reaching out his senses to touch the gleaming silver. He still could not place whatever spell it contained: it wasn't complex, but that simplicity confused him.

"Can you read any of the runes on it?"

"There aren't any." Isak held up the shield for Bahl to see, keeping a tight grip on it. Bahl made no attempt to touch it as he inspected the surface.

"Not on either side?" Isak turned it over to show his Master the inside. There was nothing, not even written on the leather straps for Isak's arm.

"I did dream of a rune the night I got this. Tila found me a book to look them up in."

"Them?"

"It—there were, ah, lots, of runes in the book. It was a core rune, meaning something like 'Merge' or 'Union.'"

"Ah." Bahl drew back from the shield, understanding suddenly dawning as he remembered the thread of magic that had wormed its way between the flagstones of the Great Hall that day. "That makes sense—although I suspect the connotations will be a puzzle."

"Why? What makes sense?"

"Best you see for yourself. Come."

The pair descended the main stairs side by side. The chaos of preparations for the army's departure was strangely absent here; the running feet and bellowed commands were distant, behind thick walls of stone. As they neared the bottom, a scampering soldier in Tebran's livery appeared before them, on an errand to his lord's chambers. Startled by the two white-eyes, the man accidentally careened into a wall, then pressed himself up against it to make room for them. As soon as they had passed, he took off again, and they heard his feet pounding heavily on the stairs as he made his way to the suzerain's suite.

In the lower level of the tower, the air was cold and dank. With no fire burning, it felt like a dungeon. Since the advancing elven army had first been drawn to their attention, the call of Isak's gifts had intensified. Bahl was sure

Isak had felt it too; more than once he had left his room in the morning to find Isak lingering at the base of the tower, instead of eating breakfast in the Great Hall.

Isak pulled his paral shirt tighter against the clammy air, which pushed the dragon brooch pinned to it to a strange angle, snout down, as though it was digging into the ground. It reminded Bahl that he had not spoken to the beast below in six months. He had no idea how it would react to Isak's presence.

The cycle of a dragon's life consisted of long periods of rest and sleep, then perhaps half a century of destruction and terror in the mating rituals. In return for a safe haven for this beast, Bahl had secured the promise of assistance in battle when it was required, and that the destructive phase would take place far from Farlan lands. It was a strange bargain to have struck, but the cost of feeding a dragon was far less than maintaining troops enough to match the dragon's worth.

Down they went, deep into the belly of the earth, far from prying eyes. Isak, now used to the tower's magic, guessed the distance to be half the height of the tower—a long way down to put a strong room; when he announced that, it elicited only a humourless snort by way of reply.

Now it was pitch black, and Isak could see nothing at all, not even the hand he reached out in front of his own face, until Bahl muttered a few words under his breath. Isak detected the dirty-sour smell of magic as a ball of flame appeared in Bahl's palm. Although the words were too quiet for Isak to hear, they rose in his memory: one of many spells he'd memorised over the past few weeks but couldn't make work.

They were in a cave, a hollowed-out space some ten feet high and wide, unfinished walls still marked by the tools used to carve out the hole. The flame gave off only enough light to see that not even an iron brand adorned the walls. Bahl led him through a hole in the wall into an undulating tunnel, wide enough only for one at a time. Isak trailed along behind, wondering where this was taking them.

He tried another attempt at conversation, something that had been nagging at his mind for a while. "My Lord?"

"Hmm?"

"When we return from Lomin, what will I do?"

"You're the Krann, you do what you like."

"That's not what I mean. If I've proved myself in battle—if I have gifts like yours—what should I be doing with my life?"

Isak knew it was a strange question, but in a nation of allotted roles, he could not now see one for him—at least until he became the Lord of the Farlan, and that was a long way ahead.

Bahl stopped, his expression hidden by his mask. "What should you be doing with your life? A good question, I suppose." Abruptly, he started walking again. "You're a suzerain. You have an estate and a shire to manage; just getting your lands in order may take years. Lesarl will provide you with records of the suzerain's possessions in Anvee—I think you'll have quite a lot of evictions, rent collecting, and deal making to do. Crops grown on your land now belong to you, no matter who planted them, your nobles will have redrawn boundaries, your shire seat will be in disrepair, your bondsmen need accounting—"

"Oh, playing with bits of paper, measuring land, counting money." Isak couldn't hide the boredom in his voice.

"Hunting, hawking, practising your magic, horse breeding, bullying old aristocrats and charming their innocent daughters; I assumed you'd enjoy it. Estate managers can be found to deal with the administrative side. Did you expect more?"

"I suppose—" Isak sounded a little diffident now. "Well, I had wondered whether you'd be sending me on diplomatic missions."

"You? A diplomat? What a curious concept."

Isak smiled at Bahl's tone, glad for any levity between them.

"There will certainly be lots to keep you busy here if you want it, but our relationships with other states are limited. We are too powerful for them to attack us, and trade agreements are already in place, so your principal official role if you want it would be patrolling our borders to discourage raiding."

"What if—"

Isak got no further as Bahl interrupted, "Another time. We're here."

Isak realised he'd forgotten to count the paces as he'd intended, but guessed they'd covered a hundred yards or more. Another twenty paces and Bahl stopped in front of the outline of a doorway hewn in the rock: sharp, irregular lines edged in the faintest of green.

As they'd been walking, Isak had been more and more aware of the presence of magic of some sort up ahead, but the scent was unlike any he recognised. As he followed Bahl inside, the smell of wet lichen, animal dung, and a piercing acrid odour grew hugely, as did the magic in the air. There were powerful streams of energy present, not building up, but attracted to this place for some reason, presumably his gifts. The smell of dung bemused him, though: it was not quite like a stable, nor a slaughterhouse, but the aroma was similarly pervasive.

As Isak took in the proportions of the room, he faltered: this was a cavern stretching off into blackness, not the strong room he'd been expecting. The faint green tint that outlined the walls and uneven floor had no apparent source, other than the magic he could sense swirling all around. The cavern was not one regular open space; the roof dipped and rose as it pleased and the floor rose up in the centre around a group of thick pillars clustered with quartz. Two large holes had been hacked into a side wall, presumably tunnels leading to more chambers. One had great chunks of rock lying broken at its entrance.

"Where are we? What is this place?" He found himself whispering.

"I keep some of the artefacts Atro collected over the years here. We cannot keep them in the palace itself, nor can we destroy most of them, for fear of releasing the magic inside—for the same reason why the Elven Waste is indeed a waste: that is where the Great War was fought and vast amounts of uncontrolled magic poisoned the ground."

"That's all? But this is a cavern, and I can feel something else down here. Gods, is there something alive here? What's that I can sense?" Isak stood still, trying to make sense of what he could smell and feel, then he gasped as he recognised the ancient air that lingered in parts of the palace, like the presence of centuries, but alive and aware, and terrifyingly potent.

Bahl didn't reply, but gestured towards the raised part of the floor, where, in the darker parts between the pillars, Isak could just make out a long lump of rock. As his eyes adjusted, he noticed a smooth arc against the irregular stone, that became a tail, huge and scaled, with a fat scimitar tip. Isak's mouth dropped open; without warning, the tail was whipped back and into the shadows, then a cold rasping rose from the lump of rock Bahl had indicated. It slid forward, the heavy click of claw on stone and the rasp of its scaled tail dragging along the rough surface announcing its living presence.

Welcome, Lord Isak.

Inside his head the words echoed and crashed, rising in power until Isak started backwards in surprise.

Do not be alarmed. I have promised Lord Bahl I will eat none of his subjects. I am Genedel.

Now a head appeared from the shadows, dipping down the slope with a deliberate lack of speed. It was fully two yards long, with a frill of bone sweeping back from the top of its head, which in turn was flanked by two huge horns that twisted back and up, another two yards long themselves. A wide snout held rows of glittering teeth; the protrusion of nostrils broke its smooth curve, and a pair of tusklike horns pointed forward from behind the frill of bone, almost as far as the very tip of the snout. Behind that lay two huge eyes, glimmers of deepest red in the underground night. The rest of the body was hidden, visible only in silhouette. Isak guessed at folded wings sitting high on each side and a relatively slender body supported by wide clawed legs.

"Ah—" replied Isak in a daze. "And how about burning them?" As soon as the words came out he realised he was being flippant to a dragon, one that was no more than ten yards from his face. It could probably flame him without even moving.

I have promised nothing there.

"Oh."

But let no man say a dragon is without a sense of humour.

Isak kept his jaw clamped shut, terrified in case his inability to shut up might anger the beast. That was something he didn't want to see.

Your gifts, young Krann; that is why you are here, is it not?

"I . . . yes, it is. We ride for Lomin within the hour."

Your first battle. It will show your true nature to your men; it is how they will remember you, yet I doubt any could forget you. Take the eastern tunnel and you will find what cries for a master.

Isak looked at the inscrutable features of the dragon, then at the two tunnel entrances. Eastern, not left or right. For a second he started trying to picture east in the palace, and then work out which way they had turned to get down here. Then he remembered where he was, and what he was looking for. Starting out towards the tunnels, he felt the keen of his gifts more strongly than ever before. The crunch of broken stone and dirt underfoot danced around the walls, sounding ever louder as his heart hammered inside his chest.

Reaching the tunnel, Isak glanced back for a moment. The weight of Genedel's presence behind him was a burn on the back of his neck he couldn't ignore. Bahl had stepped closer to the beast, only a few yards from one tusk, watching him. With a flick of its head, the dragon—Genedel—could impale Lord Bahl; it seemed impossible that even the famous hero white-eye, the Lord of the Farlan, could succeed in killing such a creature, however many tales there were of lesser men performing such a deed.

Isak tore his attention away from his Master and concentrated on the smell of magic. He took the left-hand tunnel and found himself having to duck down five yards in as the roof dipped sharply. The stone walls slewed right and spread out wide into a bowl-shaped room. There was a flat ledge against the back wall, almost waist height. Isak shuddered to a halt at the entrance, entranced by the objects before him. He didn't need to be told what they were; there was no mistaking objects constantly mentioned in myth that radiated such power he almost sank to his knees as he laid eyes on them. Only an echo of that same power from his shield kept him standing.

The dark lines of the room melted away. All he saw were the silver curves of Siulents, beautiful as a dream, even laid out in pieces. Each delicate plate and link was a craftsman's joy. The lines of each piece followed the muscular shape of a warrior's body, but with a sinuous grace that was almost inhuman. The helm was a single piece; its near-blank features showed a weirdly distorted reflection of Isak's face as he held it up to inspect. It looked like a mirror version of Bahl's mask, but not one that would mold to the wearer's face. It had two ridges, running back over the head and cold empty eye sockets, that reminded Isak of the dragon in the chamber behind him, or perhaps the rattlesnake he'd once killed: reptilian; sleek and graceful, with lethal intent.

Pushing the image from his mind, Isak moved to the sword and closed his fingers around the double-handed grip of Eolis, tightly wrapped in pure white silk and bound with an emerald filigree that emanated from the massive emerald set into the hilt. Six silver claws shaped like talons gripped the emerald securely. The guard was a circular piece of ivory that looked to be fused into the blade itself.

As Isak marvelled at the blade, he realised that the poor working Kerin had claimed was nothing more than the echo of this sword reaching up into Isak's mind. Without knowing it, some part of his soul had recognised Eolis. The smith had given the sword honest praise, but Isak knew now how far short of the mark it had fallen. The weight of the blade was almost imperceptible, yet as he moved Eolis through some basic forms, listening to the soft zip as it neatly cut the air, he felt a surge of strength in his arm. Isak realised that this blade would cut through even the pieces of rock littering the floor in Genedel's chamber.

There was a rough leather sheath beside it, Farlan-designed, of plain black leather, which presumably Lord Bahl or Lesarl had left for him. Pulling off his boots and shirt, Isak quickly dressed in the undersuit Bahl had given him. He hesitated before touching Siulents again, but as he started fitting the armour onto his body, he felt a note of exhilaration trembling; building up as each piece clipped into place. The silver took on a seductive, liquid quality as he flexed his limbs to test the freedom of movement, and even more remarkably he could not see the seams between plates, only an unbroken curve.

A smile broke over his face. This wasn't what he had expected; instead, his body felt cocooned in a second skin, only slightly constrained, and coupled with an intoxicating sense of invulnerability. Isak hesitated when only the helm remained. It was tradition that helms were only for battle; ancient belief held that a hidden face displayed hidden intentions. Wealthy knights would often have their visors made into savage and grotesque faces to further the distinction between a man of war and a person of civilisation.

Though he wanted badly to try it on, the sound of voices in the main chamber broke the spell and, gathering up his clothes, Isak bundled them together and laid them inside the shield, cushioning his helm.

As Isak entered the dragon's lair, Bahl broke off his conversation and stared, almost wavering with shock. "Gods, Aryn Bwr was well named; quicksilver indeed," he exclaimed. A rumble from deep inside Genedel's throat echoed agreement.

Isak just stood, unable to put what he felt into words. He held up Eolis, drawing it from the sheath to show Bahl the glitter of white light that shone out, even in the dark, green-tinted depths of Genedel's cavern. His expression was one of bemused helplessness.

"These really are the last king's weapons, aren't they?"

Now you know why the elves have come. The Land has envious eyes for such beauty.

"We cannot be sure of that," interrupted Bahl.

You are, as I am. The night of Isak's Choosing was one of unrest in distant parts as much as here. The creatures of the night felt it; the denizens of Ghenna knew his name at that moment. Mages and prophets have also sensed the disturbance, whether they recognise it or not. The elves have been waiting for three thousand years. They know.

Bahl didn't respond. His huge frame suddenly seemed small, deflated, even. His eyes ran down the gleaming blade, over the smooth curves of Siulents—and he gave a small nod. Stepping forward, the Lord of the Farlan reached into his belt. Isak tightened his grip on Eolis, feeling a spasm of shame as Bahl produced a piece of blue cloth.

"I have no such gifts to offer you, but I feel there is something—" He didn't finish the sentence, but held out a hood identical to his own. "May it keep you safe in other ways."

Isak nodded his thanks and placed the shield and Eolis carefully down on the ground. He slipped the hood over his cropped scalp. The silk hung loose briefly before tightening around his head, covering his nose and mouth but somehow not impairing his breath. There was an enchantment on it so subtly woven he'd not noticed it until then.

"Give me your hand." Isak cocked his head at the strange instruction, but held out his right hand, changing it to the left at the old lord's request. Bahl pulled off his gauntlet—the silver parted without resistance—and then the glove underneath.

He held Isak's hand palm up, inspecting it for a moment, before suddenly whipping a dagger from his belt and slashing down. Isak cried out in surprise and pain, but Bahl kept a tight grip on his wrist and pulled his Krann closer.

"This is my gift to you." His voice was deep and old, full of sorrow and pain. "This is the legacy that you will inherit from me; your blood, your pain, shed for people and Gods who neither know of it nor care. You will be hated and feared by those your duty leads you to protect, who will show resentment, not gratitude, no matter what you do for them. Do not expect your people to love you, trust you, or remain loyal to you. You will become the man your duty to the tribe permits, the man it forges. If you try to fight that, you will break under the weight of it."

After a respectful bow to the dragon, they returned to the main wing of the palace in silence. Isak had too much swirling in his head to speak; Bahl had no more to say and instead let his own thoughts fester. The Chief Steward met them on the stairs and bowed low to both, then offered Isak a white cape, reaching up as far as he could to set it about the Krann's shoulders. As it unfurled behind his back, Isak caught sight of an emerald dragon detailed in gold. Isak secured it himself, fastening the cloak with his brooch from the bundle of clothes. With his shield retrieved and set securely on his arm, Isak looked at the two men, waiting for their nods of approval before he set off to face his army.

A reverential whisper greeted Isak in the Great Hall. It grew and spread like a tidal wave. Bahl saw men stop dead and stare; men who had felt a change in the air and turned to watch Isak emerge into the training ground where his horse was waiting. More joined the congregation of hushed voices; the awed sound waxed with every heartbeat, echoed back by the encircling wall, then swelled to a roar into the gusting wind and growling clouds. A single fork of lightning split the sky and the men cheered, with all their hearts and souls; they raised a clamour that woke the whole of the city and sent a howl of defiance rolling east over the trees.

Chapter 11

T HE UNRELENTING NORTH WIND heaved and buffeted Tirah Palace's high walls. It brought the voices of the city up to Bahl in his lonely chamber where he sat watching the tiny figures below, a brass goblet of wine cradled forgotten in his hands as he stared out of the window. The people of the city had succumbed to the glamour of Siulents and given Isak a reception Bahl could never have dreamed of. The old Lord didn't want their adulation, but still he felt an unwonted melancholy that, despite all he had given up for them, his people had never loved him. What they cheered was a façade; a hero they could worship. Isak was the shining figurehead that Bahl had never been, but the Lord of the Farlan wondered about the uncertain youth inside that enchanted armour: was he already buckling under the weight of being Bahl's Krann? But Isak's place in the Land was not merely as Bahl's replacement. His role would be even harder to bear.

"And yet what can I teach him? What do I know of being a king?" Bahl spoke out loud to the empty room.

"More than the King of Narkang, I'll wager, and he's the only one worthy of the title these days."

Bahl jumped at the unexpected voice from the doorway. Suzerain Tebran gave him a nod as he advanced into the room.

"Kehed, you don't go to wish your son well for his first battle?"

The suzerain shrugged and eased his portly frame into the nearest chair. Few men would dare sit without permission, but Bahl would have sacrificed protocol gladly for a few more supporters as loyal.

"I spoke to the boy this morning; there's nothing more he wants to hear from me. His cousin's going to keep an eye on him. He's a sensible lad, he'll see him right. Mayhap he'll grow up in the process."

"Things are no better?"

Tebran grimaced. "Ah, sometimes I think he can't be mine. Could hardly have blamed his mother if he weren't, the number of bastards I've got. I've reached the end of my tether with that one. If this campaign doesn't wake him up to the Land, I'll ask Kerin to take him on. I'd hoped to give him a proper education, perhaps find him a seat on the city council for a few years to teach him some responsibility, but he's no interest in it. It'll be hard to let him go though. I hear his mother in every word he says."

"How long has it been?" Bahl asked softly.

"Three summers now, though I'd scarce believe it myself. The boy won't listen to me. There's nothing more I can do with him. I fear I'll have an empty hall soon enough, for I don't think Fordan's intending to come back. He sees me now and has no intention of getting this way."

The suzerain gestured down at his straining belly and stained clothes. Age and hard living was catching up with a man whose barrel shape had marked him out on the battlefield almost as much as the distinctive yellow and purple colours of Tebran. His cheeks and nose were scarred red with drink, the skin about his eyes looked heavy and tired and gout hampered every step. With the loss of his wife he'd recognised that all his friends and contemporaries were slowly fading from the Land.

He lifted a goblet and drank, wiping the wine from his chin with the grimy white stripe around his cuff that marked him as a former Ghost. Suzerain Tebran's title had never stopped him earning every shred of trust he had been given, something Bahl wished he could say about more of the nobles who owed him allegiance.

"There's always a place at my table for such a loyal friend. With your son in the Guard, I expect you'll want to keep an eye on him."

Tebran smiled in genuine gratitude and straightened himself up a little, a flicker of pride driving away his gloom for the moment.

"The Krann seems to have potential. Will he hold up in battle?"

Bahl shrugged. "We shall see. He's got the strength and skill; if we keep the elven mages off his back then he should be fine."

"And Shalstik?"

Bahl hesitated. He was far from certain in his own mind. "By the Gods, I hope not, Kehed. If the elven houses have united under the Shalstik cult, we're in for years of war."

"How likely is that?" Tebran asked, looking worried.

"Shalstik's prophecy of the last king's return has been a threat hanging over us for more than a thousand years; if that's the case, they'll fight to the bitter end to bring it about." He grimaced. "Our first defence has always been their inability to fight as a united group. We are still pretty sure the elves have ten noble houses constantly at each other's throats—I doubt any force we've met in the last hundred years has comprised warriors from more than two houses. I don't know if they have called a truce, but with an army large enough to destroy Lomin's cavalry . . ." His voice trailed off and he looked out of the window for a few moments before continuing, "The dragon's mood had better remain good over the next few weeks. We may need him."

Kehed Tebran was one of the few who knew of the truth about Genedel. His private hunting grounds, a forest at the foot of the mountain north of Tirah, was patrolled by rangers and kept as an exclusive preserve, well stocked with enough livestock to feed the dragon. Some believed that Genedel was real, and lived on the very peak of one of the mountains, under their Lord's enchantment; others saw the beast as the embodiment of Nartis, aiding them in times of need. Lesarl hadn't needed to start these rumours; the people had beaten him to it themselves. Bahl found that a little sad, no matter how convenient.

"Fortunate we have a vampire to catch too!" Tebran's laugh was empty. "Life gets harder for us all. Perhaps we should just get drunk and wait it out."

Bahl smiled wearily. "I accept. I'll tell Lesarl to find us some players, or acrobats maybe: someone to entertain us until we're too drunk to care. But first, there's something I must do while I still have my wits about me."

As Bahl walked through the top floor of the palace, he noted the dry and lifeless atmosphere with a growing distaste. Few people came up here—the guest apartments for court-ranked nobles were on a lower floor. Neither fresh rushes on the floors nor the smell of beeswax did much to change the impression of a temple, deserted yet still full of quiet reverence.

Bahl went first to Isak's chambers, then down to the library, where he paused at the entrance. He ran a hand lightly over the faded painting that covered the double doors: one of his more enlightened predecessors had been responsible for this picture, which still clearly showed his message to all who would follow him. It depicted a figure, no doubt the Lord himself, sword sheathed and carrying only a handful of scrolls as he faced down an approaching army. It was a message Atro had never appreciated, for all his acquisitiveness; few white-eyes would.

As he had expected, Bahl found Tila within, a book lying forgotten in her lap as she stared out through the bay window. The library had once been a temple to the remaining Gods of the Upper Circle before a past lord who valued learning over piety had converted it. Few recognised this room as the treasure trove it was: more than a thousand leather-bound books and dusty scrolls gathered together in a Land where fear of heresy, prophecy, and magic meant academics had to work in secret and the history of the Land was hidden in legend and fable: truth buried in myth. With daemons and Aspects—local gods subordinate to a more powerful deity—part of everyday life for some men, knowledge and the written word were as powerful as they were dangerous.

A fire crackling in the wide hearth off to his left took the edge off the cool air. Even in the depths of winter, the library was a sanctuary, away from the crowded, noisy Great Hall. The Chief Steward, using a burning log from the constant fire in the Great Hall, lit the fire in the library first, as tradition dictated. The tradition predated Bahl: it was a symbolic act that Lesarl had determinedly retained.

Bahl crossed over to the fireplace and added more logs. The noise startled Tila and she jumped to her feet, sending the book clattering to the floor. She winced, knowing full well how expensive each volume was.

"My Lord—" she started, but he cut her off with a look, then dragged a heavy oak chair closer to the fire and indicated that she should do the same. He leaned in close to banish the dismal chill in his bones.

"We should talk," he announced softly. Tila sat primly upright with her hands clamped together in her lap, waiting for him to continue, but Bahl took a minute to look her up and down first. The girl wore rather more jewellery than Lesarl usually permitted, but as most was religious, Bahl didn't comment. Unlike most Farlan, her eyes were light in colour, a soft hazel with flashes of yellow; eyes more suited to laughter than sorrow.

"You're close to my Krann." No question, merely a statement of fact.

"Yes, my Lord. He . . . Lord Isak doesn't require much of me, only that I teach him all I can, of the wars of the Houses, the Age of Gods, any small story I might have told my niece before bed." She wasn't sure what Lord Bahl wanted her to say.

"He learns quickly?"

"Oh yes! He is hungry to hear everything, I suppose because he never had a mother to—" She halted abruptly. Bahl's early life had been far harsher than Isak's; the entire palace knew that. "He also questions the stories; he wants to know why things happen."

"Give me an example."

Tila thought a moment, her lips slightly pursed. "Well, the punishments of the cursed. I'd never thought about why they were punished differently, but that interested Isak more than the punishments themselves. A couple of times last week he even corrected the priests—well, the ones who still go near him after what he did to Afger Wetlen." She hesitated again, scared that she was saying too much, or sounding like a gossip—that could cost her Isak's friendship as well as her position.

Bahl drew his cloak tighter around himself and gazed away at the shelves behind Tila's head. "Yes, that was unexpected," he murmured, almost to himself, before turning his attention back to the maid. "No matter, it brings me to what I wish to say. Isak is special, and not just as my Krann. The Age of Fulfilment is a bad time to be special."

Tila nodded, her head turning fractionally towards the bay window she'd been watching Isak from.

"A lord is blessed beyond any other mortal, but the Gods are not nurse-maids. They expect and demand unwavering loyalty. A lord should love only his patron, because to love another is to have a point of weakness." Bahl was speaking as much to the past, and giving the warning Ineh had never had. "No matter what he whispers in the night, he cannot always protect you—"

"My Lord!" she protested, a scarlet flush in her cheeks. "He's not—we've not . . ." She couldn't bring herself to finish that sentence before the Chosen of the Gods. Bahl was surprised, but she was telling the truth. No one could lie to him, not even hardened criminals or politicians.

"So you're not that close yet—but is it just a matter of time? Tell me, girl, and truthfully."

"I—" Tila lowered her eyes to escape her Master's scrutiny.

"You have feelings for him? Foolish, very foolish."

That sparked defiance in Tila. "Lord Isak and I have much in common; we enjoy each other's company," she said, a trace of bitterness in her voice. "What does it matter whether I do or not? Why else was I sent to here in the first place?"

Bahl raised an eyebrow. "Your parents will want you to secure a post in Isak's retinue and gain influence enough to be a useful bride. Lord Isak is a white-eye, not some major promoted from the ranks that you can housetrain into polite society. You could not have a family with him, could not grow old with him. Those gifts he now carries would make you the most valuable hostage in the entire Land."

Tila nodded. "I know that, my Lord. I have not even thought of discussing the future with Lord Isak. At the moment I just care that he comes back alive."

"You doubt his skills? However much he grins and acts the jester, a white-eye is born to fight and to survive; Isak's no exception there."

"I understand, my Lord," she said. "I just can't help thinking that an army in winter must want more than just slaves, and those gifts fit the puzzle. Isak is inexperienced enough without a whole army intent on killing him specifically." She released her hands for a moment to tease a thin citrine ring into a more comfortable position, then her fingers tightened around each other again.

"I am pleased that you understand," Bahl said. "Isak will need staff who can anticipate as well as organise. Too many of my nobles still say this attack is nothing more than evidence of elven insanity. Those who do recall the name Shalstik dismiss it."

Tila frowned for a moment, then understanding dawned. "Shalstik; I remember that. My mother couldn't stop boasting when a Harlequin stayed as her sister's houseguest for a week over the summer. This one apparently told the Prophecy of Shalstik every night for a week. My mother said the prophecy concerned the rebirth of the last king; but surely they cannot think Lord Isak is really Aryn Bwr reborn?"

Bahl snorted. "No, I seriously doubt even they do, but those weapons are enough by themselves to start a holy war with the elves. If they have decided their time has come, I don't know what it will take to stop them. I hope I never find out. Until then, think on what I have said. There is no room in Isak's life for romantic fancies." He stood and looked into the crackling fire. A gust of wind ran down the chimney, sending a puff of smoke out into the room. Before the curls of grey could reach Tila they stopped, hanging listlessly for a moment before fading to nothing.

Tila shifted in her seat, tucking her legs underneath her and tugging her cloak over them like a blanket. Then a thought struck her and she twisted herself around to look at the books lining the walls. "Isak knows so little of our myths and ancient history. Perhaps I could be of some use to him while he is away. If he has prophecies to contend with, the knowledge in this room could prove vital." She looked up at Lord Bahl, a note of pleading in her voice.

Bahl gave a curt nod. "I think you are a very sensible young woman; one he will benefit from listening to." He had said enough; now he left the room without another word.

Two weeks later, Bahl was preparing to start his journey east. News from
Lomin was confusing, but better than he had expected. The linked mages had
again allowed Bahl to speak to the scion, this time to follow the enemy's
movements. Vitil had fallen and had been razed to the ground, with the loss
of more than three hundred men, but more than half of the population had
been saved by a heroic effort on the part of the garrison. Their sacrifice had
drawn in the enemy attack and allowed nearby Kohm to safely evacuate along
with Vitil's civilians. Kohm's garrison saw all the refugees to the greater
safety of Peak's Gate.

With two full legions of troops there, and the townsfolk bolstering their
number, the elves would not attempt to take the fortress-town of Peak's Gate.
It would take months of siege to break that ancient stronghold, so the elves
would be content to maintain a standoff at the gates.

When the effort had again become too much for the twinned mage, Bahl
had sat in silence until everyone else had shuffled from the room. He felt a
nagging guilt about sending the army off under Isak's command. General
Lahk was more than competent; he would not allow the Krann to make any
fatal mistake, and yet . . .

And yet Bahl knew he should be out there, leading his army himself, not
walking down to the Great Hall to grab a last meal before he left Tirah. If he
took the high mountain paths shunned by most Farlan, he would be able to
travel undisturbed to his friend's deathbed. He had failed to find any trace of
the vampire they suspected was in the city; this distraction at least he would
see through.

It was evening, and muffled sounds of revelry came from behind the aged
oak doors, garbled and distant, but nonetheless welcome after the empty apartments and corridors of the upper levels. He looked at the flags adorning the
Great Hall: they were of similar age to his dying friend in the forest, and they
looked as worn as the abbot had been when Bahl had last seen him. Soon Bahl
would have to choose replacements for both as he endured yet another lifetime.

On a rare impulse he sat at the foot of the great stairway and pressed his
temple against the cold stone of the wall. As he did so, he imagined a tremble
of age pass to him from the stone, but he knew it was nothing. He ran a hand
over the worn steps and looked up at the flags, wondering when his own time

would come. White-eyes could live past five hundred summers; however much Bahl felt like an old man, he had several lifetimes ahead of him. It was hard to welcome them.

In the Great Hall, the cooking fire spat and roared as a deer roasted slowly above its flames, the scent of it thick in the air. As Bahl entered, the noise waned briefly, but he ignored the faces turned in his direction and made for the fire. A maid pulled a bowl-shaped flatbread from the cauldron behind her and heaped dripping hunks of venison and vegetables into it for him.

"You're leaving now?" Bahl turned to see Lesarl behind him and nodded as he slipped a chunk of meat into his mouth. "So is Tiniq," Lesarl continued. "He's just had a message from the Chief of Rangers; he's setting out immediately, on foot again, as always. He claims he doesn't like riding."

"At this hour? I take it the message was delayed in getting to him."

"I might have kept the ranger waiting in my office a little longer than necessary." Lesarl smiled. He knew Tiniq had piqued his Lord's interest.

"Thank you. Where is he?"

"Pack hidden under the table, trying to be unobtrusive, behind you, door-side."

Bahl nodded his thanks and gestured for Lesarl to return to his own meal, then turned to spot Tiniq, who was sitting with shoulders hunched, staring down at an empty cup. The ranger rarely came to the palace; he was here even less these days as the advancing years failed to mark his face. Tiniq Lahk defied all conventions: he was General Lahk's younger twin, a normal man, not a white-eye, and one who should have died in the womb as twins of white-eyes always did. Just as a white-eye's size would kill the mother in childbirth, so the life of any twin would be squeezed out in the weeks beforehand. But somehow Tiniq had clung grimly to life, and though a sickly child, he had grown into a strong youth. He had had a lonely childhood, fostered to a forester, and grew up suspicious of strangers. He appeared to have taken on many white-eye attributes, and no doubt he was touched by magic, a little, but just how much, he kept to himself. This was a mystery Bahl was still waiting to resolve.

Bahl's cogitation was interrupted as Tiniq noticed him. "My Lord?" he said as he rose from his seat and gave Bahl a short bow.

"I'm leaving for the Ked road now. I take it you won't be going too far off track if you accompany me part of the way."

The tone of Bahl's voice left no room for argument, but still Tiniq tried. "Actually, my Lord, I am bound for Siul."

"A few hours will not make much difference, I think. Fetch your pack."

Tiniq suppressed a sigh and reached under the bench to pull out a shapeless canvas pack and an oilskin weapons-pouch, then followed Bahl outside.

He kept his eyes low until Bahl stopped unexpectedly and spoke again. "There are tales of the Saljin Man in the deep forest. Have you seen it?"

The ranger frowned. "Just peasants being foolish. We've got enough in our forests without borrowing the curses of other tribes."

"I wonder. It's a strange thing to invent when we all know the Vukotic are as rooted to their lands as to their curses. I've heard this before, when a vampire was in the city almost a century back. Now we suspect another is here, do we call that coincidence?"

The ranger looked startled at the prospect, attempting to cover his discomfort by adjusting the baldric on his shoulder. "I understand. I'll pay attention."

"Good. Now we should leave. You must have run with your brother, I expect you to keep up." Without waiting for a reply, Bahl strode off through the moonlight to the stone fist of the barbican. The bridge was usually kept raised in times of war, but the guards had seen him standing outside the Great Hall and it was down by the time Bahl passed through the tunnel.

The wide main streets and narrow alleys of the city were almost empty. Away to the left, Bahl could hear the stamp of hobnailed boots—Ghosts on patrol. Even the gutter-runners would be holed up somewhere warm; the sparkle of frost on the gargoyles and overhangs showed how dangerous the roofs were this time of year. Despite that, the ancient city of covered streets, archways, and statues was at its most entrancing when glittering in the moonlight.

Bahl walked easily down these cobbled roads. The many towers and complex architecture made Tirah a remarkable city to behold. In the moonlight, even the most fanciful stories set here became believable. Black shadows lurked in the covered streets, under arches and around the lights of taverns. Bahl knew that not all of the eyes above were empty stone, but there was a natural order and the predators that hunted the streets at night were wary of him. They would watch him for as long as they could, like deer following a wolf pack to avoid the chance of ambush.

Up above the city, the two greater moons emerged fully from behind feathered clouds. Kasi—the lesser of the two, the hunter's moon—was halfway to the horizon. At this time of year, that meant there was less than an hour left until midnight. Off to the south, Alterr overshadowed Kasi's red tint with her own yellow eye. As followers of Nartis, both men saluted the lesser moon, kissing the backs of their bow fingers and touching them to their foreheads in a gesture whose meaning was lost, as so much else, in the mists of time.

"Strange to think that there was a time when the Land could see such great events—stranger even that we might soon return to such a time."

Tiniq looked puzzled at Bahl's announcement, following his gaze up to Kasi. The lesser moon, which appeared in the years before the Great War, was named for that most devoted of mortals, Kasi Farlan. Legend had it that Larat, the God of Magic and Manipulation, had seduced Alterr, the Moon Goddess, and persuaded her to hide her light from the sky as a party of Farlan hunters returned home. While the others found their way back, Kasi Farlan was lost in the deep forest, blinded by the darkness and hunted by Larat's assassins. When the hunters returned without her husband, the Princess of the Farlan begged the Queen of the Gods for aid. When Alterr refused to show her light again, the queen took the diamond necklace from her own neck and rolled it around the princess's ruby ring, making a single stone which she threw high into the sky to light Kasi's way home and save him from attack.

The ruby at the moon's heart was bound to Alterr's own life's blood. She was ordered to throw the gem up every night as penance, and if she failed to catch it, the stone would break on the ground, and so too would her own blood run out to the earth. To prevent that from happening, Larat took the stone from Alterr's hands the next night and threw it so hard he sent it orbiting the Land, fulfilling the bond set by the Queen of the Gods.

Now his lover need only to watch its path, and wonder whether it would ever fall.

"Would that be something to look forward to?" The ranger sounded nervous rather than enthusiastic. "The Great War poisoned the Land with its magic. If life is less dramatic, is that so bad?"

"Not at all, but it was the energies spent in anger that caused the Waste to be poisoned, rather than the Ages before the Great War. That much destruction must be avoided at all costs, but sometimes I think grand deeds like the hunter's moon might again have a place in life." He changed the subject. "You prefer to walk to Siul? It's a long way. Even for a white-eye, it would be far."

Tiniq cleared his throat noisily. "I dislike riding, and horses themselves, for that matter. It's a dislike they share, it seems—I was thrown twice as a boy in the training paddock and I've never trusted them since. I know you're wondering about my birth; that's why you wanted me to accompany you, isn't it?"

Bahl inclined his head. The two men were walking down the centre of a wide avenue through the temple district.

"Well, I'm not my brother; that's for certain, but we have some things in common. It might take me longer to get to Lomin, but the path is more direct on foot and I can outrun any normal."

"You don't consider yourself a normal?"

"Would you?"

Bahl considered that. Tiniq might look like an ordinary man, but it was unlikely he could hide his differences for long. "Perhaps not, but it would be a nice choice to have. How about children?"

"Have I any? No. I've had my share of women though, so that might be one more thing in common with your kind."

"Magic?"

"I . . ." Now discomfort was evident in Tiniq's voice. Bahl kept silent and let the man take his time. There was nowhere to run from the question. "I have some sensitivity; that is the only way I can explain it. Although my brother's magic is weak, he can perform spells. In me it's different: I can hunt and fight better than I should; my awareness is heightened, my eyes are stronger than normal men's."

"And what is the price?"

"My Lord?" Bahl couldn't tell whether that was genuine or not.

"The price, Tiniq, of these gifts. Nothing is for free. The scales must always be balanced."

"I don't know." The sentence was almost a whisper. "I think I have yet to pay it. I'll have fifty summers in the new year and I don't look older than thirty—and I'm getting stronger."

"Stronger?"

"My brother has noticed it too. When I saw him a few days ago, it was for the first time in two years. As I embraced him, he felt the difference."

"Curious." They reached the Wood Gate that led east out of the city. The frost in the air had suspended the gentle sway of the leaves; everything was still and silent. Bahl turned to the smaller man. "We'll run until the hunter's moon goes down. I expect you to keep up." Without waiting for a reply he broke into a jog, slowly building the pace to keep the ranger pushing himself to catch up. The darkness of night closed around them with a soft sigh. Under the cover of reaching branches they ran with hardly a sound, the moonlit mountains flashing in and out of sight between the trees.

After he parted company with Tiniq, Bahl met no one as he took forgotten paths through the high ground. The foothills of the mountains were the preserve of herdsmen and rangers; superstition and a lack of arable ground kept the rest away. The early winter had already sapped all the strength from the trees, leaving tired, heavy branches hanging low on the ground. Withered leaves crackled underfoot. Crabbed oaks jostled in the breeze with alders and skeletal silver birch, all hunkered down under the determined beat of rain and light snow. It wouldn't be long until the winter storms that would suspend normal life for a time.

His destination was a small monastery in the suzerainty of Ked. It was a harsh place to live: though hidden within dense woodland, it was high up, and plagued by the wind coming down off the mountain. It was a far cry from those monasteries in towns, where monks and nuns figured in all parts of the common folks' lives. This was both a retreat and a training ground, providing spiritual direction for a large number of novices as they worked on whichever path they had chosen.

Bahl was familiar with the chaplains, the zealot warrior-monks attached to each regiment, but his contact with the other sects was limited. Lesarl dealt with the cardinals who ran the cult of Nartis and Bahl had little time for the priests who performed pastoral work.

It was evening when he finally caught sight of the stockade wall of the monastery. He'd spent the morning recovering from spells he'd cast the previous night: he had been unable to bear being in complete ignorance of what was happening further east. The elven army had felt like a putrid sore on his skin when he let his senses spread over the forests. The army was keeping to the darkest corners. Split into three parts, it had a network of scouts spreading out from each section, and trails of magic reaching even further. Each one was a thread waiting to be triggered when their prey stumbled within reach. Bahl hoped he had managed to confuse them enough over the course of the night.

A stone gate was the only entrance, above which shivered the light of a fire from a small watchroom. There was a roof to keep off the snow, but the wind came in through the narrow slit that ran around the chamber. Bahl could see the huddled shape of a novice—even with the fire, it would be bitterly cold inside. After a few hours of this cold, the novice would hardly be able to raise the alarm at anything he saw . . . but a monastery was not supposed to be a place of comforts.

Bahl broke into a run, silently gliding over the grassy clearing that surrounded the square compound. The novice's head was turned away, staring at the empty trees. In one leap, Bahl cleared the spiked wall and landed on the walkway that led to the gate tower.

The guard heard the noise and fumbled with his bow as he turned, only to let it drop in amazement as he saw Bahl standing there, bow in hand and mask on. For a few seconds the novice just stared in amazement, then he gave a yelp as Bahl strode down the walkway towards him. His bow abandoned, the youth scrabbled first with the drape covering the door, then the latch, but when at last he did open it, Bahl was almost upon him. Terrified, he fell to his knees in the doorway, mittened hands clumping together beneath his chin.

"L-l-lord Nartis," he whispered with reverence. Bahl stopped with a grunt of surprise.

"Don't be stupid, boy," he snapped, moving past to the ramp that led down to the stone courtyard. He stopped to get his bearings, looking around at the interior of the monastery. Five columns of smoke rose from other parts of the building, reminding him which parts were sleeping quarters. Behind him was the gate tower, flanked by wooden stables for the livestock. On either side were the dormitories, one for novices, the other for the monks. Straight ahead was the chapel, and the flicker of candles through its rose window showed that he had arrived in time: the light that still burned for the abbot would only be extinguished when the man had passed through Death's gates.

The courtyard was only thirty paces across. A stack of cut wood was piled against the dormitory walls, as if for insulation. Cracks were visible in the stonework of the buildings; the skeleton of a creeper hung down, waiting for spring. Bahl walked to a smaller door to the right of the chapel entrance which led to the abbot's rooms. The prior had adjacent chambers running down a common wall so the large fireplaces could be shared. Privacy was not something Nartis appeared to approve of here, though certain cardinals he knew had palaces to call their own.

A rolled carpet had been placed behind the door to ward off draughts. Bahl heard the soft whisper as it ran across the floor, catching straw as it went. It opened onto a dark reception room, a traditional canvas-roll painting of Nartis the only ornamentation. It was empty and cold, normally used only for monks to sit and wait to be summoned. Three pairs of heavy fur boots were on the floor, two dropped carelessly, one carefully set perpendicular to the wall.

Bahl placed his hand on the door latch, hesitated when he heard a voice on the other side, a droning murmur of prayer, then walked in. The abbot's study showed the desk and shelves in the unused order of a dying man. On one wall were two columns of intricate pictures: twelve icons that showed the Gods of the Upper Circle. Bahl smiled at the sight of them; they were the abbot's pride and joy, exquisite images collected over a lifetime.

In the next room, the abbot's bedchamber, he found the prior standing at the end of the bed, his tall slim figure and shaven head giving him the appearance of a vulture glaring down at its dinner. He rounded on the door with a look of outrage when he heard it open but smoothly changed that into a bow when he recognised Lord Bahl. The monk sitting at the abbot's side, clearly the monastery's healer, was less composed and gaped for a moment before following suit.

"Get out," Bahl ordered quietly but firmly. The prior inclined his head and ushered the healer out with a sharp gesture. Bahl heard their footsteps go out of the study, then moved to one side of the bed. He glanced down its length to the fireplace. Through the flames he could see the prior, kneeling on the stone floor before a bow device hanging from the far wall, an imitation of prayer that would allow him to hear any conversation.

The Lord of the Farlan's face softened as he turned to his old friend, bundled up in a nest of blankets that smelt of lavender, sickness, and age. The table beside the bed that in past years had been stacked with scrolls and books now held bowls of medicine and a lukewarm broth. A strained cough from the bed summoned him; Bahl crouched down to listen. As he did so, a faltering smile broke over the abbot's face. Bahl forced a smile in reply, hiding his shock at the near-translucent skin that looked so tired.

"Forgive me, my Lord," repeated the breathless whisper.

"For what?"

"For my frailties; they shame me."

Bahl sighed. The abbot had been tall and powerfully built in his youth. To see him like this, small and withered, made Bahl feel the press of centuries on his own shoulders. "Nothing shames you. Time catches us all."

"I know." The abbot paused for breath, trying to push the blankets away but lacking the strength even for that. "I had not planned to die this way."

"Most men dream of it: to die old, surrounded by family and friends."

"One friend, not much." Bahl couldn't tell whether there was real feeling in that; the abbot was struggling to even make a sound for his friend to hear.

"It was your own choice to come here; I know you don't really regret it. The good you've done is worth that, I think, and I swore you'd not pass through alone."

"Cerrat." The word was gasped, any more swallowed by a spasm of pain that tightened every muscle in the abbot's body. His lips drew back to show his teeth as he grimaced and fought it. Many years ago, in this very monastery, he'd been taught the mantras to overcome suffering. The chaplains were the Farlan paradigms of bravery and resilience. Their lives were to serve as examples to the regiment they fought with. Only the strongest survived. Bahl could see the slight twitches on the abbot's face as he ran those devotional words through his mind again.

"Cerrat, is that someone you want to be brought?" Bahl leaned away from the abbot as he raised his voice. "Prior, don't pretend you can't hear me. If I have to leave this bed to fetch you, I swear you'll die before the abbot does."

That got the desired result. The man scrabbled to his feet and peered over the fire's flames. His calm manner was gone; the politics of a monastery rarely included direct threats of violence.

"Cerrat, my Lord? He's a novice here, training to be a chaplain. The abbot's always been fond of the boy; he's an excellent student although rather boisterous—"

"Fetch him now," Bahl ordered. He didn't need to hear any more. The face behind the flames disappeared and Bahl turned back to his friend. "Cerrat's coming." As he said it, Bahl wondered how he could help with the pain. A white-eye's magic could soothe a little.

By the time a tap came on the bedroom door, the moment had passed and the abbot was breathing again. A youth of some sixteen summers put his head around the door as Bahl called for him to enter. His alarm at seeing Bahl gave way to distress as he looked at the abbot.

"Come in, sit by the bed," Bahl told the nervous boy. "He asked for you."

"Cerrat. My bow." The novice swallowed hard and fetched the wide, flat bow from the corner. From the way he held it, he'd done this before; he'd read the inscribed passage of Nartis's words in praise of his tribe's warriors. The bow was unstrung, so Bahl dug out one of his own spare strings and handed it to Cerrat. Even after so many years, the bow he'd presented to the abbot was oiled and still strong. The abbot reached out a withered finger and brushed the curve of the bow.

"Lord Bahl gave this to me; now I give it to you." The youth's eyes widened, but he could find no words to protest. "You show great promise; as much as Cardinal Disten did when I taught him. Bahl, when he is ready, give him the position I once refused."

The Lord nodded, looking over at the young man who was overwhelmed at the gift of a bow. He had a child's face, but already the build of a man, with broad shoulders and thickly muscled arms. The abbot was a reticent man; he wouldn't have told Cerrat about the heroics that had earned that bow—anymore than he would have spoken of the day he refused the highest honour a chaplain could hold, and one rarely bestowed—that of Legion Chaplain to the Palace Guard.

Another rush of pain coursed through the abbot's body and it was a while before he could speak again. Bahl cradled the man's hand and waited.

"It's passed. How fares the Land, my friend?"

"Winter is coming. I hope you've trained your chaplains well, I'm going to need—" He broke off as the abbot cried out in pain.

"Oh merciful Gods!" The words that followed were lost, but Bahl was sure he heard "the Master calls" through the man's torment.

"Is there anything I can do?" Bahl asked, hating the feeling of impotence.

"An orb," panted the abbot. The pain was consuming him now, but this was a man who'd rallied a broken legion and led their charge with an arrow in his neck, trusting to Nartis that it would not tear the vein. He knew pain well enough; he had never submitted to it. "I want to feel power in my hands once more before I lose this battle." The effort of speaking was almost too much for him and he slumped back in his bed, a trickle of blood on his chin where he'd bitten his lip.

Bahl lost no time, for he could feel the shadows grow longer as the presence of Death encroached. Sitting the abbot up, cradling the man in his arms, Bahl began to draw his magic, letting the energies flow through the abbot's body. The old man had been a fair battle-mage in his time, as unsophisticated as a white-eye, but fuelled by his burning faith. An orb was a basic tool of training: it drew energy and spun it into a ball, an excellent way to practise control.

Bahl felt the abbot's body relax as the sudden torrent of magic coursed through his body; that much would kill him in a matter of seconds, but for those moments it overshadowed the pain, and that was enough. With one frail hand in each palm, Bahl trapped the magic between them. The room shimmered with greenish blue light while the shadows grew darker and colder. Bahl allowed the energies to swirl and dance, touching on the edge of his control before crushing them into an orb smaller than the abbot would have ever managed. This he split into three, letting them orbit each other with ferocious speed as the unnatural light flew in all directions, lapping around the edges of the abbot's magical books and lovingly stroking the hilt of White Lightning, the broadsword strapped to Bahl's back.

And then the shadows grew and the magic fled. Bahl felt a tremble in his stomach as the Chief of the Gods reached out to gather in the abbot's soul and free him from pain. His friend wore a smile as he died; remembering happier times and honoured by a single tear from the white eye of his lord.

CHAPTER 12

A LIGHT SHONE AROUND HIS BODY, tracing the curve and line of his hardened figure, illuminating scars long faded and signs of injury he could not remember. He moved with dreamy lethargy to a silent song. His armour was gone, stripped away from his flesh, but Eolis remained, secured by a bond stronger than ownership. Terribly heavy and crusted with age, it looked frail and vulnerable. Despite that, he felt sustained.

The chatter and voices that assailed his mind were muted and weak. His shell of flesh and memory was impervious to their touch, but still they gnawed, hungry for attention, or thoughts to feed off. The only one he listened to was a whisper beyond his understanding, a girl's voice that called out, searching for him in the dismal black of night. It was a language he did not recognise, words he could not fathom, but a voice he knew from deep within.

He felt the earth closing around him, as if falling into a grave, but he was not destroyed. He rose again as a shadow, unnoticed by the figures walking past him, wrapped up in their own lives. With Eolis in his hand he was suffused with calm; he patiently ignored the emptiness of death. Though broken and scarred, there was purpose in his bones, and he let them carry him forward towards the shore of a still lake and a figure, stiller than that. The breeze coming off the water brought voices with it, and the tastes of salt and cold blood. Silver shimmered in the sky and the smell of heather and wet stone was all about. He smiled as his blood ran into the earth at his feet.

"My Lord?"

General Lahk's voice jolted Isak from his doze. His eyes shot open in alarm, as vestiges of his dream made him forget momentarily where he was.

"You were sleeping in the saddle again, my Lord." Though the words contained a reproach, the tone was bereft of emotion.

"Well? What of it?"

"Well, falling from your horse would hardly be a glorious death for me to report to Lord Bahl. If it started suddenly—"

"It won't start suddenly." Isak reached out and patted the neck of the huge horse underneath him. "I know perfectly well that this is the best charger in the seven shires, and I'm not going to fall."

He rubbed his eyes, trying to keep himself awake. They had been riding for several hours that morning, but still he couldn't shake off sleep's embrace. With his blue silk mask on and his fur hood pulled up, Isak had made himself a small pocket of warmth, even while the temperature dropped further every day. The nights on the road were far from peaceful, for the bright warmth of magic of the gifts that Isak kept in reach at all times attracted lonely voices in the night. For the time being, reviving deep sleep eluded him.

He pulled his hood off to let the breeze wake him up a bit. He was always more irritable when he was sleepy, and the general's monotone brought out the worst in him. Scratching at the stubble on his head, Isak sighed and at last turned to look at the man, who sat high and proud in the saddle, his face as blank as ever. Isak had never yet seen him show emotion of any kind—what he would be like in battle was anyone's guess. It was unusual for a white-eye to go through life like that; it was inconceivable that he would be the same on the battlefield.

"So, did you wake me for a reason, or just concern for my health?" he asked, grumpily.

"I thought you would prefer to be awake as we enter the next town. It's not seemly for the Krann to be asleep when his subjects come out to cheer him. I also have word from your knights from Anvee."

"What about them? Have I offended them by not sending them orders to accompany me?" In his other life he'd found people took offence at most things, but a court rank had apparently enlarged the range of possibilities, and the things he *didn't* do were causing him almost as many problems as the things he did.

"They are your subjects. You may offend if it so pleases you."

"Enough scolding, General, I'm too tired."

"I lack the rank to scold you . . ."

"Just shut up and tell me what they said."

"They were enquiring as to whether they could present themselves to you."

Isak turned in his saddle, shifting Eolis on his back to sit more comfortably as he waited for further explanation.

"They number five hundred—an impressive number for Anvee, which of course is the intention. They are most anxious to please their new liege. The problem is that a number of the knights and most of the cavalrymen are your bondsmen." He waited for a response, but got none.

Isak sat with a blank expression. As a wagon-brat he'd never had any reason to learn the laws of landlocked men. His father had called it a collar that choked honest men into slaves. Carel had laughed at that and not bothered to argue, his chuckles indicating that Horman's opinion was so foolish it didn't even merit a response.

The general persisted. "Lord Isak, Anvee has been without a suzerain for many years. It has therefore been of advantage to pledge a bond of service to the title of Suzerain Anvee itself, since the benefits of that bond come with few of the requirements one normally expects. They are therefore now a little unsettled that a suzerain has been appointed—they now have responsibilities to you, and they are trying to keep to the letter of the law until they can judge your disposition."

"And?"

He sighed. Isak thought it was in irritation for a moment, but the reply was as bland and patient as before. "And the law states that a bondsman must secure his liege lord's permission before he can leave the shire. Technically, this constitutes desertion. They could be hanged."

Isak's face turned from confused to incredulous.

"And they are actually worried I might do that? Execute my own soldiers? Before a battle, no less?"

"They thought it prudent for me to speak to you first. You are a white-eye."

Isak felt the general's words sink like a stone in his stomach. It didn't matter that such a decision would be lunacy: they feared the monster inside him. Even General Lahk had not disputed the possibility that Isak might respond that way—it was as if Atro were still alive and every evil rumour about him had been true.

Isak felt too sickened to reply. He waved his hand in the direction of the general, telling him to get on with it, then nudged his horse away, unable to bear company. General Lahk spurred his own horse into a trot and disappeared behind the banners of Suzerain Tebran's hurscals.

How does he live like that? They must think the same about him, worse perhaps. Is there nothing he cares about? Would he disobey any order from Bahl, no matter how obscene? Would he even notice? Maybe what they say is true; maybe Nartis did burn out his soul.

· The Chief Steward had told Isak the strange circumstances of the general's birth, and how Bahl had taken him to be tested in the Temple of Nartis. Lahk was far stronger than any other white-eye, but Nartis had rejected him, scarring his body with lightning instead of raising him to the ranks of the Chosen. He was left with two choices: reject Nartis and leave, or become a perfect servant of the God. He had taken the harder path, discarding those parts of his soul that would nurture the pain of his rejection. Isak almost admired him for that, however much the thought horrified him.

A few flakes of snow swirled around Isak as he stared through the banners to see where the general was going, but his idle gaze was soon lost in the flags and colours themselves. The livery of the Palace Guard was a dour black and white—no doubt it reflected Bahl's uncompromising mind, but it seemed to suit Lahk more, especially after a few weeks of wear and dirt had dulled everything. Slowly, as they had marched through the shires collecting troops, passing through Tebran to Nelbove and Danva, then following the border of Amah and Vere, flashes of colour had begun to appear in the ranks. The Chetse called the Farlan cavalry "steel peacocks"—gaudy and arrogant, but fearsome, however much silk and lace they wore.

With the army now marched a total of eight suzerains, including the Krann himself, and eleven counts, some fifty marshals, and six hundred-odd knights. The hundreds of banners and badges, pennants and tunics, clashed in a mêlée of colour across the dull canvas of a wintry forest. Every single noble had presented himself to the Krann and had his title announced, but it was only the suzerains that Isak had remembered. The rest had been just a blur of pomp and ceremony.

That old rogue Fordan had the honour of the vanguard, ahead of higher-ranking suzerains—a decision of Isak's that had made Sir Cerse, Colonel of the Palace Guard, wince. But Fordan had proved to be both good company and a sensible advisor. Isak was less sure about Sir Cerse, the young ambitious knight from Torl who had surprised most by earning a Swordmaster's Eagleblade shortly after he joined the Ghosts. Fordan's Red Keep banner was too far ahead to be seen, as were the Gold and Green Hounds of rich Suzerain Nelbove and the Green Griffin of the odious Suzerain Selsetin. There was something about that man that set Isak's teeth on edge, even before Fordan had muttered something about both Nelbove and Selsetin being implicated in the Malich scandal. Without knowing quite what that meant, Isak did realise it made them far from friendly to his cause. The other nobles had nodded sagely at Fordan's words; whatever it was, the scandal was obviously common knowledge.

The swooping Golden Falcon of the newly raised Suzerain Danva fluttered just ahead. His brother was dead only two weeks and a book was already running on the life expectancy of his infant nephew, who would take the title if he reached adulthood. The suzerain's superb voice carried well over the breeze, and Isak could also hear an insistent debate between Suzerains Amah and Ked. The White Hart of Amah seemed to be faring well against the Yellow Lion, despite having to concede nearly twenty summers to his peer.

The last suzerain present was foremost in rank, being from the oldest family and one of the richest provinces, but to Isak's surprise, the dour, excessively devout Suzerain Torl had presented himself only briefly before setting off to ride with the ranging scouts. His Ice Cobra emblem was as uncommon as the strange and secretive suzerain himself. Just as rare was his decision to wear simple leathers, with the badge of his family sewn to his breast as a sworn soldier would, instead of the grand armour a knight was expected to be seen in. His plate was carefully packed away, as was that of his hurscals, the unit of knights that acted as his bodyguard.

At first, Isak thought the man was a coward, dressing as a simple cavalryman to avoid making a target of himself like his fellow noblemen, but as he found out more about the man, he was deeply relieved that for once he'd not let his tongue run away with him. General Lahk, not one to overly praise anyone, told Isak that when it came to battle, Suzerain Torl was always to be found fighting side-by-side with the white-eyes of the Guard.

A heavy covering of cloud kept Tsatach's eye well hidden, and a dry wind whistled past the armoured knights and the leather-clad troops to the pack animals trailing behind them. A vanguard flurry of snowflakes held a promise of far worse to come: when the ice on the road became too dangerous for horsemen, the beasts of burden would have to walk the path first, enduring the worst of the slick ground.

Isak's sharp eyes picked out red-furred squirrels watching the army from a safe distance, their thick rusty coats quivering as they tapped at the oak bark in search of insects hidden underneath. It was comforting that some life continued around them, uninterested and unaffected by the army marching east. The people of the towns they had passed through had been nervous and scared, only hesitantly cheering the soldiers. The fear of the elves had a strong grip; they had seen real anxiety even before they left Danva's borders. Seeing

Isak astride his huge white charger, silent apart from the faint jangling of the harness and the chimes of the silver chains, rings and bells that adorned the creature, seemed to inspire confidence—perhaps that was enough; their belief in him was more important than his own. If his soldiers had heart enough, his own fears would go unnoticed.

It didn't take General Lahk long to return. Trotting beside him was a black-garbed knight, his breastplate worn over his formal silks as was traditional. He was clearly wealthy: a gold damascene pattern overlaid the deep black of his armour, curling around the edge of the lion's head that sat large and proud in the centre of the breastplate. Even in his sleepy state, Isak felt a flicker of recognition. He blinked the blur from his eyes and looked again, this time realising who the man was: the Roaring Lion crest and extravagant black armour were a rare combination, and Isak knew there would be a golden helm shaped like a lion's head hanging from the man's saddle.

As the horsemen came nearer, Isak could make out the two gold earrings: the mark of a count. If his skin didn't heal too fast to make it practical, Isak would have had a similar piercing to hold the three rings of a suzerain. This was not some anonymous noble, but the renowned Count Vesna.

Vesna's reputation preceded him: every child, noble-born or wagon-brat, had grown up hearing stories of his romantic exploits: the cuckolding of an army of noblemen, the duels and rooftop pursuits . . . Carel always said Vesna was one of the tribe's finest soldiers, but necessity had required it. It was rumoured that Vesna had provided more than a few heirs to noble estates, children accepted because most feared to challenge one of the Land's most accomplished duellists: Vesna had fought twenty-four duels, and won them all. Some—a few—had tried to kill him surreptitiously, or have him assassinated, but Vesna had inherited a minor elven blade, and had mortgaged his entire estate to buy that suit of armour from the College of Magic.

A single ruby glinted in the eye of the Roaring Lion, catching what little light the day had to offer. His black hair was pulled back from his face and tied back, showing off the handsome features that had brought both pleasure and trouble. Though undeniably good-looking, with laughter-lines fanning out from his eyes, there was a hard set to his jaw, and a strength in his knowing face.

"Count Vesna," called Isak as the men dismounted and approached. The herald who shadowed Isak's every movement opened his mouth, then closed it again with a hurt expression.

"Lord Isak." Vesna's voice was like his face: a soldier's potency coupled

with a rich humour. As he knelt at Isak's feet and bowed, Isak could see blue
tattoos running down the side of his neck, the stained skin of a man who'd
been knighted on the field for bravery in battle. The title he'd inherited; this,
Vesna had earned himself.

"I was told Anvee grew cabbages and goats, not heroes." A squad of
Ghosts fell in behind Isak's stationary horse. As the rest of the army filed past,
every head craned to watch the two men. Isak heard sergeants curse their men
as the disciplined columns buckled and flexed.

"You honour me, my Lord." Isak almost laughed at Count Vesna's careful
tone of voice. How often did you have your childhood hero kneeling at your feet?
"I can only hope that I show myself worthy of that by fighting at your side."

"Enough. The first thing you can tell my bondsmen is the only men I want
at my feet are the ones I've put there. And I thank you for the respect you've
offered. I'm sure the men from Anvee will distinguish themselves on the field."

The count rose with a relieved look, the sparkle of a smile in his eyes.
Isak saw that and felt almost foolishly pleased that the man seemed to be so
easy with him. He pointed to the count's horse.

"Come on, we're slowing the army down. We can talk in the saddle."

Vesna gave a short bow, immediately all confidence now Isak's disposition was known, then gripped the horn of his saddle and pulled himself up
with a practised grace. A quick touch of his heel guided the horse around and
set it on its way.

"May I ask what my Lord has heard of the enemy?"

Isak nodded to the general as he drew his massive charger up alongside
the count's black-draped hunter. The horse had a placid and calm air to it,
not quite what Isak had expected a famed impetuous rogue to be riding. He
decided it was a good sign; that underneath the stories and the image was a
calculating intelligence. A fiery stallion pounding at the earth might be more
impressive, but this calm mare would be easier to trust in the chaos of battle.

He turned his attention away from the horse, back to the rider. "We're
too far away for the mages to scry, but we know enough." He gestured at the
general, who was happy to fill Count Vesna in on what they knew. Isak sat
aloof and let the words wash over him. General Lahk would be the one to
decide strategy when the time came, and Bahl and Lesarl had agreed that Isak
should appear detached, rather than try to field questions, as he would be
forced to defer to Lahk anyway.

"The enemy has split into three parts, all north of Lomin," the general
said. "One is at the gates of the city, laying siege, another is further west, and

the last sits halfway between Peak's Gate and Lomin. Vitil and Kohm have been burned to the ground."

Now it was always *the enemy* when the soldiers spoke, not the elves: *the enemy* was a faceless creature, one to destroy. It needed no name.

"And the people there?"

"Three hundred infantry lost at Vitil, but their deaths bought time for the rest to escape. The cavalry at Lomin we believe destroyed . . ."

"What? All?" Vesna's cool was supplanted by anger and disbelief.

"We think so. The standing guard of three thousand marched out, their annual full deployment. They did not return."

"I thought that was to be stopped?"

"It was, but since it coincided with the last day of the hunt season, Scion Lomin decided that the last year should be a special one."

"Fate is not without a sense of humour." Vesna spoke in a weary monotone that made him sound suddenly like the general: the voice of an old soldier who'd seen it all before.

They rode on in a bitter silence for another mile. Isak kept himself very still, like a child trying not to be seen. The count stared off into the distance, his lips moving almost imperceptibly. Isak could just make out the movement in the corner of his eye, but what it meant was another matter entirely. Was his new bondsman some sort of religious fanatic? Was there more than met the eye—and if so, could he ever trust any man these days? As he thought that, Isak chided himself, as he knew Carel would have.

Gods, Lesarl's infected you with his paranoia. Vesna's just praying. The man's a soldier, mourning deaths that could easily have been his own.

"I heard mention of trolls; is it true?" Isak flinched when Vesna spoke again. Perhaps it was just the loss of so many men, but the count sounded apprehensive—perhaps he had fought trolls before.

"It's true," confirmed General Lahk. "We should find out how many once we're able to scry the ground, but we must err on the pessimistic side and expect a hundred or so."

"And our heavy cavalry?"

The reputation of trolls was so fearsome that only heavy cavalry could engage the monsters head-on. That was the price of knighthood or nobility: in times like this, they took on the worst of the Farlan's enemies. It was said trolls felt no pain, even from a mortal wound. The most effective way to fight them was with long lances from horseback. Foot soldiers would struggle to reach the head, let alone hit with enough force to do any real damage:

smashing the skull was the best way to kill a troll; anything less left the attacker horribly vulnerable.

"Eight hundred Ghosts, and another seven hundred nobles and hurscals. That's all the hunters we can put on the field. The infantry legion of the Ghosts can support them, but their losses will be heavy."

The conversation turned to logistics, supplies, and troop movements. Isak had heard the days and half-days counted out interminably over the past few weeks: how fast they could reach Lomin, how soon the infantry would arrive from Peak's Gate and Lomin . . . He closed his eyes again and let the Land drift past.

The day lingered on, dully chill and boring. Pages, heralds, and quarter-masters were constantly hurrying over to talk to General Lahk, but nothing they said seemed to interest or surprise him. His replies were terse, to the point. When the army first set out, the younger pages would linger for a while at the general's heel, unsure by his tone whether they had been dismissed. They would pale and scuttle off when he turned back and told them to leave.

Vesna asked endless questions, discussing the smallest details with the general, just to keep himself in Isak's presence. It didn't irritate Isak, much to his surprise: the rich, aristocratic voice was more interesting than the slap of hooves on mud. Idly, he realised that single fact could be crucially impor-tant to Vesna's future, whether his desires were political, acquisitive, or both. It was enough to make the wagon-brat in him spit with scorn. His eyes flashed open and he scowled at the dripping trees lining the road.

As midday approached, increasing numbers lined the roadside. Hungry, drawn faces stared in mute envy at the rich clothes, healthy horses, and lush coloured banners. In full battle-dress, the column would be even more impressive—hurscals carrying flags on their backs and knights with silken strips affixed to shoulders, helm, elbow, and back. In full charge they were billowing banners of luxury.

The competition to impress was not lost on the peasants who laboured along with battered carts containing all their worldly belongings. Isak could see resentment as clearly as relief, all overlaid by dirt and fatigue. The army quelled fears of the enemy, but also highlighted how wide the gulf was between peasant and noble. Their toil in the fields was a far cry from the glamour of knighthood. Most of the nobles rode past impassive and unseeing.

"Why are all these people here?"

"Refugees, my Lord, the peasants have abandoned the land around Lomin. They know what it means to be caught by the enemy." The general sounded almost sympathetic towards the cowed, starving wretches forced off the road to let the horsemen pass. Almost. Like everything else, the peasantry didn't actually matter to the white-eye: they were just more background noise to his empty life.

As Isak watched, occasionally meeting eyes, he felt a change in the air as the numbers grew. Down the road ahead he saw huddled groups becoming crowds. He shifted in his saddle, sensing a mixture of condemnation that only now did he come to their rescue, along with fear, awe, and relief. The Farlan were a superstitious people, and the legends of Aryn Bwr lived on in the hearts of his most fervent enemies. But time plays strange tricks, and the Gods had honoured him even as they condemned him to Ghenna, for his courage and sheer genius had earned Aryn Bwr a strange place in folklore: never quite beloved, but too wonderful to completely despise. Now people were again faced with that contradiction, and no one was entirely comfortable with it.

"What are we doing for them?" Isak muttered. He twisted to look at General Lahk.

"My Lord?"

"Supplies? Food? It's winter, Larat take you! Has nothing been done for them at all? Are they just going to die out here, waiting for us to reclaim their homes?"

"Nothing has been done as yet, my Lord."

Again, no trace of anything. Isak would have been more comfortable with open contempt, anything, just to show the general was alive.

"Well, why not?"

"Chief Steward Lesarl was quite explicit, my Lord. We were to do nothing until they saw the order to come from you. Your people should love your rule as well as fear your strength." Ignoring Isak's incredulous look, he called in a booming voice to the Colonel of the Palace Guard, "Sir Cerse, my Lord wishes you to distribute our food to his subjects."

As Isak fumed he saw the knight rip off a sharp salute and gesture to his lieutenants to set about the task. The wagons of supplies appeared miraculously quickly from the back of the train and a unit of men rode at its side, handing out all they had to every Farlan who reached out eagerly.

Isak was speechless. Again he had been anticipated and manipulated. His silver-mailed fist tightened around the hilt of his blade as inside he raged at himself for being Lesarl's plaything.

"My Lord is unimpressed."

"Fuck you, Lahk. If you or Lesarl think I'll stand to be manipulated . . . The only reason I don't kill you now is that I need you for the battle."

"I understand, my Lord. Our kind does not suit such treatment—"

"And you know what it *is* to be me? Do you have my dreams? Or the Gods themselves playing with you as a puppet in games even Lesarl wouldn't dare to join?"

"We are all puppets, my Lord. The only difference is that they notice what happens to you. The rest of us do not matter so."

Isak felt a stab of guilt as the scarred general instinctively ran a finger down his neck. The jagged mess of scar ran down from behind his ear to disappear under his mail shirt. Isak couldn't find the words to reply. He returned to brooding on the eternal question of exactly what plan the Gods had for him. Since becoming one of the Chosen he felt even more constrained than when his father had dictated his life. He hated feeling like a mere pawn even more than the helplessness of his childhood servitude. It chafed as noticeably as—as his armour failed to.

Isak's mind wandered off the subject as he stroked the breastplate and wondered again about Siulents. It was faultless in design, and unmatched throughout the Land. Running a finger down its perfectly smooth surface, Isak could sense an echo of the runes that Aryn Bwr had engraved into the silver, each rune anchoring a spell of some kind. He guessed there were more than a hundred—and yet no more than a dozen suits in existence bore more than twenty runes. Lesarl had said he could snap his fingers and produce a score of men willing to spend the rest of their lives studying Siulents, and that it might take as many again twice as long.

The tales made the last king out to be noble and just, however dreadful his rebellion had been. The Gods had loved him above all others, while he was their servant. The greatest mystery in history was why Aryn Bwr had turned against his Gods.

Isak was beginning to see a different side to the man, for walking in his actual shoes told a tale that the Harlequins never had: Siulents was suited to a killer, inhuman and utterly lethal. It felt like something made by a white-eye, not the elf whose poetry had caused Leitah, Goddess of Wisdom and Learning, to cherish him above all but her brother Larat. And then Leitah had been cut down in battle, killed by a Crystal Skull that Aryn Bwr had forged.

What unnerved Isak most was the piece he had not yet worn, the helm: tradition was that it was donned only for battle—and it was one tradition with which he was completely comfortable. Those horny ridges and blank face held a promise of something he was in no rush to sample.

The strange dreams, the extraordinary gifts, the "heart" rune, the voice of a young girl calling his name through the blackness—there was a tapestry of sorts coming together, and at every turn another thread appeared to bind him further. To the peasants watching Isak as they crammed bread into their growling stomachs, he looked calm, and without a care. His horse moved with brisk arrogance, its hooves pricking up high, the silver rings and bells catching each other and singing out in a dreary day.

Vesna, watching Isak's expression growing increasingly perturbed, cleared his throat to attract his new lord's attention.

Isak scowled at his bondsman, but the count ignored it and nudged his horse closer. Now a little curious, Isak leaned down to hear what the man had to say.

"My Lord, I am your bondsman to command, and required by law and oath to protect your interests. I know these political games well, and can play them better, if that would be of use to you."

"And why would you do that?" Isak muttered, ungraciously. "Why should I trust a man of your reputation, someone I hardly know?"

The count looked startled at that. "My reputation, my Lord Suzerain, has never been one for oath-breaking." There was a cold tone to his voice that made Isak think he had taken real offence. If that was the case, Isak wasn't about to apologise. A bondsman, even a count, was not someone he had to care about unsettling.

"I am your bondsman. My fortunes follow yours, so your success is certainly of importance to me—and my reputation is all I have. To foster treachery would take that from me."

Isak sat back, impressed by the passion in Vesna's voice. "So, what is your advice then?"

"The general is not your enemy. To consider him so is a mistake."

"He's hardly friendly."

Vesna shrugged. "General Lahk is a devoted servant of his tribe. He respects the authority of Lord Bahl and his most trusted servants. He trusts that their orders are in the best interests of the tribe. Treat him as a dependable servant and he will act so."

"And Lesarl?"

"The Chief Steward is a sadist who loves his power, but he is a devoted vassal of Lord Bahl who knows that he can find his pleasures pursuing the interests of the tribe. Spies and assassins are his toys; his loyalty is assured because it affords him what he loves most. Even Lesarl's enemies would acknowledge that he is a genius of a governor. I believe he will honour you when you are his lord. Until then, perhaps he thinks you have to learn to be a lord worthy of honour?"

Isak looked again at General Lahk, considering Vesna's words. There was logic there, and though that didn't mean it was necessarily true, he would lose nothing by playing along. "So who *are* my enemies then?" he asked mildly.

"Right now, your enemies are camped outside Lomin. To forget that could be fatal."

The days passed quickly. Isak remembered little of his dreams except for the clamour of battles he hadn't fought, and that same searching voice; of the days, almost as little. He felt exhausted from lack of sleep, and was lulled into a constant doze by the uniform grey sky and the sway of his horse. Bahl had told him that he would need to draw in on himself and prepare for the battle, but Isak couldn't have done much else anyway.

The nag of the enemy somewhere ahead remained a faint prickle at the base of his skull as he ran through control exercises in his mind. He couldn't release magic yet, but drilling the theory of defending himself from it might just save his life. Half a dozen times, General Lahk flinched in his saddle as he felt a burst of energy pulse out from the Krann as he practised.

A week later there was a distraction from the normal tedium of the march, as scouts reported the enemy had been sighted moving away from Lomin to open ground. Isak didn't understand, until Vesna explained that by withdrawing early, the elves were in effect picking the battleground, to ensure they had room for their superior numbers instead of letting isolated groups be picked off one at a time by the Farlan cavalry.

Karlat Lomin rode into camp with his hurscals ahead of his foot soldiers, who were hurrying to join up with the cavalry, to offer grudging obeisance. Vesna found Isak pawing listlessly at a bowl of fatty broth and fussed over his appearance until Isak was smart enough—and alert enough—to meet Scion Lomin. Hauling Isak to his feet and buttoning his tunic had had very little effect; it was only when Vesna fractionally touched the scabbard holding Eolis that he was rewarded by a glare that showed Isak was at last fully awake.

The young wolf cut an impressive figure in the bronze and red of his family. His scarlet-stained helm, shaped like a wolf's head, glowed eerily in the firelight as he reined in by Isak's tent. He wore only half armour, cuirass and mail atop expensive leathers worked with gold and bronze thread. The wolf's head hung from his saddle like the bloody trophies Isak had once seen hanging from the walls of a Chetse town.

As Lomin slid nimbly from his saddle, Vesna moved ahead of his lord to greet the man. One of the hurscals took half a pace forward and a thin smile crept onto Isak's face as he saw the intent to stir up trouble, but Lomin raised a finger to stop the man. Clearly these two had met before.

"Good evening, Scion Lomin," called the count in a cheery tone, his palms upturned in traditional welcome. He took great care over the younger man's title, one that was inferior to his own.

The scion took his time acknowledging Vesna's greeting. Handing his reins to a page, he carefully shook out his long straight black hair and fiddled with the gold clasps on each shoulder that held his cloak. Isak could see that these too were wolf heads—interesting; they should have been the Keep device of the Lomin family. Once the clasps were arranged to his satisfaction, Lomin looked at the count, his lips thinned into a line of distaste. That one look was enough to convince Isak that Vesna would be loyal to him: it was pure hatred.

"The evening is not good, Count Vesna, and neither am I Scion."

Vesna forced himself down onto one knee as Lomin strode imperiously up to him. "Then you have my apologies, Duke Lomin," he said, reaching out to touch the ducal seal.

The duke raised a finger to cut Vesna off. "Duke Certinse, Vesna. I have decided to take my mother's family name."

Isak saw Count Vesna's shoulders tense. That Karlat Lomin—now Certinse, he must remember that—had eschewed both his own family name and that of his city, favouring his mother's powerful family, was a studied insult to Lord Bahl's position.

Somehow, Vesna managed to maintain the level of respect required of him, unclipping his sheathed sword and holding it out hilt-first to his enemy in a gesture of deference, muttering, "Duke Certinse, I apologise, and I grieve for your father. We had not heard his illness had won out."

"It didn't. Weak as he was, my father was not one to be beaten by an ill humour. A team of assassins breached the walls two nights past. They murdered him in his bed before firing the keep. Only my mother and I survived. Ten elven assassins managed to murder my entire family, fifty guards, and burn my home. The wall guards tell me some even made it back to their lines."

All around, protocol was forgotten in the horror of the news and a hundred voices murmured rage and disbelief, common soldiers and nobility alike cursing in the same breath. Only General Lahk's voice interrupted as he called for the watches to be doubled and the fires banked high. That assassins could penetrate one of the most secure of the Farlan keeps was a horrifying thought. Isak heard a knight mutter "sorcery," as he thought the same thing.

Before him, Duke Certinse stood appreciating the effect he'd had. One gloved hand rested lovingly on the hilt of his sword. At his father's death he had inherited Bloodlight and Lomin's Torch, weapons that only those of the Chosen could surpass. It was rumoured that the young man, still only twenty summers, had never had any love for his popular father, or any of his siblings. The young wolf held only his mother in his heart. He was her very image, made masculine.

Despite the shock, Isak couldn't help but wonder why only those two had managed to avoid the tragedy. "I'm sorry to hear that," he rumbled gravely. "Everyone spoke well of Duke Lomin, your father. I had hoped to meet him one day."

Silence returned to the scene and faces turned to watch the two men. Duke Certinse took in Isak, bigger even than when he'd left Tirah, and nodded curtly. He was obviously unhappy about being in the presence of someone whose image overshadowed his own. He walked over to Isak, and, as Vesna had done to him, he held out the hilt of Lomin's Torch to Isak and grudgingly touched the dragon-ring on Isak's hand. Certinse might be a duke now, and thus outrank Isak, but the Krann had been given specific command of the army and so carried Bahl's authority in lieu.

Behind Certinse, a page had the hem of his cloak bunched in his hand. The boy's pudgy face was frozen in fear and Isak's sharpened senses caught the faint stink of urine. He couldn't blame the boy, having to come to within a few feet of such a monstrous figure, but he doubted the duke would be so forgiving.

Isak reached out and touched the pommel of the weapon. Certinse flinched in surprise as Isak probed its potency, one finger resting on the figure of a wolf sleeping with nose tucked under its bushy tail. The runes he felt were strong and simple, except for one that gave Isak a sense of bloodlust, a hunger to burn and ruin the flesh of the twisted creatures now advancing.

The rune felt as if it had recoiled at his touch and he withdrew his hand hurriedly. He didn't want to know why it had done that. He might not know much about magic yet, but he was positive some forbidden process had made this. At its very core, the sword knew the taste of elves—it had been quenched in the blood of one.

"Rise; we can play formalities some other time."

"As you say." Certinse's voice was cool as he stood. "You received my man with news of their forces?"

"We did," broke in General Lahk, stepping forward to take control of the discussion. Vesna had already told Isak that Certinse would try to lead the battle if given the slightest opportunity. "Suzerain Torl has command of four legions of cavalry—he went ahead two days ago to harry their movements. How many men have you managed to bring from Lomin?"

"All the infantry I could muster: four legions of spear and one of archers. None of the town garrisons have had a chance to get here, but with luck the rangers might be able to find a secure path for some to reach the battle in time."

"We're short on archers then, with so many light cavalry away, but it will have to do. From what we've scried of the enemy, they have far greater numbers, although most are on foot. The group trying to outflank us is entirely horse; that means they won't want to move the main bulk very far."

"They'll take the northern end of the Chir Plain then."

"You know it?" Lahk waved a hand behind him and immediately one of his staff thrust a map-scroll into it. Another man brought a table and the map was unrolled on it.

"Here's the plain," said Certinse, his finger stabbing down at the map. Isak moved forward to look over Lahk's shoulder. With a grunt the general slid around the table to afford Isak a better view. The curves and lines meant little to the Krann but he kept quiet. A wagoner knew the lie of the Land from his own travels and the accounts of others, not paper, but he had to learn.

"There's a rise that runs much of that side, we can ride hidden behind it, but if they try to go over they'll be in trouble. It's too rocky to get down that slope. They will have to wait until they reach the cleft where a small river cuts the ridge. It's wide and brings you right round the other side of the plain."

"What else is there?"

"The river. That cuts through the ridge like this and runs that way—it's not deep, though. There's a steep, flat-topped rise here." Certinse moved his finger northeast of the river. Nothing was indicated on the map, but neither duke nor general looked surprised. "There are some old fortifications on top, nothing significant, but it's a safe place to have a good view of the field. Other than that, there's a slight up-slope running east and a nice big space to pick them off in."

"What will the river be like at this time of year?" interrupted Isak. He'd dragged enough horses through enough rivers swollen by autumn rain as a child to know how difficult it would be for an army.

Certinse glanced up, a flash of irritation on his face, but replied, "Not too bad; even with the rain we've had it'll still be possible to cross."

"Good," declared General Lahk in a decisive voice. "That's where we'll attack. We can take the heavy cavalry through the ridge there and hit the enemy in the side."

"Alone?"

"Not quite. Your legion of archers will be on that rocky slope, protected by one of the Lomin spear legions. We have one legion of light cavalry with our group, and a division will skirmish ahead to draw the trolls off that rise—"

"How do you know they will be there?" the duke interrupted.

"It's protected from cavalry, therefore that is where the trolls will go, ready to attack our heavy cavalry once we commit it. The division will be doused in every bottle of perfume and scent our fair knights have brought with them. My Ghosts have already searched the baggage of every man with us. Your hurscals will submit to the same, Duke Certinse."

The young man went red with anger at being ordered about by a white-eye, but Isak's question came out first. "Perfume? Have you gone mad?"

"Firstly, the scent of trolls on the wind will alarm the horses," the general explained calmly. "Hopefully, this will help mask their stench, which in turn will help us to keep our order tight. Secondly, a troll relies on scent and hearing—they can only see very short distances. The archers will also be burning all the incense our priests have. I am assured that the direction of the wind will be favourable. By moving quickly enough, and with any help the mages can provide, we can at least anger the trolls. They will follow the unfamiliar smell as much as the movement of the cavalry, and when our horses break south, out of the way, I believe they will falter in confusion."

"That's lunacy!" cried Certinse.

The general straightened up to face the duke, but still no trace of annoyance showed on his face, let alone anger at the insult. "Well then, it is unfortunate for all of us that Lord Isak has approved of the plan, and it is he who was specifically appointed commander of our army," he said quietly.

"Lord Bahl did not know a duke would be present!" snapped Certinse in return. "If my father had been alive he would have been granted command as soon as he rode in. I demand the same right, as is the privilege of my rank."

Isak raised an eyebrow at Vesna, but the count was not paying attention. His hand was creeping closer to his sword as the Lomin hurscals edged closer to the group.

It was up to Isak. "Demand whatever in the name of the Dark Place you like," he bellowed. The venom in his voice froze every man to the spot and rippled out through the air to reach the Ghosts camped all around Isak's tent. Hands reached instinctively for weapons as they caught sight of Certinse's hurscals and they immediately closed the respectful gap between men and generals. General Lahk was an emotionless bastard who'd sacrifice a division if he had to, but he'd kept them all alive time and time again for that precise reason. They trusted him as much as Lord Bahl and had no affection for the arrogance of household knights.

"The first man who draws a sword here, I'll call mutiny and run him through. That also goes for the first who tries to take my command, whatever his rank is," Isak continued. "I'll answer to Lord Bahl for my actions, but no one else commands me." He glared around at every man there. "Now, does anyone wish to take issue with the plan?"

A moment of silence followed before Certinse opened his mouth again and blurted out, "The enemy's numbers are too great. We'd have to cut our way through several legions to reach the trolls."

"General Lahk, would you care to explain further?" Isak's voice was quiet and controlled; something Bahl had said to Isak had emerged from his memory: *the eye of the storm is when men have time to fear the other side. Show your anger, and then don't use it further. They will expect it to return, and hesitate. One pause is all a soldier needs.*

"Of course, my Lord. To the south will be the rest of the foot, the Palace Guard infantry at their fore, and the rest of the light cavalry. The Ghosts and cavalry will advance, then falter at the sight of the enemy before retreating in a chaotic fashion. I would prefer to keep the Ghosts up with our group, but they are the only ones trained for this manoeuvre."

"What manoeuvre?"

"Flee under orders. Our enemy likes nothing more than a running foe; their commanders will not be able to prevent a pursuit. There can be no doubt of that. The fleeing men return to our line and reform—please trust me, Duke Certinse, I have seen to it personally that this will be done—and wait for the attack. The ground will become open enough for us to take the trolls without becoming surrounded."

"But it means we are dividing our forces against superior numbers," the duke said. "That goes against one of the most basic principles of warfare."

"And thus demonstrates Eraliave's assertion that all tenets of war are fluid and a good general must be able to adapt to the current situation," finished Vesna. The duke glared at him, but obviously accepted that this was not the time for further argument.

"Indeed, Count Vesna," the general said. "Now, with your permission, my Lord, I will give orders to the legion colonels."

Isak gestured for Lahk to leave, even giving the general a nod of respect. It was hard for him not to smirk as the other men there did the same. Certinse had no choice but to follow suit, bound by the rules, laws, and traditions of his class.

Suzerain Fordan then cleared his throat, his face a picture of innocent helpfulness. A pitcher of wine had not dimmed his intelligence: he could see that Certinse was about to leave and impose his own will on the execution of the plan. General Lahk was known for his utter obedience to authority; the last thing they needed now was for him to have to face down a superior.

"Duke Certinse, Lord Bahl wrote to me recently expressing a concern that soon the dukedom of Lomin might be without an heir, knowing how ill your beloved father was. Since this unhappy situation has now arisen, and we have so many of your peers at hand, this would seem the perfect opportunity to discuss a betrothal."

The duke squirmed for a moment and then shrugged. He had the sense to know when he was out-manoeuvred and forced a smile at the craggy old man, who beamed in return. It was over an hour before the matter was settled: a magnificent dowry would accompany his marriage to Suzerain Nelbove's daughter. Nelbove was close to Tirah, and the suzerain knew he was suspected of treachery so he'd not risk angering Lord Bahl further.

With the evening's work done, the nobles retired to await the morning.

"Now then, my lady, don't you think you've spent long enough in here for one week?"

Tila flinched in her chair, hands reaching for the armrest to push herself up until she realised it was only Swordmaster Kerin standing before her. He grinned and eased himself down into the seat opposite, sighing with pleasure as he turned his attention to the fire. Tila had kept it banked up throughout the day; by Kerin's reaction she guessed it was bitterly cold outside now night had fallen. The Swordmaster was dressed in his formal uniform—as he had been every day since Lord Bahl's departure—and it didn't look nearly as warm as the leather and woollens he normally wore.

"I've spent quite a lot of time in here," Tila admitted, rubbing the tiredness from her eyes as she inspected the Swordmaster, "but I don't have any real duties until Lord Isak returns—and as you can see, I've quite a way to go yet." She gestured at the books and scrolls on the walls with a weary smile.

"You intend to read them all?"

"I intend to read anything I think might be useful to Lord Isak." She raised the book resting in her lap so Kerin could read the curling writing on its cover. "A collection of prophecies about the Saviour." She grimaced.

"Do you think—" Kerin began.

Tila cut him off. "No, but there's been talk of all kinds since Lord Isak received his gifts. You must have heard the preachers out on the Palace Walk."

"I've heard *about* them," Kerin said, "but I've got better things to do than listen to a bunch of unkempt madmen. Anyway, as Knight-Defender, I can't leave the palace until either Lord Bahl or a general relieves me of my duty; otherwise it's desertion of duty and that means a trip to the nearest tree and a quick drop." They both smiled: the thought of Swordmaster Kerin even considering dereliction of duty was laughable.

"My men have been bringing back reports of all kinds of preachers throughout the city, and talking about the Saviour isn't their only favourite subject. There's been no trouble though; they're not rabble-rousers, just barking mad."

Tila sniffed. "You might find one of them to be a real holy man, then you'll be in trouble for dismissing them all as insane."

"Oh Gods, they'd be worse!" Kerin exclaimed, leaning forward in his seat to emphasise his point. "As any man involved with keeping the peace will agree: merciful Gods, save us from the religious."

"And what do you mean by that?"

"I mean I've seen how some who claim to be truly religious behave, and I tell you, Lady Tila, no creature of the Dark Place would ever turn on its own kind for such small reasons as these will. Religious folk'll burn or hang a man for smiling wrong." Kerin wasn't smiling now. He sat gripping the armrests of his chair and glaring fiercely.

Tila thought better of trying to explain the difference between fanatics and the devout: some people had no interest in seeing one. "Well then, if people are going to act that way, it would be sensible to be prepared for it," she said calmly. "We should be able to recognise whatever dogma they're obeying." She tapped the open page of the book. "Have a read of this one and tell me what you think."

She handed the book to Kerin, who frowned as he scanned the lines of text. The prophecy she meant had come down on a stableboy in Embere two hundred years ago; apparently no one, not even the scholar who had written this book, knew quite what to make of it. The Swordmaster's lips moved as he read—Tila recognised that amongst the palace's soldiers who'd come late to education—and his expression became graver at every sentence.

"Well I don't understand half of it, but this is no Saviour I'd like to meet," he growled. "*A shadow rising from the faithful of the West; his twilight reign to begin amid the slain.*"

"Comforting, isn't it?" Tila took the book back, placed it on the table beside her, and stood up. Automatically, Kerin rose as well. "But it is better to know what madness our enemies might follow than to wallow in our ignorance." She presented her arm and nodded towards the door. "Come on then. If you think I've been locked away in here too long, let's go and find some form of entertainment."

CHAPTER 13

FROM ONE OF THE TOWERS STILL STANDING he saw the damage to his beautiful home. From up there the ruin had an almost glorious quality, an air of decadence. Like paint on canvas, great sweeps of the brush had carved rents in the ground and spread the stones of the fallen towers with careless abandon. He remembered the rage of his return, and the misshapen beasts capering in the destruction. Heavy jutting muzzles gnawed with relish; curling tongues lapped at the dark pools of dirt and blood. They'd screamed as they died, knowing agony for their crimes, and yet there had been so many. Wounds unhealed had been overlaid by fresh burning hurts, and as he lay beside those dear to him, broken and alone, they tasted his blood.

A name had saved him. A single word that hung thick in the air and ate into the stiffening wounds on his body. The sweet stench of corruption and loss lingered still, long after it had twisted his attackers into grotesque ruin. He felt himself contaminated, infected with something there could be no cure for. Desperately he searched about for some means of escape, some possibility of redemption. Running down corpse-strewn corridors he came to a decaying garden—so recently his refuge from the horror of life. Now it was dead, along with the creatures that had once been his beloved pets. Some no doubt had fled, but most lay in stinking heaps, their bones breaking with tiny snaps under his heel as he walked to a clear, serene pool. Looking in, he caught his own reflection—and felt the grip of damnation as he saw a face that was not his own. The face screamed and he heard himself echo that scream as the colour faded to black.

In a tangle of sodden blankets, Isak awoke with a gasp. The clammy touch of early dawn whispered over his skin and a shiver ran down his back while the memory of his wounds from the dream burned hot on his body. It was dark inside the tent, and distances were treacherous in the weak light, shapes shifting subtly in the corner of his eye. He closed his hand around Eolis—the blade always found its way to his side as he slept—and raised it to see his reflection. The silver gave him a slightly distorted picture, but he'd settle for anything resembling his own face after that dream.

His hand trembled with the effort and when a figure at the entrance twitched at his movement he almost dropped Eolis in surprise. The hairs on Isak's neck prickled with panic and the long blade was drawing back, ready to strike, even as he recognised General Lahk. The white-eye's hands were demurely clasped together, a strange pose for a knight in full armour.

"What're you doing, General?" Isak thought his voice sounded drunk and uncertain, but the general gave no sign that he had noticed.

"It is time. We must ride before dawn." He was staring intently at Isak, as though he was trying to see what had set them apart—what qualities Lahk was lacking to set this boy above him. "Do you want me to fetch a page to help you with your armour?"

Isak frowned for a moment, then remembered why he had refused a page in the first place. Grabbing at the blanket, he pulled it high up to his neck, re-covering the scar on his chest. "No, I'll be fine. How soon do we ride?"

"When you are ready, my Lord. I have told the infantry to be prepared within the half-hour. I received a rider in the night from Suzerain Torl; he engaged the enemy twice yesterday and forced them to change direction both times."

"We're still going to be badly outnumbered, though."

"Not greatly. You have not seen disciplined troops standing against a rabble. I would happily form the foot legion of the Ghosts into a square and let five times our number of untrained men attack all sides. The enemy are cowardly and weak. If there are members of different houses, then it is even possible some troops will never engage but abandon the field, take their booty, and return to usurp those they abandon."

"And the trolls?"

The general paused at that. He opened his mouth a fraction, then paused again, before saying, "They are animals, not soldiers. They were one of the warrior-races created by the Gods during the Great War—they were not intended for sophistication, nor intelligence, only to be driven towards the enemy. They like to destroy; they like to fight. They won't run like the others."

It looked like he wanted to say more, but nothing came. Isak waited a few heartbeats, then realised they were wasting time. "Go and see to the men, I'll get ready."

"Yes, my Lord." A short bow and Lahk was gone. Isak could hear voices calling for the general's attention, but they didn't intrude on his space and he was glad for it. He relieved himself into the brass pot by his bed, then jammed a dry crust of bread into his mouth and began to fit his body into the undersuit laid out next to Siulents. As Bahl had predicted, the larger one was now a better fit. Once that was on and the toggles fastened, he swallowed the last few pieces of bread and clipped on the mail skirt and codpiece that would lie underneath the main plates of armour.

Carel had said that a cut to the groin was one of the fastest ways to bleed to death. Now that Isak was dwelling on that image, he could feel the hot pulse beating under the leather. Next came the cuirass. He opened the hinge to fit the two plates around his torso. As it snapped shut, a close fit molded to the curve of his muscles, the seam and hinge melted from view. The fact that he'd grown in size didn't seem to bother Siulents one bit. Isak couldn't resist running a finger down that line one more time, feeling edges that his eyes couldn't detect.

As the pieces came together, a warmth settled into his skin, driving away the morning chill and bringing the hint of a smile to his face. For the moment, trepidation was a distant memory. Shrugging his shoulders inside the plate, Isak felt hardly any restriction or weight. The illusion of a seamless liquid-metal casing over his body increased his confidence in his own strength and speed. Passing Eolis through a few strokes, Isak felt his already supernatural skills enhanced even further. The weapon in movement felt like it was fused to his arm.

Even sheathed, Eolis felt alive and hungry for action. Isak strode out with a cold grin on his face. His blue mask was slipped over the padded hood of his undersuit. His armour shimmered in the grim grey light while the dragon symbol on his long cloak danced and raged in the breeze. Though the Ghosts had seen him in Siulents before, the effect on the men he passed was electrifying. He stopped and met their amazed faces, then snapped an order to get back to work and smiled as they jumped like startled rabbits.

He looked around. Neat lines of mounted men waited on all sides while more readied their horses and checked weapons. Pages and servants ran in and out of the forest of tents that covered the ground. Most of the mounted men were Ghosts. Many of the things Lahk had drilled them in were basics, but details like that could mean the difference between victory and defeat, and a general who didn't get bored was ideal to drill men until they were perfect.

Count Vesna, fully accoutred, hurried over to Isak as he watched the troops moving with purpose and grim efficiency. Here and there a voice was raised in laughter, but most men were lost in cold deliberation. The fleeing commoners and the assault on Lomin had provoked a deep anger within the troops.

"My Lord, your charger is ready." Vesna moved with the uncomfortable swing of a man in plate armour, but quickly enough for it to be obvious that the black-painted metal was enchanted. His hair, plaited, was wrapped around his neck, covering up the tattoos.

Isak's view of his horse was obscured by a knight draped in yellow and white who was gesticulating wildly at his page. Isak glanced at him as he stalked past and the man froze in midsentence.

White drapes hung down over the horse's armour, with Isak's dragon emblazoned on its flanks. A steel spike rose out through the cloth on its forehead. As Isak approached, the horse twitched a step towards him, pulling taut the reins held by the figure beside it. The horse tossed its head nervously.

A sudden sense of danger screamed in Isak's head, and a memory flashed up: his page was smaller. The figure holding the reins threw back its cloak and leapt forward, unfolding long limbs from a slender body. Isak blinked— and the figure had covered the ground between them, stabbing forwards as it moved. Unbidden, Eolis darted up to meet it as the figure hit Isak full in the chest and threw him off his feet. As his shoulders slammed into the ground, he kicked off, desperately feeling for solid ground underfoot. Distantly he felt blows slam into his stomach as his left hand grabbed a thin arm that squirmed with amazing strength.

Then the attacker broke away. Isak rolled onto his knees and threw himself left, sheer instinct, as two thin white spears stabbed into the ground where he'd been a heartbeat before. He hacked through one before hurling himself away again. An inhuman screech tore through the air and Isak felt a weight slam onto his back. Scarcely thinking, he flung his left arm up to protect his face and felt something score his vambrace instead of his throat.

He stabbed Eolis up over his shoulder and felt it grate on bone, then the weight was gone. He jumped to his feet and spun around, cutting up as he did so, but now his assailant kept just out of reach. For a moment he locked eyes with the creature. Mandible jaws on either side of its mouth twitched as it peered back at its intended prey. It stood on three legs; the fourth was shorn off and dripping black blood. More blood ran down from its right shoulder, but the arm ending in a bony blade was still ready to strike.

Before any of the watching knights could move to attack it, the creature leaped again, every limb swept back and ready. Isak slid away to his right, leaving Eolis in his wake to slash up as his attacker passed. He felt chitin split and the sword cut deep before his movement brought it out. He gave the creature no time to recover from the second cut, dropping down to kick away its legs. The savagery of the blow snapped something and brought Isak right around, Eolis already hacking at the figure on the floor before he had even focused on it. A second blow sheared through one of the bladed arms and a third stabbed straight down to impale the creature on the ground.

Isak staggered backwards, crashing into Vesna as he did so. He turned, raising his empty sword-arm for a moment before his senses returned. Behind him the figure thrashed and spasmed, but they were the movements of a dead thing.

"My Lord, are you hurt?" Vesna dropped his sword and grabbed at the huge white-eye as Isak lurched again. Finding his feet, Isak gripped his bondsman's shoulder and steadied himself. The surge of adrenalin blurred his sight for a moment, then his vision snapped back into focus. Isak found himself staring at the tattoo on the count's neck. Taut muscles distorted it into a bizarre shape.

Isak sucked in a huge gulp of air and felt his hand tremble as he replied, "I—I think so." Looking down at where the creature had been hitting him in the stomach, Isak could see only one tiny break in the armour, and that sealed up as he watched. "Am I bleeding?"

"You—" Vesna stopped and looked Isak over. The attack had been so fast Vesna had hardly seen the blows, but apart from a deep groove on Isak's arm-guard where the creature had tried to cut his throat, there were no signs of damage. "No, it doesn't seem to have pierced the armour anywhere."

"What was it?"

Both men turned to look at the corpse. As they did so, a Ghost ran his lance down into its throat to make sure it was dead. When there was no further movement, the soldier pulled Eolis from the body and offered it over his arm to Isak. The Krann stared at it for a moment, surprised at the formality, but judging by the faces of every man there, they had been impressed with the fight.

"That, my Lord," supplied General Lahk from behind Isak, "is an Estashanti warrior. It's one of the hybrid races bred by the Gods for the Great War, then discarded when their talents were surplus to requirements." In the shock of the aftermath, Isak thought he detected an air of bitterness about the general's voice.

"It explains how the enemy managed to kill Duke Lomin. Buggers use them as assassins," muttered Suzerain Fordan. As he gave the corpse a kick, a golden gorget fell away. The chain had been neatly severed. Isak felt a surge of magic leave the ruined object: that was how it had managed to get past all the guards.

"Gods, if it had got here yesterday . . . Without Siulents I'd have been gutted in that first attack. If we were not riding to battle this morning—"

"You'd be dead, my Lord. But before you offer thanks to the Gods, we do have another battle to fight. It can only harm our cause to let this delay us further." General Lahk didn't wait for a reply as he turned to a herald at his side. The herald was several summers younger than Isak and the only one there in light armour. He had a large round shield on his back and a hunting horn in his hands. His job was to stay alive to sound orders for the troops. Isak could see puke on his clothes already—perhaps he'd been thinking about meeting a troll.

"Sound the order to move out," Isak said, and mounted his horse, which was calm now the Estashanti was dead. Vesna handed him the cold, blank helm that Isak had dropped in the attack. A smear of mud marked the crest.

"My Lord?"

Isak turned to see the general raise his helm slightly. Looking around, he realised they were all watching him. He was leading this army, so tradition dictated the order come from him. Every boy of the tribe shouted the words out as they played; even those without friends felt the words in their heart.

Isak wheeled his horse around, held up his helm for all to see, and called out as loud as he could, "My Lords, we go to war—your helms!"

Amid a great cheer Isak slid his own helm over his head and felt the lip of the collar meet his cuirass. At his side Vesna rammed home the golden wolf's head and slid the faceplate up to look at his liege lord. The count muttered a few words of shock that were lost in the cheers from all about. Isak didn't wait to hear any more. He spurred his charger ahead, through the rows of mounted Guardsmen, with war cries ringing all about.

CHAPTER 14

A S THE KNIGHTS FOLLOWED THE PATH of the shallow river and reached the ridge, Isak noticed a scent on the wind he couldn't place. Winter had muted every flavour that reached him, and it came only when the breeze momentarily cleared the heavy musk of horse. Whether it was just too faint to recognise, or something new to him, Isak couldn't be sure. These parts were too remote to have been of any interest to a wagon train. This area looked unspectacular, but still Isak wondered what he would miss as he passed through, how much he would never see of lands that would one day belong to him. Anvee itself was nothing more than a name at the moment, and that was just one suzerainty—what about when he became Lord of the Farlan?

Off to the left fluttered the archer legion's colours; the men around the pennant stood with shoulders hunched against the wind at their backs. As the cavalry approached, one man raised his longbow in a salute and disappeared down the slope to report their arrival to the legion's commander.

"My Lord?"

Isak realised he'd been turning in the saddle, into the wind coming from behind them. It carried elusive snatches of that scent he was suddenly determined to identify. Vesna had followed his gaze and found only soldiers, grave eyes encased in steel and black iron. Isak sensed his confusion and turned his thoughts away; there was nothing in the air except the scent of men wanting to avoid what was to come.

Isak reached out and gripped Vesna's shoulder plate. "I'm fine," he said, "just thinking about this place."

"Don't—it distracts you from the battle. Every man does that the first time. I know what you're thinking and you mustn't. Imagine the enemy, and nothing more. Think of the path your horse will take, the way you'll make your first strike. Picture that rank of enemy crumpling and freeing your path to ride away while Certinse's wing hits the other side. Picture wheeling and forming the line again."

Isak grinned. "Yes. I understand."

In the distance they heard hunting horns—the command calls of the light cavalry—echoed by the drums of the foot legions. Behind Isak, men shifted in their saddles, impatient to be off.

"It begins," commented General Lahk, from the front. The heavy cavalry was in three groups, to better negotiate the ford, with Isak's Ghosts at the fore. Behind him were another five hundred knights, under Duke Certinse's command, and the final group, led by Suzerain Ked, followed closely behind, a mix of black-and-white-clad Guardsmen and brightly coloured nobles. Once the first two parties were caught up in the fighting, Ked would lead these men hard and straight into the trolls, a final shock movement intended to drive the beasts away.

Seeing the heavy cavalry together in one place brought home to Isak the beauty of the Farlan system. Though the general had grumbled that the turnout should have been significantly higher, it was unlikely any other nation or tribe in the Land could field more than half the number of heavy cavalry that the Farlan could muster. The tribe's entire social structure worked to keep this war machine operating at peak performance.

A knight of battle age who didn't maintain a full suit of armour would be stripped of his title and lands. However impoverished his family might be, the knight's hunter would be well fed, and ready to carry him into battle at any moment. Any tenant who could shoot an arrow from horseback and hit four out of five times was entitled to a small wage from his landlord, whether he were a landlocked serf or a local poacher. Drilling was of paramount importance for every healthy Farlan male; as children, they play-acted the battles they would fight as men. It was in their blood.

The horns sounded again, over a rising clamour in the distance. High in the patched blanket of cloud, Isak could see birds soaring—scavengers of some sort, kites and buzzards, no doubt. A handful of crows were cawing in the trees to his right, disturbed by the movements below but refusing to be driven off.

"What's that call?"

"Strike left, strike right," replied Vesna automatically. "The light cavalry has found a target."

"They're not supposed to engage, though."

"But it is to be expected. The captains know they can engage if they can still break and continue with the plan. They'll fall back quickly and move south to open a path for us, but there's always the chance they can rout an enemy division before they do."

"Where's the herald with the flags?" A white flag would mean the attack could go ahead as planned, red that the enemy was advancing en masse. If that happened, the plan was to ride out and attack whatever troops presented themselves. Red meant salvage whatever they could, and buy the rest of the army time to regroup.

"There."

Isak fell silent. His fingers skittered over the surface of his armour as he waited for their signal. He was burning to be off and into action himself: he needed it to start. More horns came, fainter this time, and the heavy beat of a battery of drums. Isak's head twitched up as he felt magic burst from the ridge ahead: the battle-mages were joining the attack.

Even from the other side of the ridge, Isak could feel their elation at the release. The mages had kept their distance from him for the whole journey, no doubt Afger Wetlen's death strong in their minds.

Isak's impatience grew as the prickle of magic went down his spine. He could feel the blood pumping through his body, the memory of his muscles in movement; he could imagine the power and animal heat of the huge horse charging. He blinked and felt his hand tighten about the reins. The edge of his shield pushed on his thigh and he forced it down harder, glad of the pressure as a distraction. It kept his mind from wandering, kept his eyes focused on the figure ahead.

Then—finally—the flag was raised and frantically swept from side to side. The horses surged forward as one, even Isak's, as he paused for a moment to check the colour of the flag. Against the grey sky it was hard to make out—then he realised that red would have been clearly visible. Things were going to plan.

As they clattered over the stones of the riverbed and urged their horses up the small bank, Isak saw nothing but disorganised crowds. Farlan horsemen were outstripping their pursuers, a tidal wave of elves following them south. Between the horsemen were the ranks of infantry, running back in disorder, but Isak could see the gaps between the lines, the spaces that would allow them to reform, even if it looked like they were fleeing in terror from the enemy.

A minute later a horn rang out. The leading rank of Ghosts apparently running away stopped dead and turned to face the enemy. The second rank, behind them, did the same, and the third, until the men were in line, forming a shield wall and ready to take on the elves again.

Isak tore himself away—they knew what they were doing; they didn't need him—and concentrated on the hulking grey shapes two hundred yards away. His charger picked up speed. All he could make out were wide, heavy bodies and long thick arms, and deep, bestial growls that turned to bellowing as they heard the horsemen.

Isak's horse thundered to the head of the group without any encouragement from its rider. On either side lances edged down as they began to close the distance. The trolls loomed large and a few took hesitant steps forward, but most, confused by the sudden appearance of the cavalry, stood still, apparently unaware of what was happening—until the horses were almost upon them.

Isak stood up in the saddle. He was the only man there without a lance; he'd refused one without really knowing why. Buoyed by the energy of the knights behind him and the streams of magic bursting around the trolls, Isak felt a euphoric power run down his arm. Only now did he draw Eolis, holding the sword up high as though drawing strength from the heavens. The Ghosts behind roared their approval as he towered over them all, a divine figure ready to strike down the cursed.

Then he threw it. Eolis flashed through the air like an arrow and slammed into the nearest troll. One of the light cavalry had already hit it— a red-feathered shaft struck straight up from its shoulder. Isak couldn't tell whether the troll had even noticed the first wound, but when Eolis buried itself into its chest, the creature shuddered and gave a guttural groan. It looked down in surprise, one hand sluggishly reaching up to touch the hilt. With a thought, Isak called the weapon back to him. Eolis slid back out with a gush of black blood and the troll collapsed.

There was no time to cheer the first kill. Eolis returned to Isak's hand just as they reached the first line of trolls, those that had advanced early. Leaning out in his saddle, Isak slashed one as he passed, not even noticing the spurt of blood that spattered his thigh. Before he was clear another stepped out, swinging its arm up to swat him off his horse. Barely in time Isak wheeled away and chopped downwards to cut through the thick limb. The massive hand slammed into his shield and threw him back in his saddle, then the arm fell away and he was clear.

Behind Isak came the meaty thump of lances piercing flesh and breaking bone. A horse screamed, but when Isak turned to look, he could see nothing more than a whirl of men frantically urging their horses away.

From the bodies on the floor it was clear that many had failed to drive their lances deep enough. One troll bounded forward with frightening speed, seeming not to notice the three lances in its body. A Ghost saw the movement and moved in behind the creature, but it had anticipated him and, turning, crashed a huge fist down on to the horse's neck. Its forelegs crumpled into the ground and the Ghost was catapulted forward, rolling over and over until a second troll hopped forward and stamped down on his head. His armour provided no defence against so foul a death; Isak heard the man's scream cut off and winced, then looked to the living again.

As a group of trolls started towards where the Ghosts were stopping to turn, Duke Certinse came hurtling onto the field, howling madly, at the head of a long column of knights. His lance thudded smartly into the skull of his chosen target, then he tore Lomin's Torch, his family's ancestral sword, from its scabbard and claimed another before riding away.

The plan had been to ride past on the first run, then cut deep into the trolls' ranks on the second pass, but the trolls ran forward so quickly that there was nowhere else to go. General Lahk saw the charging knights absorbed. He wasted no time finding his herald but grabbed his own horn from its sheath on his saddle and blew a shrill volley of notes.

"Form line," he roared, the words hardly carrying against the clamour of battle, "form line!" The general spurred his horse hard to get in line with Isak; his Ghosts streamed past, then reined in hard. There was no time to fetch spare lances: the nobles would be slaughtered unless help came immediately. The Ghosts, calmly and efficiently, formed a line around the general as he drew his axe and held it up for them all to see. Isak watched men on either side heft spiked hammers and crow-bill axes; a savage mix of crushing weapons sprang up all down the line.

Off to their right the ordered ranks of Suzerain Ked's party, their lances raised, waited for the general's order. As soon as the Ghosts were ready, a double blast of the trumpet sent them into a headlong charge, straight into the trolls. Once they were in full gallop, he called the charge, indicating with his axe the left flank of the expanding group of trolls.

Isak kicked his spurs in hard and his charger surged forward. Distantly he heard a voice shouting to hold the line, but a cold rage suffused his mind and Isak barely noticed anything, other than the creatures that had sullied this place he called home—beasts that would pay for this at his own hand.

The sickening, wet crunch of lances meeting flesh and bone, human war cries, and monstrous roars filled the air as Isak led his men into the beasts, hacking left and right with the fury of a madman. Abandoning all pretence at grace, Isak slashed and stabbed with mechanical precision, snarling with rage. The buzz of magic filled his mind as the lumbering horrors threw themselves at the knights with an animal hunger.

Though attacked on three sides, the trolls ignored the numbers piled against them and swung their huge arms tirelessly, crushing and breaking horses and soldiers alike. As each troll fell, another rushed forward to take its place in the front line, fearless and frenzied. Isak didn't care, he wanted them to come. Unaware of his comrades, Isak drove deeper into the creatures. His rage consumed everything, dulled the pain, cowed fear and desperation—he didn't even notice the blows that rocked him in his saddle.

With the ecstasy of hatred came the release he craved so desperately. His arms filled with warmth, the sharp tang of magic was acidic in his throat. Tentative flickers of lightning lit up the mud-spattered grey hides clustering around him and lashed forward to tear into them. Fingers of spitting fire worked their way into the troll's throat and nose, stabbing down through the troll's small ears and reaching through to its thick spine. Lifting it up in his sorcerous grip, Isak roared with laughter, then threw the dead body into the trolls' ranks.

Before he could focus on the next victim, a massive weight slammed into his side as a fist punched him from his saddle. Distantly he felt the snap of ribs breaking, but still his fury eclipsed all. Isak rolled as he hit the ground and came up with Eolis ready to take out the first enemy in range. Leaving the blade buried in its skull, Isak stretched his arms out wide and embraced the clamouring energies that coursed through him.

A nimbus of bright white light enveloped his body. Whipping sparks danced over his armour and arced from one fist to the other. He rose up on an effusion of wrath. The air shimmered and wavered as he held the rampant magic tight in his hands, then unleashed the spitting bursts of light on his enemies.

With the sparks and screams fell a haze of rain. He heard someone calling out, a name, but didn't know if it was his own. He didn't care. That part of him that had a name was hidden—now, he was an avatar of death, glorying in the majesty of his work. Words came unbidden to his lips, gathering those sparks and raindrops together. He pulled Eolis from the dead thing impaled upon it and cut it through the glittering swirl he'd created. It became a storm of golden shards of glass, spinning faster and faster, until he threw it forward to slice and ruin.

As the magic drained from his body, Isak felt something else ahead, something growing with ferocious speed and burning with the same anger he felt. The air grew hot around him and dirty grey wisps of smoke appeared from the churned ground. A shape, orange and white, burst into life on the ground, a creature of flame bound by hatred. A memory forced its way into his thoughts: a Chalebrat. He was facing a fire elemental. As Isak gasped, he felt scorching heat run down his throat. He staggered back, the fringes of his cloak alight, and held his shield high to protect his exposed eyes as swirling hot trails danced in the air and a crushing pain pressed in on his skull.

He struck out—and hit nothing. A long arm of fire swept him off his feet, but again Isak hit nothing. The blade trembled in his hand, frustrated. Though unstained by the flames it cut through, Eolis could find nothing to destroy. In the searing heat Isak cowered back, away from the legion of fiery pinpricks that razed his skin.

Now he felt the Chalebrat looming over him, insubstantial, but deadly, closing for the kill. He felt a shadow pass over his body and the light dimmed—only a little, but enough to relieve the pain for a moment or two. He tensed every muscle in his body and tightened his grip on Eolis, readying himself for his one chance to survive—

A terrific blast of rushing air screamed down towards Isak, followed immediately by the earth-shaking thump of a massive weight hitting the ground. Isak was jerked up into the air by the impact, and as he dropped back down, he realised the intense heat had faded to nothing. Cool air rushed in around him as he lay crumpled, face-down on the muddy ground, the rain spattering on his armour. A moment of calm descended. The bitter scent of burnt flesh drifted to Isak's nose, stirring brief panic as he wondered whether it was his own. He listened to the raindrops falling . . .

. . . until a thunderous roar broke the quiet, a bellow so loud that Isak recoiled from the sheer force of the sound, scrambling to his feet to face this new monster. As he did, a huge head snapped forward towards him. Isak ducked, dropping down to one knee, and heard the terrifying crunch of huge jaws. He got to his feet and as the dragon raised its head and shook the troll in its mouth before tearing it in two, he recognised Genedel.

The deceptive shadows of its underground lair had not fully prepared Isak for what now lay before him: a long serpentine body covered in shimmering, near-translucent scales, a glittering kaleidoscope of magic and light that married a shocking beauty to awesome, lethal power. The dragon's speed was phenomenal as it ripped into the trolls, biting, spearing with its horns, raking with wicked talons and chopping left and right with its axelike tail.

Even the tough hides of the trolls were no match for this dazzling storm of claws, horns, and teeth, and at that moment, Isak recognised the vision in

Aryn Bwr's mind when he shaped Siulents. This was the image he wanted others to see.

From a saddle on the dragon's back slid the Lord of the Farlan, as graceful as a dancer moving through familiar steps, before the crackling edge of his sword sliced through the bodies around him. On his head was an old crested helm that Isak had never seen before, but that was far from the greatest difference. Lord Bahl moved without hesitation, blending magic and devastating strength with a skill that made Isak shiver at the enormous gulf between them.

Bahl struck and drew back, struck again as a grey barrier appeared to deflect a swinging fist. Another kicked out and Bahl simply stepped up sideways, turning his body horizontal in the air before pushing off the chest of another troll and launching himself through the body of the one that had kicked at him. Isak gasped as he felt the massive burst of magic from Bahl's enchanted armour. The Lord's body seemed to fade into insubstantiality as it passed through the troll, only to return to normal as Bahl turned to hack into its spine. He spun in the air as another reached for him, stepped up onto a dead body, and grabbed the next with his free hand, swinging his blade around to slash the troll's throat.

Under such an assault, and penned in on three sides by the heartened knights, the trolls could face no more. Growls of panic and fear rang out on all sides as they turned, like a startled herd of bison, and fled the field. Those few who lingered in confusion were mown down by the rejuvenated soldiers. Genedel gave a triumphant bellow. With one great beat of its wings it took to the air, spitting gouts of flame down on the fleeing creatures, while the Ghosts cheered the dragon on.

"General, enemy to your rear," shouted Bahl as he stood on a grey corpse and scanned the field. "Our infantry are not close enough; we'll be boxed in."

"Herald," cried the general. Isak followed the voice to see the general, battered and bloody, with his herald cowering behind him. The general pushed up his visor and pulled the boy round to face him. "Sound infantry advance to flank."

The herald coughed and scrabbled to bring his horn to his lips, but he could find no breath to produce a sound. General Lahk, losing patience, grabbed the horn from his hands and sounded the five quick notes then, thrusting it back at the herald, scowled and ran to his Lord's side. To the right, Sir Cerse raised his battle-axe, pointing off to the left of where the trolls were fleeing.

"Ghosts, form line east on me!" The order rang out loud and clear.

Isak joined Bahl and the general as they took in what they could of the battlefield.

"The foot are holding, the enemy is too disorganised to break the line, and the cavalry have prevented a flanking attack," Bahl said. "Isak, you did well there, but now trust your arm only. You've drawn on so much magic that any more could overwhelm you."

Isak nodded, wincing slightly as he pushed against the armour over his ribs.

"Hurt?"

"Not badly enough to stop me."

"Good. Find yourself a horse. We can finish this battle now, with luck."

Already the Ghosts were in some sort of order. Duke Certinse was standing in his stirrups, his burning sword raised high as he called the Eastmen to him. Isak watched liveried hurscals and knights make for Suzerain Fordan as he did the same, shouting for the men of the Heartland. The regions were old forms of allegiance, a relic of the fractured realm Bahl had inherited. Isak had not realised until now that they had been preserved for the battlefield, but he recognised a quick way to regroup amid the chaos of combat.

"General Lahk, sound the infantry advance and take the Ghosts to their brothers," Bahl ordered.

The general saluted crisply and turned without waiting to hear more. Before Bahl could speak again, the general was shouting for his troops to turn west. The infantry and knights of the Ghosts would carve an army in two to join their brothers. The delay while the soldiers reformed would be more than worthwhile.

"My Lords." Isak looked up as Count Vesna approached, leading two horses. The man looked pristine, not a dent or scratch on his armour and hardly a fleck of dirt or blood on himself or his horse. Isak could smell the mud and gore on his own armour—if he hadn't seen Vesna ride into the mass of trolls himself, he'd have thought the man had never been near the battlefield.

Bahl nodded his thanks and took the reins from Vesna. He kept the bay in the black-and-white of the Palace Guard, his own colours, and offered the jet black mare draped in yellow to Isak. The Krann struggled for a moment to get back into the saddle, his shield and damaged ribs hampering his efforts. He didn't bother asking after the owners of the horses.

"Lord Isak, your cloak . . . are you sure you can fight?" Vesna pointed at

Isak's cloak. The once-pristine white cloth was now grey with dirt and soot, and burned away to the bottom of the dragon symbol. Below it, scorch marks were visible on the surface of Siulents.

"I'll be fine," he said, sounding more blasé than he felt. "Genedel's shadow made the Chalebrat pause. It could have killed me, but it hesitated."

"Shadow?" interrupted Bahl. "We came in too low to cast a shadow on you."

Behind them a great voice rang out from the assembled Palace Guard. "Meh Nartis!"

The three men turned to see the general raise a pair of battle-axes above his head as his soldiers took up their war cry: *The Hand of God, the Fire of the Storm, the Reapers of Men.*

"Enemy advancing," warned a voice from behind them. Bahl snapped a look at Isak, then swung up into his saddle. "This is not the time to discuss shadows," Bahl said before raising his voice to a roar. "Eastmen, Knights of the Heartland, to me!" His deep voice carried to both groups, and Certinse and Fordan immediately repeated the order. Isak was glad to see Duke Certinse had not hesitated to obey his Lord, however much of a traitor he might be.

Bahl sat in his saddle and waited for the men to catch them up—the Palace Guard moving through and around them had caused the knights to sit and let them pass. From his vantage point he could see two units of several thousand elves advancing towards them. To the left, the spearmen of Lomin were running up to make up the distance.

"They're not close enough to protect our flank," Bahl muttered to himself. "Let the enemy come to us."

Isak looked at the old lord and realised the thinking aloud was for his benefit. If he was ever to lead the Farlan, he needed to know about distances and lines of attack, and all manner of things that were difficult to learn except on the field of battle.

"So we need to slow them down or they'll swamp us with numbers."

"Exactly. Victory sometimes depends on nothing more than illusion," Bahl replied. Sheathing White Lightning, he reached out his hands and muttered under his breath. Isak felt the words slide out through the air as they were spoken, rushing forward to the advancing elves. The magic inside him was crying out to be wielded again, but he resisted, heeding Bahl's words.

Up ahead, a line of fire flared up from the grass in front of the nearer enemy unit. Isak could hear the screams of fear and alarm as the flames grew taller, and the whole mass of figures struggled and fought to a halt. Bahl shuddered suddenly as the enemy mages dispelled the magic and the illusion vanished from their path, then he chuckled dryly to himself. "That was a stupid thing to do. Don't they know dragons like the taste of mages better than trolls?"

A ripple of magic echoed out from the rocky ridge behind them. Isak turned in the saddle; he was just able to make out the scarlet robes of the Farlan battle-mages within the ranks of archers. They'd seen what Bahl had done and followed suit. The subtlety of illusion came much more easily to a mage than a white-eye, while they in turn lacked the strength to hurl real fireballs as Bahl could.

Soon shapes started appearing in front of the hesitant troops, who crept forward slowly: a gigantic ice-cobra reared up and lunged at them. A pair of huge eagles began to circle above the further unit and that too faltered.

"And now to actually hurt them." Bahl began to mouth words again, but this time Isak could see the sounds escape as wisps of black smoke from the Lord's mouth. They fell to the ground and began to merge into one, growing as Bahl repeated the words again and again. A fat oily cloud was forming, turning and wriggling like some awful blind maggot, until it suddenly appeared to get the scent of the elves ahead. With a dreadful rustling slither it began to glide over the plain with deceptive speed, its thin tail propelling it onwards with each grotesque flick.

By the time the elves noticed Bahl's magic they had no time to move. The shape surged on into their ranks and sudden shrieks of pain began to come from the enemy lines. Isak saw the elves fighting with each other to get out of the way, frantically swatting at their arms and bodies to try to remove whatever was hurting them. It looked like those whom the shape passed over had been sprayed in acid as they screamed in agony and panic.

"What was that?"

"Something nasty. Who's got a horn?" Suzerain Fordan, riding beside Lord Bahl, offered his. Bahl waved it away so Fordan shrugged and raised it to his own lips and looked to Bahl for his orders.

"Sound the full charge."

"But we're not formed up yet," he protested.

"It doesn't matter. What does matter is that we hit them now, while they're wavering."

Fordan nodded his agreement and sounded the order, which was echoed by the infantry's drummers. Bahl looked around, then raised White Lightning and kicked his heels into the flanks of his horse. The men around him followed suit and a throaty roar spread through the mass of horsemen as they hurtled after their Lord, headlong into the enemy ranks. Paralysed by the spells cast upon them, the elves stood still and unprepared. The powerful hunters, their armour turning each one into a battering ram, smashed through the infantry lines, kicking and stamping, while their riders split skulls and lopped off limbs with equal ease.

As he cut and slashed the scrawny elves, Isak could hardly feel any impact in his arm. The light armour they wore had no effect on Eolis—he could have been hewing a path through a field of nettles rather than living creatures. The sensation stirred something inside him. These elves were nothing more than long grass rustling against his calves. As his armour turned aside spears and arrows and his sword cut limbs into bloody chunks, the gnawing beast of magic in his belly screamed to be released.

A spear thrust under his horse's armour, drove deep into its lung. The animal reared up, screaming in pain, and Isak tumbled off. As he rose to his feet, unhurt, three elves lunged for him at once. He dodged the first blow, then beheaded the second enemy and turned the third elf's spear with his shield. None of them got the chance for a second strike. The elves were the size of children next to Isak; their shoulders were hunched by the curse of the Gods and their features twisted.

Isak hardly needed his sword. His huge arms were saturated with lethal strength and raw magic. He forgot the steps and strokes Carel had drummed into him since he was a child; the press of bodies meant all he could do was to strike out at everything within reach. Nearby he heard Suzerain Fordan's throaty laughter. He had lost his helm somewhere, and his horse: the barrel-chested man was on foot, swinging a huge war-hammer so powerfully that it was taking elven heads clean off.

As Isak watched, the man's broad smile faltered as a spear spitted him, piercing the join between his breastplate and backplate. The suzerain staggered and tried to lift his hammer again, but the elf twisted his spear in the wound and a paroxysm of agony flashed over Fordan's face. He fell to his knees and another elf stepped up and stabbed down with a short but lethal stroke. Before Isak could move, Duke Certinse's burning sword flashed into view, cutting through both elves, before he was off and moving deeper into their ranks. Behind him followed three of his hurscals; there were mounted knights behind them.

Isak turned and launched himself at the enemy again. The choking odour of death, sweat, and excrement made his human self recoil, but there was something else to replace it. He tasted magic on the air and embraced its fury. Encased in the liquid grace of Siulents, Isak flowed over the bodies and started dealing death with an artistry that belied his brutish desire.

He hardly noticed when the enemy began to flee. The slow-moving elves died, whether they faced him or ran. Eolis sliced through swords and shields to reach the flesh. Fire and fury burst hot and savage from Isak's fingertips as a torrent of magic lashed and swirled around him. Spectral shapes hovered at the edges of his sight as he killed again and again. The ground itself opened up to receive the dead, deep furrows in the earth groaning open like yawning funeral barrows.

Finally a burst of pain in his skull stopped Isak dead. A cold weight appeared at the back of his head, as though he'd been clubbed, and his body was shocked into numbness. As he dropped to his knees the beast inside him faded, sated by the destruction it had wrought. Isak gasped for breath he could no longer find. Dropping Eolis and throwing aside his shield, he scrabbled desperately at his helm. For a moment he couldn't move it, through weakness or some sort of resistance, and then off it came.

Tearing off his hood, Isak sucked in great heaving gulps of air. He had been so immersed in the sea of battle that he had almost drowned in its dark depths. Now pain lanced through his body and his lungs cried out for more air while his mind howled at the slaughter around him—and the pleasure it had spawned in him. He bent over and retched, tears of pain and anguish dripping to mingle with the blood that ran from his body. With the taste of puke still in his mouth, he pitched forward and collapsed onto the ground, not even feeling himself hit as a numbing darkness washed over him.

CHAPTER 15

DRAGONS SOARED OVERHEAD, emerald, diamond, and sapphire scales shining in the summer sun. The monsters radiated an unearthly beauty as they gouged and tore each other apart. He laughed as he plunged his blade into beautiful men with wings for arms, their soft feathers charred and matted with blood. Insectoid figures bearing huge bronze hammers leapt eagerly to their deaths. The sun cast rainbow hues off their dark chitinous bodies. The coppery tang of magic melded the panoramic riot into an intoxicating and corrupting exhilaration. He crafted agony in his hand and cast it out among the mortals beneath him. The song of fear rang out in his mind, drowning out the wind and the clash of steel. The sun itself drew back and hid from the slaughter. And still he laughed. Still he killed.

Daylight slipped hesitantly through Isak's eyelids. A dull ache pervaded his body and when he tried to raise his head, a stab of pain flared in his temples. He fought to open swollen and caked eyelids. At first, everything was a blur of fogged shapes, but eventually the fragments of light creeping through the fabric of the tent began to trace lines he could understand. Colours wormed into focus and, tentatively, he began to take stock.

Someone had stripped and washed him, dressed his wounds, and left him to sleep under a heavy pile of furs. He flexed the fingers of his right hand. The numbness began to fade as he worked it into a fist, then opened and closed it a number of times. With his shoulder screaming in protest, Isak edged his arm higher and higher up his side until he could pull it out from under the furs. When one arm was free, Isak began to remove the furs and assess the damage.

His ribs were bandaged tightly, high enough to cover his scar, though Isak could feel no reason why the dressing needed to go quite that high up his chest. He guessed at two cracked ribs, painful but not dangerous, or he'd be in a much worse state by now. The scent of sweat-soaked linen rose up to meet him as the last fur slid off. While he'd been unconscious, someone had not only cleaned the filth and blood off and dressed his wounds, they'd even tended to his scrappy beard. He remembered nothing of it—not even the discomfort of being moved and manipulated had been strong enough to wake him. All Isak could recall was the sensation of a hurricane in his mind, and the rampant magic picking him up and tossing him to the four winds.

Continuing his personal investigation, Isak found his left arm below the elbow so swollen he could hardly move it: blow after blow had obviously been too much for the muscles of his shield arm. It looked like a spear had sliced into his thigh, but the wound didn't feel too deep, and while the sheets were far from clean, there was no smell of contagion.

Every movement hurt in some way, from neck to toes. He'd been surprised by the lack of minor cuts on his body until he caught sight of several sickly yellow patches on his skin—his remarkable capacity to heal had obviously already kicked into action. It appeared Siulents must have been pierced on several occasions.

"So much for the fabled armour," he croaked with a wry smile. His voice was barely a whisper; anything more felt beyond his strength. "Now, how long have I been here?"

As if summoned to answer his question, the shadow of hands appeared on the canvas at the tent's entrance. They fumbled for a while, then a page in Vesna's livery ducked through the gap, a large wooden bowl in his hands. He stopped so hard when he saw Isak awake that the contents slopped up onto his tunic. Before the Krann could muster any words the boy had dropped the bowl on the floor and rushed out. Distantly, Isak heard the page shouting, but the actual words eluded him.

As the voice faded into the background noise of the camp, Isak tried to work out how to ease himself into a more upright position. His left arm couldn't take any weight, so he had to use his right hand to pull some of the furs up behind him and create some sort of pile to lean on. By the time Vesna poked his bruised face through the opening, Isak lay panting, his head and shoulders elevated so he could at least see who came in.

"My Lord," Count Vesna greeted him, "dare I ask how you feel?" He took a step towards Isak's bed, followed by Suzerain Torl, the scowling features of

Duke Certinse close behind. Isak looked up at Torl, his light cavalryman uniform apparently untouched by the battle. The grim lines of his face hadn't changed; the dour, pious air he wore was impervious to such things.

"Awful. How long have I slept?"

"Three nights, my Lord," answered Vesna. "Lord Bahl assured us you just needed the rest, that there was no fatal wound, but we had begun to fear—"

"Well, I'm awake now," Isak broke in. "Is Lord Bahl here?"

"He commands the sweeping for elves," Certinse growled. "We have all been leading hunting parties to pursue those who fled the field."

"Except me? Because I've been lazing around on my backside for the last few days? If you have a problem with me, Duke Certinse, just say so." The sour emptiness in his stomach and throbbing behind his eyes told Isak he'd done more than he should have, but though he felt too drained to argue or fight, a drop of venom remained.

"Your Grace," interrupted Suzerain Torl before Certinse could rise to the bait. "I should be riding out in a few minutes, but Lord Bahl requested I take the Krann to him as soon as possible. Would you do me the honour of leading the party in my place?"

Certinse looked surprised for a moment, perhaps at the unexpectedly gracious tone, then grunted agreement. Shooting one last malevolent glare at Isak, he turned and swept out, leaving the wolf's head on his cloak to snarl at those remaining.

Torl watched him go, then turned back to the Krann with a sad shake of the head. "I hardly think you are in any condition to pick a fight with Duke Certinse," he told Isak. "You might be Krann of the Farlan, but that doesn't mean civility to your peers is impossible."

"Fuck Duke Certinse, and fuck the rest of you too. Now you're my peers, when it gives you a reason to complain. The rest of the time, I'm just some damn white-eye."

"Only if you behave like one. My son was a white-eye, and he still managed to hold a conversation without throwing insults every few minutes."

Isak slumped back down onto his bed. "By the Gods, I'm too tired for this. I'm not going to waste the energy explaining myself to you."

"Well then, conserve your energy and get dressed. You will have to explain yourself to your Lord. Being just a white-eye, you seem to have forgotten that our nation is only recently rebuilt. Reopening old wounds for no reason hurts us all."

"Actually, I do remember," Isak said crossly. "I just don't intend to deal with it through a veil of pomp and breeding. I was told that in war you play to your strengths—well, politics isn't one of mine. Strength is, and now, authority. If I have enemies within the tribe, that's what I'll use to deal with them." As he spoke, Isak levered himself up into a sitting position and pointed to his clothes.

Before he could ask, Vesna passed them over and helped Isak to dress. In the thick woollens, he looked more like a monk than a suzerain, but he didn't relish the idea of the tightly buttoned tunic around his ribs. He pulled on a pair of winter fleece boots, then belted on Eolis. He stopped before he reached the tent flap when he saw his white cloak hanging up. It had been cleaned of the mud and gore, but no one had been able to repair the burned material. As he rubbed the charred edges with his fingers, a piece came off in his hand, leaving a swirl of soot. He traced a shape too faint for the others to make out, looked at it intently for a few seconds, and then rubbed it away on his shirt.

The sky outside was overcast. Isak blinked as he took in the state of the camp. Long lines of tents were now missing, and the forest of colourful banners much reduced.

"Vesna, isn't that Fordan's banner?" he asked. "I saw him die, I'm sure of it."

"He did, my Lord," the count said sadly, "but his son was among his hurscals and survived, so the banner remains. As for the others, well, Danva took a spear in the thigh and bled to death on the field, and Amah had his skull crushed by a troll."

"How many did we lose?" A breath of air on his neck made Isak shiver suddenly. The wind was cold but listless; it felt to Isak as though men had been carried away by the breeze, along with their tents and flags.

"In total? Roughly three thousand. One hundred and fifty of your own men, three hundred Ghosts, counts from Torl, Ked, Tebran, and Vere. We've lost another three hundred chasing the survivors down."

"Did any good come from this?"

"For those who died?" asked Torl icily.

Isak looked over to the suzerain, but Torl obviously had nothing more to add.

"I meant for anyone," Isak said. He shrugged. "I'm famished: I need to eat before I see Lord Bahl."

He followed a column of smoke around a tent to where a huge pot bubbled over a fire, but when he tried to lean down he winced, clutching his ribs tenderly. "Can you give me some of that?" he asked the man attending it. The man bobbed his head, eyes wide with fear as he slopped some broth into a sturdy wooden bowl.

Isak accepted the bowl with a broad smile. "Bread?" The man reached in to the bag hanging from a post and handed him half a loaf. As soon as the man saw Isak's attention return to Suzerain Torl, he began to back away and after a few steps he turned and hurried off, getting out of sight as soon as he could.

Isak frowned and sniffed at the bread suspiciously. "What was that about?"

Vesna kept silent, eyes on the ground, while Torl stared past Isak's shoulder. "Ah, Lord Bahl, good morning," he said smoothly.

"Torl," acknowledged Bahl, then turned to Isak. "What that was, my Lord, was your legacy from the battle."

The old Lord had shrugged off the air of weariness that normally surrounded him. He looked alert, rejuvenated, even in full armour. The crested helm, an ancient-looking bowl-shaped piece of grey metal with a Y slit at the front for eyes and mouth, was tucked under his arm.

Bahl walked up to Isak and placed a hand on his shoulder, a public gesture of comradeship. "How are you feeling? You've been recovering a long time. We were starting to worry."

"I feel exhausted. Drained." He gestured to the bowl. "And famished."

"Drained is a better word than you might realise. The more you draw on the magic, the harder it is to resist the flow and stop. If you're not careful, part of you will be swept away with it."

Isak didn't reply, but nodded as he crammed a soaked corner of bread into his mouth. A murmur of pleasure was the only sound Bahl heard, but he took it as a cue to continue; the boy didn't seem to understand quite how it had looked on the battlefield. "You forgot yourself out there. The men were expecting to see a white-eye in battle, but they saw worse than that. You fought like a daemon, and more than once you almost killed one of your own men through sheer bloodlust. If you hadn't collapsed, I don't know how we'd have stopped you."

Bahl kept his voice low but there was no mistaking the anger there. Isak stopped chewing and looked into the Lord's eyes. They said clearly enough: *there was one way to stop you, and I was tempted. You didn't just shame yourself there.*

"I . . . I don't know what to say." Isak dropped his gaze. "It felt like my dreams, like I wasn't quite myself."

"What do you dream of?"

The question took Isak by surprise. He didn't think the question was as idle as it sounded.

"Sometimes just that I'm somewhere else, looking through another man's eyes. It's as though I'm remembering things I've not done."

"Hmm. What about your magic? Has it been released or was it just the battle?"

"I don't know, I hadn't thought of trying it again yet."

"Well, do so now. Nothing grand, just draw energy into your hand and imagine it as fire."

Isak did as Bahl ordered. For a moment he felt nothing. Suddenly, energy rushed to his hand, coursing like a stream of water over every inch of skin and into his hand. The air shimmered and swirled, yellow threads building and spinning together until a flame shot up from Isak's hand.

"Good, that's enough. Now stop."

With a slight reluctance, Isak halted the flames and they melted into nothing. He flexed his fingers, savouring the tingle of magic in them as it faded away.

"Well, it looks like your block has gone, whatever the problem was. I'll start teaching you the finer points of control when you're feeling stronger."

"Thank you." Isak paused. "Lord Bahl, I'm sorry. It won't happen again."

"I know you didn't mean it, but you do need to make sure it doesn't happen again. Next time it'll kill you." There was an edge to his words that chilled Isak.

"Just so you know, it was I who bandaged your chest."

Isak's stomach clenched. This wasn't a conversation he wanted to have. He didn't have any answers himself, so explaining it to someone else would be next to impossible.

"I don't expect you to tell me all your secrets," Bahl said. "There are some things that are your own business. But tell me, here and now, whether there's anything I need to know. I will not allow anything that might endanger the tribe or work against my rule. There is nothing you will have done that is so foul that we cannot counteract it, as long as we know where the problem lies."

"There's nothing," Isak muttered. "I don't understand it myself, but I don't think it's anything for you to be concerned about."

"Good, we seem to have enough of that already. Just remember that others feel the same about their own affairs. Some of my business has nothing to do with you. You will extend me the courtesy of neither asking nor investigating."

"Of course, my Lord. What did you mean when you said 'enough of that'?" The two white-eyes were walking slowly west and Isak suddenly realised that they were close to where the battle had been fought. This was where the cavalry had passed to reach the stream . . . The wind caught Bahl's long white cloak and carried it high, away from the packed mud of the ground and off towards the heart of the mountains where home lay. Count Vesna and Suzerain Torl and a couple of messengers trailed behind them, all waiting for a moment of their Lord's time. None of them looked hopeful of being acknowledged soon.

Bahl looked up at a wood pigeon winging its way high over the camp to the woods beyond. From their left, a sharp-eyed falconer set his charge after it: an army always needed more food, no matter how small—but the pigeon was gone by the time the falcon had climbed far enough. Bahl nodded enigmatically, then as Suzerain Ked appeared and began to speak urgently, he nodded at Isak, who fell back to give them some privacy.

"He agrees with you, said almost the same as you did about fighting on your own ground," said a voice from behind Isak. The Krann turned in puzzlement. Suzerain Torl had a satisfied expression on his face, as though he had been testing Isak and was happy with the outcome.

"There are also enemies within the tribe, and now we've dealt with these elves, at least for the meantime, Lord Bahl intends to adjust his focus," he said to Isak. "I assume you did appreciate the fact that of all those who owe Lord Bahl allegiance, only eight suzerains and eleven counts answered the call to battle?"

Isak nodded. He hadn't wanted to comment at the time in case it was normal behaviour and he looked a fool for saying anything.

"We have the same number again whose whereabouts illness or infirmity cannot explain. You must have learned enough by now to recognise that any victory should be followed by decisive action, lest subsequent events make it hollow."

"Unfortunate accidents—?"

"Are always a possibility in this life, yes," Torl finished for him. "It's something you should take a keen interest in."

"Me? If you are trying to tell me that Lord Bahl—"

"Hah! I'm not *telling* you anything, young man. I am, however, *suggesting* that it would be good to let men know you are more than what you showed on the field, and . . ." The suzerain's voice tailed off.

"*And* what?" demanded Isak, scowling.

For the first time, the man actually looked a little uncomfortable. He lowered his voice to make sure only Isak and Vesna could hear. "When we searched the enemy bodies, we found—well, people will draw their own conclusions. A lot of them had a scroll hung about their necks, written in Elvish, of course, but Ked is enough of a scholar to read some of the runes. It was apparently something he had to translate when he was studying the language as a boy. I don't know the full text, but we've all heard the rumours."

"What is it, for the love of Larat? You look like a scared child."

Torl held up his hands to mollify Isak's impatience and cleared his throat. "My Krann, it's called the Prophecy of Shalstik, supposedly the most significant prophecy about this Age, but written thousands of years ago. This army we have just faced down was an army of the prophet's disciples. With an Estashanti in their ranks, and the sheer numbers, from different houses at that, the elves must have organised themselves as soon as you were Chosen—perhaps even before that."

"Anyone with money will be able to find a translation somewhere," interrupted Vesna. "Every scholar of ancient languages will have one version or another, or at least know where to find one."

"What does it predict?" Isak asked weakly.

"The return of the Last King, who they believe will come to take his revenge upon the Gods—and he was the last mortal before you to wear that armour. My Lord, they seek to reclaim their holiest of relics and I fear they won't stop at this defeat. Ked could only remember the first line properly. He said that all Elvish is open to interpretation, but—" Now Torl looked pained, his face that of a man bringing bad tidings, "but that line was: *In silver light born/In silver light clothed.* For the Last King to lead them in their revenge, they need that armour."

Isak didn't reply. He didn't trust his voice. All he could do was turn and look back the way he'd come, back to his tent where the cold lines of Siulents seemed to shine through the cloth and into the pit of his stomach.

Oh Gods, whatever horror they bring down upon us, it will all be my fault. And I don't just have to worry about people resenting that, what if a duke or suzerain thinks to ask someone from the wagon train? Not even Carel would see any harm in telling them I was born on Silvernight.

CHAPTER 16

"I'M TOO OLD FOR THIS. Why haven't I retired yet?" General Chate Dev looked around the empty spaces of the temple plain and once satisfied there was no one in sight, he trotted over the dry, packed ground to the looming structure in the centre. He'd lived in Thotel all his life, but the immense pillars of the Temple of the Sun, hewn from a single pyramid of stone, always made him marvel.

"Because you'd be bored to death, Chate!" a deep voice chuckled from the temple.

The aging Chetse walked over to the nearest of the four gigantic pillars as Lord Chalat stepped out from behind it. The base was a stone block eight feet high, and the pillar itself slanted up towards the centre of the pyramidal temple, dwarfing even Lord Chalat. The white-eye almost looked humbled in its presence.

In the dark, General Dev could just see the hint of a smile in the light cast by the eternal flame. So no mourning there, then—not that it surprised the general; it was common knowledge that Lord Chalat had barely tolerated his Krann, so the news of Charr's mortal injury wouldn't have grieved him overmuch.

Chalat was dressed in a simple warrior's kilt that reached halfway down his calves. His torso was wrapped in thin white linen and his massive arms were bare, other than a number of copper bands set with lapis lazuli. The scars on both arms marked him out as having passed the five tests of the Agoste field—not that anyone could possibly have doubted that. Tsatach would never have Chosen a Lord found wanting as a child. Strapped to Chalat's back was the ancient sword Golaeth. A large ruby at his throat glowed in the weak light.

"My Lord," muttered the general as he reached Chalat and dropped to one knee at his feet. As he did so, he was distinctly aware of the empty plain behind him. No Chetse much liked the dark, and with the unyielding weight of the temple in front of him, he felt even more uncomfortable.

A shallow trench, no more than a foot deep, marked the boundary of the blessed ground of the temple. Everything within was illuminated by the eternal flame; the rest of this eerie, ancient place was black and hidden, as if a wall of stone stood there instead of a trench.

"Get up, Chate. Now, why by Tsatach have you summoned me out here in the middle of the night? It might be magnificent in the light of day, but right now it's a nightmare."

The general murmured his agreement as he rose. The many temples of the plain were disturbing to behold at night: there was an awful sadness that lingered after dark. The temples dedicated to Nartis and Alterr were situated on top of the rocky cliffs at the north end so even those priests engaged in nighttime rituals didn't have to walk the plain at night.

The general had chosen this place for that reason. "It is indeed, my Lord. I thought it best not to have a crowd of onlookers ready to spread gossip. It may be that the eternal flame may help us in understanding the facts."

"The eternal flame? Who do you suspect of lying?"

"The witness, my Lord." He looked around, and continued, "My men are bringing him along now—I thought you should know the facts, or as much as we know—before he arrives."

Chalat made an irritated noise, then led the way back around to the inside of the pillar. The pair sat down on the wide steps cut into the rock.

"So Charr wasn't hurt in battle, then?" Chalat began.

"In a fashion yes. But his guards' story is—well, unusual."

"Unusual?"

"They were in the hunting grounds of the Black Palace—this was almost two moons ago—when one of the scouts saw people walking through the grounds towards them, half a dozen foreigners, from the north."

"Well, of course they were foreigners—no Chetse's going to defy the hunting laws." He sounded irritated again.

The general continued quickly, "Exactly, my Lord, so Lord Charr decided to ambush the party."

"Hah! So the stupid bastard jumped right into a trap. He deserves to die for that."

"Yes, my Lord. In any case, the guards attacked and killed a number of the foreigners, but Lord Charr was hit by an arrow—straight into the heart— and no one even saw the archer. They loosed the hounds immediately, in the direction the arrow came from, but no one found a thing."

"If he was hit in the heart, how is he still alive?" A gust of wind rustled over the smooth temple floor, on which the general smelled age and sorrow.

In the background, the white shaft of the eternal flame, burning down from the apex of the temple to the altar, hissed quietly, as it had done for more than a thousand years.

"We have no idea. Several surgeons inspected the wound: they all agreed that the arrow was lodged in the heart and he would die. They carried Charr to the palace chapel and left him there to die with his God. My Lord, Charr's guards are devoted to him, but they agreed that there was nothing that could be done."

"So everyone was surprised when he was still alive in the morning?"

"Quite so, my Lord. They fetched a priest and he claimed the wound was magical, that the fight for Charr's life was a spiritual one, for his soul. The priest said that the arrow itself was made out of soot, enchanted to be as hard as iron."

"A spiritual battle? Useless shit's buggered then." The white-eye laughed callously.

"Quite so, Lord." The general waited patiently until his Lord showed no further sign of interrupting. Chalat was like a mountain: he moved for no man. You worked around him, or broke your hands on his edge.

Chalat waved him to continue.

"Armed with this information, the guards decided to bring Charr back to Thotel. If he was going to die anyway, they believed it would be better to be as close to the Temple of the Sun as possible."

"Pious of them. Stupid, but pious."

"They brought with them the one surviving member of the group they'd ambushed—as soon as he saw the arrow hit, he ran, but he surrendered later, once he judged their blood had cooled somewhat—he spoke Chetse; told them he had information about the assassin. His behaviour was strange enough that they decided not to kill him immediately—instead, they trussed him like a lizard and put him on the cart next to the Krann."

"And it's his testimony you want me to hear? What did he tell you?"

"If you don't mind, my Lord, I'd like you to judge it for yourself. He's less likely to lie to you with his hand in the eternal flame. He knows our language well, no doubt why he was chosen for the bait, so he must know about the flame. He did say that he'd been under some sort of enchantment, but that's a detail we can decide later. It's the assassin that I'm worried about."

"Worried he's lying, or that what he says might be true?"

Harsh voices from the darkness prompted the general to clamber to his feet and walk out to the front of the temple. As Chalat joined him, the shapes of three men slowly appeared from the gloom. Two were Lion Guards, from General Dev's personal legion; the third was a little taller and much more slender, even with the thick cords of rope that bound his arms to his body and hobbled his feet.

Both guards carried crossbows, and had battle-axes slung on their backs. The larger of the two also carried an iron-shod quarterstaff, the foreigner's weapon. They threw the prisoner onto the floor and stepped over him to kneel at their Lord's feet.

"Cut those bonds from his hands," ordered Chalat, "and bring him to the flame." Their footsteps echoed strangely over the polished surface, getting quieter as they reached the centre, as if deadened by the constant whisper of the eternal flame. The prisoner had hair dark enough for a Farlan, though he lacked the height or the tribe's distinctive facial features. He stumbled along after the white-eye as best he could. Though the guards kept prodding him along, he couldn't help looking up at the astonishing temple. His mouth fell open in awe as he followed the four pillars up to the apex, almost eighty yards above the altar in the centre. Nothing supported them; the thin white shaft of the eternal flame was the only thing that connected the peak and altar.

An open walkway that ran around the pillars at the midpoint was strictly the preserve of Tsatach's priests. Anyone else who dared enter the stairs in the pillars that led to the walkway—even General Dev—would be executed on the spot. The walkways were supported only by air and magic: anyone other than the temple's priests might disrupt the spells that supported the thousands of tons of stone and kill the pilgrims congregating below—on a feast day, they numbered in the thousands.

Chalat wasted no time when he reached the altar. He'd been enjoying himself with four of his favourite concubines and he fully intended to return to their delights as quickly as possible. Grabbing the foreigner by the scruff of the neck, he picked him up bodily and deposited him next to the flame.

"Do you know what happens to liars who put their hands in the flame?" he asked cheerily.

The man nodded, a little nervous, but remarkably calm—the general thought he looked as though he'd resigned himself to execution and had made his peace with the Gods already.

Chalat nodded in approval and took the man's hand in his own. As the Chosen of Tsatach, the flame would never hurt him. If the foreigner lied while his hand was within the flame, his entire arm would be consumed. If he was quick, it would be just the arm.

"What is your name?"

"Mihn ab Netren ab Felith. I am called Mihn."

"Where do you come from?"

"I was born into the clans of the northern coast. I have wandered the Land for several years now, often in the Wastes."

"Tell me who the assassin was." Chalat had better things to do than waste time on pointless questions.

"He—he called himself Arlal."

"What sort of a name is that? Farlan?"

"No, Lord, elven."

Chalat gave a cough of surprise, letting go of the man's wrist for a moment in his astonishment. General Dev shrugged when Chalat looked at him. He looked at the flame; the man's hand was still there and he had not even attempted to pull away, though the flames licked and danced over his skin. Even if Mihn were a sorcerer, he'd still not have the power to stop his hand burning. He must be telling the truth.

The man kept his hand in the centre of the flame, a defiant look on his face while he waited for the next question.

"Arlal was an elf?"

"A true elf, my Lord."

Now the white-eye gaped. "You were in the company of a true elf called Arlal? The one storytellers call the Poisonblade?"

Mihn paused, considering how to frame his reply so it was completely true. "It is possible. I don't know how many true elves there are in the Land, but it is most likely. The Poisonblade is said to be an assassin."

"Did he tell you who paid him?"

"No. He said little, other than to give us orders. He had some sort of amulet around his neck, I didn't even consider disobeying him."

The sound of footsteps running over the plain made them all jump. The two soldiers had their crossbows raised and ready to fire when a voice hailed them from the gloom, sounding far too scared to be a threat.

"General! He's awake!"

"It's Gerrint. Put your bows down," General Dev ordered. "It's my adjutant, Lord Chalat. I left him in charge of the Krann."

The soldier pounded his way over the temple boundary, nearly tripping as he remembered how disrespectful it was. He stumbled to a halt, looked around as if expecting a furious priest to appear from the pillars, then walked as fast as he could to the altar.

"My Lord, General Dev, the Krann has recovered!"

"Don't be ridiculous, Gerrint; he was all but dead when I saw him."

"I know, sir, but he's up and walking around. But he looks different my Lord, changed. The wound is a black stain on his chest, nothing more. The medic said that the arrow crumbled to soot suddenly and stained his skin—then Lord Charr got up and threw out everyone but his personal guards. I came as quickly as I could, sir, my Lord."

Chalat frowned, looking deeply concerned, and drawing his sword, walked away from the altar.

The coppery surface of Golaeth glinted in the light of the eternal flame as Chalat used it to score a circle on the floor almost two yards in diameter. A faint black trail followed the path of the sword while Chalat whispered the words of a spell under his breath. That done, he sat down, cross-legged, within the circle, looking faintly comical as he carefully tucked his thick legs under himself. He nicked his finger on Golaeth's edge and placed the sword across his knees, then caressed the ruby gem at his neck with the bloody digit.

General Dev walked nervously around his Lord, keeping far enough away that he didn't disturb his work but, as always, fascinated by the magic. He shivered as the open space suddenly became darker and a sharp chill appeared in the air. Chalat's breathing slowed until it was almost imperceptible. The Bloodrose at his throat smouldered brighter, then blazed for a brief moment before the air around Chalat returned to normal.

"He's at his homestead. There's a darkness surrounding him, something I don't recognise." Chalat's voice sounded hollow and distant, as though his Lord had been somewhere else and part of him hadn't fully returned.

"I can have the Lion Guard ready in half an hour, the Ten Thousand within the hour—" He stopped as Chalat held up a hand.

"What's that sound?" The Lord blinked owlishly at the darkness, cocking his head to one side.

Everyone listened hard as a sudden rushing noise came from behind, like a rogue gust of wind. The general turned as a wet gasp cut the air, instinctively diving away from the oncoming shape. In a blur of movement he felt a figure slam into him, and he saw the two guards fall dead behind it. Pain flared in his arm as a blade cut deep, then he was smashed out of the way. His head thumped against the ground and stars burst before his eyes.

The figure, the shape of a Chetse man, but with long claws and spiky protrusions along its limbs and shoulders, crashed bodily into Chalat and knocked the white-eye over. As the Lord tried to rise again, the creature threw itself upon him, flailing madly as a ruby light enveloped the two for a moment. The general felt hands on his back, urging him down; though he tried to move, his body betrayed him and he could only submit as Mihn, now free of his bonds and armed with his staff, advanced.

Chalat kicked his attacker away and the Bloodrose flared again as it absorbed another wound. Mihn immediately swung at the creature, but had to fling himself back when he missed, trying to avoid the raking claws. He waved his staff in a wide half circle, not daring to risk another strike at the monster, but trying to distract it. The twisted perversion of a man had bony growths pushed through the skin; it looked daemonic, and the furious snarls sounded like the dying breath of a ruined throat, amplified by rage.

With the creature's attention on the foreigner, Chalat had the time he needed. Golaeth's coppery surface blazed in the light from the eternal flame and Chalat roared as he hacked down at the creature. The blow was somehow turned by the creature's arm, but it could do nothing to stop the sword when it lanced forward into its belly. Razor-sharp claws lashed forward as it tried to shred Chalat's flesh, but the white-eye had already withdrawn. He struck again, and this time cut off one of the monster's arms, then as he chopped deep into its neck, it collapsed, flailing violently before falling abruptly, rigid. One last twitch came, then it was still.

Chalat looked up at Mihn and bared his teeth in some sort of a smile.

"Well done." He sounded husky with barely restrained aggression. Chalat hardly cared for the duties of state, but fighting in his tribe's need was always joyfully done.

"See to the general; those three are dead." Chalat stood over the corpse for a moment, then stabbed his sword down into its chest, driving it on into the rock below.

The foreigner jumped at the sudden sound, then crouched down over the general, peering into his eyes. He nodded to himself, and took the general's dagger from his belt. With an assured movement he cut away the sleeve of the general's shirt and tied that above the bleeding arm; the other sleeve was similarly removed and used to bandage the wound itself.

"It's a clean cut, but deep," he told Chalat. When he received no reply, he looked up from his charge. The Lord was squatting by the creature's head, muttering something, one hand placed flat against the ground. A tremble ran through the stone beneath their feet, rippling towards the white-eye, and then a face appeared on the temple floor. The flat stone billowed up, as though it was nothing more than a sheet of silk held up against a man's face, though the face was far from human. Though the eyes were overly large and the thick jaw extended too far back, somehow there was a beauty in the curve of the nose, cheek, and forehead that redeemed its strangeness.

"What happened to him?" Chalat muttered to the face, ignoring the foreigner's presence. "These regimental tattoos mark him as Charr's bodyguard, but—" The white-eye's voice tailed off as he gestured over the body. "Has the same happened to Charr?"

The being in the ground rose up a little further so that the tops of its shoulders were now protruding from the rock. There was no seam between the being and the stone floor; they were made of the same substance. Mihn stared at the Ralebrat—the earth elementals were known to be allies of the Chetse, but he had never heard of them being seen outside of battle.

"Your Krann is dead. Something else possesses his body now." There was a smooth quality to the Ralebrat's voice, sand running over stone. Something underneath the corpse reached up to tap one of the horns. The nearly decapitated head twitched under the movement as the elemental cocked its head to one side.

"I couldn't sense it as it attacked," Chalat said. "If more than a handful have been changed, I cannot kill them. Can your kind help?"

"We dare not. The Gods are at play, and others. We will not be involved this time."

Chalat seemed to take the refusal with remarkable calm. The Ralebrat had allied themselves with Aryn Bwr during the Great War—clearly the slaughter on both sides had taught them to keep clear of anything similar.

"You must leave."

"What?" Chalat was surprised.

"You cannot fight these daemons; you must leave for the sake of your people. We have expected this Age for a thousand years—we will go deep into the earth until we are called by one who is known to us."

"How can I leave Charr to rule the Chetse?"

"You cannot avoid it. The only question is whether you will be alive when the time comes to save your people." An arm appeared from the ground, rising up as though from a perfectly still lake. It pointed at the foreigner. "Take that one with you."

"Him? Why?"

The Ralebrat emitted a sound like sand brushing over steel; it was amused. "Fate intervened to put him in your enemy's path. He is marked, that one."

"Marked for what?"

"For suffering and service. What he has lost from his soul, he must confront and surpass. If he does as he must, his name will be honoured for a thousand years."

"I don't understand." Chalat now stared at the foreigner in curiosity and fascination.

"It is not yours to understand. He belongs to another." With that the Ralebrat slid back down into the ground, disappearing without trace.

Chalat stared at the blank stone for a moment, then a gust of wind tugged at his hair and stirred him to movement. He stood up and cleaned his sword on the clothes of the dead bodyguard.

"It looks like we both have some long years ahead of us. If you're not my business, I don't want to know any more. I know the Ralebrat well enough to keep my silence. How badly injured is Chate?"

The foreigner looked down and shrugged. The man had passed out and he pushed back the man's thinning silver hair to show Chalat a ripe swelling visible on the general's hairline.

"Right, then. I'll carry him to the Temple of Asenn; they'll be around soon for the dew rituals and it's next to the Temple of Shotir. Then we go north."

CHAPTER 17

KOEZH VUKOTIC WATCHED THE BEACONS on the walls struggle against the unremitting wind. The flames sent faint shadows cavorting over the glistening cobbles of Daraban's streets, but they made little inroad into the coating of liquid darkness that had descended upon his city. Bulging clouds obscured his sight of the moons; he preferred it that way, without Alterr's watching eye.

But the shouts and calls out there, the clank of iron and drum of hooves, they were all sounds of another life, aspects of a time when he had been truly alive. The long years of his curse were an indistinct ache, quite separate from the sharp years of mortal life; as few as they had been. Though they were mere seconds compared to the long years that followed, their light still burned fiercely.

Out there, men preparing to die thought of their wives, their children. They smiled over those years that had been their span, hoping, praying, for a few more, however cold and harsh life might be in the Forbidden Lands.

It sickened Vukotic that his people would die in winter. The season was long here, long and harsh and violent, and he believed this attack had come about because a Krann was desperate to prove his worth. It was fear of meeting some unfortunate accident now that Lord Styrax's own son had come of age that had driven Lord Cytt to risk marching to the Forbidden Lands in winter. He was obviously trying to emulate Lord Styrax's great victory here.

Vukotic imagined ten thousand men, stamping their way over treacherous frozen ground, their fingers and toes black and festering, lost to frostbite and gangrene before they even reached these walls. What lurked in the shadows of these streets would only compound their misery: bright eyes and twisted smiles, and pale skin that barely noticed the bite of winter flushed in grotesque anticipation of the slaughter to come.

He could feel his breed slipping through streets and alleys now, nostrils flaring, tasting the first blood on the wind. Many were close enough for him to sense individually, more lingered at the fringes of his mind, and as each recognised his presence, they begged permission to join.

He rarely let them take part—he wanted them to have as little to do with his citizens as possible—but they would always be there on the edges. Most were worse than animals, beautiful, degenerate daemons that preyed on those they would now be protecting—for this was different. This battle had nothing to do with the people of the city, and Vukotic saw no reason why they should suffer any more than necessary.

As he turned away from the window, echoes of lusty jubilation rang out with revolting familiarity. He steadied himself on the desk and lifted a foot to tug at the black mail covering it. It had been several years since he last wore his armour and the leather padding was chafing at skin more used to the finest silks. The curse gave him enormous strength and resilience, but his senses were likewise magnified. Pain was something he had learned to endure; his many deaths had provided more than sufficient practice.

A little more comfortable now, Vukotic eased himself into the sturdy leather chair before him and pushed aside the stack of papers on the walnut desk that were awaiting his attention. Now was not the time for civic affairs, not even the most pressing matter, a legal dispute between minor nobles—he found himself hoping one or the other died in the coming battle. It might not be a humane solution, but few would ever accuse a vampire of excessive compassion.

His eyes wandered the room, lingering on the gold threading that now lined the shelves of his bookcase. The housekeeper had a free rein when it came to decoration and each time he returned, the room was different in some way. Perhaps to ward off the harsh winter, she had chosen bright reds and oranges, as well as a liberal use of gold leaf far beyond the finances of most; the new colour scheme certainly cheered his dull spirits. If he hadn't had the rest of his armour sitting on a chair behind him, the evening might not have been too unpleasant . . .

He sighed and trudged over to the pile of plate armour, picked up a piece, and, grumbling to himself, began to strap it on. He winced as he pulled the cuirass over his head. His left hand gave a twinge as he raised his arm, the legacy of his recent death at the hands of Lord Styrax. For some reason, that injury had not entirely healed during his dark sojourn. His pale brow furrowed as he recalled not only being bested in single combat—extraordinarily—but the humiliation of slowly dying while his armour was roughly stripped from his body as it rotted to nothing. What he was donning now was his father's armour, but it was identical to his own bar the monogrammed initials.

That Lord Styrax had beaten him in single combat was truly remarkable; the Menin Lord was the finest warrior Koezh Vukotic had ever faced. He sighed. He very much doubted Styrax's Krann, rumoured to be dim-witted, even for a white-eye, would be of the same calibre.

A soft knock on the door dispelled his thoughts. Vukotic shrugged his shoulders to ensure the cuirass was straight and comfortable, then called for the servant to come in.

"Forgive the intrusion, my Prince, but you have a visitor and your tea is ready," the elderly man said as he bowed as far as his load and age would permit, then shuffled forward and carefully placed a heavily laden tray onto a small table beside the fire.

"If it is one of the scouts then send them to Duke Onteviz; he has command of the walls," said Vukotic before he noticed the second cup on the tray. A visitor was rare enough at any time, let alone when an army was attacking the city. It couldn't be his brother—Vorizh wouldn't dream of announcing himself to a servant; he preferred them to not even see him. Conceivably, his sister had returned from playing with the politicians of the western cities. She was more likely to visit than the others, perhaps the White Circle politics had bored her even quicker than she'd expected.

He paused, lost in thought. Strange he hadn't sensed whoever it was when he spoke to the rest of his breed. Just in case, he looked at the sword belt hanging from the back of the chair to make sure it was easily accessible if some treachery were afoot.

"I hardly think you need that," someone outside the room said firmly.

The voice brought a smile to Vukotic's face and he dismissed the servant who had been waiting with hands anxiously clamped together. Aracnan leaned on the door frame. "It's good to see you well again."

Vukotic snorted. "You make it sound like I had a cold."

"Nothing you would not recover from. Complaints are not princely."

The vampire smiled and straightened up from fitting the plates about his shin to grasp Aracnan's huge hand and squeeze it tightly. "Nor is much that I do, and yet this is the company you keep. How are you, my friend?"

"Well." Aracnan shook off the black bearskin draped over his shoulders and sat down beside the fire with a satisfied sigh. His taut, pale skin glowed in the firelight, though his large black eyes reflected nothing. "But I do not expect to be popular in the west, so I thought I might call in on an old enemy and see how he's getting over his cold."

Vukotic sat opposite him, leaving Bariaeth in its scabbard on the other side of the room. "Why?"

"Well, it appears I tried to put an influence charm on the Saviour."

"What?" Vukotic nearly jumped out of his seat. "The Saviour? I've heard none of this. When? Who?"

Aracnan gave a whispery chuckle and, ignoring his friend's sudden animation, poured two cups of the steaming tea. The cup looked tiny in his hands as he wrapped his chilled fingers about it.

He took a sip and smiled, then said, "Patience; and I will tell you. He is Farlan—Nartis has two Chosen again. I was given instructions to fetch him and announce it to Lord Bahl, but he would not come."

"Why not?"

"I cannot say exactly, but I felt a sudden hatred for the boy as soon as I laid eyes on him and I believe he saw that, or maybe felt the same way, but why? All I remember is that he wears a halo of trouble. He's wild, and that makes me fear for what he might do—"

"And you still keep a trap-scroll with you for when you meet interesting strangers," finished Vukotic, with a smile. "You've become a creature of habit, my friend. Age has caught up with you at last. But it's sensible enough. The influence will remain dormant and undetected by most mages."

"Except it was never activated. The scroll was given to Lord Bahl, who knew not to open it. I followed the boy to Tirah—I wanted to understand why I'd felt him to be different, and I wanted to deliver the message at least to Lord Bahl, even if I couldn't deliver the boy."

Vukotic looked at the immortal sitting opposite him. They called themselves friends, though that was not the simple truth. The story was likely to be less innocent than Aracnan was suggesting, but he had done the same many times. They both had their own agendas, their own games to play and what were a few lies between immortals? As the years swept past it was good to see a familiar face, so they both ignored much to ensure that continued.

He prompted Aracnan. "And?"

"And I was attacked, again and again—attacked in my sleep by some Yeetatchen witch, of all things. Whenever I neared the boy she came after me. I've been warding my mind ever since, but I think she only wanted to drive me away. I was out of the city by the time I heard about the Krann's gifts and realised what he was."

"What would the Gods gift their Saviour with?" Vukotic wondered out loud. "He's Farlan, so it would ultimately be Nartis's choice . . . so it would be an aggressive one, without thought to the consequences, but not whimsical. Amavoq would have given a dragon, no doubt, but not the Night Hunter." He sighed. "So. Siulents and Eolis are back in the Land."

"My friend, you have too much time on your hands." The mercenary chuckled. "But you are, of course, quite correct."

As he rose, slowly unfurling his body from the chair, the vampire wondered, as always, if Aracnan was a native of *anywhere*. His almost inhuman, hairless features were starkly different to Vukotic's own, and unchanged over the millennia. His ears, unadorned and unscarred, were prominent against the smooth lines of his skull, which added to the generally outlandish impression. He was not of any of the tribes of man, but neither was he similar to any of the warrior races created by the Gods.

Vukotic sighed to himself, remembering those poor creatures bred only for war and the part he had played in exterminating them: the feral Manee, the beautiful Angosteil whose shining faces had stirred the envy of the elves, and the bizarre, green-carapaced Voch. They had killed them all, and more besides, in ambushes, with terrible spells, unleashing unnatural plagues. The elves had been as vicious as their Gods; perhaps even more ruthless, because they understood hurt in a way immortals couldn't.

Vukotic's memories were interrupted by a sudden discordant clanging from the walls that got louder as more hands fell to the task of warning the city. He shrugged at Aracnan. "It seems I must wait for whatever other news you have of the Land. The Menin's Lord Cytt demands my presence so he can prove his worth to the rest of his tribe."

"As if there is anyone else in the Menin who has not accepted Lord Styrax's son as their future ruler," Aracnan scoffed.

"Will you join me? Together we could deal with the man before he wastes his soldiers on the walls. I'm sure your reputation would be furthered by the death of Lord Cytt surrounded by his entire army."

Aracnan laughed out loud and nodded his agreement. "We both have reputations to further, do we not—in dark times, who knows what use they might be? After, we must make plans to leave in search of summer."

"Leave the Forbidden Lands? Events have progressed that far?"

"They have gone far enough that we must deal ourselves into the game, or be left behind."

After they had left, the shadows slowly lengthened as the lamps died down. When a servant came to clear the cups and tend the fire, he was struck, suddenly, by the feeling that he was not alone. The room grew cold for a moment and he shivered as he looked around, but there was no one there and, feeling foolish, he dismissed it as an old man's fears.

Outside, on the blanketed plain beyond the city, two shapes moved silently over the snow.

CHAPTER 18

ISAK PAUSED OUTSIDE LORD BAHL'S TENT and looked up at the eagle standard that battered at the wind as though trying to escape its bonds. Bright slashes of orange on the horizon cut through the clouds, while higher up, the sky was stained pink and purple, with twists of gilt-edged cloud overlaying the colours. It was an arresting sight, belying the drab day and biting cold.

He pushed back the hood of his heavy cape and felt the rushing breeze over his newly shorn scalp. He'd spent the whole day hiding from the chill; it seemed only fair that he embrace it for a moment before night asserted itself. Twilight was always Isak's favourite time: it wasn't to be trusted, it played tricks on the mind, and yet he loved it.

General Lahk had informed Isak that he would be taking his evening meal with Lord Bahl—that meant something was going on, for he ate with his Lord more often than not, and neither required a summons to the other's company.

"Lord Isak," called a voice behind him. Isak turned to see Sir Cerse approaching. "Am I to have the pleasure of your company at supper too?"

It looked like Isak was right about the young colonel of the Palace Guard: he knew the man to be ambitious and politically minded, but he believed Sir Cerse could most likely be trusted. He was of minor gentry stock from Amah, as loyal a region as any. The significance of the dinner invitation had obviously not been lost on him: power lay within the lord of the Farlan's inner circle, and he was being given the opportunity to show himself worthy.

"Among others, I suspect." As he spoke, Suzerain Ked and Count Vesna appeared from different directions in the growing gloom, both wrapped against the cold in heavy, plain cloaks. They were alone, and trying to draw as little attention as possible. Isak nodded to both, then entered the tent ahead of the other three men.

Inside Bahl and Suzerain Torl were already seated, while General Lahk stood over a steaming pot, ladling what smelled like venison stew into bowls.

Isak stopped suddenly when he caught sight of a copper-haired woman standing to one side—the last thing he'd expected to see out here in the middle of nowhere was a strange and very beautiful woman. He ignored Sir Cerse's polite cough behind him and caught Bahl's eye, hoping the woman's presence would be explained.

Bahl couldn't fail to notice his Krann's interest. "One of my Chief Steward's agents," he said dismissively, "bringing me information that does not concern you."

Isak remembered Bahl's warning after the battle that there were some secrets he was not privy to. He nodded in acceptance and moved further in, allowing the others to enter.

"My Lords, gentlemen," Bahl greeted them once all four were inside and the hide flap fastened against the wind.

Isak caught the scuff of boots on grass outside: Ghosts, he guessed, loitering outside to prevent eavesdroppers.

"Please, make yourselves comfortable, for we have matters to discuss."

There were stools enough for all while Bahl sat back in a campaign armchair, one that was easily folded for transport but strong enough to support his massive weight.

Isak took an overfilled bowl of stew and picked out a hard lump of bread, then sat himself on Bahl's left. The general paused, then found himself another stool, his face impassive, as usual. Isak hoped the others hadn't seen it as a deliberate slight—Bahl never gave anything away, so he'd wanted to be able to watch every other face there. He hadn't intended to be deliberately rude to the general. Vesna secured the place on Isak's other side.

"Sir Cerse, you may speak as a peer here," Bahl said quietly, and the Colonel gave a nod of appreciation at the courtesy—as the only man there without court rank, he would otherwise have had to stay quiet unless directly addressed.

Bahl didn't waste time. "The Malich affair is not quite over. You will all have noticed the failure of some to answer the call to battle, and the problems the cavalry have been having with the blood stocks. My authority still lacks the weight in some places that I would wish."

"My Lord," interrupted Ked carefully, "I have had my best man watching the young wolf, but he reports nothing of this importance. Certinse left for Lomin today."

"I have also heard nothing to say those suspected—" began Torl.

Bahl raised a hand to stop him. "Neither have I, but neither do they rush back to the fold. My lords will need convincing, it seems, and that is what we will do."

"Lesarl?" asked Isak with a faint smile, looking quickly at the woman, who was crouching easily at the side of the tent. He noticed that Ked wore a look of pained resignation. No doubt he'd hoped the time for savage measures had passed.

"Legana has other duties," Bahl said. "She will be returning to Helrect, where she will join the White Circle. We have little information about them or their plans because they have been so hard to infiltrate. We have few female agents of Legana's talents; to waste her on this would be foolish. In any case, Lesarl will have to restrain his feelings for Duke Certinse for the moment. I do not destroy powerful families lightly, for that would, I think, come back to haunt us."

"And counts?" prompted Vesna quietly.

"Kinbe and Solsis should both disappear. There's no doubt that they are guilty of murder and heresy, though we've never had evidence enough for a public trial. That should send a clear message to Duke Certinse; after that, we will have to watch how he reacts. I will have Suzerain Nelbove in my pocket by the time his daughter marries Certinse. His allegiance to Malich was only ever intended to further his fortune."

"Count Vilan and those marshals of his," supplied Sir Cerse. "The count sent ambiguous letters to my predecessor—they were delayed and by the time they arrived the colonel had died and a relative in the city had claimed his personal papers. There is no reason for Vilan to know his letters were not burned, as I'm sure the rest were. I've known him for years, so I doubt his importance to the general plot, but it would send a message to anyone thinking of pulling strings."

The grey-haired Torl blinked in surprise. Vilan was one of his subjects—and one of his most important. "I had no idea," he said, looking at Bahl. "It's true I have never been on the best of terms with Vilan, but I've had no reason to think him a traitor. His family have always supported mine; he's my second cousin." The suzerain pinched the bridge of his nose and sighed heavily. Isak watched, fascinated at the effect of this revelation on the normally granite-faced soldier. "If you would be good enough to show me the documents, Sir Cerse?"

The knight nodded. "Of course, sir. They are under lock and key in Tirah. If it helps, it mentions your hidden armouries at your hunting lodge and River-bree Manor—I assume that was information he shouldn't have shared."

"Vilan was the only one outside my family to know of those, damn him. I *will* deal with him, but I want it to be seen as an accident. The Vilans have done my family good service over the years; I don't want their reputation to be stained because of one man."

"May I ask something?" asked Isak. He looked around at the expectant faces and felt the memory of his display on the battlefield rise in his throat. He'd been trying to avoid being the centre of attention since he regained consciousness. "I'm sure you've all grown up discussing this sort of thing, but I didn't. It's obvious there is disloyalty, and problems with the Cult of Nartis, but I still don't know what Malich actually did. Could I get the short explanation before we decide who to murder?"

A barking laugh came from Suzerain Ked, not mocking but brotherly, as if Isak's request had made him appear human again. There were smiles all round and the sombre mood evaporated.

The colonel cleared his throat to attract Bahl's attention. "I think that perhaps I might be the best person for that, my Lord. I know enough to give a brief outline." His tone was respectful but bold as he warmed to his new position in Bahl's inner circle. He could make a good guess at the sort of man the Lord would value.

Bahl gestured for Sir Cerse to continue.

"The scandal was brought to light by a Cardinal of the cult of Nartis, Cardinal Disten," he said. "He was once chaplain to a cavalry regiment in Amah. He discovered daemon worshippers spreading a cult devoted to a being called Azaer, mostly in the Cardinal branch, but they were slowly gaining control of the whole cult of Nartis. It was rumoured that the Dowager Duchess Certinse was at the centre of the plot, taking orders directly from Malich. I heard that the men who found Suzerain Suil's body were on their way to arrest him for high treason. They were preparing for a full-scale rebellion when Cardinal Disten uncovered the plot last summer."

"But how could any Farlan rebel against the Chosen of Nartis?" demanded Isak, unable to keep from interrupting.

"Firstly, if you'll forgive the observation, my Lord, even a white-eye of Lord Bahl's ability cannot face an entire army. With necromantic powers augmenting their forces and the military support of those nobles they controlled, the danger was very real."

"But surely most are loyal still?"

"Possibly, but by rigging the election of one of their own to High Cardinal of Nartis they have great authority over the people, as well as the ability to declare Lord Bahl Forsaken."

Isak sounded confused. "What does that mean?"

"Forsaken means abandoned by the Gods. While we are servants of the Gods, they rarely pay much attention to us. Nartis is like any other God of the Upper Circle. The Chosen must be able to protect both their positions and persons, otherwise they do not deserve his blessing. If the Cardinals declare Lord Bahl to be Forsaken, then they can order those loyal to join them or stay away. Not all would obey, but enough. Lord Bahl is head of the cult of Nartis, but the Cardinals speak with divine authority. With intelligence and magic they could manipulate the mood of crowds; they could turn public opinion even against the chosen Lord of the Farlan.

"Half the tribe seems to have been implicated by one rumour or another. Mostly these have been false—petty revenge or family feuds, such is court life—but some must be true. I believe that there was a large faction of Devoted involved."

Sir Cerse looked at Bahl for comment but received merely a blank stare. He coughed and continued quickly, "To best Lord Bahl in battle, Malich would have needed to control at least one duke and five powerful suzerains. That's the only way he could be confident of defeating the loyal troops. The true extent of how many were involved we may never know, but the tribe has been severely weakened by suspicion. Many have failed to maintain proper, lawful levels of stock, trained soldiers, campaign supplies . . ." His voice tailed off as gloom overtook the tent once more.

Isak looked around at the faces staring at the ground. Bahl's own naturally grim expression was reflected on the faces of Torl, Vesna, Sir Cerse—even the beautiful assassin, Legana. Suzerain Ked, normally a calm and reflective man, had his jaw clamped tight and anger tightened his brow.

With a start Isak realised their dismay was not at the task facing them, but shame that their own people could turn on each other in such a way, and against the will of the God.

Insurrection was nothing new, but plotting the downfall of the entire nation was a completely different matter. Their tribe had remained strong by relying on its own—an arrogant and xenophobic way of life, possibly, but one that had kept them whole nonetheless.

"Thank you," he said quietly. "Now I understand what's at stake, of course I'll be part of it—I'll do anything you need."

Expressions faded to acceptance and resolve. The next few hours saw each man writing a painfully long list while outside, winter tightened its grip on the mountains they called home.

A discreet knock came at the dining room door. Amanas raised an eyebrow at his wife, but from her expression Jelana knew nothing about it. The Keymaster frequently spent all day in the Heraldic Library, or at official functions. Dinner was *their* time: they would eat together and undisturbed every night unless it almost was a matter of life or death. As absentminded as Amanas was, he knew his wife felt strongly about this. He actively dissuaded visitors at the best of times; the evenings were sacrosanct.

The butler entered, casting an apprehensive look at his mistress before saying, "Sir, I apologise for interrupting, but you have a visitor who demands to see you urgently."

Amanas didn't have time to reply before a voice came from the open doorway and a man stepped into the dining room. "My apologies, dear lady," he declared, bowing low and kissing her theatrically on the hand. The man was tall and slim, with a distinguished touch of grey in his hair, dressed fashionably, if on the young side. "I'm afraid the matter could not wait. I must drag your husband away for a while."

Jelana Amanas gave a curt nod of the head and rose, patting her husband on the shoulder on her way past. She said not a word to the newcomer. When she had left, the man took her seat and leaned forward, fingers interlocked, as he studied Amanas with a predatory expression that reminded the Keymaster of the Chief Steward.

"So, Amanas, how is life in the Heraldic Library?"

"As it always is, Dancer. You have interrupted my dinner for a good reason, I hope?"

The man called Dancer chuckled at the use of that name. He was one of Lesarl's personal advisors, a member of the Chief Steward's very personal coterie. Few knew that name for him; it was reserved for business done well away from the public eye.

"You have a set of files here that my employer asked you to prepare a few years ago; you have not destroyed them?"

"Files?" Amanas asked. For a moment he had no idea what Dancer was talking about, then he realised. "The Malich affair? Yes, I still have them, though I resent the Chief Steward using me as his personal blackmailer. Why do you need them? Surely we're no longer in danger of civil war now that Malich is dead."

"I have just received a message from the army in Lomin. Duke Lomin is dead."

"Murdered?" Amanas asked, aghast.

"By elves, not by Farlan hand. The problem is his son, Scion Lomin. He has taken the name of Duke Certinse." Dancer's eyes narrowed. "The Certinse family now directly controls a suzerainty, a dukedom, the Knights of the Temples, and it may soon control the Cardinal branch of the cult of Nartis."

Amanas sighed and heaved himself to his feet. From the sideboard he picked up an oil lamp and used it to gesture towards the door. "Well then, you'd better come with me. We have a long night ahead of us."

CHAPTER 19

ISAK'S HORSE ALMOST SAGGED WITH FATIGUE. The snowflakes turning to water as they landed on the cloth covering weighed down the poor beast even further as it laboured on through the dirty sludge that passed for the forest highway. The local suzerains employed roadmen to maintain these routes, but several thousand horsemen coming through in the depths of winter made it impossible to tell whether those duties had been neglected or not. Since they were in Amah, a rich and prosperous suzerainty, it was likely there was someone sadly shaking his head as the troops passed, wondering how he'd ever get his road back into top condition.

"Remind me why we need to do this," Isak muttered, eyes fixed on a single snowflake that was precariously balanced on the rise of a seam.

"Because wintering in Lomin would be as inconvenient as it would be fraught with complications." Vesna's reply sounded mechanical: he was quite as bored and cold as the Krann, and he had answered this question half a dozen times already. "Quite aside from the fact that you'd probably end up fighting Duke Certinse, Lomin is eight hundred miles from Perlir. With life as it is, that's too far. Duke Sempes hasn't caused trouble for quite a while and the Chief Steward is probably mad with suspicion by now."

"Have we reached Danva yet?"

"Soon. The next village we come to should be flying red banners."

"Why red?" Now Isak looked a little more interested. "Surely it should be white if they're mourning their suzerain?" He looked at his bondsman, who looked significantly more noble than his master—Isak's heavy fleeces were stained with mud after an ignominious spill from his horse when the hunter had stumbled and fallen badly. At least they'd had a decent meal out of it—the break had been too bad for the horse to be of any further use and the Farlan were a practical people. Horses were the lifeblood of their nation, valued by all, but they were a tool. Isak had heard the Yeetatchen treated their horses like family, but the Farlan were much more sensible.

"No, my Lord, they fly the red when the suzerain dies in battle. I thought everyone knew that." Vesna looked puzzled. "Where were you born?"

"On the road to the Circle City. My mother went into labour just as they sighted Blackfang, I'm told. That's where she's buried, at the foot of a willow by the road." There was a tinge of pain in Isak's voice. Like all white-eyes, he knew exactly why his mother died.

"I'm sorry—"

"Long in the past," replied Isak, shaking himself free of the memory. "I might not remember her, but at least I've seen where she was buried—that route was my life for ten years. Three trips every two years, and I had to sneak off to visit her grave and get a whipping when I returned."

"Your father hates you that much?" Vesna sounded like he couldn't believe a parent would act that way, but Isak had seen men worse than his father. At least Horman had a reason to hate his son. Some men did worse, for no cause other than that they had been born vicious.

"Father never forgave the loss of my mother. He named me to mock Kasi Farlan—maybe he hoped the Gods would take me young because of that. Without Carel to keep me in check I'd probably have hung as a result of our combined tempers."

"I've heard you speak of Carel before; who is he?" the count asked.

"Carel—Sergeant Betyn Carelfolden," Isak said. "He taught me everything I know, not just how to fight, but to rein in my temper, to think before reacting—it may not look like it, but I could have been much worse!" He laughed, then explained, "Carel was a Ghost, so he was fair. He didn't despise me just because I was a white-eye, and he didn't hate me for killing my mother like my father did." He smiled, remembering. "He's probably the reason my father and I didn't end up killing each other."

"Why don't you send for him, this Carelfolden, if he's your friend?" Vesna asked curiously.

Isak shrugged. He'd thought of doing just that from time to time, but somehow he'd never actually done anything about it—he wasn't sure why that was. Carel's smile and gruff voice composed almost the entirety of Isak's good childhood memories. He was the one who had urged Isak to be more than just a white-eye, who'd borne in silence the brunt of a young man's frustration as it boiled over. Carel was almost the only person Isak gave a damn about, and the only person he wanted to be proud of him. Still something held him back.

"My Lord? Would it not be good to have another man you could trust?

One whose opinion is worthwhile? If he was a Ghost, then he'll be trust-worthy and capable, and will already know that the life of the nobility is often less than noble. You'll need men of your own, men who are loyal to you before anyone else."

"Are you saying I can't trust whoever Bahl does?"

Vesna shook his head. "Not at all. But the Chief Steward is the servant of the Lord of the Farlan, no matter who that is. Suzerains like Torl or Tebran, or Swordmaster Kerin, they're devoted to Lord Bahl himself: they're friends as well as vassals. I'm not saying they're a danger to you, not at all, but you have to recognise that you now wield great political power in your own right. But you're only one man, and a young one at that. I'm loyal to Lord Bahl, and Nartis of course, but my bond is specifically to you, Suzerain Anvee. My point is: Lord Bahl has his own people to worry about his interests, and friends to act as confidants."

Isak held up a hand to stop the count, already convinced. He didn't want to think too hard about the political situation right now: all the secret agendas and wheelings and dealings were still a mystery; he was having a hard enough time remembering who could be trusted and how much now without adding a whole new layer of intrigue. "You're right, you're absolutely right. I'll send for Carel—don't ever call him Carelfolden; he saves that for formal occasions only. Can you send a messenger for me? Probably best to leave it at the Hood and Cape in the Golden Tower district." He didn't add "before I change my mind," though the words were lurking at the back of his throat.

He sighed. Carel had truly made him what he was—he recalled as if it were yesterday, his fifteenth birthday, when, after yet another brawl with the other boys of the wagon train, Carel had taken him aside, dismissing Isak's whining complaints with one sentence: *You have to act as more than the colour of your eyes.* Those words imprinted themselves onto Isak's heart, and when worry or anger clouded his thoughts, he tried to cling to that conversation to help him come to his senses . . . but now he had the memory of his behaviour in the battle. His disadvantages might not be obvious, but Isak knew they were there, and that he had to overcome them.

Bringing Carel to the palace was the sensible course. His mantra when-ever Isak's fiery temper got the better of his brain was more soldiers' wisdom: *You're not perfect, life isn't perfect. There are more important things to be pissed off about, so save your temper for a real problem.*

"I'll do so immediately," said Vesna, relieved. "He'll be good for you to have around. If Carel knew you in your previous life, he'll give his opinion to the man, not the title."

And is that what I'm afraid of? Isak wondered. *Do I want Carel to continually tell me I'm wrong? Do I want to be the errant child all my life?* He turned back to the road ahead, and to the same view they had had for the past two weeks. Only the Palace Guard and one legion of light cavalry were returning with them, and to the casual observer it looked as though every Ghost held the reins of a spare horse. A fog of gloom surrounded them: their losses had been severe, both on the field and in the days following as men succumbed to their wounds. When they arrived home in Tirah, the citizens would have to tread softly for a few weeks.

"And to what do you give your opinion, the man or the title?" There was an edge to Isak's voice that he'd not intended. Uneasy nights as growing pains racked his body coupled with the relentless days of travel were making him irritable and restless. His newly developed muscles were crying out for exercise beyond hacking chunks from unfortunate trees that he passed by. With Bahl in a similar mood—albeit for different reasons—Isak fought extra hard to keep control of his temper, but there was always a trace of pent-up anger when he spoke.

"To both, my Lord." Vesna's reply was assured and immediate.

"Both?" Isak laughed, a little bitterly. "You're remarkably honest, especially when compared to your peers. They watch me like a wolf that's just arrived in camp."

"That's because they are not from Anvee; they are not *your* bondsmen. You have no reason to trust them; they have no need to earn your trust."

"And you do?"

Vesna smiled and nodded. "As my liege and holder of my bond, you could destroy me with a few words. You are also one of the most powerful men in the tribe, so as your star ascends, so will mine. That means I speak to your title in part, but not all. If I'm going to tie myself so closely to your cause, I might as well try to like you; I can always fall back on being owned by you if that doesn't work."

In spite of his mood, Vesna's words made Isak laugh out loud. He did like the man, for his confidence as much as his honesty. All he needed was a reason to trust him, and this one sounded as good as any. Bahl certainly seemed to approve; Isak was quite sure he'd have made any disapprobation clear if he thought Count Vesna to be a danger. Isak had been glad of his presence over the last week or two: he was proving to be a useful man to have around.

He made a decision and turned to face his bondsman. "In that case, Vesna, I would be grateful if you would not forget that I have a real name. It might not be impressive, I might not like it all that much, and it might have been given as an insult, but it's mine. Isak is who I am. If you're to be a friend of mine, you had better remember that."

"I will, my Lord. Thank you."

Isak turned sharply, in case he was being mocked, but found only a broad smile on Vesna's face. "Unfortunately, I suspect I have more enemies than friends," he said, quietly. "I don't pretend to understand why I was made Krann, or why I was given these gifts. I'm far from being a Saviour—"

"Perhaps it is something you have to become, rather than be born into?" Vesna didn't sound particularly enthusiastic.

"Me? Not in this lifetime!" replied Isak with a bitter laugh. "But it doesn't matter what I think. Within a few hours of being Chosen, two men I'd never met tried their best to kill me. That's too much of a coincidence for me."

Vesna looked surprised. "I heard about the training ground, but I met Sir Dirass Certinse several times. I can't see him offering to be assassin for anyone—and his family would hardly have wanted him to do it that way if they'd been involved."

"I know, which makes me think there's someone watching from the shadows. They both looked like rabid dogs, like they were not themselves."

Vesna made a choked sound and his face paled. "That sounds like the sort of magic necromancers play with."

"Let's not get too excited. Half the Land is worried about what I might be—either Aryn Bwr returned to life, or an obstacle to his rise. How many of them would think it better I just died?"

"True enough. If you weren't Farlan, I'm sure the Chief Steward would have your murder planned already. Anything else that might make sense of all this?"

Isak hesitated. There were some things he didn't mean to tell anyone, not until he understood them himself—he had no idea what was significant or not. The Gods didn't work in obvious ways; the Age of Fulfilment was just that, an Age. It could last centuries. Still he found himself saying, "There is one thing. A voice."

"A voice?"

"I hear it in my dreams sometimes, a girl's voice. I think she's calling me, but I can't understand her."

"Looking for you? I doubt that would impress Lady Tila." He winked.

"Tila? You've never even met her!"

"You forget that soldiers gossip worse than washerwomen." Vesna laughed. "From what I hear, your pretty little maid's taken quite a fancy to you."

"Then you're as bad as the rest of them," he growled. "In case you hadn't noticed, I'm a white-eye. She isn't."

"*She* might not mind what you are, not all do."

"And not all have parents expecting to marry their daughters off well, and expecting children. I may well live long enough to fight beside your great-grandson, but I'll never have one of my own."

"I'm sorry, my Lord—Isak. I didn't mean to offend."

Isak gave a sigh and stretched his arms up into the air, then rolled his shoulders forward and back, attempting to work the stiffness from them. "I know, and I'm not, really, but Tila's nothing to do with all this, so let's keep her out of it. As for the girl in my dreams, I feel I recognise her, and yet I don't."

"What are you going to do?"

"What can I do? It's just another mystery about me that I can't do anything about. Maybe it's just designed to drive me insane wondering about it. But I *will* find out one day, there's no doubt about that, and all I can do is be ready for whatever's waiting."

The following weeks saw the army getting ever smaller as knights and hurscals slipped away in small groups to their own holdings. The rest of the troops searched the horizon for the peaks of Tirah's towers as the miles passed away beneath their tramping feet. When they reached Fordan, the sombre mood deepened. The new suzerain, a greying man of forty summers, had struggled into his father's armour despite a deep wound in his shoulder. Now he walked before the coffin, leading the cortège home.

That evening, the suzerain crammed as many as possible into the manor's great hall and spoke for a few minutes with dignified grief about those they had lost. As a last gesture to his beloved father, he ordered up the contents of their cellars, and barrels of beer and wine were rolled out for the endless toasts to the regiments who'd fought and the men who'd died. Everyone knew the late Suzerain Fordan would have hugely approved of having a hundred drunken soldiers as his memorial.

Isak sat back from it all, feeling out of place, though he'd been as much a part of the battle as any of them. A pang of guilt ran through him as he saw a tear in the new suzerain's eye as he raised a glass to his father's memory. That was something Isak would never be able to do—not even if his father managed some great feat of heroism. Isak doubted he'd feel much at all when Horman died.

His hands tightened into fists as part of him cried shame. Rising abruptly, he slipped away from the increasingly drunken mourners, following a servant's directions to a tight spiral staircase that led away from the hall. He told himself he didn't belong there, belting out marching songs, and stepped out on to a high terrace overlooking the fields. The crisp quiet of evening, with the hunter's moon dropping behind the distant pines, was a better place to remember the dead.

Isak idly caressed the emerald set into Eolis's pommel. The cut surfaces were silky in the sharp winter air; the silver claws that held the stone were wet with cold. The wide river that cut through the neat lines of fields looked calm in the moonlight, but it ran both swift and dangerous. Isak watched the phantom clouds of his breath push out over the crenellations, then they were swept away into nothing.

A finger of cold suddenly flashed down Isak's spine and he flinched in surprise. Then an icy prickle on his neck made him look abruptly over his shoulder. The terrace was only ten yards long, and it remained resolutely empty. Alterr's light from high above had cast a deep shadow on the wall behind him, but no one—or *thing*—loitered in it, as far as Isak could see. There was no window where someone could observe him, and when he embraced a sliver of magic, he was assured that there truly was not a soul nearby.

Still Isak felt uncomfortable, as if there were a physical presence standing at his shoulder. The bite in the air crept inside his clothes, and the shadows grew deep and ancient. His hand closed tight about Eolis. Still he could see nothing. A flicker of panic set in. As a cloud moved over Alterr's face, Isak shuddered: this bitter, dark place was not for mortal breath. He turned and hurried back inside.

From the shadows, the boy's precipitous flight was noted with some amusement. His uncertainty, melancholy, and jumbled fears left a sweet aroma lingering in the air.

So blind, still, but have no fear. Not yet. You hardly know who you are—you're not yet ready to know my *name.*

CHAPTER 20

ISAK WAS GLAD OF THE SILK MASK COVERING HIS FACE as the column of horsemen clattered their way through the streets of Tirah. The crowds had braved a brisk wind and swirling eddies of snow to line the streets all the way to the palace. Under scarves and caps skin was reddened and raw, but lifted by the smiles and cheers that greeted the troops. A victory parade through the city always brought out the people, if only to gawp at the Farlan cavalry in all their colourful finery. Even the Ghosts had made the effort to look their best, and the knights were as gaudy as ever, but it was Isak who drew everyone's attention.

At Bahl's request, the Krann was in full armour, the only concession to the cold a bearskin around his shoulders. He managed not to shiver too obviously. No matter how uncomfortable, he could not deny the effect he was having on the people—*his* people. They might still be fearful of what lay behind these particular gifts, but the sight of Siulents and Eolis, and the proud emerald dragons decorating the flanks of Isak's hunter, were irresistible.

The people of Tirah cheered their army, and they cheered Isak at its head. Bahl was beside him, but Isak felt their eyes on his back long after he had trotted under the barbican gate. Flaming brands lit the thirty yards of dank stone tunnel, then the column emerged into the familiar surrounds of the palace grounds, to be received formally by the entire staff and residents of the palace and barracks. Guardsmen and recruits, all in full dress uniform, stood in neat ranks off to the left, with the palace staff lined up on the right. Fearful wives and children, still not knowing who had survived and who had died, huddled behind the ranks.

Swordmaster Kerin, standing before his men, saluted, beaming, as the troops clattered past to the sound of his men cheering. Even the noblemen and officials grouped beyond the palace staff added their voices to the tumultuous reception.

Bahl, having acknowledged his Swordmaster, ignored the rest and slipped from his horse as soon as he reached the steps. Lesarl had already broken away from the group of officials, a pair of clerks in his wake, and fell

in with Bahl as he strode into the palace. It was left up to Isak to acknowledge the greeting, bestowing on each group a regal wave or a smile before he
was able to dismount.

The Swordmaster took that as the signal to dismiss everyone and his curt
order was echoed by the bellow of a sergeant-at-arms. The orderly lines
melted back to their barracks and duties as a stream of weary knights trotted
past and onto the stables on either side of the south gate.

Isak gave his horse one last pat on the neck and smiled at Kerin, who
saluted him again as he passed, on his way to Sir Cerse. The colonel of the
Ghosts turned with a smile as Kerin patted him on the shoulder, then Isak's
attention wandered to the hundreds of reunions going on across the ground,
with friends, families, or lovers. A touch of sadness stirred in his belly as he
watched some collapsing in tears, others laughing in relief.

He was about to head off to his chambers when he noticed a figure out
of the corner of his eye, standing motionless in the teeming crowds. The man
was staring straight at him, not moving a muscle, even as a woman behind
him bewailed the loss of a husband. With a shout, Isak tore the mask from
his face and sprang forward as the man broke into a broad smile and stepped
forward to meet the bounding giant.

"Gods, boy, look at the size of you—I wasn't sure it was really you for a
moment there!" exclaimed Carel as Isak reached him.

Not waiting for any formal greeting, Isak discarded his gauntlets and
reached down to hug him. Carel was now significantly shorter than him. Isak
lifted him off his feet with fierce affection.

"Aargh, put me down, you ox!" cried Carel as Isak squeezed the breath
from his body. He took Isak's hand in his, feeling the hard muscle under his
palms. Looking him up and down, Carel's expression was one of amazement.
"Isak, boy, you've grown near a foot since I last saw you—and if you fill that
armour out the way it looks—Such a change in half a year! Merciful Nartis,
your hand feels like it's been carved from oak!"

"And you look smaller than ever," Isak countered, grinning widely.

Count Vesna walked over from his own horse, a satisfied smile on his lips
as he watched the reunion. It was the first time he'd seen the Krann like this.

"Hah, and I'm softer in my old age too. Don't hug me like that again,
please, you might snap me in two. Don't think you'll be feeling the back of
my hand any more now either—your skull was always over-thick even before
you were Chosen. Gods, even now I can hardly believe I'm saying that. You,
one of the Chosen—"

"I know, but you can save the jokes for later."

"Those'll wait." Carel stopped and reached up to grasp Isak by the shoulders. "I'm not joking now, boy. I hope you realise the honour done to you."

"The honour of having half the Land after my blood?" Isak laughed at Carel's expression and stuck his tongue out at him in mock petulance. "Oh don't scowl at me like that, I know what you mean. I'm just glad you're here. I was afraid that you'd have gone off on another trip."

"No, with the attack on Lomin, work stopped dead. I wouldn't have gone anyway. I resigned my position; took work as bodyguard for a merchant. All you need's the white collar to do that without fear, and I knew you'd be needing my help sooner or later."

Isak stopped and looked down at the ground, guiltily aware of the length of time since he'd seen his old friend. "I'm sorry, I—"

Carel shut him up with a wave of the hand. "Boy, I know your mind better than you do. I'd have been able to tell you on your first day that you'd start it off alone. And now I see you like this—oh Gods, I'm so proud of you. You've nothing to apologise for, *nothing*. You've settled in, and now you've realised you're in need of someone to clip your ear from time to time—took your time, but you got there in the end."

Both men turned to Vesna as the count stifled a snort of laughter. "Ahem, my apologies, Lord Isak."

"Tsatach's balls! You're Count Vesna?" Carel grabbed the man's hand and continued, "An honour to meet you, my Lord. Wait a moment—" He looked from Vesna to Isak, then another smile broke over his lined face. "You took a bond of service, didn't you? Because of the College of Magic. You're from—Hah!" Carel suddenly laughed so hard the men behind him jumped in alarm. "You're bonded to this great lump of wood?"

"I have that honour, sir," replied Vesna smoothly, his eyes twinkling as he recognised a kindred spirit. "But can I suggest we continue this conversation inside, away from the troops?"

"That's a good idea," agreed Isak quickly, realising that the two were going to get on well, probably at his own expense. He draped an arm over Carel's shoulder and turned towards the main wing where hot food would be waiting. "I see you're well, then."

"As well as can be expected for a man who feels his age around all these boys." Carel waved his hand towards the soldiers, unconsciously touching the white collar on his tunic as he looked at them. Only then did it occur to Isak that Carel was better dressed than Isak had ever seen him before. A fine coat of short black fur reached down to his knees, edged in pristine white fox fur. Under this were bleached soft leathers and a fine pair of high green boots, all of which seemed unusually foppish for the former Ghost.

"You've taken advantage of our hospitality then," Isak remarked, touching a finger to the coat's edge.

"I've been here only a few days, but your maid has been looking after me—since you're the Krann, I thought I'd better get myself some new clothes; didn't want you to be ashamed of me." Carel gestured towards the approaching figure of Tila.

"Welcome back, my Lord," the girl said, curtseying neatly to Isak, then bobbing her head and adding, "Count Vesna."

"Have you two met before?" Isak asked, curious.

"No, my Lord," Tila said, "but the count's armour makes him easy to recognise, and of course his reputation precedes him."

The count hesitated a second, then bowed low to kiss Tila's hand in formal greeting. "My Lady."

As Tila's face remained impassive, Isak remembered she wouldn't share a soldier's admiration of Vesna's reputation.

There was a frosty edge to her voice when she at last did speak. "Your apartments have been readied, but unfortunately there has been some storm damage to one of the court apartments, and the other two are already allocated. I hope you will not mind using guest chambers instead. I have had your belongings delivered to the rooms beside Sergeant Carelfolden's, since you are both of Lord Isak's party."

Isak gaped at the meek girl he had said goodbye to. The hostility was not open enough to be insulting, but it was obvious all the same. It was the first time he really saw her as a Farlan woman, taught from birth that her position would never be equal to that of a man. For the Chetse, that meant women held no opinions; they were docile, obedient, and polite to their masters, never even raising their voices. The Farlan were different, for Farlan women-folk turned weakness into strength in classic military manner: they ran everything from behind the scenes. It wasn't shaming for a man's peers to know his wife made the decisions, and girls with wit and fierce intelligence were well educated and keenly sought in marriage.

"Who's in the other apartments?" Isak demanded when he found his voice.

To his surprise, her gaze never wavered, even in the face of his obvious anger. She stared him down as she replied, "Suzerain Tebran is still techni-cally in residence, and Count Vilan has been allocated the other apartment."

"But we met Tebran at his manor. And Vilan? Fetch Lesarl, now," Isak snapped.

The count raised a black velvet-clad hand. "My Lord, I am quite happy with the arrangements. I believe Sir Cerse invited Count Vilan here, and I would hate to interfere with that."

Isak looked at his bondsman for a moment and then realisation dawned. He nodded briefly at Vesna, then turned back to Tila and said politely, "My lady, the arrangements are most satisfactory. Please convey my warmest regards to the Chief Steward. I'm sure he would have given me a stable if he could."

Tila curtsied again and swung about to return to the palace.

Vesna breathed in deeply as a brief gust of perfume washed towards him. "I think she likes me."

"She has certain opinions, about—" Isak blushed, and continued, his voice softer, "about sexual relations. I don't think you quite meet her standards."

Vesna laughed dryly. "I should hope not. Those sort of 'relations,' as you so coyly put it, are not for unmarried girls."

"I feel sorry for your wife when at last you do marry," Isak said with a laugh.

"Why? If I get all my dalliances out of the way beforehand, she will reap the benefit of my hard work and practice!" He smiled, and Isak didn't push the subject further. It was clear Vesna had reeled out his defence time after time, whether he actively believed in it or not was not Isak's problem.

"Anyway, enough of this," the count continued. "I can decide how to win Lady Tila's heart some other time. What's more important is that Count Vilan is on a certain list in my possession."

"I know; just don't be too impatient to get his chambers; understood?"

Carel watched Isak. Whether the boy knew it or not, he was growing into his position as much in attitude as he was in body. He felt a welling of pride in his heart, and gladness: for once his wild boy didn't have his usual look of wariness on his face. Now he didn't have to keep out of the way, or keep one eye open for a passing blow, nor did he have to endure the scowls and distrust of everyone he met.

Isak stood tall and proud. He'd shaken off the slouch he'd adopted as a child to disguise his height and he looked more alive than he ever had. No longer would Isak have to skirt around society: now life would shape itself about his battle-hardened figure. It was more than the child Carel had first met could ever have dreamed of. Now, with an enchanted blade hanging casually at his hip, a dragon on his cloak, and clad in magical armour, he would be the envy of every boy in the tribe.

As Carel's gaze paused on Eolis, Isak's head snapped around. The youth's face was suspicious for a fraction of a second, then he forced out a smile again. "Enough of business; we need food and wine." He ushered Carel and Vesna towards the Great Hall, where the men crowding around the roasting boar parted respectfully. Isak piled as much food as he could carry into his bowl, then directed Carel to the head table with a nod of his head.

Once they were all comfortable, he asked Carel, "So what news do you have?"

Carel looked up from his food and hesitated for a moment, trying to read the Krann's face, but finding nothing, started, "Well, Valo finally got around to marrying Faean, Jedah gave birth to a baby girl a day shy of midwinter—"

"That's not what I meant."

"Well then, just ask. How can I guess whether you want to hear about Horman or not? You've been living with politicians for half a year; you've grown one of their blank faces."

Isak looked startled, then his more familiar expression of slight anxiety spread across his face.

"So, is he glad I'm gone?"

"What do you think?"

"I expect he misses having someone to bully. I expect he's got less to complain about, so he's drinking rather than talking."

"Close enough to the truth there. But of course he misses you. You're still family, even if you can't stand each other. You've got your whole life ahead of you, and quite a life it'll be now. His ended when your mother died. Whatever he thinks of you, you were the last link to her. Many's the time I've got drunk with him and he's not said a word, just run that green ring around and around in his hand for hours."

"Well, don't expect me to see him," Isak growled.

"I don't."

Isak looked surprised at Carel's easy acceptance. He snorted and slapped his palm on the table. "You're surprised? My boy, you're not the only white-eye I've known, and I damn well know you better than any man alive. You're as proud as you are nasty sometimes. On top of that Horman, my friend as he still is, has done little to deserve your love."

"Little?"

Carel waved a finger at him. "He looked after you better than some I've heard of. Whatever else you say, and however begrudgingly it was given, you never went hungry. Deny that and I'll slap you so hard your armour will fall off. There were some all for giving you a child's portion at meals, instead of more than Valo could manage. Not one would have dared say that to your father."

"Why not?"

"Well, for a start, no one wanted to talk about you unless they had to—they were your mother's folk, and a superstitious rabble, then and now. You look like your mother, and everyone knew what she meant to Horman; he took his loneliness and frustration out on you for that, but he'd not have seen you starve, whatever words his temper might put in his mouth."

"Perhaps. But I'll be more alone than he ever was—at least he had someone once; he had a child, even if it was a white-eye."

"And look what the loss did to him."

Isak didn't reply, but Carel could see from his clamped jaw that the boy understood more than he was going to admit. Before the conversation could continue, Tila arrived with a second bowl of food for Isak.

Vesna rose at Tila's arrival, a smile on his lips, but Tila, feeling like he was mocking her, pointedly ignored him and sat down next to Carel, who waved a spoon in greeting. She had immediately warmed to the aging soldier: there was a warm generosity about him, a feeling of dependability and reassurance, like a loving uncle, perhaps—quite unlike the handsome charms of Count Vesna, whose glittering eyes were not exactly indecent, but they were most certainly predatory.

Tila wore a simple, warm dress, but with a glance and a smile Vesna managed to make her feel as though she were dressed fit for a summer ball. She had no intention of trusting a man like that. His face was too comely, his words too welcome, his presence too magnetic.

"My Lord, was the battle as much of a success as we have heard?" she asked, breaking her concentration away from Vesna.

"Was that really all of the Ghosts returning today?" Carel asked before Isak could finish his mouthful and reply to Tila's question. He sounded concerned; Carel had been a Ghost; he knew what a full complement looked like and was well able to guess their losses.

Vesna nodded. "Near enough. Some stopped at their homesteads, but with those killed in battle and winter picking off the injured, we're almost four hundred down. Success? My Lady, it was, but at a high price. Still, Isak led well in his first battle and that's a good sign for the future."

Isak said nothing—he still felt guilty whenever the battle was mentioned—but Carel took his silence as lamenting the dead. "Don't think about the fallen, Isak," he said. "From what I hear, there would have been even more widows without you: Lord Bahl and the dragon broke the trolls, but they would have been too late if the Ghosts hadn't held—and without you, they would have been overcome before Lord Bahl got there."

Isak looked up and met his friend's gaze: Carel had never been adept at lying, nor had he ever made allowances for the feelings of an outcast. He had guessed what happened, and understood.

A sudden draft from the tower corridor heralded the Swordmaster's arrival. Kerin's grim face brightened when he breathed in the aroma that filled the Great Hall. The Swordmaster hadn't yet returned to his training leathers; under his coat was the dress uniform of the Ghosts, including a heavily braided, double-breasted tunic of black linen woven with gold thread.

He secured a bowl of the stew from the huge cauldrons nestled inside the stone hearth of the great fire and a haunch of the spitted boar, then joined Isak and his friends. He came straight to the point. "Lord Bahl has been filling me in. You can use magic now?"

Isak's heart sank. From the gleam in Kerin's eye, the Swordmaster had a whole host of new routines already devised. "Barely," he said quickly, "nothing with any skill, just the most basic of energies, not real combat magic at all."

Kerin smiled. "Barely will do for me."

"Magic?" asked Tila sharply. "What do you mean by basic energies?"

"Do you know anything about magic?" Isak asked. He knew a little more of the subject than when he had left the palace.

"Only that white-eyes are different to wizards."

The others had leaned forward slightly and Isak smiled. Few people really knew anything about magic—it was the preserve of a select few—but who could fail to be interested? "Well, it's complicated, and I don't understand most of it myself. From what I've read, there are three types of magic, the basic energies—"

"Like creating lightning?" Vesna interrupted with boyish eagerness. Any man who had seen Bahl fight knew how destructive that could be.

"Yes," Isak said, "although I don't think it's exactly the same as real lightning, but we're the Chosen of Nartis so that's how this works. Creating fire is possible but takes more energy—Lord Chalat or his Krann would be able to do it more easily because of their patron."

"It's all the same energy, but different people turn it into different things, lightning, fire, or whatever," said Kerin, who had far more experience of his Lord's skills.

"That's how it ends up," Isak agreed. "You'd have to ask a wizard from the College why. I don't understand most of what they say, but apparently I don't need to. Anyway, the three types are called energies, enchantments, and spells. Enchantments are very simple spells, so simple that even white-eyes can do them. It's just using the energies more carefully, shaping them to a purpose and binding them to stay, rather than releasing them in a single burst."

Isak could see from his audience that his lecture was beginning to lose them. He tried an example. "Do you remember the story of the jeweller and the rope snake?"

"The children's story?" replied Tila, starting to understand. "So the rope was enchanted?" Seeing blank expressions on the faces of the three men she smiled and began to explain. "A jeweller asks a wizard to protect him from thieves—I forget what happened, but the wizard gave him a piece of rope to leave in his shop at night. It would wander the rooms and if anyone else apart from the jeweller came in, it would tie them up."

"Exactly," said Isak. "There's more to it than just that, of course, but that's as far as I've got. As for spells, apparently they aren't something most white-eyes can do. There's something called 'covenant theory,' but I didn't really understand that."

As they all opened their mouths to speak at once, Isak's name was called out from the door. They turned to see the Chief Steward, flanked by his clerks.

Lesarl lowered his voice now he had their attention. "Lord Isak, the master wishes to see you now, alone. Kerin, there's work to do." He didn't wait for a response. He was fully up to date now with the events of the last few weeks and there was a mountain of work to do. Quite apart from his normal duties of effectively running Bahl's lands, he was in charge of securing and paying for everything Bahl felt the army would need. The lack of horses was his problem to resolve; his spy networks needed briefing; and now he had to look at securing the loyalty of the Farlan nobility from an economic perspective. He had a big staff, but keeping control of so many threads was a task more demanding than most men could manage.

"That there is," said Kerin to the general company as he rose from his seat. "With your leave, my Lord."

Isak waved in assent as the grey-haired man lifted his legs over the bench and went back to work. Isak finished his last mouthful of bread and stood to leave. "Vesna, I doubt this will take long. Round up some men, recruits, whoever, with practice weapons and armour. Kerin will have to be there for single combat practice, but I'm desperate to stretch my limbs. I'll meet you by the training posts—Tila, can you show him around?" He smiled at her.

Tila didn't look overly pleased at his request, but she and the count were going to have to get on, no matter what she thought of him. Isak suddenly realised then that whatever feelings he had held for Tila had changed. There was still a close affection, and appreciation, for she was beautiful, but now she was a friend, no more. Whether she felt the same remained to be seen, but to Isak, his maid had become the sister he'd never had.

The realisation had been sparked by his lack of jealousy at Vesna's interest in Tila, despite her obvious scorn for the famous—*infamous*—count. Things had changed since the battle, and now he just wanted to see Tila happy. There could be no match with him, but Vesna, on the other hand . . .

Carel watched the Krann go to the door with a smile on his face. He wondered whether Isak had noticed that he walked with one finger resting on Eolis always. He hoped the youth would take that armour off soon; he didn't seem quite human with it on. Still, if he was going to do weapons training he'd have to—Kerin had taken great delight in showing off the suit of armour he'd had specially made for Isak.

The Swordmaster had described it as the opposite of Siulents, a thick steel frame with each piece coated in lead to add to the already significant weight. The Krann's practice blade was to be a steel tube filled with lead. The idea was that the weight would slow the boy down so he would have to pay more attention to his technique. Kerin was still unimpressed at being bested on Isak's first day; he was looking forward to a little friendly revenge.

As Carel chuckled to himself at the image of Isak in a lead suit, Tila broke her silence. "Count Vesna, how is it that you call your master Isak, and yet he still uses your surname?"

Vesna dropped his gaze in embarrassment, his veneer of charm suddenly stripped away. "I, ah . . . well, to be honest, Lord Isak has yet to think of it. He has only one name, and it is good enough for him, so he thinks it is good enough for everyone."

"But you do have a name?" A nasty grin crept over Tila's normally gentle features; she was sensing a weakness in the famous Count Vesna's glamour.

"I do, but I do not use it—"

"You will tell me," Tila insisted to the squirming warrior.

"I—"

"Otherwise I shall feel honour-bound to put the idea in Isak's head, perhaps during the banquet tonight—"

"No! No need for that, Lady Tila. I will be glad to tell you." He paused and took a deep breath. "My name is Evanelial, Evanelial Vesna." He watched Tila glumly as she burst into sudden laughter.

"You mean as in the story?" Tila began to laugh again, her usual calm deserting her as she tried to smother her giggles in her voluminous sleeve.

"The very same. The story was written for my grandmother, but according to my parents, it used to be a man's name."

"Oh yes, very masculine—oh dear, look at me," exclaimed Tila, suddenly aware that the eyes of the entire room were on her. "I'm sorry, I shouldn't laugh, but with your reputation? Every boy in the tribe wants to grow up to be you, to be the consummate brave knight, the dashing rogue . . ."

"I know. And that's precisely why I don't tell people my first name—though most of them wouldn't admit to recognising it."

The count's pleading tone got through and Tila began to feel quite sorry for him. She had two brothers and knew how cruel boys could be to their friends. The martial life was not a forgiving one, and even less so for those who shone brightest.

"You're right, I apologise. I shall not say a word. Please forgive me for laughing." There was a smile on her face still, and Vesna nodded eagerly.

"Forgiven, Lady Tila, if you in turn will forgive me my reputation."

The smile faded from Tila's face, but she could see nothing to provoke her earlier dislike. She inclined her head regally and stood. "Perhaps I should not listen to tales. You appear loyal to Isak, so I shall not judge you yet. In the meantime, I believe I should be showing you to the barracks."

She felt a pang of guilt towards Isak for being so friendly, but only for a moment—when Isak had greeted her earlier, she had seen great affection in his eyes, but nothing more. She wasn't quite sure how she felt, but if there had been something there, it had already faded for Isak. At some point they would have to talk alone, but there was no rush. She smiled wryly: Lord Bahl would be pleased.

They said their farewells to the veteran Ghost, then Count Vesna, bowing slightly, ushered her out of the room with all the grace of a practised courtier. Carel watched them go out side by side: at that moment he felt very old, so out of touch. That thought stirred him into action and he got up to go in search of Chief Steward Lesarl's offices. Surely there was something even an old man could do.

The guardsman on the door outside Bahl's study nodded to Isak and eased the door open. The old Lord had removed his hood and Isak could see the concern etched onto Bahl's face. The light from the stained-glass windows was weak, and a number of huge candles were already alight, their flames casting strange shadows on Bahl's furrowed brow as he sat at his desk.

"You're glad to have your friend in the palace?"

Isak smiled inwardly. Bahl was not one for small talk, but Isak hadn't been the only one to notice that he was making an effort—a minor thing, but it made him less remote. The people of Tirah had all heard the last joke Bahl had made at his Krann's expense, and that had helped dispel some of their fear.

"I have more friends here than I've ever had in my life, but it's good to see Carel again," he agreed.

"He was a Ghost, was he not? Well, he may be more use than just as a friend."

Isak tried to stop his Lord: "I don't want to have to ask that of him. He retired to a quieter life for a reason. I don't want to be ordering him to kill, or to spy for me."

"I understand, but never forget that he was a Ghost. I hear he thinks of you as a son."

Obviously Lesarl would report on every new face, but it still rankled that Carel—*his* friend—had come under the Chief Steward's scrutiny. He didn't say anything, but dipped his head slightly in acknowledgement.

"I suspect he'll demand to be involved soon enough," Bahl continued, then changed the subject as swiftly as always. "You know Count Vilan is in the palace to see his old friend, Sir Cerse?"

"I do, but I've told Vesna to be patient about getting court apartments," said Isak firmly. "I'll deal with Vilan soon enough."

"Good. If you need a man to do it—or woman, he has several quite capable—then ask Lesarl. I know you don't like him, but you don't want blood staining your livery."

"I'll be careful. Was that what you wanted to see me about?" He was puzzled that Bahl would bother summoning his Krann for something they'd already discussed.

"No. There are two other things. Firstly, I have decided you should leave Tirah."

"Leave?" spluttered Isak, incredulously. "But I've only just returned! Why would I want to leave?"

Bahl held up a hand to silence Isak's protest. "You will hear me out first. I will not force you to go, but I believe it is for the best."

"Was this Lesarl's idea?" snapped Isak, unable to keep quiet.

"I said *listen!*" bellowed Bahl, half rising from his seat. His great hands gripped the mahogany desk as he leaned forward into Isak's face, the curl of a snarl appearing from nowhere. Isak matched it, rising himself. The shadows darkened in the room and the copper tang of magic suddenly filled the air as Bahl's anger flared. Isak's mirrored it, his eyes blazing, but before anything more could happen he felt a near-irresistible demand from Eolis. His hand twitched down of its own accord before he snatched it back in horror.

The shock restored his senses and he leaned heavily on the desk as the strength fled from his body, hardly aware that White Lightning was now nestled in Bahl's grip. The old Lord narrowed his eyes. He had expected an attack, but Isak was so stunned by the power of what had just happened that a breeze could have toppled him.

Isak looked up, slowly recognising Bahl's own readiness; his great blade was swept back and ready to strike. The younger man dropped to one knee, realising how close they had come to blows for no reason other than his own impatience. There was real contrition when at last he found his voice. "My Lord, forgive me. I—I don't know what came over me."

Isak slowly unbuckled his bleached leather sword belt, a gift from the new Suzerain Fordan, and let it drop to the floor. Only then did he dare lift his head.

Bahl hesitated, wary of a ruse; it was a moment or two before centuries of instinct let him relax again.

Only then did Isak stand and retrieve his chair, waiting for Bahl's consent before sitting again.

"That's one reason why you should leave for a while. We've had enough of each other's company for a while. Also, with this Shalstik matter, I think it is safe to say they could try again. I want you to go west, to Narkang. It'll be a long way for trouble to follow unnoticed, and that aside, King Emin would be a good ally."

Isak considered Bahl's words. He knew a little about Narkang, the emerging kingdom in the west, where all of the cities were populated by people of mixed blood, not pure-bred members of any of the Seven Tribes. The tribes had always looked down on half-breeds, but King Emin had created a nation to rival them all.

"Emin Thonal took the crown at the age of twenty-one, and three years later he conquered Aroth, the larger of his neighbours," Lord Bahl said. "Two years after that the renowned warriors of Canar Fell surrendered on the field rather than face utter destruction, and five years on, Canar Thrit bowed to economic pressure and voted to join Thonal's kingdom. In the space of twenty years, Narkang has grown into one of the largest and most prosperous cities in the entire Land.

"King Emin could be a valuable ally. Our man there is sure that the king has halted his expansion and there is room now for friendship. He could be vital if there's more trouble on the horizon, and you'll find more to learn about court politics in Narkang than even Lesarl could teach you here."

"I will do as you command," said Isak quietly, bowing his head again.

"I don't want you to do as I command," Bahl replied, softening his voice a little. "I want you to understand why this is a good idea. We've spent too long together on the journey back; I do not wish to let bad blood come between us. You're still young and hotheaded, I am perhaps rather set in my ways."

Isak kept his eyes on the floor to hide his smile in case the old Lord had missed the humour in his words. The Krann knew he was rash, but Bahl's temper was at least as much of a danger to those around.

"Then I do agree, my Lord. I have no wish to be a prisoner in the palace, constantly on my guard for the next Estashanti assassin. And who could turn down the chance to visit Narkang?" He forced a smile to diffuse the last of the tension.

"Good. We will discuss this again later, but there is a rather more pressing matter, one that will, to a degree, explain your short temper. Tell me, do you feel anything different? Anything out of place?"

Isak shot his master a questioning look, unsure what Bahl was expecting from him. The Lord sighed.

"No matter, I was not sure whether you would be able to actually tell, but I think it is affecting you anyway. You'll no doubt recognise it in future, once you've felt his presence more strongly."

Isak's face remained blank. Bahl stood and spread his hands in exasperation. "We have a visitor. I only noticed him once we had driven the elves out, but now he's in the city and about to arrive at our gate. Pick up your sword and come with me to greet him. Just keep your temper in check. He isn't as forgiving as some."

Isak looked for a name, but was ignored as Bahl walked around him, a slight smile twisting his mouth, and opened the door. The main wing of the palace was four storeys high, with a warren of cellars extending beneath. Bahl's chambers, which occupied much of the small top floor, had a balcony running around them to give a view of the city over the peaked roof of the Great Hall. The palace was rather more functional than the name suggested, lacking the decoration that characterised the homes of the richest noblemen in the city. Only small things, like the number of glass panes, belied Tirah Palace's martial image.

Both men wore soft leather boots; despite their size, they padded down the main staircase as stealthily as panthers, shocking the soldier and maid who were chatting conspiratorially at the bottom. Both jumped when Isak cleared his throat just behind them, bowing as Isak smirked, then moving swiftly out of the way as Bahl strode past imperiously.

In the Great Hall the two white-eyes drew curious glances, but those were cut off when the warning horn sounded through the clear winter air. Men jumped to their feet, bowls, glasses and goblets, and cutlery flying in all directions as they scrabbled for their weapons. A pair of guardsmen had been just entering when the horn rang—by the time the louder steel clang of the attack alarm followed, they were ready, their weapons drawn.

Bahl, a vision of calm, walked through the open door, Isak still close behind him. The stone steps that led to the training ground were icy and treacherous, but he trotted briskly down and made his way straight to the barbican. Isak noticed a bright light flaring from the normally murky depths of the tunnel.

As he hurried to keep up with Bahl, a wave of awareness broke over him and rocked him on his heels. He could feel a burst of magic echo out, an alien feeling that set every nerve screaming danger. His hand flew to Eolis so quickly that the Ghosts scrambling past leapt back in surprise.

He had half drawn the blade when he realised that the old Lord was still quite unconcerned. No doubt he could feel the same, but he appeared not to mind. Ramming Eolis back into its sheath, Isak broke into a jog and caught up. Now he recognised the difference that Bahl had mentioned, the feeling of something that was out of place.

As they entered the tunnel, they saw six men with weapons drawn, frozen into silhouette by a gigantic figure. A deep bellow of laughter echoed towards them while massive flames danced from the outstretched hands of the monstrous visitor. Isak felt Bahl draw magic into himself and followed suit, fighting the urge to tear Eolis out and charge straight in.

As he closed, Isak took a better look at the newcomer, and realised with a gasp that it was a Chetse white-eye, a huge man whose barrel chest almost surpassed description. The Chetse was shorter than Isak, only a hand taller than the guards levelling drawn bows at him, but lack of height did not detract from his unbelievable size.

All Chetse were muscular compared to the Farlan, and this man could have been a caricature if it hadn't been for the aura of raw, limitless strength that surrounded him. He was cackling with sheer pleasure as the leaping slices of fire raced up to the roof and played in loops about his arms.

"Lord Bahl," boomed the man as he saw the pair approaching. The Ghosts almost sagged in relief as Bahl motioned for them to lower their weapons.

"Lord Chalat, welcome to my palace," replied Bahl warmly as the Chetse released the magic. "May I present to you my Krann? Lord Isak—Lord Chalat, Chosen of Tsatach."

Isak bowed awkwardly, his obvious discomfort merely widening the Chetse's grin. Bahl then cocked his head to one side and Isak tore his gaze away from the white-eye, finally noticing the curious sight beside the Chetse: pinned up against a wall was a fully armoured guardsman, his weapons on the floor at his feet. The foot of some small foreigner was planted firmly on his throat. The little man held a steel-tipped quarterstaff ready and showed no sign of putting up the weapon. Looking over to the other Ghosts, Isak saw one was sheepishly wiping blood from his mouth and another looked less than steady, his helm knocked askew.

"And your companion?" continued Bahl after a pause. "And why is he trying to kill one of my guards?"

Under that gaze, the small man bent his leg at the knee, keeping his stance for a moment before lowering his leg. He stepped back, adopting a rather less aggressive pose, but still impressively proud in the face of a white-eye almost two feet taller.

"Ah, now there's a man with a story," replied Chalat in heavily accented Farlan, his good humour undiminished. "Offer us food and drink and we'll tell you all."

CHAPTER 21

"**A**ND THERE YOU HAVE IT," declared Chalat, ending his story with a flourish. The enormous man sat back in his chair, hurriedly fetched from an upper chamber, and took a last bite at the leg of lamb in his hand, then tossed it over his shoulder with a satisfied air. The bone slapped on the wall behind, falling to the ground where a hound fell upon it. The sound of the dog's teeth on the bone was the only thing to break the silence as the small audience considered Chalat's words.

The eight men sat around a circular meeting table in the chamber at the base of the Tower of Semar. Bahl had limited the attendees to his closest aides, Kerin, Lesarl, and Lahk, but Isak had brought Vesna with him—it would probably give rise to complaints by the other nobles in the palace, but Bahl had pointedly ignored the count's inclusion. Vesna had mentioned in passing a debt and some sort of assistance given to him by Lesarl. Clearly the count owed a favour, and Bahl was happy for him to be attached to Isak.

As for Carel, Isak decided to have a long talk with the old man before dragging him into the Land's politics.

"Mihn," Isak said suddenly. The Chetse's companion intrigued him. The man's manner was so quiet and calm; it spoke of great confidence in his own abilities. "Lord Chalat said you were from the clans on the north coast." Mihn inclined his head.

"In that case, how is it you speak Farlan so well?" Isak was determined to get more than a nod from the man. There was something about Mihn's speech that nagged, something Isak couldn't quite place yet.

"All the clans speak Farlan," Mihn said, almost doubling the number of words he'd uttered since his arrival.

"But why? You must be too far away to have any contact with us."

"Farlan is the root of our language, and with the Great Forest a week's ride away we have to keep close ties to the other clans," the man said.

"All the Land's languages come from the same source," interjected Lesarl contemplatively. "Since Mihn speaks Chetse too, I'm sure we would not be surprised at how quickly he could pick up others."

Mihn's face was full of suspicion; the Chief Steward was watching him carefully, scarcely even blinking. Isak knew Lesarl was distrustful of everyone, but this time he agreed—and suddenly he knew the answer . . . but it gave rise to yet more questions.

Perhaps the nobles hadn't noticed, but even after six months, Isak still found their words overly pronounced: Mihn spoke like a nobleman. His cadences and rounded syllables were too cultured for any barbarian clansman. He certainly wasn't Farlan, but he was more than he let on.

"My Lord," said Kerin, breaking the thoughtful silence hanging over the table, "this daemon-arrow sounds like powerful necromancy to me—but Malich must surely have been dead too long to set this in motion. I was under the impression that Malich's skill was an extremely rare thing. So that makes me think this was done by an acolyte, or he's returned from the grave somehow."

"I would be surprised if he had," Bahl said. "Denying death is more difficult than animating corpses or incarnating daemons. From what I know of raising the dead, I think we disposed of the body well enough for that to be an option." There was a hint of a smile on his face. Isak remembered the sight of Genedel gulping down corpses on the battlefield and shared the old Lord's smile.

"Well then, either way we have a problem," continued Vesna. "Either Malich had an acolyte strong enough to cast this himself, which surely we'd have realised, or—"

"Or this has nothing to do with him," finished Kerin.

"I agree." General Lahk looked extremely uncomfortable as all eyes turned towards him. He kept his distance from Isak and Bahl whenever possible. Sharing a room with three white-eyes, each vastly stronger than he, was not a comfortable situation.

"This weakens your army considerably, Lord Chalat. Charr is still young for a Krann, and from what we hear, lacking much intelligence at the best of times. That's how the elf was able to draw him out in the first place. I doubt a possessing daemon would have any more understanding of how to lead an army."

"Siblis?" barked Chalat. Isak felt a wave of anger radiate out from the Chetse Lord as he spoke the word.

"We know they have sent parties north to search for weapons. Perhaps they found allies instead. The elves could have created the weapon they needed. To kill you, Lord Chalat, would have been incredibly difficult, and hardly enough to win the war, since your generals are still there. But to control the commander and direct the war from both sides . . ." The general's voice trailed off, leaving the conclusions to be imagined.

Chalat clenched his fist furiously, the slabs of muscle in his arms showing a tracery of angry veins. By contrast, Bahl, resting his elbows on the table, was vaguely glum, lost in thought.

"Your point is a good one, Lahk," Bahl said after a grim pause. "I cannot think of a more likely reason. It makes me wonder what else the Siblis might have bargained for, and what price was asked in return."

"Well, such things are beyond me. Charms, curses, enchantments, bugger them all. That's not how I've fought my wars," Chalat growled loudly.

"But it seems you need a change of tactics." Lesarl ignored the scowl he received. "I know the man you should speak to."

"Well, who is he?" snapped Chalat. "Where is he? At your College of Magic?"

Lesarl smiled briefly. "Unfortunately not, though I'm sure the Archmage will be more than willing to help you in whatever way he can—if you can manage to look less like a white-eye, because he rather despises your kind."

Isak expected a bellow at that, but Chalat merely smiled. The white-eyes who reigned for a long time were obviously the ones who could control themselves.

"The true expert is rather closer to his subject matter. Invriss Fordal has been the authority on elven magic for decades now. I'm afraid he is considered rather eccentric, being one of the few who actually engages in expeditions into the Great Forest, but he is certainly the man to assist you. I'm sure the Duke of Lomin will be delighted to have you as his guest for as long as necessary."

"Lomin. So if I were to grow bored and need something to kill—"

"Then the Forest is sufficiently close, and I hear the Festival of Swords has been rather a dull event of late."

"Hah. Still, I hear the Duke is a good man, at least—"

"Ah." Lesarl's smile didn't waver for a moment. "There I'm afraid we have bad news."

Chalat snorted, he knew Lesarl's reputation as well as any Farlan. Turning to Bahl he found only a smile. The Chetse Lord threw up his hands in amused exasperation.

"Very well, no doubt you'll have a favour to ask of me, something small, very little effort . . . Just don't blame me if I end up giving the new duke a sound thrashing. I get bad-tempered when it's raining, and it always bloody rains here."

Lesarl was unable to prevent a look of delight spreading across his face. "Lord Chalat, I'm sure it would not even be mentioned."

Bahl rose. "Lesarl, arrange quarters for Lord Chalat; I'm sure Tirah can provide some entertainment for him so see to whatever he wishes. Isak, you have your own preparations to make. Take as many guardsmen as you need to carry your maid's wardrobe. Lesarl tells me that new chargers will arrive within the week. Until then I believe Kerin has some plans for you."

The room rose as one, Mihn placing himself in Chalat's shadow as the Lord was led off. Chalat saw him do so and stopped suddenly, turning sharply to Bahl once again. "I do have a request, Lord Bahl."

Bahl raised an eyebrow.

"Mihn has some strange sense of honour; he insisted on becoming my bondsman. I'm too old for some pious shit trailing me around, but as your guards can testify, it would be a waste just to kill him."

"What is the bond for? Luring Charr out?" Bahl glanced towards Isak. From what he had seen in the tunnel, Bahl had not expected Mihn to be the quiet unassuming figure he'd appeared as so far. What had been clear was that Mihn carried himself with enormous grace, even more so than Count Vesna who'd been trained as a duellist since he could hold a weapon.

"Exactly—not as if I liked the bastard anyway. But Mihn doesn't think my opinion is important. I do know that he's got some future to play out, though, and that it's not with me."

"Well, we can hardly have a guest inconvenienced. I suggest the bond be transferred to my Krann." He turned to Mihn. "Your language skills could be valuable on his journey."

He paused to allow the man to speak, but Mihn merely bowed his head in acceptance. He hardly seemed to care, which made Bahl curious. He'd have to ask Isak to learn what he could of Mihn's story before they went—only then did it occur to him to ask Isak whether he objected, but a look over the table brought a shrug of acceptance. Isak was about to speak to his new bondsman when Kerin appeared at his side. Rubbing his hands together in affected anticipation, the Swordmaster clapped them down on Isak's huge shoulders.

"Right, my Lord Krann, I have a new training régime for you. You'll be glad to hear I've had a pipe filled with lead for your sword, and a suit of armour commissioned specially for you. You're going to love it."

Isak groaned and sank back down into his chair. Kerin laughed and gave the chair leg an ineffectual kick. "Come on, boy, I'm your Lord for the next week, so jump to it."

CHAPTER 22

A BRIGHT BLANKET OF CLOUD HUNG OVER THE CITY, somewhat lessening winter's sharp touch on the still air. Isak could hear the city beyond the walls as people took advantage of a lull in the bitter weather. Covered bridges and walkways kept the city alive in the depth of winter. Though there was little fresh food to be found on the stalls, the cold stores beneath the city meant the handful of enclosed markets still did a brisk trade. The crisp afternoon light would not last long and then the city would return to hibernation.

Isak, sprawled on the stone stairs, let his practice blade clatter onto the bottom step and stared longingly over at Eolis. The weapon hung in its scabbard from a post nearby. Isak knew he was safe, but he just couldn't shake the need to have the sword at hand. His feelings were rather more ambiguous about his armour, left under guard in the Duke's Chapel. Siulents reeked of the last king, both his sorcery and his mind, and since the battle Isak had never quite been comfortable in it. Eolis was different: the sword was an extension of his body, the edge to his anger more than its instrument.

As the Krann sat panting, a group of guardsmen nursed their bruises and laughed with Kerin. The Swordmaster leant on a blunt-tipped spear and tugged a fleece around his shoulder. The rest, Ghosts in full plate armour, removed their peaked steel helms as they also caught their breath. The winter air ached in their lungs, but it was worthwhile for the beating they'd given Isak. Most had fresh dents in their armour, but Isak had definitely come off worst, and they'd all enjoyed themselves immensely.

"So, my Lord, you're finally learning some balance," commented Vesna from the sidelines. The count had refrained from taking part, but a pair of fencing blades dangled from his fingers for when Isak was exhausted.

Vesna looked at Mihn, standing firmly between Eolis and the rest of the world, who inclined his head in agreement. The small man had interrupted the exercise twice to correct Isak's movements. Vesna was beginning to wonder what the others of Charr's "bait" had been like. Each correction had presented Isak with the best range of available strokes—but as far as Vesna knew, Mihn had used no weapon but his staff . . .

Before he could pursue the thought, Tila trotted down the stairs, giving Vesna a courteous nod before crouching next to Isak and quietly asking, "Did you hear what happened last night?"

"You mean Count Vilan? A terrible shame that," Isak replied in a lazy drawl, leaning back against the stone steps. His chest seemed to heave up even further as his breastplate was pushed up by the angle of the steps. Grunting slightly, Isak raised himself up and shifted it into a more comfortable position.

"How can you be so uncaring about it? A man died last night, on these very steps."

"I know, but it was hardly surprising. He had been drinking heavily, and these steps are icy even during the day now."

Tila narrowed her eyes. "Is that all that happened then? You're acting very strange; was this something of Lesarl's doing? Oh Gods—"

"Hush," urged Isak. "This isn't something to be gossiping about, unless you want to help matters by encouraging the maids to gossip about how much Vilan drank last night. Let's just say this accident was convenient, but there must be no talk that it was anything but an accident."

Tila's eyes widened for a moment. This was as close as she'd ever been to the blunt end of politics. Looking down at the steps she was standing on, she pulled her cloak tight about her body and checked the soldiers, but none were close enough to hear. "Do you know why?"

"The count was a traitor," Isak replied simply. "A legacy of the Malich affair."

"But then why not arrest him? There was no call to murder someone, and to push him down these stairs? If he'd survived Vilan could have had the man prosecuted for attempted murder—that would bring the whole scandal down onto Lord Bahl."

"I know. That's why I broke the bastard's neck before he fell."

Tila's hand flew to her mouth. A tiny sound escaped her lips, the careless way Isak had said it shocking her as much as the admission itself. Isak sat up, hurriedly reaching for her arm, but she slapped him away. She swallowed and took a deep breath, trying to force the bile in her throat back down. She held up her hand to stop the Krann from speaking further.

"Vesna," said Isak over his shoulder. "Take Tila in, explain to her."

Revulsion flooded her face and Isak felt a sudden pang of guilt. The count nodded to Isak and took Tila gently by the elbow, but she pushed

Vesna away, muttering curtly that she could manage, and turned her back on the pair of them. The door slammed behind her. Isak's eyes stayed on the quivering oak for a moment and then he looked up at Vesna. The count shook his head and turned back down to the training field.

"She'll get over it—she's a delicate girl, that's all. Killing isn't a way of life for her; even soldiers tend to have an opinion on murder."

"But—"

Vesna held up a hand and Isak let the sentence die unsaid. "You two are close; she forgets, as I do, that you are a white-eye. It's hard to remember that you're different, and hard not to judge. Give her time to be angry, then I'll go and speak to her. She'll remember that she loves you by this evening."

"Loves me?" The remark caught Isak by surprise, but Vesna only chuckled.

"Of course, my Lord, but only as a brother. I suspect you love her like a sister, you've just never known the feeling enough to give it a name. Certainly I hope—" It was Vesna's turn to flounder now, blanching as he realised he could have been dangerously wrong. To his intense relief, he hadn't.

"Don't worry," Isak said, "I've seen you two together. It's actually a relief—one less concern in my life."

"One less concern?" Vesna could not hide his incredulity, but Isak merely smiled and wagged a finger in admonishment.

"Now you're forgetting I'm a white-eye again. Think about it, my faithful bondsman: in less than a year my life has changed beyond recognition. The Gods only know how many people are actually *planning* to kill me, let alone those who would *like* to. Not even the greatest wizards pretend to fully understand the gifts I've been given. I murdered a man last night for a cause I have only a vague grasp of, without seeing actual proof. Trying to understand my feelings, or Tila's, would just . . ." Clearly Vesna understood, so he left the sentence unfinished.

"But are you not disappointed that—" Vesna looked up to the sky, wondering how to phrase it without sounding condescending.

"Perhaps a little, but lacking something I've never known? I don't think white-eyes are made for regrets. Anyway, enough of this. How are the preparations for our little jaunt to Narkang going?"

"Well enough, though of course there's been no time for the messenger to even get to King Emin. We'll be off within the week, I think. Two horses arrived this morning from Siul, fine beasts, both of them, or so the stablemaster tells me—the best he's seen in years, he claims. We'll go and see them once we're finished here. I've picked the escort, Tila's chaperone has presented her requirements—"

"Chaperone?"

Vesna laughed. "Oh yes. You forget that Tila's father is an important man in the city. For her to travel to foreign parts in the company of soldiers . . . well, her mother is less than impressed, but I've informed Lady Introl that it is your specific command. I think she was mollified somewhat when I mentioned that Tila would be your political advisor in all negotiations with the Kingdom of Narkang and the Three Cities."

"But is the chaperone to ward off the attentions of the uncivilised white-eye, or the notorious Count Vesna?" Isak smiled and sat up, tugging at the lead-coated armour with a slight groan. "So how many are we going to be?"

"Well, an escort of thirty soldiers and two rangers to scout for us, you, me, Mihn, Lady Tila and the battle-axe who's going to carry Tila's makeup, and Carel. Thirty-eight in total."

Isak lifted the shoulder plates over his head and tossed them to the ground. "That's too many—we'll be too slow."

"Our speed will be dictated by Tila's chaperone and the availability of riverships, not numbers. She's the wrong side of forty summers, and I doubt she's much of a horsewoman."

"Then I'll leave her behind," declared Isak. "She'll ride well enough when she sees us disappear over the horizon."

"My Lord, some day we really must teach you about diplomacy," Vesna drawled, an amused smile on his lips.

Isak made a face. "Lesarl told me about it—don't think I want to associate with that sort of thing."

"Ah. Like 'tact' and 'manners,' is it?"

Isak beamed. "Exactly. Now, how long is it going to take us to get to Narkang?"

Vesna sat down a few steps up from his Lord so they could speak on the same level. Mihn came and stood at the foot of the stairs, his body angled slightly towards the training ground, close enough to be part of the conversation while still on silent guard. Mihn was obviously not simple-minded, but he was certainly monosyllabic.

"With luck, less than a month. There are several stages we're planning to do by river—one will take us to Nerlos Fortress, on the border, another should cover much of the Tor Milist territory we'll have to pass through, and I believe a third could take us much of the last stretch to Narkang itself—

but only a few vessels are large enough to carry so many horses, so we'll have to throw money at the captains."

"Less than a month?" Isak was pleased. "Hardly any time at all—by wagon it would take the best part of half a year, I guess. I've never met anyone who's done that route, but that's one of the reasons we're going, I suppose. Lesarl is going to brief us on everything tonight, including the disputed lands we'll have to travel through, but Bahl thinks that my gifts will dissuade attack rather than encourage it."

"The Lord's right. I doubt any of them have the numbers to trouble us. The Ghosts have a fearsome reputation, and there'll be little more than brigands where we're going. Alone, we'd see off double our number of horsemen, more of foot soldiers; with your growing skills and magic, I can't see anyone putting enough men together to get anywhere."

They were interrupted by the door behind them slamming open and the three men turned to see Carel making his way down the worn steps. "Isak, there's a seamstress looking for you," he called.

It looked like Carel had just come from seeing a tailor himself. He wore a long elegant coat the colour of fresh grass, trimmed in sable, with gold-chased ivory buttons. Only the white clay pipe in his hands harked back to former days, but even that was new.

"What's this?" cried Vesna. "Don't tell me we might get our master to look rather more like a nobleman of some substance?" It was a source of constant amusement to the count that Isak had chosen to dress like the hermit lord they served.

Isak made an obscene gesture as he replied, "I didn't summon one, what does she want?"

"I believe she was summoned for you—by Tila, I assume." He pointed with his pipe to the soldiers Isak had been training with. "She had some maids with her, all carrying bundles; I think they're uniforms for your guards."

"Uniforms?"

"Of course. We can't have them in their usual colours when you meet King Emin." As Carel spoke the door opened again and a flurry of white linen burst through, talking rapidly before the door had even fully opened. The men backed off in the face of such bright and busy determination.

"My Lord Isak, at last I've found you. Now, these are not entirely completed and we have the riding garments coming later, but I have the armour drapes for your men. If you could ask them to form up here, I'll start my measurements."

Isak stood there bemused for a moment, staring down at the ruddy face wrapped in a spotless white headscarf. The seamstress might have been dressed like a servant, but she had the poise of a duchess. Despite Isak's huge height, he found himself wilting under the sheer force of that impatient stare. Behind her stood five maids, each with a wicker basket clasped tightly to her chest and eyes fixed firmly on the woman at her head.

"Who are you?" he wondered aloud in amazement. Vesna had an equally bewildered expression on his face, while Carel smiled approvingly at the lack of fawning usually so prevalent among the servants. Only Mihn matched her gaze with an impassive stare, his eyes running coolly over the woman and her attendants.

"I, my Lord? I'm the head seamstress. I was instructed that your men would require a uniform to match your crest and colours. We've done most of the work, but we now need to take measurements. If it would be convenient, my Lord." Her tone indicated that if it were not convenient, she would want to know why.

Isak asked Vesna, suppressing a laugh as he saw the count's expression, "Well, Count, if it would not inconvenience you too greatly?" As he spoke, he saw the soldiers had formed up in two ranks—as always, it looked like the entire palace knew about his plans before he did. Kerin had drifted away, presumably to fetch the others, while those who had been giving Isak a beating began to strip off their armour.

The maids fanned out among them, ignoring the comments they got from the soldiers as they helped them undress. From the baskets the girls produced cream leather tunics and breeches, decorated with green braiding. Isak's dragon, outlined in green and flecked with gold, was emblazoned across the chest and shoulders. The dragon itself was an altogether more impressive sight than the austere black and white of the Ghosts. Isak couldn't imagine the full two legions of the Palace Guard wearing this, but it still affected him to see his personal guards so richly dressed.

The others trotted along now, faces Isak recognised for the main part as the men who'd been attending his rooms or eating with Carel. Clearly the veteran and Kerin had handpicked the thirty who were now his guard, split evenly between hardened veterans and the best of the younger Ghosts. The unit looked tight and confident, apparently delighted at their appointment as they joked with each other and held up their new uniforms to show other Ghosts who'd begun to drift over. Isak felt unaccountably awkward as he saw men discard Bahl's livery.

He rose and pulled off the sweat-soaked tunic he'd been wearing underneath his armour. His bruised body complained at the movement and the chill air rushed over his skin, prickling up the fine hairs and dancing down his spine. A thick woollen shirt sat rolled up at the foot of the steps. Hurriedly he slipped the dark blue material over his head, tugging it down as fast as he could. The cold didn't upset him, but showing his torso just highlighted how different Isak was to the other soldiers there. Isak's muscles were so sculpted it was obvious that the Chosen were not just human. He was careful to hide the scar on his chest, but still there were a few stares. People who'd grown used to his size were still taken aback by the sharp lines of his body.

Isak was now the best part of a foot taller than most of his guards, and more than double their weight. He could only guess at the difference in strength, but even thinking about it worried him. He was used to being different, but living with such strength in his body unsettled him as much as it elated him. It was so easy to forget how much more powerful he was—he had once, and he still didn't trust himself not to do so again.

He straightened the shirt and took Eolis from Mihn, running a loving finger over the claws that imprisoned the emerald. Drawing the blade a few inches, he stared down at the surface, just able to make out the runes, faint and shifting, even under their master's gaze.

Snapping out of the trance, Isak looked over at the assembled guard, most now dressed in the new tunics and parading for admiring eyes while the maids tried to check the fit. It was a slight shock to see Carel among them, but the veteran's look of defiance told Isak that his opinion was not invited. Isak scowled at the Land in general and stalked over to the palace smithy, Mihn, at his heels. He could hear muted voices from inside, but they broke off when he gripped the door handle and opened it up.

He ducked through the doorway and stood inside, blinking as his eyes adjusted to the dim light. Three faces looked up at him, but with no words spoken, two rose and left. The third was the head smith, a taciturn man who tolerated the presence of few outsiders in his domain. The first time Isak had gone in, he'd received a glare that made nothing of his rank of suzerain, let alone Krann. After a minute of matching Isak's stare, the man had shrugged and gone about his work. Isak had watched, fascinated by how a hammer could be used in such a controlled way. On his third visit the Krann had taken up a hammer of his own and mirrored the strokes on the second anvil.

Now he crossed the forge and removed a block of black iron from the rack on the far wall. The smith watched him select one by stroking the small rectangular pieces until suddenly his hand paused over one. Those blocks were made of the finest steel, reforged by the College of Magic in some jealously guarded process. Each blank was waiting to be turned into a sword of black iron, so expensive to produce they were rarely done.

"Goin' to teach me somethen' new?"

As the confusion of his new life crowded in on Isak's mind, the simple, solid forge had increasingly become a sanctuary. There was no idle chatter, no swirl of politics here. The smith respected ability with a hammer and didn't give a damn about much else. He was happy to tolerate Isak's presence, though the young lord had yet to say a word to him. There'd not been any need—and the smith was a man of few words himself.

Isak didn't reply. His eyes were already lost in the black iron and the smith immediately gave up his place at the fire. There was purpose in those eyes. The smith recognised it and knew not to disturb Isak. He secretly hoped that Isak would forge with magic one day, something he'd dreamed about but never yet been permitted to witness.

The smith picked up the bellows and began to stoke the flames. Isak sat before the fire and waited, lost in the dancing surge of heat. The image of Carel beaming down at the dragon on his tunic loomed large. Isak knew that Carel still kept a Palace Guard tunic among his effects for the day he died. He couldn't imagine the man wearing any other. The arrogant dragon symbol had been fine until Carel put it on, but then it looked a sick joke, one that would come back to haunt him. Isak had been tempted to go and ask the Keymaster what he'd seen in his future, but something told him it would be futile.

A slight cough from the smith brought him back to reality. Taking the long steel tongs, Isak withdrew the glowing brick and held it before him. Looking deep into that bright burst of colour, his eyes began to water from the heat. As the image blurred he saw the shape this weapon should take: a slender, curved sabre with symbols he didn't recognise etched and inlaid with gold. The rounded pommel was to be carved with a hawk's head. The dusky steel would contrast with Carel's cream glove.

With a sigh, Isak nodded to himself and laid the metal down on the battered anvil. The first few strokes were hesitant, but he soon found his rhythm. The smith stood and watched the sparks fly, mesmerised by the sweet ring of the hammer. It was only when Isak stopped to return the metal to the fire that the smith realised his eyes had been closed after that rhythm had been reached. Though his bladder was pressing, the smith couldn't drag himself away. It was pitch black outside by the time he did leave, drained by the effort of watching. Isak didn't notice him go.

After the evening meal, Carel found himself a stool in the forge and puffed away on his pipe while Isak worked. The seamstress had been dealt with earlier, storming off in a huff when Isak refused to stop to be measured for his own uniform. Carel didn't disturb the boy, but Isak did acknowledge his presence. It was almost unbearably hot that close to the forge; Carel could see Isak's chapped lips underneath the glisten of sweat, but knew he'd not accept any water. Once the sword had gone back into the fire, Carel offered his pipe to Isak, who smiled to himself and accepted. He drew on it a few times, then pulled the sword out again and started hammering. As he did so, he puffed out the smoke from the pipe over the glowing surface and then struck it again, repeating the process until the tobacco was finished.

Carel had half risen from his seat to reclaim the pipe when Isak slipped it under the cooling metal and smashed the hammer down again, shattering the fired clay and sending pieces clattering out around the room. Carel opened his mouth to protest and then closed it again. Isak had clearly done that for a reason, just as there had to be sense in the way the boy had repeatedly gestured towards Carel as though he was wafting the scent of the sword towards him.

Abandoning the Krann to his labours, Carel went into the frosty night air, a heavy fur draped over his shoulders, and sat himself down on a rough wooden bench against the wall. It gave him a good view of the deserted training field, which glistened frostily in the moonlight.

Mihn's eyes swept over the veteran, then he returned to his own distant thoughts. The foreigner had left the door of the forge only to fetch a fur for himself once the cold night air started to bite. As a cloud covered the gibbous face of Alterr above, Carel fumbled through his pockets for his tobacco pouch, which also contained the scratched wooden pipe that had accompanied him on every campaign of his life. He filled and lit it before offering the pouch to Mihn.

"Come and sit down, man," he said, patting the bench. "Isak doesn't need a guard at this time of night."

Mihn stared suspiciously at both Carel and his offering, shaking his head to the pouch, but he did leave his post to cross the few yards to the bench. He made no noise as he walked, even across the iced grass. Carel was a Ghost; he had worked with the biggest and best of the Farlan, men who combined skill and grace with more deadly skills. Mihn was shorter than every soldier there, and slender too, but he stood out to the trained eye. The man reminded Carel of the black leopard he'd seen once in Duke Vrerr's menagerie in Tor Milist. The animal had hypnotised Carel: it moved with an almost supernatural elegance. A drunken soldier had got too close to the enclosure and in the blink of an eye the leopard's pose had changed from lethargy to lethal purpose.

"Have you been watching him?" asked Mihn suddenly, bringing Carel back to the present with a jerk.

"I—ah, yes. I don't know what he's doing now, but that'll be one fine weapon when he's finally satisfied. The shape's there already, but he keeps beating at it."

"Is he speaking?" There was a slight anxiety in Mihn's voice, but Carel saw nothing in his face.

"Nothing I could hear, but I saw his lips move from time to time. Why?"

"No matter. Is he going to engrave it too?"

"If you're so interested, what're you doing out here?"

Mihn ducked his head slightly and Carel immediately regretted his tone.

"Sorry, lad, my mind's still waking up. Feels like I've been in a trance while watching him. I think he's going to engrave it, yes. He's got some tools beside him—though I've never seen him do anything like it before."

"I doubt he has."

Carel drew deeply on his pipe. "Being as mysterious as ever tonight, I see. Care to tell me?"

The smaller man shook his head, blinking away the smoke.

"Then let me tell you something then," said the veteran, his voice a low growl. Mihn caught the tone immediately and sat stock-still, his body almost quivering with readiness. Had it been almost any other man, Carel would have grabbed him by the tunic, but the image of the leopard rose in his mind once more. The drunken soldier had died.

Mihn had already proven his skill publicly. A friend of one of the soldiers he had felled in the barbican tunnel tried to secure some measure of revenge. He was a hulking brute, but a skilled one. His wrist was so badly dislocated the surgeons at the College of Magic had to be called in to repair the damage. A rib, snapped under a well-placed knee, was still giving him trouble. Carel had seen that Mihn had the killing blow ready and waiting. Luckily, it had not been needed.

"Whatever penance you're doing, I don't care, see? I've smacked his arse and wiped his eyes; I've taught him when to fight and when to stand back. Even if you'd give your life for him, that's nothing big to me. If you know something, if you even suspect it, don't you dare hide it, not from me. In case your nose has been so far up his arse you haven't noticed, Isak's a white-eye. He's a stubborn and wilful shit for much of the time, but I love him like a son and I know his mind better than he does. He can protect himself from others, but he's no defence against himself."

Mihn stared into Carel's eyes and then, without warning, wilted. "I understand," he said quietly. "And I apologise. I held my tongue because there are those who expect great things, or fear them. I should trust you as he does."

"And so?" replied Carel, a little mollified.

"And so I believe he is beating magic into that sword. Whether he recognises it or not, Lord Isak seems to be something of a mage-smith."

"How can he not know it?"

"If he has the skill, it will come naturally—not the complex spells of Eolis, which would take weeks of preparation, but a white-eye's version. I've heard that mage-smiths go into a near-trance when they forge. I think Lord Isak is pouring raw magic into the blade to help it last, or be lighter to use. With a mind for forging, and his powers developing very recently, it's an unsurprising outcome, but—"

"But that's not what people are likely to think," breathed Carel. "They'll see the greatest mage-smith in history, practising his craft once more."

"Exactly. Does Lord Bahl have mages he can trust? Could we summon one to be here? It would be best if it were someone willing to take any credit if the sword does have any magic in it."

"I'm sure there will be. Go and wake Lesarl—he should be able to organise something like that."

As Mihn slipped off into the chill darkness, Carel turned back to the closed door of the forge. The memory of Isak labouring away, his eyes closed and a smile on his lips, confirmed Mihn's suspicions in his own mind.

"Ah, my boy, you'll be the death of me yet. I should be abed by now. Instead I'm playing nursemaid and waiting about in the dead of night for some fat mage." He chuckled to himself, pulling his fur tighter around him and taking slow puffs on his pipe until the night air grew too cold for him and he retreated inside the forge. Isak was as he had left him, but this time

Carel sat closer and paid greater attention. He still couldn't make out the words Isak was muttering over that blade, but they didn't sound Farlan.

When the old man did finally retire for the night, it was with worry etched into his brow.

CHAPTER 23

TWO DAYS LATER THEY WERE READY. The cold heart of winter seemed to have thawed for a moment, and a rare sparkle of sun had lit up the previous afternoon when Isak finally emerged from the forge, happily exhausted. Fetching a mage from the College of Magic had turned out to be a real blessing, for Chirialt Dermeness, a strong, fit man of forty summers, was an authority on magical forging.

The man was not what Isak had expected. Even the battle-mages tended towards the portly, but Dermeness had realised that to be a mage-smith meant first of all being a capable smith. He himself had beaten out every piece of Count Vesna's armour before engraving the necessary runes into its surface.

Mage Dermeness had, in a brief time, taught Isak much about the basics of the art. Isak had an image of the end result in his mind, and the mage had improved the reality. It had taken a full day of engraving, sharpening, sharpening again, and finally detailing with gold-leaf before the sword was ready. Then Isak had staggered away to sleep while Tila prepared his baggage and got everything ready to be off the next morning.

A bright, clear dawn found the Krann and his companions checking over their horses, waiting only for Bahl's signal to be off. Isak stood between his two chargers, comfortable there as they hid his size a little. The smaller, Megenn, was close to eighteen hands in height, the second, named Toramin after a famous Farlan warhorse, was a shade off nineteen. Horses this big were ruinously expensive animals, frequently produced just to demonstrate a breeder's skill. Crossing hunter stock with the largest breed of carthorse normally produced one viable charger in a dozen, but both of Isak's were a horseman's dream: incredibly powerful, and swift enough to keep up with hunters half their size.

Isak felt the eyes of the whole field on him, and the glare of Tila's chaperone most pointed among them. Resisting the temptation to pull on his hood, he busied himself with checking Toramin's saddle. He would have to get used to people staring; he'd endure far greater scrutiny than this in Narkang.

The crash of the doors to the Great Hall drew all heads as the Lord of the Farlan, hooded, but for once dressed in all his ducal finery, came through, Lesarl at his heels. Bahl's eagle was emblazoned in white on a deep-red tunic, the sleeves of which were slashed to reveal the white silk underneath. Silver embroidery and pearl detailing gave the richly coloured fabrics texture. No one had expected the normally sombrely clad white-eye to make such an effort.

"Sergeant Carelfolden," called the old Lord as he approached. The veteran stepped up, a quizzical look on his face. Isak was close behind. Bahl took in the crowd watching with an air of approval before his eyes settled on Carel.

"Lesarl reminds me that Narkang is a city of crass foreigners who respect only rank and wealth. You seem to have neither, so it would look strange for you to wear the same uniform as the guardsmen you command when you're old enough to have fathered most of them. It would be more fitting if your presence in Isak's party were justified by something more than the fact that you're the only one who can tell him when to shut up."

Carel smiled with the rest of the crowd. Bahl had been extremely impressed when, one evening in Isak's chamber, Carel had clipped the youth round the ear for a typically impious comment. The old Lord had been more impressed that Isak had accepted the chastisement without even a flicker of anger.

Later he'd told his Krann that his relationship with the old man was something to be cherished. Bahl had said nothing about the danger it posed; that they both recognised all too well.

"There's supposed to be some ceremony for this, but most of it is unnecessary. I know Isak is keen to be away. Betyn Carelfolden, please kneel."

Carel dropped to one knee immediately, his head bowed low, almost hiding the surprise on his face. Bahl reached to his hip and drew White Lightning. The massive broadsword looked a little incongruous next to the lush velvets and silks. He lifted the blade and laid it down on Carel's right shoulder. The veteran raised his eyes as the blade stayed there, instead of moving over to his other shoulder, as would happen with a knighthood. Less than a foot from his eye was one of the spikes that curved out from the wide base of the blade. It was hard to fight the prickle of nervousness as that lethal edge sat so close.

"I don't believe a mere knight should lead the Krann's personal guard. Anvee has few enough nobles at the moment, and more than sufficient land to grant, so I dub you Marshal Carelfolden and confer upon you the manor of Etinn, together with all its rights and revenues."

Carel gasped in surprise, as did the crowd looking on. There was a heartbeat of silence as the weight on his shoulder seemed to grow too heavy and he swayed forward. Then the sword was lifted and the dragon-liveried guardsmen cheered. Isak reached forward and took Carel by the arm, making a show of congratulating him as he helped him up.

"I—My Lord, I had not—" Carel stuttered. The estate of Etinn made him a wealthy man in his own right; it was the last thing he'd been expecting. "I thank you, my Lord. I shall try to be worthy of the honour."

Bahl nodded curtly, then turned to Isak. "Everything is in order?"

Isak nodded, his eyes darting down to the sword hanging loosely in Bahl's hand.

The Lord caught the movement and sheathed the weapon. Isak recognised the twitch on his close-fitting hood as a smile. Their friendship was not yet so close that either would be comfortable when, facing each other, one held a naked blade.

"I think so, though the preparations have all been made for me. Tila has the letters of introduction, Vesna and I carry the gold, in various currencies, gems, and promissory notes. Lesarl has fully briefed us on agreements and treaties, such as there are."

"Good. When you are in Narkang you will be extended as much credit as you require. Lesarl's great-grandfather spent many years restoring our treasury; the money is there to be spent if it secures us the links we need to Narkang. I care about two things: that you don't start a war, and that Narkang thinks of us as friends rather than arrogant neighbours. King Emin is too intelligent a man, and too powerful, for us to allow that view to continue." He kept his voice low so others would not hear the exchange.

Isak followed suit. "Understood. I believe Tila intends to teach me to be charming and witty, in anticipation of the hundreds of social events we'll be invited to."

Bahl gave a snort of amusement. Isak's vocal disregard of Tirah's high society showed little chance of Tila succeeding in that ambition. "If you come back charming and witty, I'll make her a duchess. If I hear that she's even managed to stop you from being directly offensive to those you dislike, I'll give her a state wedding here when she marries."

Isak glanced down at Count Vesna. "I think there might be a need for that sooner than her parents realise," he said with a smile.

"Really?" Bahl looked a little surprised; he hadn't realised the romance had progressed that far. "Then she'll deserve a title just for getting *him* under control, let alone you."

"He's smitten, so there's hope for both of them," Isak said fondly.

Bahl's eyes lingered on the two for a moment longer. "They have your blessing?"

"They do." Isak's smile showed that he was glad about it; he had not just accepted the situation. "Before, I had—well, this is the best way for all of us. The battle changed me, and we both realised it as soon as I returned here."

Bahl held up his hand. He knew well the lonely life of a white-eye, and he was glad that the friendships had survived. "Very well. Best be on your way now, for the days are short and you've a long way to travel."

He turned to his Chief Steward, who had stepped away to afford them some privacy. "Lesarl, give the gifts for King Emin to Count Vesna, if you would be so kind."

Isak cocked his head at the long wrapped bundle in Lesarl's hands. "What are they?" He could feel magic surrounding them, not as powerful as his own gifts, but far from insignificant.

"Snake jewels for the Queen of Narkang, and a book for the King. Our man there tells us that King Emin has a passion for history, particularly its darker side. A man I've known for many years, one who could have been High Cardinal, wrote this. Even today he's a force inside the cult of Nartis— you'd do well to meet him one day. I believe King Emin will find this account . . . diverting."

"That's not what I meant."

"Ah," Bahl smiled. "I'm glad to see your senses are improving. That was part of Atro's personal collection. It's no elven blade, but it is a fine weapon nonetheless, created by the mage Sorodoch. Have you heard of him?"

Isak shook his head.

"An interesting man, one of only a rare few Chetse mage-smiths. I assumed you would have read the histories of forging we have in the library. No matter; when you return. He was a talented smith who produced minor weapons, but they last well and are dependable. This is an axe, called Darklight in the Chetse dialect. It will make our friendship clear to King Emin, while not being powerful enough to put you in danger from him. I suggest you leave it alone, though. It might be little compared to Eolis, but we do get attached so easily."

Isak nodded. The stories about Atro were ample warning.

"Enough of this." Bahl held out an arm that Isak took willingly, gripping the man's wrist warmly as the old Lord clapped a fatherly hand onto his Krann's shoulder. "Return when you will. Best to winter in Narkang and set out again a year from now, I think. You know the kind of stories you might hear from home, so make it clear how long you intend to stay and show to the whole Land that we're united."

Isak held onto the man's arm a moment longer, acknowledging that he understood the trust Bahl was placing in him. With the clandestine campaign Bahl and his Chief Steward had already embarked upon, letting the Krann out of his sight showed a great degree of faith—the count had explained how easy it would be for Isak to start a civil war once free of the Lord's watchful gaze.

Isak saw a flicker of understanding in Bahl's eyes and smiled. "There is just one more thing," he said, and turned back to the newly made Marshal Carelfolden of Etinn. He beckoned to a page standing at the side, who brought over a curved sabre sheathed in a plain leather scabbard.

"Marshal," he said to Carel, taking the sword from its sheath and presenting it hilt-first, "it is only fitting that your new rank is marked with a new weapon." He grinned and said, so quietly that only Carel could hear, "And I tried to temper it the way you tempered me!"

The joke relieved the high tension and Carel smiled proudly as he accepted the sword, a misty shine like smoke wreathing the blade.

"Boy," he said softly, "this is the greater honour." Then, to the watching crowd, "I will wield it in your name, and the name of the Lord of the Farlan, and of our God Nartis." He bowed low and backed away, returning to Isak's waiting group.

Isak turned back to Bahl, relieved to see the old Lord's smile of approbation. They gripped wrists firmly one last time, then Isak bowed low and backed away.

The rest of his company did likewise, and then mounted at Isak's cue. They cut a fine sight, the colours of their new livery bright in the cloud-filtered sunlight. Isak stroked Toramin's mane, then raised his arm to signal the advance. He sat tall and proud, his white cape draped over his shoulders. Though the battle's mud and gore had been cleaned off long ago, this was the first time Isak had worn it since—he had insisted that the cloak be repaired instead of replaced, to remind him always of a creature that was little more than burning bloodlust made flesh.

He looked around at the smiling faces. Mihn rode just behind, his face as guarded as ever, but Isak had grown used to that. The man didn't seem to be brooding, but he was among strangers, and he knew well how much interest there was in him. The onlookers smiled as they waved last goodbyes, and the mood of optimism and cheer extended even to the horses as they pranced after Isak.

A ringing clatter echoed down the barbican tunnel and Isak drank in the sights and sounds he wouldn't experience for at least a year. The people of Tirah stepped back and watched, awestruck, as the splendid party cantered down Palace Way and struck out for the south. As they made their way through the ancient streets, each rider fixed the images of home firmly in his or her mind: the bridges and towers, the engraved stones that adorned all but the meanest of buildings, every reason for loving their city.

Within what felt a very short time, they had reached the outskirts, where long straight roads led off to distant lands. The peaks of the Spiderweb Mountains rose on both sides; ahead were river valleys and open fields. Isak smiled at the sight until he remembered what might be lurking in the shadows. They'd spent hours discussing each and every possible danger.

He sighed, and prayed for a dull journey, something he knew only too well from his previous life. These days, the prospect wasn't as dismal as it had been then, but he still couldn't bring himself to believe that it would be so easy this time.

The first day was easy enough. At times it felt more like a parade than the start of a long journey; they overnighted at a manor belonging to Suzerain Tebran, where they were treated like royalty. By noon of the second day they were still travelling at the same pace and Isak's patience was beginning to wear thin.

"It's slowing us down," he said, exasperated. "Did you really think you could get to Narkang like that? Do you realise how far it is?"

Tila regarded him with a cold eye, refusing to dignify that with an answer.

Isak struggled to control himself—it was as if the girl knew instinctively how to infuriate him.

"No matter how far it is, my Lord, she's an unmarried woman," snapped Tila's chaperone, a woman of fifty summers or so. She had introduced herself as Mistress Daran and given no first name, so, titled or not, Vesna and Carel had no choice but to address her as such, though it was a respect her station hardly afforded. Tila called her Nurse, and Isak was very proud of himself for managing not to say out loud the name he'd privately given her.

"She could be a sniping old harridan for all I care, as long as she uses a real bloody saddle." Isak's retort almost had the desired effect, but the women managed to hold back. They stood in a small circle, away from the soldiers, who were watching the entertainment with great amusement.

"Isak, *all* unmarried women ride sidesaddle," Tila repeated with exaggerated patience. "If you can't work out why, then I'm sure your bondsman will draw you a diagram. It's apparently something of a speciality of his."

The count's broad smile fell at this, but Carel chuckled softly. For her remark, Tila received a hurt look from Vesna and a slap on the wrist from Mistress Daran. She won back the first with a smile and ignored the second, planting her hands firmly on her hips as she squared up to Isak.

Isak shot a look of irritation at Carel, who ignored it and suggested, "perhaps you should use Tila's spare saddle as penance, my friend." The looks he received made him throw up his hands theatrically and stomp off to join his men, who were supposed to be changing horses and eating, but were more interested in the little drama playing out a few yards away.

"Tila, we need to move faster, or it will take a few months to get there. Even if you *could* manage the pace on that thing, you'd be hurting so badly we'd have to stop for you to recuperate," he said more calmly now.

"But there *is* no other choice," Tila explained again. "You seem to have forgotten that the only reason my parents allowed me to accompany you was because they think it will mean a better marriage for me afterwards. That'll be worthless if I'm damaged . . ." Her face was bright red and her voice trailed off. Did she have to draw the wretched man a picture?

"And you seem to have forgotten how long and hard this journey is going to be." Now Isak was beginning to lose his temper. "Even using a normal saddle, the first week will be hard enough. You'll be sleeping in a tent more often than not—"

"My Lady will stay in a proper bed in a good inn every night," Mistress Daran interjected.

Isak glared at the woman. He didn't like conversations with two people in the first place, whatever the subject, since he ended up not being able to concentrate on either. Mistress Daran was not as old as he had first assumed from her permanently sour expression, but she treated everyone—even Carel, a landed marshal, no less—like a foolish child.

"What my Lady requires is of little concern," Isak snapped. "We travel until *I* decide we should rest, and *if* there's an inn when we stop, then that's where we will stay, but once we're past Nerlos Fortress, there won't be many and not all towns are going to welcome a party of armed men."

"Lady Introl was most specific as to her daughter's requirements," muttered Mistress Daran, her lips pursing. Isak saw exactly what the woman thought of white-eyes.

"Lady Introl does not interest me in the least." He checked his words for fear of insulting Tila's family too much—however cross he was, Tila *was* a friend—but he couldn't control the look on his face: the wretched woman would not last much longer if she continued to irritate him. "What does interest me is getting to Narkang before bloody Silvernight," he growled.

He was pleased to see Mistress Daran flinch, presumably fighting the instinct to admonish him for his language. He determined to see how often he could make that happen on the journey to alleviate his own boredom.

"Isak, there's nothing you can do about it, so if you want to make good speed, then let's eat now and not tarry too long." Tila shifted as she stood; she was already feeling the strain of her new saddle.

Isak shrugged at her and walked off angrily to see to his horses instead. The argument would have to wait until Tila was too tender to be obstinate. Let's see how she felt after her first night on the ground. He swapped the packs from one horse to the other and readied Megenn's saddle.

Isak patted both animals affectionately, then rubbed down Megenn's chestnut flanks where the packs had rested. They had very different temperaments: Toramin was a fiery young stallion of unbelievable strength, while Megenn was older, a gelding, and as biddable as could be wished. Both horses appeared to cope with his weight without complaint, but Isak felt only Toramin was desperate to gallop on. At times he could feel the muscles bunch under the rich, dark coat and he'd have to tighten his grip to remind the horse who was in control.

Isak turned to watch the others for a while. Carel had already won over the Ghosts with his humour and his undeniable skill, still sharp, no matter his age; Vesna's reputation almost guaranteed respect in any barracks.

The soldiers kept apart from Mihn—the only company he sought out was that of the two rangers. Now the three were sitting slightly apart from the others, Mihn carefully positioned so he could see both Isak and the road ahead. Rangers were all strange, reclusive, often to the point of surly disregard for any who might not match their own high standards. Mihn fitted in perfectly. The bulky northerner, Borl Dedev, was the more talkative. Jeil was a native of Tirah, a wiry man only slightly taller than Mihn. Jeil had probably been orphaned to the palace as a child, judging from his lack of family name. A number of rangers and Ghosts in Bahl's service had been left as babies at the palace gates by mothers who felt they couldn't cope. Without a parent to claim them—or denied by a spiteful father, as in Isak's case—they had no family name. Like Bahl and Isak, Jeil had had to make his own name.

Isak made up his mind: now was the time, before they got too far from Tirah. He called for Mihn, and the small man was already rising, his staff in hand, almost before Isak had finished speaking. Isak led him away to a place where they could speak without being overheard, ignoring the curious faces that watched them. Borl had cropped Mihn's hair close to his scalp the previous night; it suited him better, highlighting the dark gleam of his eyes.

"We're going to be away for a long time," Isak started. "Longer than a year." He tried to think how to phrase what he wanted to say. His lack of eloquence was already annoying him. "I don't know what's going to happen, and every day, I feel like I know even less." He sighed. He'd have to be blunt. "I want to know your history, Mihn. You've avoided telling anyone very much, and when I don't understand my own shadow, I've no chance with the rest of the Land."

"My Lord," he said, quietly, "I've told you that I come from a small tribe on the northern coast—"

Isak bared his teeth in irritation. "That's not what I mean. You're saying so little you might as well lie to my face. No common tribesman speaks perfect Farlan. Your accent is more refined than mine. No normal moves the way you do—not even any man of Kerin's, and he's trained our best. I doubt many of the Chief Steward's agents would survive long against you. And the man practically went down on his knees to Lord Bahl to get you working as an assassin for him—he promised he'd have the entire tribe swearing oaths of loyalty within six months."

Mihn flinched; if anything, it looked like the idea sickened him, though Isak knew he didn't have qualms about violence. Mihn wouldn't meet his gaze and his fingers shifted and flexed round the shaft of his staff as he stared at the ground.

"Well? Have you got nothing to say? I've seen you fight. Either you're a very short true elf, a Harlequin, or—" The words died in Isak's throat as Mihn's entire body jerked at his words and his eyes went wide with shock. Isak realised that the man was caught somewhere between anger and terror, then the strength drained out of his body and Mihn sank to his knees, gasping for air.

Isak gaped at the change in his bondsman, then crouched down beside the man, placing a hand on his shoulder to steady him as much as calm him. Before he could think of anything to say, Mihn choked out a handful of words. "Please don't send me away. I have nothing—I am nothing now. My life has been . . ." His voice trailed off into a language Isak didn't recognise, his own tongue, perhaps.

Finally Isak understood. "You're a Harlequin?" It was scarcely possible to believe. No one knew very much about the Harlequins—not even where they came from, let alone how they were able to remember every story and song they had ever heard. The androgynous storytellers carried a pair of slender swords and dressed in diamond—pattern clothes and white masks were as mythical as the tales they told.

"I am nothing," Mihn repeated, as if in a trance. He looked up to meet Isak's eyes for the first time and calmed himself a little. "I'm a failure. They had such high hopes for me; all the elders said I would be the best they had ever seen. I had surpassed the masters with the blades by my eighteenth summer."

"Then what happened?"

"I failed the last trial. There were only three of us. Those who are allowed to take the test should be certain to pass. But I failed."

"How?"

"The last trial is to tell one of the sagas, in full, one that should last for a day at least, but I . . . I could not remember my tale, not a single word, not a name, not a place. I had spent my life training for this, learning every language in the Land, all the dialects and accents and idiosyncrasies, repeating the stories the Gods taught us, practising each step of every play, the voices of animals and accents of man and woman. But at the test I could not remember one word of my favourite tale, one I had memorised before my tenth summer."

Mihn leaned forward, his chest pressed down on his thighs. "I was cast out. The mask I was to put on was burned, my blades broken. I vowed never to wield an edged weapon again, as penance for failing those who had trained me and invested their faith in me."

"One story? One forgotten story and your life is over?"

With a bitter laugh, Mihn replied, "A Harlequin who cannot remember? The Gods themselves wrote our laws in stone, carved into the wall of our holiest place. A Harlequin is emissary of the Gods. Without perfection in thought and word, it would be blasphemy."

Isak gently grasped the broken figure by the shoulders and lifted him up. As he felt a shudder run through Mihn's body, he realised it was just as well Mihn had come with him: he was too similar to Bahl—left alone, he'd end up a shadow, walking the corridors of the palace like a restless phantom.

Mihn's face had crumpled into complete hopelessness. He was searching for something to give him meaning again.

"One moment of pain can rule you, but it doesn't have to. Lord Bahl has been dwelling on the death of his love for so many years that it has become his life and might even be his death," Isak said. "Listen to me. Harlequins may be wonderful; they may be blessed—but you can be more than that."

Mihn gaped at his lord, mouth half open to protest, when Isak went on, "Think about it. What do Harlequins do? They teach us where we came from, and *hope* we heed the warnings of history. They have so many skills, but they hardly use them. They have so much knowledge, but when do they ever exploit it for the good of anyone, even themselves? You have all of these gifts, and *one more*—you don't wear the mask."

"I don't understand," Mihn muttered.

"The Harlequins' masks hide them from the Land. Unlike a Harlequin, I can't hide behind my mask forever. I have to be a part of the Land—it's up to me whether my influence will be for good or bad. You might not be able to tell the stories, but you can influence them. Tila is forever laughing at my ignorance, but it could be a crucial failing if the Gods involve themselves in our lives. You can fight better than any normal I've met, but it's your knowledge of the Gods, of the entire Land and its languages, that I need—and I won't find that in any other soldier."

Isak realised that he was trembling. The whole subject of being a failure was a little close to his heart. "Think it over. We'll be back in the saddle soon, but you have until we leave Nerlos Fortress to make up your mind. After that, we'll be outside Farlan territory. You can decide to become a ranger, or an assassin, or a court jester, or whatever you wish, but if you want purpose in your life, here it is, for the taking."

CHAPTER 24

As THE FIRST COLD RAYS OF DAWN reached out over the Land, a figure made his way onto a deserted stretch of battlements on the south-western corner of Nerlos Fortress. He was dressed only in a rough black shirt and billowing trousers, hardly suitable for the cool morning, but as he padded on to the corner platform between two stretches of walkway he appeared unperturbed by either the wind or the cold stone against his bare feet.

He knelt, facing the sun as it crept up towards the cloud that covered most of the sky, then bowed and, eyes half closed, whispered a mantra. The words drifted away on the wind as he repeated the bow and the prayer ten more times, his voice smooth, almost hypnotic.

He sat back on his heels and beamed contentedly at the sunrise for a few minutes, then closed his eyes again and stretched out his right leg, laying it flat against the stone pointing north, then extended his left leg to the south, all with apparent ease. More words slipped through his lips, less formal, per-haps, but still full of reverence, as he leaned forward and placed his hands against the stone floor, tensing slightly, and eased his weight onto his palms. His legs wavered for a moment as he found his body's centre of balance, then he drew them together, pointing straight up.

He straightened his arms and moved his weight onto one hand, twisting so he was facing down the empty walkway. In times of peace there was only a single lookout on the highest tower and no one else had risen with the dawn. He bent his body into a crescent shape, then propelled his body around and back up to a standing position.

"And what was that?" The voice made Mihn pause and he peered into the darkened doorway suspiciously until Isak stepped out into the crisp sunlight.

"I was praying."

Isak raised an eyebrow. "Praying? I've never seen a priest do that."

"You don't need to be a priest to pray, my Lord. Every child should be taught the devotionals to each of the Upper Circle."

"No doubt they should—I can probably even remember some of them—

but what was that last bit? If everyone had to do that at temple I might have gone more often." Isak's laughter died when he saw Mihn's grave expression.

"That was a personal prayer, something we were taught in our tribe. It's different for each person, a way of giving thanks for something you enjoy, or a particular ability—"

"So I should be killing someone each morning? That's all they made *me* good for." Isak immediately regretted snapping, but Mihn's calm was not disrupted.

"Not at all. I believe you have several things to be grateful for: your strength, your health, your position. And there are your gifts—"

"Fine, I understand, just stop preaching. If you've decided to stay and piously whine at me as your life's calling, I take everything back." Isak shifted uncomfortably. It hadn't even occurred to him to say a prayer of thanks for his gifts. There had been little chance when Nartis was invading his dreams, and then he'd got caught up in his new life . . . one had to hope that the Gods weren't like people. Isak had seen family feuds grow out of those feast days where gifts were traditional. The idea of appearing ungrateful to the God of Storms was not appealing.

Mihn broke into his reverie. "Then I will try not to piously whine at you every morning—but yes, I have decided to stay with you. For a man whose first recourse is violence, you can be eloquent at times. The casual listener might believe you had given the subject some thought."

Isak grinned. "If you've quite finished, you can go and fetch me some jugs of water."

Mihn narrowed his eyes. For all of his power, Isak was still a young man, and one who'd rarely had a chance to enjoy himself at that. "Some might think Carel's observation that he found it hard to wake up early these days was not intended as a hint."

"I know, but they're the sort of people who pray every morning. I, on the other hand, have no morals—by divine mandate. And who am I to defy the will of the Gods?"

Mihn sighed. "Who indeed?"

Jeil moved swiftly through the trees, his bow held ready. Over the rushing sound of the river nearby he heard a faint birdcall, the short double-trill of a goldcrest, and he stopped to crouch behind an ancient hawthorn. Borl's mimicry of birdcalls was brilliant, one of the reasons he had been picked to escort Isak to Narkang. It was the perfect way to keep his companions informed of enemy movements without giving himself away, and it meant Jeil, who was faster, could hunt them down from his calls.

This was the first person they had encountered since disembarking from the riverboat they had used to travel the border between Tor Milist and Scree towards Helrect. It was an obvious ambush point, as only coracles could traverse this section of the river, and they were no use for transporting horses.

The goldcrest trilled again and Jeil tensed, ready to step out, when a second call sounded from somewhere up ahead. He swore silently: either Borl's mimicry was too good and had attracted a real bird, or their prey had caught on. Jeil hunkered down and kept completely still, listening hard. The Land was unnaturally quiet—until a piercing whistle broke the stillness, no bird sound, this, but a warning that Jeil had been seen. The ranger rose and drew his sword, stabbing it into the earth within easy reach before fully drawing his bow.

"Enough of the birdsong," called a voice no more than thirty yards ahead. "I know you're there, so come out."

He heard footsteps crunching over dead branches advancing towards him and stepped around the hawthorn, still certain that no one could have seen or heard him. The silk of his bowstring caressed his cheek as he caught sight of the speaker. He wasn't much to look at: dressed in roughly patched leathers and a ragged wolf's pelt, with a longbow slung over his shoulder and a short-handled axe at his belt.

"I'm alone," he said. "I've been waiting for you all morning." He looked about fifty summers, with traces of white on the week's growth of beard. An easy smile hovered on his lips, one that put Jeil on edge.

"The border with Scree is a strange place to be waiting alone and on foot," Jeil replied, keeping his bow raised. "A boat couldn't have brought you to this stretch of the river and you don't look much like a local waterman to me."

"Send the other ranger back to fetch your Lord," the man continued. "I would speak to him." He didn't sound like he was a native of these parts. His accent was awkward, as if his own dialect were markedly different.

"What's your business with my Lord?"

"Someone sent me to speak to him. Look, boy, I knew you were coming, I could have ambushed you all if I wanted him dead. Just send your friend to tell them I'm here and then we can relax with a pipe until they arrive."

Jeil eased the tension in the bow enough to free up his right hand.

Without taking his eyes off the man, he raised his arm and motioned in the air. A whistle told him that Borl understood. Still keeping his eyes on the man, Jeil backed away and retrieved his blade; the arrow stayed nocked.

"Don't get comfortable," he warned as the man squatted down on the roots of an oak and pulled out his tobacco pouch. "We'll go some of the way back, this way." He pointed back to where he'd left his horse.

The stranger sighed theatrically and pushed himself to his feet. A mocking smile remained on his lips as he passed the ranger. Jeil couldn't help but wonder just what he had found instead of an ambush.

"So who are you?" Isak's hand rested very obviously on Eolis's emerald-studded hilt. Standing face to face he dwarfed the man, but the stranger showed no sign of discomfort. Either he was mad, or there was a lot more to him than met the eye. The man seemed vaguely interested in Isak's gifts, but no more—the white-eye's hooded face drew more attention than either Siulents or Eolis.

"Greetings, brother," the stranger said, with a laconic bow. Isak saw his own confusion echoed on the faces of his companions. "My name is Morghien, but that will mean little enough to you, I'm sure."

The Krann grinned under the blue silk as he caught Mihn's eye. The small man shifted in discomfort, but did not hesitate to speak. "You are called the man of many spirits."

Morghien arched his eyebrows in surprise, the smile fading momentarily, much to Isak's satisfaction, but he didn't falter for long. He shrugged his shoulders, causing the moth-eaten pelt to twitch as if in the final spasms of death, then said, "Your man knows his stories. I did not realise my fame had extended to the northern clans."

It was Mihn's turn to be surprised now, but Morghien simply chuckled and continued. "And now the introductions are out of the way, perhaps we can get to business."

"What business do you have with us?" demanded Carel. "How did you know we were coming this way, and why did you call him brother?"

"Explanations can come another time, but as for how I knew you were coming, let us say the girl of his dreams told me so."

Carel laughed, but he saw Isak tense. There was a strange assurance about Morghien that worried the veteran. The man looked younger than Carel was himself, but he had an almost otherworldly air; he suited the strange title Mihn had used: *the man of many spirits*.

"Should we talk alone?" asked Morghien softly. Isak nodded and waved the others back, never taking his eyes off the man. Carel recognised Isak's mood and moved off without a word; Vesna and the soldiers followed his lead, but Mihn didn't move. He tightened his grip on the steel-shod staff in his hand.

Morghien turned a sympathetic eye on him. "It's all right, lad. If you know about me, then you'll know I wouldn't stand a chance against him."

Mihn kept very still for a moment and then bowed his head in acknowledgement. He joined Carel, but kept his eyes on Morghien. When the older man reached out to touch his arm, Mihn jumped in surprise.

"What was that about?"

When he answered, Mihn's voice was distant. "Have you heard of the Finntrail?"

"No, who are they? Another northern tribe?"

Mihn shook his head slowly. "No. I will explain later. Though I don't think he poses a threat to Lord Isak, that man is dangerous."

"Now we're alone, tell me exactly what you mean." Any mention of Isak's dreams put the white-eye on edge. How a stranger could know about the girl's voice in them was something Isak couldn't fathom.

"I'm not sure entirely," Morghien began, but the words died in his throat as a silver gleam appeared at his throat.

"No riddles, old man," warned the Krann in a low tone.

Morghien swallowed and nodded as best he could. "I am afraid I may not have as many answers as you would hope. Four times now I have had dreams that are more than dreams."

"You said the girl of my dreams," Isak said impatiently. "Explain that."

"My dreams have been of a girl, talking to me. She told me about you and asked me to come here to meet you. I assumed you must have dreamed of her too, for her to know who you are and where to find you."

"Who is she? How does she know me?"

"Her name is Xeliath. She tells me she has been looking for you for over a year now, hardly knowing for whom she was searching, until you put on Siulents."

"She can sense Siulents?"

Morghien ignored Isak's scepticism. "She is, I think, scared to tell me how. She said that Siulents is like a giant beacon, shining out through the Land when she sleeps, but that your dreams are guarded too well to let her enter them. She hopes that by telling you this, you would perhaps open yourself up to her."

"I'll need more reason than that. Continue."

"She's Yeetatchen, I think, though I have never been there: her skin is as brown as a hazelnut. Xeliath is young, perhaps as little as fifteen winters."

"What does she want with me?"

"I believe she wants only to help you. She persuaded me that I should too."

"How? What help do you think I need?" Finally Isak lowered his sword, satisfied that the man neither could nor would do anything to harm him. Isak looked a little deeper into Morghien, feeling an unusual mix of power within the man. His strength was curious, unlike anything Isak had seen before, but it was not great enough to concern him.

"Preparation for troubles ahead, Xeliath said." At Isak's expression Morghien raised a hand and continued hurriedly. "She has not told me everything, and though I think I understand what she meant, telling you might make matters worse."

"Worse? I've still half a mind to kill you so what will be worse than that?"

"You having less than half a mind," replied Morghien simply.

Isak opened his mouth to respond and then saw the stranger's expression. He was being deadly serious, even if he was as insane as he sounded. The white-eye looked back to the rest of his party, then walked over to the moss-draped form of a fallen tree, indicating that Morghien should follow. He straddled the trunk and sat down, facing his companions so Morghien had to sit with his back to them. He pulled off the silken hood and ran a gauntleted hand over his cropped scalp. The cool whisper of silver on skin sounded like the breathing of wind through the trees.

"You want to help me, and you want me to trust you, without knowing what's going on?"

"It is a matter of destiny, and a man learns his fate at his own risk." Morghien shrugged.

"Damn my fate," Isak snapped back, "I don't believe the future is fixed—"

"And it is not," interrupted Morghien firmly. "Which is why you cannot know what I mean. Xeliath is some sort of prophet or oracle, but it doesn't take a prophet to know that a white-eye isn't going to follow his fate willingly. Whether knowingly or not, you'll fight against any outside forces in your life; it is what you are. But you can perhaps be prepared for what is to come."

Isak hardly noticed that he had bitten his lip. "What do you propose?"

"Xeliath thinks herself your guardian spirit. She told me, "His armour may keep his body alive, but I must watch over his soul." It is clear that the threats to you are greater than you know."

"I have enough enemies, I think," said Isak bitterly.

Morghien ignored him and continued. "Xeliath has seen your death in the future and hopes to avoid it. To that end, she has asked me to help."

"What can you teach me?" Isak snorted at the idea. "You don't look much of a swordsman to me."

"Indeed I am not. But your death is one of the mind, not the body. If you are to be attacked in the mind, then perhaps I *can* be of use."

"Why you?"

"Because, as your man back there will tell you, I am possessed."

A cough of laughter escaped Isak's lips, but it died soon as he saw nothing but the truth in the man's face. "You're serious?"

"Completely serious. I'm not inhabited by a daemon, and the possession was voluntary, but yes. Remember what your man called me?"

"The man of spirits? Something like that?" Isak fought the urge to stand up and step back from this madman. His hand tightened for a moment around the hilt of his sheathed sword.

Morghien caught the movement and a smile of understanding crossed his lips. "The man of many spirits. Perhaps now is not the time, for my story is a long one, but the short answer is that I took pity on a local Aspect of Vasle. Her stream was going to be dammed, and when the water stopped flowing she would have faded to just a voice on the wind. I offered what I had out of compassion. When the last of the water stopped flowing, she entered my soul. The others—well, they were similar stories. I have a generous heart."

"Mihn looked like he thought you were dangerous."

"Me? No, not I, but one of those within is a Finntrail, that's true enough."

"And that is?"

Morghien smiled uncertainly. Obviously his choices in life had made him an outcast. Trusting his secrets to strangers was not a comfortable thing to do. Isak could sympathise there.

"I—Ah, well, the Finntrail are a sort of ghost, I suppose. Not the ghost of a human, but something older. I don't know exactly what they are, for they cannot remember. What could have happened to Seliasei did, I suspect, happen to the Finntrail. They are only shadows of whatever they used to be, but to retain even that much means they must have been very powerful."

"And they are dangerous?"

Morghien looked thoughtful for a moment, searching for the right word. "They are angry, perhaps that's the best description. As long as they are capable of anger they exist as more than just a faint echo; it sustains them, whatever else it does. But, they are all subservient to me; even the Finntrail has accepted my dominance. The sensation of being alive again more than makes up for that."

"So what do you propose? I'm not sure I want to know how you can help me with some vicious little shade running around in your head."

"Call it a new experience. Trust me, it will hurt me more than you— there's no doubt of that. I don't pretend to be able to read those runes on your armour, but Seliasei fears them. All I ask of you is that you hold back as much as you can—and perhaps put your sword out of immediate reach."

Isak stared at him for a moment, suspicious again, but then he closed his eyes and opened his senses to the world. An awareness of the Land about him began to filter slowly into his mind and a spreading numbness flooded through his body, a cool breath of fresh damp leaves and moist earth. In only a few seconds he began to feel the gentle shape of the ground about him, the faint pinpricks of life from his companions, the curious medley of souls about Morghien that justified the strange name Mihn called him.

Isak smiled to himself as he experienced the peace of opening himself to the Land. From the comforting immovability of the earth beneath his feet to the vibrant swirl of air high above; all this took him away from the pulse of anger buried under his skin, however briefly.

"I'll trust you." He forced his eyelids open to disperse the dreamy contentment in his head. Drawing Eolis, he threw the weapon and embedded it in a nearby elm. The silver blade drove a foot deep into the trunk and sat quivering, emitting a low hum. Even in the dull light of a cloudy morning, Eolis sparkled as if dusted in morning frost.

Satisfied that the blade was out of reach, Morghien took a moment to calm himself. Isak felt a pulse of something, maybe the Aspect's concern at what was to come. Even a weak spirit would be aware of what it could lose.

"I'm no scholar," Morghien began, "and I don't pretend to understand much of spirits or daemons, for all that a friend in Narkang has tried to explain matters to me, but I can feel from the spirit's point of view. The first thing you must learn, Lord Isak, is that they are not as powerful as people believe them to be."

Isak's focus returned somewhat at Morghien's respectful use of his title. The man had felt just how strong he was; the mocking smile was gone and Morghien now looked like Kerin did on the training field. Isak reminded himself what that meant: just because he could kill Morghien with little effort said nothing about what he could learn from the man.

Morghien, unaware of Isak's mental discussion, carried on, "Part of a spirit's power derives from how it is perceived. The myths you learn, the fear and awe you experience when you encounter them—magic is a force in itself, and though different in every way to nature, it can still create a form of life . . . perhaps *existence* is a better word.

"So in the fashion that you and I are created from the same matter as the earth and trees, so Gods and daemons have a common source in magic."

"How is this helping?" The mages from the College of Magic, in their attempts to educate the Krann, had not found fertile ground. They had made the mistake of telling him that theoretical understanding of magic would be of small use to a white-eye. Isak had taken that as a reason to pay no further attention.

Morghien's look of irritation faded quickly as he remembered his ultimate goal. His brow furrowed as he sought a more appropriate explanation. "When you fight, there is more to know than stabbing a man, no?"

Isak shrugged and Morghien continued. "Of course there is—not only must you know your strokes, your stances, and your weapons, you must also know your enemy and the land around you. Now think of magic as this battle.

"Your weapons and strokes might be spells or curses. They must be practised and refined so your crude swipes become deft cuts and concealed moves. Knowing your enemy—how his armour slows him or how great his reach is—is as important as knowing how the mud underfoot will slow you, whether you will slip on a particular stone, or can kick him off-balance after he has struck.

"You are aware of the slope of the Land, the rain coming down, his relative size and strength. These things you understand as naturally as you know how to chew and swallow, and as you must with magic. Magic has rules that follow their own sense—those that might ignore the warmth of the sun, but could be affected by moonlight—"

Isak held up a hand. "I've had these lessons already, I remember enough on the nature of magic. You're starting to sound like those excitable lecturers."

Morghien stared at him curiously. "You don't find the nature of magic interesting at all?"

Isak shrugged again. Magic was intoxicating, exhilarating, to such a degree the rest of the Land faded away. Talking about it was less so. It was like discussing sex. Some people got excited enough about it to talk for hours on the subject. Isak could find no enthusiasm for just talking.

"Well, I shall say no more then, other than you must remember they grow strong from illogical sources, that their image is often greater than their strength. There are some that are very powerful, but that is the same with men. You would not notice a man if he were not remarkable in size or strength or skill. But if that same man went berserk, he could cause a shocking amount of damage, and if he attacked a race that had never seen a man, he would terrify them."

"I think I understand what you mean. When I feel the presence of Nartis I'm paralysed . . ." Isak trailed off, unable to describe the sensation.

"And that gives him strength over you. It is intentional—the Gods project a shining image because it inspires wonder. And the more you are awed, the more powerful they grow; not only over you, but part of what sustains them is belief and praise. Gods are made stronger by belief: that you see them as greater, and worship them accordingly. And that is one of the things that separates Gods from daemons."

"One of the things?"

"That is not an encouraged topic of conversation. The state of my eternal soul is debatable in any case when much of my time is spent hunting down followers of Azaer; I have no desire to be actively impious on top of anything else. King Emin will know men who will be happy to have those discussions. For now, you should accept that a daemon or ghost will try to terrify you, because then you open yourself to it and lend it strength."

He raised his hands to his face and rubbed his palms over his cheeks, the rough skin rasping against his stubbled face. "I think it's time for a practical demonstration."

Isak stared in fascination, reaching out with his senses to feel the shape of what was happening to Morghien. The man started to hold up a hand to halt the Krann's efforts, but it was not necessary: one look at Morghien's features had been enough for Isak to draw back hurriedly and grasp the ghost of Eolis at his hilt.

The man had changed. Subtle weaves of magic had smoothed out the lines of his face, softening the ruddy colour of his cheeks and reducing the size of his nose. It was still Morghien, but Isak could see the features were now almost those of a woman.

His voice had altered too. "Keep your defences strong, don't leave yourself open," Morghien said, but a musical note had entered his previously rough voice.

Isak felt his mouth dry as he tried to respond, but then he remembered Morghien's words. With an effort he could see past the glamour to the man's true features: and he was right, nothing had changed except for Isak's perception. With a smile he dismissed the weaves of the projected image.

Morghien shrieked in pain. His hands flew to his face as though Isak had just slashed him with a knife. He threw himself off the log and crashed facedown onto the ground. Isak jumped to his feet in alarm and Mihn rushed over with Vesna and Carel close behind. He held up a hand to them.

"No, get back—keep away from him. He didn't attack me."

They did not look impressed with the order, but they complied sullenly. Morghien remained on the ground as they moved away.

A tense silence fell. Isak could hear the keening of a hawk in the distance, and the skitter of dead leaves as a gust swept them up and settled a few on Morghien's back, like the first effort to bury a man who was lying as still as a corpse.

At last he breathed out, sending a single leaf tumbling end over end. He took his hands away from his face with careful, deliberate movements and pushed himself up from the ground. His face was disturbingly pale and calm, all trace of the Aspect gone, though his cheek and eyebrow seemed to be trembling very slightly. Then he breathed again and the calm was abruptly broken as he gulped down air, his shoulders shaking with the effort.

"I'm sorry," Isak began, "truly. What did I do?"

Morghien felt his way back to the fallen log again and pulled himself onto it. After half a minute, some colour returned to his face and he began to explain. "The fault was mine. I should have explained more of the nature of glamour. But there is no serious damage done."

"Are you sure?"

"I am. Seliasei was hurt rather, but I think it's shock more than anything else. The glamour is part of what she is; a local Aspect is still a God. It is not vanity, but part of her very essence. When you cut through those weaves it was like slapping my face to distort my features—except I have a shape to revert to. Seliasei has only the image of herself to define her. Without the strength to extend it to a physical form, any distortion of that image makes her forget who she is."

Isak looked stricken. "I think I understand. I'm—Er, could you apologise to her for me?" He would have felt stupid saying that, but for the glimpse of fear and pain on Morghien's face. One thing he did remember was that death for a God was the loss of identity. A divine force could not be truly killed, but as Aryn Bwr had shown with the Crystal Skulls, it could be reduced to a voice on the wind, weakened to the point of nonexistence and capable only of remembering that once it had been so much more. Isak had shivered at the prospect of eternity like that: a sense of loss the only sliver of self left.

"She will recover, but she will not come out in your presence again. Even before that she was terrified of you. She's a local God, an Aspect, sharing some memories with Vasle and his view of history. They see the present in a completely different way to mortals. To her, you are partly to blame for the death of Vasle's brother, for it was partly you who proved Gods could be effectively destroyed."

"Ah. And then I did something akin to just that. I'm sorry."

"There's more of a problem than that. She had agreed to touch your mind, to help you understand how Xeliath thinks you will be attacked. Now . . ." Morghien's voice trailed off. His eyes lost their focus as if he were listening to a faint voice behind him. Isak watched silently.

"We can but try," he said aloud finally. Isak was burning to ask what had been decided, but he'd caused enough trouble—and besides, he was too impatient to listen to more explanations.

"Please, sit again." Morghien motioned Isak to the fallen tree. Once they were facing each other again, Morghien closed his eyes and started breathing deeply. When he looked up to Isak again, he appeared calmer, still himself, but ready for whatever lay ahead.

He reached out and touched his fingertips to Isak's forehead. The white-eye recoiled slightly, then leaned forward so Morghien wouldn't have to stretch quite so far. As he did so, Isak realised that the muscles of his shoulders were rigid with anticipation, ready to strike out. He made himself relax and opened his thoughts again.

A chill breeze touched his cheek, like the caress of winter fingers. He closed his eyes to focus on the smooth sensation as it trembled over his skin. A tingling began on his forehead where Morghien was touching him, trickling down through his right eyebrow and into the cheekbone. The delicate sensation grew in strength and Isak felt the warmth of his body begin to seep from his skin. This time he was careful not to disturb the shade that was greedily leeching off him. Whatever it was, it lacked the strength to cause him any hurt, whether it was intended to or not.

In his mind, Isak was aware of an ancient odour—not actually unpleasant, but not enjoyable: the dry scent of a tomb, the smell of undisturbed years rather than a corpse, but still a dead place. The prickle of ice increased, sliding its way down to his jugular.

Now Isak stopped it gently, reaching around the helpless spirit to bind it and keep it still so he could see what he was dealing with. It was still terribly weak, but it had drawn enough strength for the image of a man's face to appear in Isak's mind. He could perceive features etched in a white mist— a thin jaw, deep-set eyes, hair receding from a smooth forehead: the first things the shade could remember of itself.

As with Seliasei, identity was the first concern. Once they had a face, a name, a memory, it helped bring the Land back into focus for them. Until a sense of self could be produced, desires and emotions couldn't matter because there was no reference for them. As the shade struggled in vain, Isak felt a moment of pity. There was no malice in its desire for the warmth and strength of his body, only a desperation that Isak found achingly sad. Once he had cradled it for a while, Isak realised he understood enough and ushered the spirit back to Morghien. As he did so he sent a thought to it, almost an apology, as it fought his grip. *Let go. Life is for the living.*

As the misty shape faded away, a blackness leapt up from nowhere and enveloped Isak's mind. A stab of pain flashed through his head as the invading spirit took him in its numbing grip and fed savagely at his throat. This was no half-forgotten Aspect: Isak felt as if he had fallen into an icy stream. Each time he moved he felt his strength being sucked out of him. The cold kept flowing over his skin, drawing out heat, drawing out life.

Isak began to panic as each breath grew harder, as his body faded away into a deadened memory. Images of hungry eyes and long thin fangs flashed before his eyes. He felt the Finntrail's desire, its anger and loss fuelling the enveloping strength. He was afraid of becoming that hollow.

Then Morghien's words came back to him: such creatures *were* hollow; their strength was partly what you gave them. This suppressed the alarm clouding his mind. He looked again at the feeding spirit and saw it was insubstantial. He saw the mist of its form and how easily he could push through.

The numbing ceased as Isak reached out with his mind, ignoring the desperate, but now feather-light, retaliation. He reached out all around him and gathered the inky strands in tight. The Finntrail struggled and raged, but it was powerless. With a furious scream the shadow was expelled back to Morghien and the wanderer withdrew his hand and smiled weakly.

The Krann didn't meet Morghien's eye. Looking round to his companions he saw Mihn, Carel, and Tila watching as before. Nothing appeared to have changed, but Isak shivered slightly. The air felt cooler than before, as if the night's frost had returned. He rose and began to walk the ten yards to retrieve Eolis before stopping short suddenly. He whirled around, but he could see nothing different—but it felt as if they had been joined by another. Beyond the road the trees were empty and quiet. The sky above held only a few birds, too distant to recognise, but still Isak felt uneasy. He wrenched the blade from its resting place but didn't sheathe it. The others gave him uncomfortable looks, but Isak ignored them, glad of the security Eolis lent.

An unheard chuckle crept out from the overhanging branches of a yew. The birds nearby were startled into flight as they sensed malevolence all around. Only the wind heard and it swept away after the birds, dead leaves and damp crumbs of earth skittering away in its wake.

"Life is for the living? Sometimes I think you say these things solely for my pleasure. Will you remember those words, I wonder?"

CHAPTER 25

ISAK OPENED HIS EYES AND LOOKED AROUND IN ALARM. The last thing he remembered was huddling close to the others in front of the fire, Tila curled into the warm lee of his body and a skin of wine snug in his hand. Now he was here—wherever *here* was. The clouded sky swirled uncertainly above a rolling plain of long grass. A few moments ago, he'd been surrounded by trees.

Dawn shadows covered the ground, but Isak couldn't see the sun anywhere. He couldn't even tell which direction was north—and he'd *always* been able to do that. It was as if he wasn't in the Land any longer . . . and that thought chilled him more than the cool air. He watched as a breeze rippled through the grass, but he felt nothing on his skin. It reminded him of the palace he used to dream about, otherworldly and uncomfortable.

"With all your ability—all your potential—and it just takes a skin of wine to open your mind. Typical."

Isak jumped: behind him stood a girl, her beauty taking Isak's breath away almost more than the shock at her sudden appearance. Her skin was as Morghien had described, as smooth and radiant as polished walnut wood, darker than anyone Isak had seen before, darker even than the Chetse desert clans.

While the Yeetatchen were their neighbours, living off the Farlan coast, there was almost no contact between the two tribes: most face-to-face meetings had been on the battlefield—and those rivalled the Great War for savagery.

Isak was mesmerised just by the sight of her: with such rich brown skin, her white eyes were even more astonishing. "You're Xeliath?"

"And you're the cause of all my troubles."

Isak narrowed his eyes, one hand moving instinctively to his side before he realised he was wearing just the rags from his life on the wagon train. Eolis was still hanging from his belt, but Siulents and his fine clothes were nowhere to be seen.

"Just a reminder, of who you once were," Xeliath explained. She gave him a stern look, studying his reaction at the torn, dirty clothes. Suddenly she broke out in a girlish smile and skipped over to plant a kiss on his lips. Isak gasped in surprise. The sweet scent of her skin was almost over-whelming. Instinctively he reached out and slipped his hands around her waist, but she skipped back and the smooth skin of her hips slid out of his fragile grip. Now her face bore a look of pure delight.

"Ah, it's been a while since I could do that." She danced over to a mossy rise and sat. Isak scarcely noticed that he'd not seen the rise earlier.

"What—Ah, why?"

"Why has it been a while? Well that's your fault, but the story is a long one." From her manner, Isak realised that Morghien had been correct in her age. She was tall as any white-eye, with a healthy strength in those long slender limbs, but hardly past girlhood, for all her remarkable beauty.

"But I've never met you," Isak protested as he struggled past the memory of her lips.

"No excuse." Her tone was playful, but she clearly meant it. "I had kissed quite a number of pretty young men before someone decided to make you the Saviour—"

"Now wait," Isak snapped. "I'm no Saviour and I don't intend to be."

"What you intend has nothing to do with it!" With the snap in her voice came a distant rumble of thunder. Isak immediately realised that the two were linked, and that they both could rage much closer. Even female white-eyes had a temper bubbling under the surface.

Xeliath ignored the interruption. "What others intend is the matter at hand. Unfortunately for all of us, you've become a nexus for those intentions."

"What are you talking about? I've been given no quest by the Gods. Carel always says I've got the piety of a dead ice-cobra. Just why do people think I've been chosen to lead a crusade, or whatever other damn stupid idea they have?"

"And therein lies the problem."

Isak cocked his head at the strange girl. For such a young woman she was amazingly confident and assured. "How did you learn Farlan anyway?" That was one of the things nagging at him about this girl: her accent was not just excellent, but native.

"Can we please keep to the matter at hand? If you need an answer, I didn't, I can't. I'm speaking directly to your thoughts. Whatever you hear is how your mind chooses to represent those thoughts. This is just a dream, Isak, your dream. The conversation *is* happening, but this place doesn't exist."

"Then how?"

"I'm not sure whether I should tell you, but I don't suppose you'll pay attention until you get an answer. You were Chosen last year; I already had been. Lady Amavoq came to me in a dream. I wasn't made Krann or given a title, but my gift was rather special. Lady Amavoq told me to watch over you. I was intended to be your bride and royal assassin."

"What was the gift? Why only intended?"

"The gift was the Skull of Dreams, the one owned by Aryn Bwr's queen. That's how I'm here: other than warded minds, I can enter most people's dreams—and once there, I can kill them. As for *intended*, well, things went astray there, but it's only been since I met Morghien that I begin to understand why.

"I'm now a prisoner in my dreams. When I accepted the Skull, my fate was entwined with yours—but unfortunately, you have many fates . . . and none. Either way, it was too much: it broke me. Oh Gods, did it hurt— you've no idea just how much something like that could hurt." She stopped for a moment, her pain showing in her face. Isak didn't know how to respond; he felt guilty for something that he knew nothing about.

Xeliath shuddered. "For a moment, an instant, I saw a thousand futures ahead of me. The Skull stopped my mind being completely destroyed; it cushioned the blow, somehow, but it could do nothing to stop me screaming. I looked like I'd been struck down by madness." She sighed. "My family believe I have been called as a prophet. Now I'm kept confined and drugged."

"And this is my fault?" Isak couldn't keep the incredulous edge from his voice, but Xeliath gave no sign that she had noticed.

"In a way. When I was following your mind, I found Morghien, passing close by, and I entered his dreams out of curiosity. The man of many spirits: he is well named. I found *more* answers than I'd expected, and answers that I had *not* expected." She sighed. "There were so many prophecies about the Age of Fulfilment—so many hands trying to affect the future—that it looks like they may *all* have failed."

"How? You're not making any sense." He was beginning to feel stupid: should it be this hard to grasp?

She smiled and patted the ground beside her. He sat, feeling the soft ground give slightly under his weight, and Xeliath leaned against him, slender and frail, but curiously warming on his skin.

"You know about prophets, yes? That they speak in riddles and every- thing has to be deciphered? Well, they don't see the future, they see what is possible, and then those visions are translated according to the viewpoint of the scholars who study the prophet."

"So the scholars could be lying?"

"If only it were that simple." Xeliath gave a rueful chuckle and took his hand, patting it affectionately before interlacing her fingers with his and squeezing them. "Sometimes they are correct, sometimes not. But you must remember that there's a power in words, there's a power in belief. Men work towards what they believe—Gods are sustained partly by the belief and devotion of their followers. You should know that words can affect the Land—whether it's logical or not, we see the Land through words, stories, and beliefs. The course of history itself can be shaped by these words. You might want to tell your father that. Honestly, giving a white-eye such a name . . . it just pushed you further from the intended path. He might find himself explaining his decision at the Gates of Death to an annoyed deity."

"*I* didn't pick my name . . . and I still don't get what is this to do with me." Now he sounded plaintive.

"You're at the heart of it all. 'Saviour' is just a name, but it's loaded with enough power to affect those who are associated with it. Names can be used by men and Gods towards their own ends. You've become the centre of the prophecies of the Saviour, whether you like it or not, but the laws of magic are not the same as those of nature.

"Everyone with any power has tried to influence your birth, to create the man they needed. They failed. Between them they gave you the power to change the Land around you, to bend fate to your will, but they forgot the difference between nature and magic: when forces of nature meet, either one wins outright, or they cancel each other out. When forces of magic meet, they corrupt and change each other.

"The result is that you have the power without the desire: no dreams of conquest, no grand schemes, just an emptiness of ambition. Destiny has twisted about you and snapped."

Isak took a deep breath. He had no idea what questions he should be asking. His mind was blank. "I—How can I know you're telling me the truth?"

Xeliath smiled, understanding his suspicion. "Well, first of all, you recognise my voice don't you? I was watching that first night in the Tower—though I didn't know where you were, I could feel your soul entwined with my own. I've been with you since the beginning of this new life of yours."

Isak's eyes widened in recollection and he opened his mouth to speak, but Xeliath placed a finger to his lips and hushed him. Then she put her hand on his chest and pressed her fingers against the scar there. "And I know you can feel it within yourself. You've been Chosen, yet you hardly care, do you? It's not affected you: whatever sense of purpose you feel comes from your intelligence, not your instincts.

"I—" Xeliath looked around suddenly, alarm flashing over her face.

Isak looked too, but he could see nothing in the empty landscape—then he remembered this was just an image in his mind. He closed his eyes and reached out cautiously.

It was as if there were two Lands, laid one upon the other. He could feel his friends asleep around him under a canopy of trees, and the grass, fluttering out on the plain. He focused on the dream scene—and found the source of Xeliath's concern. A shadow swirled around them, like fingers of cloud drifting past the unseen sun. Isak recognised the sensation; it was what he'd felt on the battlements, at Suzerain Fordan's feast.

"I must leave," Xeliath began, "don't worry; I'll deal with whatever that is. Did Morghien give you letters for the King of Narkang?"

Isak nodded, his mind still on the shadow.

"Give them to King Emin in private; he will explain in more detail. I don't know him yet, but the king's mind shines as brightly as yours and he could be as important as you are. Shadows fear him. I will come to you again, when I can." She hesitated, her confidence melting away as she stared up into eyes that mirrored her own.

Tentatively she drew herself closer, breathing in the scent of his body, and placed a tender kiss on his lips. Isak felt her tongue flicker against his own, and then she pulled back. She looked sad.

Isak saw her completely open and vulnerable. The scar on his chest burned with shame and lust. "Wait," he cried, feeling himself drifting awake, "if I've broken your mind, then why are you still helping me?"

Now all he could see was the outline of her face against the starry sky. The melancholy in her voice was almost more than Isak could bear. "Because it's what I am. It's all I have left."

CHAPTER 26

HE FURTHER SOUTH THEY TRAVELLED, the more winter lost its edge. Nights were cold, especially when they slept on board the riverboat, but the familiar bite of snow in the air was gone. The Farlan felt summer on the horizon as they left the shadow of the mountains and crossed wide empty plains. Narkang lay to the southwest, but they had no intention of going near either Vanach, which had strict religious laws too easy to break unsuspectingly, or Tor Milist—no one knew what reception Isak might get there.

Instead, they travelled on the river that marked the border between Tor Milist and Scree for much of the way. There was a small risk of trouble, but their party was well able to deal with any problems they might encounter.

It was strange to wake without a mountain somewhere on the horizon, but the presence of the early morning sunshine more than compensated. The sight of thin wisps of cloud above, all edged in gold, brought a smile to Isak's lips. He began to remember the pleasure to be found out in the wilds. With the warm memory of Xeliath in his head and friends surrounding him, Isak found himself enjoying life more than ever. Only the lingering memory of what the dark-skinned girl had said troubled him, even though he had determined not to worry any more about it until he reached Narkang and the brightly shining King Emin. Still he couldn't quite shake off the feeling of unease.

As they skirted Tor Milist's official border, those they met reported that the civil war had started up again in earnest. Duke Vrerr had suffered two minor defeats already that year, though he had barely escaped with his life, it appeared the rumours of his death had been exaggerated. The duke had placed an enormous bounty on the head of the witch Leferna after her attempt on his life, but so far, no one had claimed it. The peasants hated their Lord with a passion, for he was already appropriating people's crops—at this rate they would have nothing to store up for the winter.

And court gossip was passed on too: a Chetse mercenary was providing plenty of talk amongst the gentlefolk of Tor Milist, for he had apparently succeeded in cuckolding the notoriously jealous duke.

"I can believe that well enough," Vesna commented as they relaxed in the common room of a dockside tavern they had graced with their presence.

"And why's that?" Tila's expression went unnoticed.

Vesna stared at his drink and scowled at the bitter aftertaste. "Well, I went there as part of the negotiations over the last border raids, a famous name to distract the duke."

Isak smiled. Vesna hadn't admitted to Tila *all* the reasons for being sent on such missions: no only did men tend to get distracted when the famous adulterer was around, but Vesna had been trained by the best poisoners in the Chief Steward's employ. Many negotiations had been swiftly resolved by the timely passing of an obstructive old man.

"I met the duchess only once, but she—" Now he caught sight of Tila's face. "Ah, I mean—Well, you know what they say about the Chetse . . ." The count's brain caught up with his mouth and he shut up.

"No," said Tila, innocently, "what do they say?"

"I, er . . . they say—" He looked around the smiling faces and scowled. "Oh leave me alone, I never went near the woman, despite her offers. She smelled so bad I couldn't bear being in the same room."

Carel gave the downcast count a pat on the shoulder, but Vesna got up and headed for the door.

"I think it would probably be quicker to just ask him which women he *has* gone near," Carel told Tila, a merciless grin on his face.

Tila could see why the count kept his first name from everyone, even his friends. "And I think you should keep quiet, old man," she snapped back. "At least Count Vesna's trying to be respectable. You're the one encouraging him—not to mention throwing all your money at trollop barmaids."

The laughter was less raucous now: the guardsmen filling most of the bar weren't going to risk enjoying themselves too much at their commander's expense. In any case, Tila had a treacherously good memory for those with a sweetheart at home and a local girl on their lap. Since she'd had to give in to Isak and use a normal saddle, Tila's tongue had been sharper than ever and the men trod carefully around her.

Carel snorted and turned away and Tila stormed off to join Mistress Daran at a table away from the increasingly rowdy soldiers.

"So you're goin' south to the borderland from here, my Lord?" asked the barkeep hesitantly, taking advantage of the lull in conversation.

Isak turned to look at the man. Just for a moment his temper flared as he recalled all the inns like this he'd been excluded from in his old life. Then the memory of the shadow took over, and he grimaced at the thought that still his life was not his own.

The barkeep began to sweat as Isak glared at him, twisting a grimy cloth tighter and tighter around his pudgy hands.

"Do you normally let white-eyes in here?"

"I—Er, well, some o' tha mercenaries we get in these parts, it don't matter whether they're white-eye or no. Duke Vrerr pays for men who'll follow any orders and that al'ays bring scum—men as'll kill you soon as look as you."

"So you think I'm respectable enough for your establishment?"

"My Lord?" enquired Carel, sternly.

Isak kept the terrified barkeep frozen to the spot for a moment longer, then shook off his bad mood. He acknowledged Carel's admonishment and tossed a gold coin onto the bar.

"I'm sorry. Please, keep the beer coming. If you have brandy, then you look like you could do with one yourself."

The man looked down at the coin with suspicion, then nodded and swept it cleanly into his apron pocket. "Thank you, my Lord. Will you be wantin' a bottle yoursel'?" He was obviously still uncomfortable, but gold was gold.

"Yes, thank you, and we are going south through the borderland, if that's what you call the disputed lands south of here—why? Have you heard anything?"

"I—Well, nothin' new. But you might like to know they're a touchy breed south o' here. They fight Tor Milist *and* Helrect if either tries to claim the region. They see a lot o' soldiers passin' through, so a uniform they don't know, like them dragon badges, you'll get arrows every step o' the way. They'll prob'ly leave you alone if you don't boast your colours—and if you're goin' nice and slow and obvious-like towards Ghorent. That's the heart o' the borderland and some respec' to'ards the town should see you left in peace."

Isak nodded and muttered his thanks, then touched Carel on the arm and indicated he was going out to speak to Vesna. Carel nodded and turned to watch one of the guardsmen's efforts to engage Mistress Daran in conversation. Their evening amusement frequently revolved around a bet on who could draw the chaperone into an obscure argument and how long it could be strung out—that woman did like to argue once she had a glass or two of wine in her. So far they'd managed to conceal the actual betting from Tila.

Out of the corner of his eye Carel saw Mihn follow Isak outside. He smiled: at last his boy had friends, and ones who'd watch out for him at that. It was just what Isak needed, some friendship and reassurance in his life. But he still lay awake at nights worrying about how long it would last. Isak would always be a white-eye. Even if they stopped him looking for trouble, trouble would still find him one day.

A curtain of pink washed across the eastern sky as dusk closed in. A long tear just above the horizon glowed ruby red and to the west, towards the Gods, the sky was dark and forbidding. The bloody shard seemed to be pointing out the group's direction; the Gods ignored them. Behind them, in the north, a mass of clouds were ready to sweep down over the plains and pound them with sleet. The boats were waiting for them on the river, but Ghorent itself was still half a day's travel over the floodplains. More than once over the last few days, parties of bowmen had appeared at the side of the river to watch them pass. They were in no doubt that their passage was being carefully monitored.

Ghorent had to be close now, Isak reckoned—despite the sense of menace that hung over the borderlands, he was looking forward to a night in a town, anywhere with clean beds and fresh food. All those years as a wagon-brat had been wiped out by a few brief months in Tirah Palace, he laughed to himself, until he saw movement, a jerking shadow in the evening gloom.

He readied himself unconsciously, relaxing only when the shadow resolved into Jeil to answer his unspoken prayer. The ranger reined in just before reaching the party and called out in a clear voice, "My Lord, there's a fortified town up ahead with scouts watching the road; do you want us to announce you?"

Isak looked to Vesna and nodded. The count reached out and touched Tila on her gloved hand, an apology for cutting their conversation short, before handing her the reins to his second horse and cantering forward. Jeil wheeled about and then sent his stock pony in eager pursuit.

"Do you want to approach under a flag?" Carel knew the answer already, but Isak must confirm all decisions. The white-eye might not care about minor details like where they camped, knowing that if he did object, his word would be heeded, but he had to get used to the protocols of Farlan life.

So when the rangers pointed out a possible campsite, the greying soldier would turn to Isak and ask whether he would like to stop.

"No," Isak replied. "Somehow I don't think that would be appreciated here."

The villagers around here saw Ghorent as the heart of these disputed lands. This was where most of the inhabitants came for guidance or justice. The town council was respected precisely because it had no authority and expected none. The arrangement seemed almost absurd to the Farlan, who were used to rigid laws and conventions: there were no taxes paid, no real system of governance, certainly no army. What the people of the borderlands did have was a fierce pride in their way of life, and respect that bordered on affection for the views of Ghorent.

"Clearly not: they would see it as a boast of strength. Humility and respect is what these people want," Tila said from within the pale blue folds of her cape, wrapped around her to keep off the evening chill. Isak bobbed his head in agreement and nudged Toramin into a brisker pace.

"Well, let no man say I'm lacking in respect. We had better not keep them waiting." As the charger kicked forward into a canter, he heard Tila mutter something to Carel. The words were too soft to hear, but when they caught up and drew level with him they were both smiling.

It wasn't long before they caught sight of Ghorent's three towers and the wooden palisade that encircled the hilltop town. The gateway itself was made of stone, set into the tallest of the towers. Beacons shone out against the encroaching night, illuminating a line of bowmen who watched their approach with keen interest.

Vesna and the two rangers waited a hundred yards from the gate with two men, also on horseback. As they approached, Carel gave a signal and the Ghosts riding ahead split into two columns to allow Isak to the fore.

"Welcome, Lord Isak. You honour Ghorent with your presence," called the better-dressed of the two men with the count. His Farlan was heavily accented. His choice of words reminded Isak of an observation Tila had made a few minutes before: *The people see Ghorent as an entity.* "We" were not honoured, *Ghorent* was. She was right. It was Ghorent that was respected, not the individual people. A foreign dignitary would be unlikely to find such unity in Tirah.

"I am Councillor Horen, this is Captain Berard," the man continued. "Please, enter Ghorent as friends. We've been looking forward to your arrival."

Isak cocked his head, wondering if they would comment on their very effective tracking system.

The councillor noted Isak's face and smiled. "All will be explained when you meet the Seer. He has asked that you be brought directly to him before being presented to the Council."

Without waiting for a reply, Horen turned his horse and indicated for them to follow. Captain Berard, dressed in mail with a sheathed sword at his side, smiled in a guarded manner. He looked tough and proud, a professional soldier rather than just a mercenary, but his long dark hair drawn back from his face revealed a welcoming face. Life here must have been strange, considering neither man appeared either awed or surprised—most people were taken aback by Toramin's monstrous size even before they got to Isak.

Isak nudged his horse to follow and Vesna dutifully fell in beside his Lord, moving closer when Isak learned over to whisper, "The Seer?"

"I'm not sure. A mage of some sort, I assume. That might account for the town's prosperity."

Isak looked up as they approached the town walls. Vesna was right. The walls might have been of wood, but they looked strong and well maintained. The councillor was dressed as a Tirah city official might; he didn't look like the wealthy tradesmen who populated most town councils. As they passed through the gate, Isak and his party were watched by guards who betrayed little emotion: these were obviously disciplined men who trusted their leaders. They had no form of uniform or livery but they were clearly a strong and ordered unit.

Within the walls were tidy rows of wide, solid houses, well built and well maintained, for all their lack of decoration. Isak concluded that the security Ghorent offered had attracted men and women of many different skills. There were too many curls of smoke rising from squat chimneys to count: whoever had organised these people had a very tidy mind. If the Seer was the one running the Council, he must be a dour man of facts and figures, to keep this town so well ordered, Isak thought.

The houses this close to the wall were no more than two storeys high, but Isak could see taller buildings further in. Councillor Horen led them down the wide main street and past a tavern that looked like it was doing good trade—until sight of the visitors stopped the noise and bustle.

Toramin noticed the audience and picked up his feet a little more, showing off his well-muscled shoulders and flanks. Isak had no need to make an effort to impress; he gave the beast a tap on the neck, but Toramin responded by tossing his head haughtily and continuing to prance. In Kasi's dim light, Isak's white-sleeved cape took on an ethereal glow. The deep blue of his hood looked even more forbidding to the onlookers. More than a few found that dark face disturbingly similar to the icons of Nartis in the temple. They all heard the mutters that sounded like prayers in the sudden quiet.

Once past the tavern, Isak smiled slightly at the voices behind. It felt good to stir excitement in others. The wagon-brat had come a long way: now his presence in town was an event—he would be remembered wherever he drank or spent a night. The innkeepers would be able to say to customers, "I'll give you the best room in the inn, Lord Isak himself slept in it." More curiously, people would care that he had.

Up ahead, Isak saw that the road ended abruptly at a copse of trees standing at the centre of the town, where he would have expected a market square. The undergrowth had been cut back enough to allow passage and the councillor and captain went straight on in without pausing. Isak and Vesna exchanged glances. The trees were not densely packed—there was no cover for an ambush—so they followed their guides into the gloomy thicket. Isak could make out carved stones, sitting upright in the ground. They formed no apparent pattern, but were evenly spread—Isak could sense some echo there, a faint presence lingering in the copse. He guessed that this was dedicated ground, probably a temple of sorts to an Aspect of Amavoq or Belarannar.

On the other side, no more than thirty yards away, they rejoined the street, now dominated by a large building, the smaller houses looking almost as if they were keeping a respectful distance. By the standards of Tirah's wealthy the building was modest, but it was a surprising sight in Ghorent.

The councillor stopped at the ornate door and turned to his charges. "My Lord, I leave you in the capable hands of Ahden, the Seer's man." He gestured to the emerging figure, a tall, gaunt man who appeared from the bright interior. He padded down the stone steps, hands piously clasped together.

The manservant looked rather less impressed with the Krann than the tavern folk had been. "Lord Isak, welcome to Ghorent." Ahden gave a small bow to the white-eye as he dismounted. "My master is coming to greet you as I speak, but in the meantime might I offer you and your men food and wine?"

Isak made a show of stretching his back and shaking the stiffness from his broad shoulders. There was something about the staid figure with his thinning hair scraped carefully over his head that Isak didn't take to. When at last he deigned to give Ahden his attention, he was cut off by a voice from inside the house.

A second man burst through the door, gesticulating seemingly at random while he gabbled on in a high reedy voice. "Lord Isak, at last you've arrived. Come inside, your rooms have been prepared. My grooms will see to the horses; we have much more important matters to discuss. My study will be suitable."

The white-eye found his arm determinedly grasped by the scrawny hands of the man—presumably the Seer—who looked about to be engulfed by his billowing linen shirt.

Isak shot a bemused look to his companions. Few people outside his immediate circle of friends would dare touch the Krann, yet this odd little man was trying to escort him away like a child. Isak raised a hand to tell Mihn his presence was not required and allowed the Seer to drag him inside. As the man struggled to hurry Isak up, he launched into a discussion on the quality of horses they bred in Ghorent, happily providing both sides of the conversation.

The interior was markedly different to the houses in Tirah. Bright swathes of colour adorned the walls and the high hallway was filled with all sorts of wicker birdcages, hanging from the ceiling, from wall brackets, and mounted on beautifully ornate carved stands. Isak slowed to marvel at the room and take a closer look at the nearest bird, a delicate green creature the length of his finger, crested with the most glorious golden plume.

As he neared it, the bird cocked its head towards him and sang out, a rich liquid warble. The hallway erupted into a cacophony of song as the other birds took their cue and Isak turned in a circle to watch the sudden riot of noise and exotic colours. Tila, hearing the commotion, came after Isak and stopped dead, beaming with delight.

"My chorus seems to have taken a shine to you, Lord Isak. They rarely sing at night. They say the creatures of the forest have astounding abilities of perception—interesting that they do not seem afraid of you, a white-eye no less. When an Alyne cat crept in one night, ah the chaos!"

"You keep them all caged?" asked Tila, seeing how small some of the cages were.

"Certainly not; they spend the day in the trees of the town. We're rather well known in these parts for our exotic birds. When the nights are cold we tempt them into cages in the evening; the tamest do not migrate at all now." The Seer gave an expansive smile. His manservant glowered from the doorway as Vesna and Mistress Daran craned past him to see better. No doubt Ahden was the one who had to clean the cages.

"Did you know that the King of Narkang has a similar passion? He's carefully cultivated his gardens to attract the migratory butterflies that go up the coast from Mustet to summer around Narkang. I hear it's quite a sight—

the dusted blue is apparently most beautiful." The Seer stopped abruptly and his brow furrowed. "But this won't do, we must get on. Please excuse us, dear ladies, dear sirs. Ahden, bring up food and wine to my study when you have served the Lord's companions."

He took hold of Isak's arm once more and led him up the wide stairway to a corridor, at the end of which stood a pair of tall decorative doors. The polished wood was a creamy coffee shade, intricately carved with a fantastical pattern of animals and trees, but Isak had no time to study the doors further as his host swept him on into the room.

Piles of books and scrolls were spread across the floor, while jumbled brass instruments littered the many shelves, along with bits of pottery and odd stones, all broken and stained with age and dirt. A large open cabinet housed ancient-looking jewellery, and a few amulets and charms. Isak could tell that they were of very modest magical strength—he recalled the scornful way the mages from the College of Magic had dismissed such things as "low magics," suitable only for village wisewomen or forest witches.

The Seer flopped into a chair, only to bound up again as he compared his to the other chair in the room and considered Isak's bulk.

"How is it I've not heard of you when you seem to rule this region?" Isak blurted out as he took the seat offered and gingerly eased himself into it.

The Seer smiled and sat opposite, suddenly calm. He bridged his fingers as he gazed deep into Isak's eyes. "I certainly do not claim to rule anywhere; I merely offer advice—and only then when it is asked of me. As for having heard of me, well, I'm afraid it has been frequently observed that the Farlan do not take much interest in foreign politics unless conducted by a titled man. I would expect you have been told little more than that these lands are claimed by both Tor Milist and Helrect, but possessed by neither."

Isak nodded, not offended: he understood the friendly sarcasm. The Farlan were one of the greatest powers in the Land, and they set great store by their traditions and their strong feudal system. A man of noble birth had power and status; anyone who won power would soon receive a title and thus become part of the system. Men such as the Seer were simply not accommodated.

"Let me begin very simply," the strange old man continued. "Historically, this region has been either self-governing or conquered and under the thumb of some neighbouring Lord. In the current climate it serves the purpose of both Tor Milist and Helrect to not actually take the territory—first because they would find it no easy task, and second because they would then share a border with long-standing enemies."

"Can we start with you?" Isak interrupted. "I don't even know your name."

"Me? Ah, of course! Forgive my rudeness. My name is Fedei, Wisten Fedei, and folk here call me the Seer."

Fedei smiled to avoid that sounding a theatrical boast, but Isak just nodded for him to continue.

"I am a scholar. My history is rather long and complicated, but in brief, I had a modest amount of magical ability and training as a youth, as well as schooling in the more natural arts. Then, when I was twenty-five or so, I started displaying the classic symptoms of becoming a prophet—" he paused, waiting for Isak to interrupt, but this time the white-eye just nodded.

"That's where you are supposed to say, 'surely that's impossible?' the Seer said dryly.

"It is? Oh, right." Isak looked bemused.

Fedei chortled like an amused child. "Well, most people do. If you had received any formal schooling in magic you would know that is impossible."

"Probably," Isak replied, haughtily. "Would my formal schooling have been wrong about everything else too?"

"I—No, not at all. In this case, the theory still bears up to scrutiny, but as many of us find, the reality of the Land is often very different. In any case, as I'm sure you can tell from the lack of frothing and violence, I'm not a prophet. Somehow it was controlled by my magic—"

"Wait a moment, what magic? I can't feel anything."

The Seer bobbed his head in acknowledgement of the objection. "My abilities were almost entirely stripped in the conflict. I can still produce simple potions, and I can sense magic, but little more. What I can do is gather insights as a prophet, though only regarding the immediate future, and actually explain to others what I see. Think of it as having visions of impending events. They are not entirely clear, but your arrival, for example, was simple enough to understand. The ripples of your passing are profound even for me."

"So can you do any fortune-telling for me?" Isak hadn't intended it to sound sarcastic, but Fedei stiffened nonetheless.

His voice was frosty. "Perhaps later. For now, I would like to hear about you."

Isak nodded quickly, annoyed with himself for putting the Seer's back up when the man had been so welcoming. "Of course—though I doubt there is much you don't know."

"Did you meet Morghien on the road?"

Isak jerked in surprise. He had expected questions about his gifts. Only then did he realise that, unlike most people with any magical ability at all, the Seer had hardly glanced at Eolis. Like Morghien, he actually sounded more interested in Isak.

"I, ah, yes. How did you know that? Did you send him?"

"Send Morghien? Hah! A man such as that isn't sent by the likes of me. I just knew he was in these parts, and Morghien has always had the habit of casually meeting interesting people. He's a curious one, that's for sure. I first heard his tale when I was studying as a young man; I'm approaching seventy summers now." He laughed at Isak's sceptical expression. "You find that so strange? Those who live unnatural lives often find the effects of time slowed. You yourself will stop outwardly aging around thirty summers.

"In any event, Morghien visited me less than a fortnight ago. I don't know much about him, but his interests frequently coincide with my own, and he is interested in my enduring well-being. I'll wager he told you only the bare minimum about himself."

Isak nodded. "Is there much more to know?"

"I'm not sure myself," Fedei said, "but what I do know could endanger others, so this isn't a topic lightly discussed."

"How? What enemies could you have?"

"The Knights of the Temples, for a start. They dislike academics on principle." Now Fedei gave his guest a nervous smile, his fingers anxiously working at the trim of his shirt. "And the dear ladies of the White Circle: they appear to be courting power for reasons I cannot yet understand and I doubt they will be so tolerant of this region if they succeed in taking Tor Milist."

"No, there's more to it than that," Isak pressed. "What are you involved in?"

The Seer sagged visibly. "I dislike this; we've been so careful for years," he muttered, more to himself than anyone else.

"Dislike what?" Isak was getting increasingly confused.

He straightened up. "You know of Verliq, the mage, yes? What you perhaps didn't know is that he founded a school, one unlike any the Land has known since before the Great War. To ensure his teachings were not lost, Verliq sent many of his works away with his pupils, before the Menin invasion; that's how the West knows of him at all. His students were persecuted in every city, but they endured, and taught pupils of their own, in secret. Among those who know, they're referred to as Verliq's Children. In every city-state in the Land there are men who have his works hidden in their libraries, who believe that learning should never be heresy, even if it contravenes political dogma of the day."

"And why are you telling me this? If anyone represents political dogma it's me." Isak felt a familiar uncomfortable stir in his gut. There was more to this than he was being told; he could practically taste schemes, plots, and secrets.

"And that is why I dislike this, but Morghien says we must trust you."

"Morghien? He'd not even met me then—and why didn't he tell me this when he did find me?" Isak knew he was sounding petulant, but he was trying hard not to lose his temper.

"Morghien takes his time over everything. You'll never learn the full story in one sitting from him, sometimes for his safety and sometimes for your own. It doesn't take a Seer to know that we've entered the Age of Fulfilment, and we should fear it. What little powers I do have show me a shadow falling over the future."

"What sort of shadow?" There was something in Fedei's tone that Isak recognised all too well.

"*Everything* I see is overlaid by a shadow, and the further I look, the thicker it gets. It masses on the horizon like a storm cloud. I don't know enough to explain what it means; King Emin is the one for that. He and Morghien are preparing for something. You are important and I must help you in whatever way you need."

"How does Morghien know so much?" Isak asked, crossly. "The man looks like a tramp; how in Nartis's name is he in league with the King of Narkang?"

"There is more to Morghien than is apparent: he and Emin are a pair in that sense. It dates back to an expedition into the Elven Waste more than a hundred years ago, led by one of Verliq's Children. They went to explore a ruined castle, with a division of Knights of the Temples providing escort. The locals were supposedly friendly, but . . ."

"So they never came back from the Waste? That's not even surprising, hardly some dark mystery."

"Morghien came back, alone. I doubt anyone but Emin knows the truth of what actually happened, but if you mention the expedition to Morghien— Well, best that you do not. It was after that Morghien started travelling the Land, tracking down Verliq's Children, keeping the links between them alive. King Emin employs a handful of men who assist him in this, perhaps only twenty or thirty in all, but they're as lethal as Harlequins, and utterly loyal to him."

"You've met them?"

"They deliver messages, ask for news, offer help if I need it—"

"Help?"

"I have no use for them myself, but I've heard rumours: competitors disappearing, mysterious fires, city rulers suddenly going back on decisions. There's never anything definite, of course, nothing that could be laid at their door, but they bring letters whenever they come and sometimes I can trace the hand of fortune to their footsteps.

"There's a famous gang of criminals in Narkang, the Brotherhood. That's the name they use. You can recognise them by a black tattoo on their left ear, very small and easy to miss, an elven rune meaning 'heart'—though I don't know the significance."

Isak's entire body went rigid and only by a huge effort did he manage to prevent his hand from going to the scar on his chest. How many years had they been using that symbol? Could they have known? He was certain Xeliath had been telling him the truth, for the connection to her was undeniable, burned into his skin and quite sensitive enough to recognise a lie.

Isak barely registered the knock at the door; it was Fedei who jumped at the sound, flushing guiltily as he hopped up from his seat. Isak saw the panic on Fedei's face: this man who'd taken a white-eye by the arm and virtually dragged him inside was nervous even talking about the Brotherhood.

"Come," Fedei eventually called and Ahden strode in with a tray piled high balanced carefully in his hands. Isak helped him lay out the dishes on a side table, then set about them with a will, suddenly starving, and glad of the interruption. The scar on his chest felt tight, constrained, against the beat of his heart.

Eventually, Fedei could stand no more and noisily cleared his throat. "Speaking of symbols, I see your crest is a crowned dragon. Did the Heraldic Library properly appoint it?"

Isak nodded. "What of it?"

"Well, the dragon is a portentous symbol. I suppose it is to be expected, but those who have also worn it include Deverk Grast and Aliax Versit."

"Versit? The Yeetatchen Lord who sacked Merlat?"

"And was only defeated within sight of Tirah. That was him. Grast was the Menin ruler who almost wiped out the Litse, before forcing his tribe to take the Long March. Both men were followed by destruction their entire lives."

"Did either have a crowned dragon?"

Fedei squirmed under Isak's gaze. "No. I've never heard of any man to have that," he said quietly, staring at the floor.

"Tell me about your work," said Isak suddenly.

Fedei began to relax as he detailed a variety of projects, chattering on for the best part of an hour while Isak ate his fill, then sat nursing a large goblet of warmed wine. It was clear that Fedei relished the opportunity to talk to someone who showed a real interest in him; most of his colleagues were correspondents rather than visitors. While Isak couldn't provide much in the way of intelligent questions, he did display sufficient enthusiasm, and the Seer made the most of it.

Finally Isak interrupted him, changing the subject entirely. "So if you're a Seer, can you tell anything of my future?" He remembered Xeliath, and what Morghien had said, but he couldn't resist hearing what Fedei might be able to tell him.

The Seer nodded slowly and reached out to take Isak's hand. He closed his eyes, and started breathing deeply, rhythmically. Isak felt more than a little foolish; had it not been for the focused, entirely serious expression on his host's face, he might have pulled his hand away and laughed it off as a joke.

Fedei's hand was perfectly still for a time, then it twitched suddenly and Isak flinched at the unexpected movement. For the first time he felt a slight rush of magic from the Seer, just a trickle. The candles guttered under a draft that didn't touch Isak's skin; he sensed rather than saw a movement, something flashing around the shadows of the room. He twisted in his seat to follow it over his shoulder, but there was nothing out of the ordinary. He would have dismissed it as fancy before he saw Fedei looking in the same direction.

"What was that?"

"I'm not sure, my Lord." The Seer's voice was level but Isak could smell his fear. He shivered and took a deep breath. "When I touched your hand, I had a vision of some sort—not a portent of the future, but something else. I saw Aryn Bwr—or perhaps you, but the figure seemed lighter, less substantial than you are—fully armoured, with dragon horns on his helm. He casts a perfectly black shadow. He stands within a circle of twelve crystal columns, each one twisted and bent into some awful shape. Facing him is a figure, a knight with a fanged sword in one hand and a hound's leash in the other."

Isak couldn't suppress the shiver that ran through his body as he pictured the knight in black armour and his massive fanged sword. He could remember the icy bite of its edge all too clearly from his dreams.

"The leash runs to two figures that sit at his heel, a naked Chetse on one side and a winged daemon on the other." The Seer's voice shook a little.

"What does it mean?" Isak could hardly bring himself to ask the question, but he forced out the words.

The Seer, pale as a ghost, slowly swivelled his head to match Isak's gaze. The movement appeared to break the stupor he was in and he sank back into his chair as though drained of strength.

Isak got up and moved quickly to his side. The Seer's breathing was shallow and for a moment Isak thought his heart had given out. He lifted him into a more comfortable position and asked what he should do to help. He felt useless.

"I feel so weak. Please, ring for Ahden," the old man whispered.

Isak found a bellpull beside the fire and tugged it hard, setting a jangle of bells going in other rooms. Within a matter of seconds, Ahden was storming into the room, ignoring Isak as he made his way straight to his master's side.

The servant told Isak curtly that his companions were waiting for him downstairs. Maids would show them to their rooms. Isak looked at Fedei and said softly, "Feel better. We'll be fine." He received a wan smile in reply.

Isak rejoined his friends, who were gathered together in a stately but comfortable room, chatting. He said little for the rest of the evening, the image of the dark knight and his fanged sword weighing heavy on his soul.

CHAPTER 27

THE DESERT SMELLED OF AGE. Looking around at the withered trees clinging to the rocky ground, Kastan Styrax felt his own fatigue even more strongly. The ghost of an evening breeze yawned past his face as he removed his helm and looked at the cultivated scrap of land that, astonishingly, had warded off the desert long enough for the houses here to grow old and dilapidated.

Unhooking the golden rings of his belt from the great padded saddle, he slipped down from the wyvern's back and onto the dusty earth. The freezing air high above had left his muscles cold and stiff, but it took only a few careful steps to recapture his balance. He flexed his huge shoulders twice and then drew the fanged sword from behind his back.

He stretched his back, arms, and shoulders by working through forms, slowly, assuredly. As the massive blade hissed through the cool air, the grunting wyvern behind him turned its head, then returned its unblinking eyes to a figure trotting towards them from the distant houses.

The moves completed, Styrax returned the obsidian black sword to its sheath and sucked in a great gulp of air. The scent of the desert was more apparent down here, where the air was warm and calm, and he stood still for a moment to savour it. He spotted a miniva, one of the strange, dust-coloured plants that flourished all over this desert, providing food for animals and humans alike. Styrax bent down to examine the delicate fronds of the miniva leaf that absorbed what little moisture there was in the air. Lifting the flattened leaves, he exposed the deep-red plant stem. The tiny fruits were pale, not yet ripe, but he plucked and ate one, savouring the sharp sourness. A smile hovered on Kastan Styrax's lips as he waited for his vassal to approach.

"My Lord," said the arriving soldier. He removed his black iron helm and dropped to one knee. His hair fell down untidily as he bowed his head. When he peered cautiously up he had to shake the long strands out of the way. After a pause he was motioned to rise. The man was small for a white-eye, and it was even more apparent when he stood before the Lord of the Menin.

"Duke Vrill. Everything proceeds as planned?"

"As well as I could hope for," replied the duke. He cursed himself as he heard the nervousness in his voice; however slight, Lord Styrax would notice. In recent years their rare meetings had been in the comfortable surrounds of Crafanc, and Anote Vrill had forgotten just how overwhelming his master could be, particularly when dressed for battle. The soul-sapping, weirdly curved armour grated on the edges of the duke's soul as much as the vile air of malice radiating from the sword Kobra. He shivered.

Styrax said, "You've had problems with the centaurs. The Dark Knights are about to return home. Suzerain Zolin ran a sword through one of his own bondsmen, and a mage of the Order of the Five Black Stars was murdered last night."

If any other man had said that, Vrill would have gaped in surprise. The duke prided himself on being better informed than his peers, yet his Lord always managed to surprise him. It had often occurred to Vrill that, in another age, he would have been Lord of the Menin, for no one, nobleman, merchant, or politician, could match him for intellect and plotting—with the exception of Lord Styrax. As it was, Duke Vrill's lust for power had not overshadowed his intelligence and it was clear that Lord Styrax was at least equally adept at intricacy and cunning. Even the Mages of the Hidden Tower lived in fear of his skill. Only a madman would exercise the Menin right of challenge—though that most ancient of laws stated combatants should use identical weapons, it would make no difference. Styrax had won his right to rule at the age of twenty when he had killed his predecessor, who had ruled the Menin for three hundred years. The old Lord had wielded Kobra. Kastan Styrax used a steel broadsword. His prowess was unsurpassed and soon the entire Land would come to recognise that.

The duke put his musings to one side and concentrated on what his Lord was saying. "How did you know about the mage?"

"I told Kohrad to do it. The man was a necromancer, and my son relishes any chance to practise his own arts." There was a hint of laughter in that statement, but Styrax was a man who laughed alone. He didn't joke for the sake of others.

"So that's why he burned a falcon. I hadn't realised there was reason to it."

"That was the reason. Kohrad is not completely gone yet, but I am hoping he overextends in the battle. Pitting him against the Order of Fire might amuse him enough to draw more magic than he can control. If that happens, Gaur knows what to do. You will assist him however he wishes."

Vrill nodded, then ventured, "Is Kohrad dying, then?"

The white-eye Lord drew in a sharp breath at the question, but Vrill had proved many times that he knew his place; that he intended to find greatness in Styrax's shadow. He could be trusted, as far as Kastan Styrax trusted anyone.

He answered the question. "Eventually it will consume him, but I have no intention of losing this battle—or any other."

Vrill nodded and bowed low, discreetly withdrawing from Styrax's presence. "I will have a man bring you food."

Styrax nodded distantly, staring away to the fading sun. As wisps of cloud stretched away like the sun's smoky trails, dusk wrapped the landscape in chill shadows. "Make sure he's young, and of no consequence."

Vrill hesitated, surprised by the command, then nodded curtly and marched back to his men. Styrax returned to the wyvern and unbuckled the saddle—none of his beastmasters were there to tend to the creature, and a hungry wyvern wouldn't let a common soldier see to it. Once the ornate saddle was removed, Styrax took hold of the creature's nearside horn and roughly pulled its head towards him. The wyvern resisted for a second, then moved. Styrax peered into one massive green-veined eye and checked the shine and dilation of the pupil for a moment. He gave a grim smile, satisfied the beast remained sufficiently in his thrall.

He ran his fingers over the massive, blue-green scales that covered the wyvern's head. His left hand, snow white now, was bare, as always. He felt little sensation through the skin since the day he'd won his armour on the battlefield. He ran a red-stained fingernail down the edge of one scale, teased out a small parasite, and crushed it. He tapped lightly, listening carefully, and found two more of the potentially lethal parasites. There was no time to check the wyvern's entire body so he stopped once the head was clear. That would do for now. From his saddle he withdrew a large, tightly wrapped bundle and untied the leather straps that held it together. He shook the bundle out and laid it on the ground. The woven silk looked creased and worn in the fading light. He didn't bother pulling out the waxed tent cloth. There would be no rain tonight, only a biting cold that the many layers of silk would keep at bay.

The wyvern stamped one clawed foot and dragged a furrow through the ground, then shook its large horned head at Styrax, stretching out its wings to their full extent. He silenced it with a short gesture, but it was clear from the glare it gave him as it hunkered down that the wyvern was not wholly cowed. A minute or two of foraging found an armful of sticks, not enough to keep him warm throughout the night, but sufficient for his needs. Once the wyvern settled down for the night, it would willingly allow him to curl up against its belly.

Styrax divided the sticks into two piles and waved a hand over one of them. It burst into flame. He smiled, wondering idly when he had last lit a fire by natural means, until a snort from the wyvern made him look up towards the buildings in the distance. A figure trudged slowly towards him, a bulky soldier carrying a bag in one hand and a skin of wine in the other. He was tall and well built but as he drew closer, his youth became apparent, as did his fear.

Styrax could imagine what was going through the young man's head. The Menin attitude to sex was open and permissive—the male form was rightly admired in a warrior tribe—but the youth looked less than pleased at the prospect. That wouldn't matter soon. What Styrax had in mind was something rather more unfortunate than buggery.

He turned quickly and retrieved two small leather bags from a larger one. Drawing a rough circle in the parched earth with his foot, he emptied the smaller of the bags into it. A dozen or so white objects tumbled onto the ground. Styrax quickly checked that none touched the edge, then pulled a pinch of black withered herbs from the other bag. As the youth covered the last few yards, Styrax raised his fingers to his nose and breathed in the sour, sickening flavour of deathsbane that had been soaked in blood and left to dry. It was a truly repulsive smell, but he had to ensure the herbs retained their potency.

The soldier reached him and dropped to one knee, but was immediately ordered up and told to put the food and wine by the fire.

The boy kept his gaze glued to Styrax's face. The wyvern snorted and hissed in the background, weaving its head from side to side until a second glance from the Lord quietened it down. Styrax stood at one edge of the circle and beckoned the youth forward. One pace, then a second and the boy was standing inside the circle.

With no warning, Styrax's hand flashed forward and the soldier gave a gasp of shock, his hands flinching up to his chest as his entire body swayed with the unexpected impact. Styrax withdrew his hand and the youth wheezed in fear and pain as he saw a dagger buried to the hilt in his chest. Tiny noises escaped his throat; his knees trembled, but somehow he stayed upright. His shaking fingers reached up to touch the ornate bone handle that blossomed from his sternum.

Styrax reached forward with the treated herbs on his upturned palm, the desiccated plants twisted and cracked with the pain of being plucked from the ground. He raised his hand to the man's face and ignited the herbs as the soldier touched the hilt of the dagger. The agony of his mortal wound suddenly hit him and his eyes rolled as a hot lance of pain ran through his entire body. With one last gasp of horror that sucked in the dirty smoke of the burning herbs, the man crumpled down. As Styrax whipped the dagger from his chest, the soldier's descent halted with an unnatural jolt.

A gloom fell over the rough circle, the calm breath of the wind shivered to a halt, and time itself seemed to shudder and slow. Despite himself, Styrax twitched as a chill ran down his spine. He stared at the corpse jerking uneasily back to an upright position: he could feel the void of death close by now. He sighed. Only a madman would be comfortable around this.

The boy's face looked hollow, drained. His lips were drawn back tightly over his teeth and his tongue lolled out, useless. The limp head angled its way up to meet Styrax's gaze, dropped down to check the circle that contained it, and then returned to the impassive white-eye.

The dead features somehow managed to convey a hint of anger that it had to crane its head up to face the white-eye. "You bind me?" The voice was grating and harsh, bubbling its way past the still-warm blood in the body's lungs: it clearly came from the corpse, though there was a strange, distant echo.

"I bind you," confirmed Styrax. "I have no interest in seeing you slaughter an élite regiment, not to mention my most valuable general."

"Your promises are empty. You offered a river of souls, yet I have had a mere handful. I think you forget with whom you have made a bargain."

"I have not forgotten. Your river of souls is gathering, and when it comes, the dead will number in their thousands." Styrax stared down at the corpse and felt contempt. The daemon was a prince among its kind, incredibly powerful and as old as time, but it didn't care why he wanted its help. It was content with the deluge of death and destruction Styrax had promised. Its abilities far exceeded its desire and for that, Styrax could only despise it.

"But when?" The corpse's slack lips quivered.

Styrax could hear the hunger in that inhuman voice. "Soon. We've cleared a path to Destenn. Soon the destruction will begin. If we are to win a decisive battle we need to catch the Chetse army out in the open and under-strength. Your servant had better have done its job correctly, or Lord Charr will not march out as soon as he hears of our presence."

"Lord Charr weeps in the dark place; he cares not for his tribe. What inhabits his body loves battle. It will need no encouragement."

"Then skulls will be heaped at every crossroads and your name spoken over them."

At that the corpse gave some perverse representation of greedy laughter. Styrax felt bile rise in his throat. He had to resist the urge to draw Kobra and remove the creature's head. Instead he nodded along. He would not need to pander to this obscenity much longer. Already he had the strength to defy it; soon he would make it fear him, and beg to fulfil his every whim. Soon it would have nothing he could need.

"And in the north?" Styrax pressed.

"The haunted does not sleep; the cries of the lost ring out through the night. He has sent the boy west and searches in forbidden places. He will do as you intend."

"The boy has gone west? Do any in the mountains remain bound to your name?"

"Those who have sworn cannot escape their bonds. You would do well to remember that. To forswear is to draw down our wrath."

"Then fill their dreams with glory and riches. If both of the Chosen are far from home then the Farlan are ripe for revolt. Find a man who would be king."

"Tear down the temple and speak my name there." The corpse sagged as Styrax began to drive the daemon from its host. Styrax nodded his agreement and caught the daemon's final words, almost too faint to be heard. "Then tonight, Lomin will dream of his crown."

The clicks and buzzing of night's creatures filled Styrax's ears as the air around him returned to normality. He felt his body tremble with the power he'd expended. To raise a daemon was no great effort, but they were other-worldly and aside from the march of time; to keep it long enough to hold a conversation required strength, more each time.

He turned to the fire and sank down, his white hand almost touching the flames as he sought to absorb its warmth and purge the daemon-cold. Almost as weak as an old man, he waved in the direction of the wyvern. With a snarl, the creature scrabbled to its feet and fell upon the dead soldier, scimitar claws making light work of the man's leather armour. Soon savage teeth were tearing chunks of the boy's flesh away.

"I see you, shade," called Styrax wearily, keeping his eyes fixed on the fire. "You take a great risk, spying on a prince of your kind. I wonder why."

"*My kind?*" The voice was entirely unlike any daemon Styrax had previously encountered. "*And yet not. I hardly feel kinship to such an introverted creature, so unable to see beyond its own needs and obsessions it could almost be human.*"

Despite himself, Styrax laughed, a cold, weary humour. This was a daemon after his own heart. "Then why are you here? Do you wish to bargain with me?"

"*I require no covenant, but perhaps you would appreciate a warning. The Farlan whelp will not be the only one to return to a cold reception.*"

Styrax considered the words, and the voice that spoke them. From the corner of his eye he could see nothing more than a shadowy outline. The voice, though rich and cultured, sounded both ancient and sinister.

"And who gives me this warning?"

"*An observer of events. An approver of ambition. He who is hidden conceals more than you might assume.*"

"How much do you observe?"

"*Much. 'In flames, destruction found.'*"

Styrax stiffened. "That's a line from the prophecy of Shalstik?" Inside, he was raging. If one daemon, however unusual, could discover his secrets, then others could, others that might be bound to his enemies. Styrax was not yet strong enough to challenge the Gods, and ownership of a Crystal Skull was not encouraged, even among their greatest Chosen.

There was no reply.

CHAPTER 28

DORANEI IDLY SCRATCHED AT THE STUBBLE ON HIS CHEEK, keeping his eyes low and disinterested as he eavesdropped on the next table. He sat alone in a dark corner of the inn, sipping weak beer and occasionally checking the scarf had not slipped from his neck. The bar was warm and the tightly wrapped scarf had attracted some attention, but Doranei didn't have the sort of face that encouraged questions. The next table was occupied by a group of farmers discussing the topic that occupied everyone else in this town: word of Lord Isak's imminent arrival had come two days ago, and he was expected this evening. Tongues were wagging.

"Can't see that one sending the Krann away if they've fallen out. He's a mad bastard when he's roused—"

"They all are," interrupted another. From Doranei's brief observation of the trio it seemed this speaker had been born surly. Only bitter little miseries had passed his lips throughout the evening. "A traveller told me that the Krann was too ashamed to leave his tent for three days after the battle of Lomin. Even for a white-eye he'd fought like a blood-crazed daemon." The man was bent over his drink, staring into the near-empty pot with a resigned air.

The inn was hardly the best this small town had to offer. The wooden walls were cracked and warped; the stench of sweat and mold and old smoke and spilt beer filled the air. Doranei was well used to sleeping under the stars or in a stable, but the ingrained grime nagged at his mind.

Face it, Doranei, he thought with a wry smile, *the king's made a snob of you. This is the sort of tavern you spent far too long in when you were younger.*

"So why's he coming, then?" urged the youngest of the three. The dirt wasn't yet ingrained into his skin like the others. A spark of interest in the Land remained yet.

Doranei knew the answer. Underneath his scarf he was concealing the bee emblem. He was dressed in studded leather and mail, but that was common enough here; no one would take much note of a soldier. The bee device would mark him out as a King's Man. Dark things were whispered about the King's

Men, rumours that they were above the law, which was actually one of the few truths told about them. With the bee in full sight, honest men would go silent in his presence and wonder what indiscretions they might be accused of. No magistrate would dare touch Doranei, no matter what the crime, in case it bore the royal sanction. It would be futile to explain to people that the king demanded absolute selflessness of service from his men. He punished corruption savagely—and had an uncanny knack of rooting it out.

"The Krann's probably here to sign some treaty," declared the first farmer after a thoughtful pause. "Everyone knows the Farlan have claims on Tor Milist, probably they don't want a war with us, so King Emin and that Krann, what's his name again—?"

"Isak, they say. His father named him out of spite—typical bloody Farlan. Probably regretting that now his son's Krann!" The surly individual laughed at his own words as his companion nodded.

"Isak, that's the one. Bet he's here to draw a line down Tor Milist and offer the king half. Bastard'll probably take it too, another few towns to hang his colours in."

Doranei's fist closed instinctively. The three farmers chuckled on, unaware of how close they were to a beating, when a trumpet rang out through the night. This was a border town, with lookouts on constant watch. The men looked at each other, the smiles falling away: riders approaching. It was a fair guess that one of them would be the Krann.

Talk in the tavern quietened, then stopped completely as folk looked at each other to see who was going to move first. They all wanted to see the white-eye in his fancy elven armour, but no one wanted to be the first to rush off and stare at a foreigner. Farlan arrogance wasn't appreciated here, not now that Narkang's strength neared that of Farlan and Chetse.

Doranei stood slowly, the scrape of his chair drawing all eyes. He unwound his scarf with deliberate care, drawing great satisfaction as the three farmers started shaking at the sight of the golden bee on his collar. He pulled on a worn pair of gloves, retrieved his cape from the spare chair at his table, and then made his way out. In his wake Doranei felt people stir, but he had reached the stables before he heard eager footsteps run for the walls. He ran an affectionate hand down his horse's grey neck; she turned to nuzzle at him, then nosed his hand, questing for food.

He draped an arm over the horse's neck and, looking straight into her hazel eye, said, "Well, my friend, shall we go and see this Krann who's got everyone so excited?"

The mare snorted and shook her head. Doranei chuckled and patted the creature. "Ah, you could be right there. However, it will be as the king commanded. The Krann might be bringing dark times, but that's been our life for a spell anyway." He swung himself easily up into the saddle, then the tall grey mare started out at a brisk trot towards the gate tower.

"Hey, where do you think you're going?" demanded the watchman belligerently. Behind him, Doranei could see a collection of men eyeing him nervously. One was riding a handsome hunter, probably the local suzerain. He was old, but he could obviously still wield the blade at his hip. The others were town councillors, nervous and sweating under the ceremonial finery of their offices. Doranei suppressed a smile—their opinion of all Farlan as peacocks would hardly extend to a white-eye.

"I've been sent to greet the Lord Isak and put myself at his disposal."

The watchman advanced with a curse on his lips before noticing the emblem on Doranei's collar. He reined in sharply, eyes narrowing in the dim light. "You're a King's Man?"

"No, I just wear his badge because I hear he's a good man to irritate," Doranei snapped. Without waiting for a reply he directed his horse around the man and advanced on the others. To one side a mounted figure stirred, only to be stopped by a raised hand from the suzerain.

As Doranei reached them he saw the figure in the shadows was wearing fine clothes, but his gauntlets betrayed mail underneath. Doranei guessed it was the nobleman's son. That was all he needed now, a provincial hothead who was yet to learn he couldn't be rude to everyone he met. The old soldier who'd sired him obviously had wits enough to be cautious. The king was very specific about his men getting the right amount of respect due their position. If that meant fighting duels with incautious noblemen, he was happy to pay the price.

"My Lord Suzerain," Doranei called, inclining his head respectfully to the man. He made a point of ignoring the others, turning his back on the councillors as he rode past them.

"I'm Suzerain Coadech," confirmed the older man. "And you're no royal herald. Why would the king send a soldier to greet the Farlan Krann?"

Doranei kept his face impassive. Though he would prefer to be friendly with the suzerain—and he had heard good things of Coadech—his job meant he stayed apart. King's Men were an unknown quantity to all but the king himself.

"He would not; he sent me instead. However, I'm sure he would prefer you, his most venerable subject, to ride out and greet the Krann."

The son made an indignant noise, but the suzerain merely smiled. He'd seen enough of life not to react to a small jibe, given in a friendly way. King's Men held no titles, but their power rivalled any subject of the king's.

"Then I would be pleased to. I hope the king would not find me impertinent if I don't offer your *services* to his honoured guest, other than as a guide—it might appear strange to put *all* of your skills at the disposal of a foreign power."

Doranei's eyes narrowed. He was very aware that many believed the wearers of the bee to be little more than royal assassins—but there was a crinkle of humour around the suzerain's mouth. He returned the smile and gestured for the elderly man to take the lead. A whistle from above set the men opening the great ceremonial gates. The suzerain trotted forward, followed closely by his scowling son so there would be no room for Doranei. The King's Man ignored the youth and turned to the councillors.

"Wait here. If the Krann has had a long journey, he might not want to meet a whole line of officials before he's even got off his horse."

They looked dismayed at his words, but found no courage to protest as he tapped the hilt of his sword impatiently.

Doranei followed the suzerain out and allowed his eager grey mare to catch up to the horsemen fading into the twilight. Up ahead he could see a neat troop of soldiers, bright against the shadows in their white tunics. At their heart, riding the biggest charger Doranei had ever seen, was the Krann, gleaming in what light remained of the evening. Even Doranei caught his breath at the sight. The Krann was masked to resemble the blue face of Nartis, but it was the liquid silver that encased his body that made him appear like a God looming in the dark.

The soldiers around him were in full battle dress, yet their drapes were not the austere colours of the Palace Guard but a dragon design Doranei recognised only from the reports they had received. With the eyes of the forewarned, he picked out the black and gold of Count Vesna riding just behind the Krann, and a startlingly beautiful woman, obviously noble, close to the hero. Behind them rode a thin woman of middle age and proud bearing, a chaperone, presumably, given Count Vesna's reputation. Who the man riding alongside her was, Doranei could not imagine. He wore the dark, functional clothes of a scout instead of armour, but two rangers already flanked the soldiers.

Well, this is a curious collection we have here, the King's Man thought as he watched the formalities unfold. Suzerain Coadech reined in and the Krann's guards split neatly to allow their Lord to pass through them to the front. The drill had obviously been well practised, Doranei noted with a soldier's eye: there was not a horse's hair moving out of step.

The Krann trotted forward with serene grace, towering over them all. *Already I'm wondering how many stories are playing out here, and I've yet to meet the man at the centre.*

"Lord Isak, Chosen of Nartis, Heir to Lord Bahl, and Suzerain of Anvee," called the suzerain in a clear voice. "On behalf of Emin Thonal, King of Narkang and the Three Cities, I bid you welcome to his realm."

Isak looked out of the window and down on the rows of tables set out in the square below. The old suzerain had given them his own house to use—the finest in town, from what Isak could see. A bath sat, grey and cooling, behind him as he surreptitiously observed the feast being prepared below. The servants were scurrying about, flowing neatly around the town official whose efforts at ordering them around seemed to be creating only disorder. A raised platform stood at the far end of the square, cordoned off from the rough benches where the townsfolk would congregate and toast the health of any foreigner whose arrival prompted free beer.

The platform itself had been draped in white linen and carefully decked in flowers. There was enough room for at least eighty people to sit. Isak sighed heavily at the thought of all the preening nobles and officials lined up and oozing affected pleasure at his presence, but he knew there was nothing he could do about it. Bahl wanted him to be comfortable in court life. Perhaps he intended to reduce the distance that existed between the Lord of the Farlan and his nobles; perhaps he just didn't want to do it himself.

Isak watched the view while drying off, then let the towel drop to the floor as he ran his hands over his head. It was strange to have hair again. Tila had advised him not to keep shaving his head, pointing out that he looked intimidating enough without highlighting the blunt lines of his skull. Turning back to the room he eyed Siulents on the armour stand that had been provided. He took a step towards it, and then caught sight of himself in the mirror.

The armour forgotten, he stood before the full-length mirror and angled it up to observe his naked frame. His reflection had always fascinated Isak: the image he presented to the world was so different to how he saw himself. The stranger in the mirror peered back with equal curiosity, looking for the slender child Isak still pictured himself as. Neither his increased height nor his added bulk looked quite right. He didn't particularly care to look as brutally powerful as he obviously did. He sighed. He *did* like the power residing in his limbs. That would have to be compensation enough.

A knock on the door caused Isak to jump and his gaze flew immediately to Eolis, hanging from one corner of the four-poster bed.

"My Lord?" Mihn's voice sounded from behind the door.

Isak grabbed at the fresh underclothes that Tila had laid out on his bed, pulled them on, and then called for his bondsman to enter. Now he knew Mihn's past, Isak found himself remarkably secure in the failed Harlequin's presence. He'd kept all other enquiring eyes from the scar on his chest—the mark of Xeliath's affection, as he joked to himself—except for Mihn, who had seen it and said nothing. Bahl considered it Isak's own business, and Mihn would stay silent until Isak was ready to talk about it. Isak wasn't sure whether he should involve the others to such a degree—Carel, Vesna, Tila: they still had the option of another life.

Vesna grew more devoted to Tila each day. Just watching them share a joke, or smile tenderly at each other, spurred a pang of guilt in Isak. He knew he might well have to ask a lot of his bondsman in the years to come: would he be able to endure Tila's silent condemnation if he called upon the father of her children to commit murder—or worse?

He felt a different shape of guilt at how he might use and abuse Mihn, but he understood the need, and Mihn had nothing else. The foreigner shared something with Xeliath: another broken life Isak carried as a burden, another damaged soul he'd use as a weapon when the time came.

That thought made Isak pause. Even *he* was beginning to think that he had a purpose in life . . . In the darkest hours of the night he lay alone and worried that the assumption the Land made, that he had a cause for which to fight, would bring destruction, that any prophecies would be self-fulfilling. Could he cope with what might be required of him?

Mihn entered the room, took one look as Isak, and slammed the door shut behind him. Isak's eyes darted up in surprise. "The man Doranei has come to speak with you. He will wait."

Isak pulled on a linen shirt and cream trousers similar to those worn by his guards. "Send him in," he ordered. Picking up the tall cavalry boots sitting at the foot of his bed, Isak sat and began to fit his feet into them. Doranei sauntered through the door and past Mihn, checking the room for whatever he'd been excluded from seeing before his eyes settled on the Krann. Mihn cut across his path, forcing the King's Man to stop dead, and knelt at Isak's feet to help him with his boots.

Isak gestured to a chair and Doranei drew it up, carefully placing it to one side of Mihn before sitting.

Isak left the boots to Mihn and inspected his visitor. "That's an interesting tattoo on your ear."

Doranei stiffened slightly and turned his head slightly away. Isak couldn't see the actual shape, but he didn't want to make it appear that he was too interested. He'd have bet the entirety of Anvee that he had something to match it.

"Merely the product of a wayward youth, my Lord. I trust everything has been to your satisfaction thus far?"

"It has, but I don't think you're here to see I have enough blankets. So would you like to tell me what a member of the Brotherhood is doing here?"

Doranei didn't blink. "I, that is, the king, merely wishes to ensure your passage to Narkang is as unimpeded as possible." Doranei's Farlan was fluent, with barely a trace of an accent. Lesarl had told them that Farlan was fast becoming the country's second language. Most traders in the northwest spoke Farlan, and the keen merchants of Narkang took even greater pride in their linguistic proficiency. It showed how cosmopolitan Narkang was.

"And I had been advised that these lands were remarkably lawful. Or does the king expect any trouble in particular?" Isak asked.

"Of course not, my Lord. However, I wear the king's device and that gives me the right to commandeer supplies or lodgings on his behalf for your party. Some might also say that our laws are rather more permissive than those of the Farlan. There are several, sometimes competing, parties who call these lands home." He paused. "The Knights of the Temples, for example."

"Well then, I trust there will be no unpleasantness on their part," Isak growled.

"I am sure that will be the case. The Knight-Cardinal has submitted a request via the king for an informal meeting, but as such it can be refused with little offence given. In part, my visible presence will ensure that those you meet will not have another guise unknown to you."

"The king's spies are that efficient?"

"They are more than competent. Our enemies cannot be certain of what we do or do not know—that limits them in itself."

Isak rose and took the dragon-embossed tunic from Mihn. As he pulled it on and fastened the toggles he retained eye contact with the King's Man.

"You have an unusual manservant, my Lord."

A flicker of discomfort passed over Mihn's face.

"Really."

"And Count Vesna rides with you too. I'm sure he will be as popular with the husbands of this town as that attractive young lady will be with the wives."

Isak made no reply as he fixed his long white cloak about his shoulders with a dragon clasp. The evening was going to be quite long enough without having to banter words now. He turned to the mirror to see how the Land would view him now. There was no hiding the bulging muscles and massive frame, but the reflection was as civilised as Isak had ever looked. A smile appeared on his lips.

Apart from his first fitting of this suit, back at Tirah Palace, this was the first time he had worn his crest like this. He spent a wordless minute following each and every line of that dragon image, the golden curls of its claws and proud rampant stance.

"So tell me about Morghien. I hear he is more than he appears."

Doranei chuckled at that, scratching at his freshly shaved face as he smiled. "To tell you about Morghien, that is where I would start. Unfortunately, it also explains how I would end. Did the Seer tell you about him?"

"No, he was waiting for me on the road." Isak caught Doranei's reflection in the mirror, but saw nothing more than vague surprise on the man's face.

"I learned a little about Morghien—and you—from the Seer, but not enough, I suspect. What did interest me was that Morghien gave me a letter for your king."

"And you read it?"

"I could hardly believe that was not the intention. It's there, in that pack by Siulents."

Isak pointed to the one he meant and Mihn retrieved the scroll. Doranei opened it and scanned the first few lines. "Velere's Fell," he muttered to himself.

"A year ago I would have thought that to be a ghost story, but not since

I heard about the Malich affair, about the Azaer cult—" Isak saw the hardened soldier flinch at his words and knew he'd scored some sort of hit.

"Please, my Lord, now is not the time. As it is, I am not the man you should speak to about this . . ." His voice trailed off as Isak held up a hand.

There was an angry glare in his eyes. "Let me guess, the king is the one I should speak to. I've heard that before and it grows old." The white-eye took a step forward, but Doranei managed not to shrink away from the looming figure.

"Then I can only apologise. I am a servant of the king and I know only what I need to know to perform whatever function is required of me. As you can tell, King Emin is a man who keeps much to himself—but from this letter, from my presence, I can only assume he intends to provide you with answers. I understand your frustration, but please, be patient and enjoy our hospitality until we reach Narkang."

Isak grimaced, but made no further comment. He swept the sheathed Eolis off the bedpost and fastened the sword belt about his waist. With one hand resting on the emerald hilt, he cocked his head at Doranei and forced a smile on to his lips. "Well then, lead on to this hospitality."

CHAPTER 29

THE JOURNEY TO NARKANG WAS SWIFT AND PLEASANT. The Farlan party was carried by a luxurious barge down the Morwhent River, accompanied by a merry procession of boats of all shapes and sizes. To Isak's immense surprise, he found the noblemen who welcomed him into their manors each evening to be likable and open people; King Emin's rule was now twenty years established, but the titles were still held by those who had supported his conquest. In the place of the old nobility the king had installed merchants, ambitious minor nobles, and more than a few pirates and smugglers who'd joined the war effort. It was said that Emin Thonal couldn't resist the friendship of an arrogant rogue, though a number of those had found to their cost that the king was not a man whose trust could be abused.

The Farlan saw a vibrant nation, proud of their successes and unashamed that they had no particular one of the seven tribes to call ancestor. It was a long way from how the Farlan liked to think of the "lesser peoples," but that it worked was undeniable. When they exercised their horses each morning and evening it was with an escort of élite Kingsguard who clearly held the Ghosts up as their benchmark and were keen to prove themselves their equal in horsemanship and sparring. The competitions were good-natured and cheered on by the local people whose adulation of the Kingsguard was marvelled at by the Ghosts. Leaning over the barge's rail, watching the fields sliding past, Carel pointed out that it wasn't only Isak who had something to learn from this nation.

Isak cantered gently up the slope, studying the King's Man waiting for them at the top of the ridge. They were approaching Narkang, so they'd spent the whole morning in the saddle: tradition dictated that Farlan always ride into a foreign city and Isak wasn't about to break with custom just yet. Doranei had taken himself off that morning, riding ahead of the party to ensure its path was unhindered.

Despite Isak's initial suspicions, Doranei had proved good company as they travelled through the country he loved. The man knew when to talk and when to keep a comfortable silence. The Krann suspected he had a few secrets of his own—perhaps all of the Brotherhood did—and they had taught him the value of silence.

There was a sparkle of spring in the air. A brisk breeze ran over the fields and whistled over the road before shivering through the branches of a bank of ash trees on the other side. Through the trees Isak could see neat rows of crops and a manor house in the distance. Boys lazed on a paddock fence, coaxing horses over to them, while the cattle they were tending drifted aimlessly in the meadow. As Isak and his companions neared the peak of the rise, the wind changed direction and brought the taste of salt from the ocean.

They reached Doranei, who stretched an arm out to present his city.

"Behold, my Lord: Narkang, First City of the West."

Beside Isak, Tila gasped. A wide, open plain stretched out before them, painted the vibrant green of spring and dotted with dark copses of copper beech and elm. In from the east came the Morwhent, the river that had carried them most of the way to the city, now running wide and slow. A pair of high arches spanned the river to a small island in the centre, which allowed the sandstone city wall to run unbroken even by the river's passage.

From the banks of the river the wall followed the curve of the ground up and around in a gentle undulation to encircle wide regular streets of purple-slate rooftops.

Occupying the higher ground deeper inside was what could only have been the White Palace, its twin silver-capped towers glittering in the sunlight. The lower ground of the western side, where the river entered the city, was hidden by the walls, but a great copper dome shone in the sunlight. Past that, faint in the distance, Isak could see a soaring slender tower that would have been remarkable even in Tirah.

And somewhere even further beyond, vague and grey in the distance, lay the ocean. Isak could feel the immense weight of water lurking at the back of his mind, an old and powerful presence, but comforting nonetheless. The magnificence of the ocean, stretching out to the distant horizon, beyond which lived the Gods, overshadowed even the glory that was Narkang.

A thousand flags fluttered and whipped from the walls of the city, a dis-

ordered mix of colours and shapes, and a huge banner hung above the
Southern Gate. The banner was almost as large as the massive copper-plated
gate itself, and even at this distance, the visitors could easily make out the
golden bee with its wings outstretched over the green background.

"It's a fine sight, is it not, my Lord?" continued Doranei as the remaining
Farlan soldiers vied for position to take in the view. "Visiting foreign climes
is an easier thing to do when you've Narkang's smile to return to."

"A fine sight indeed." Vesna and Carel nodded their agreement. The city
was confirmation that Narkang's power equalled that of Tirah, and they all
knew it.

As if Narkang was not enough, the low plain in front of the city was a
hive of activity. At least ten great pavilions and stands were being erected,
while long swathes of tent cloth lay out on the ground, ready to be raised.
Hundreds of cut posts lay in stacked piles; cables and ropes snaked all over
the ground and a veritable army of people scurried in all directions with
wagons and livestock. Flocks of sheep were being herded to the joyful yaps
and barks of the hounds protecting them, drowning the calls of the shepherds
and those in their path.

"The Spring Fair, my Lady," supplied Doranei as Tila cast him a questioning look. "It's due to begin in two days, the day before the Equinox. It will
be the biggest yet. I believe the entire city will rejoice at your visit, Lord Isak."

"I see a scarlet banner over there. It's hard to make out, but I'm guessing
it's the Runesword of the Devoted?"

"It is, my Lord."

"And you still think I'll be welcomed by all?"

"I doubt the Knight-Cardinal wishes to make an enemy of you, my Lord."

"After what I did to his nephew, I hear he wants to make a corpse of me."
Isak laughed grimly.

"His personal feelings are still secondary to the requirements of his office,
my Lord," Doranei said sternly. "First, there is the fact that you might be the
Saviour his Order has been waiting for; second, the Devoted are not so powerful as to openly defy King Emin."

"Surely the existence of Piety Keep is a fairly obvious point of defiance,"
interjected Vesna. The Fortress of the Devoted was jokingly referred to as
Piety Keep, a nickname the Order despised. Lesarl had warned them all that
using it in Narkang could easily result in big trouble.

Doranei scowled. Isak guessed that he didn't mind about the name, just
that politics intruded on the pleasure of returning home. "The matter is not

quite so simple, but I'm sure the king would prefer to debate it himself." He broke off as the two rangers trotted up with a third man, dressed like Doranei, right down to the bee at his throat.

Doranei smiled, and said, "My brother, Veil, has taken word to the king that you have arrived. Royal processions take a little time to get moving. I'm sure you understand."

Veil didn't dismount, but touched his fingers to his lips and forehead in salute to the followers of Nartis, struck his fist against Doranei's, and then whipped his horse around to return. Despite the similarity in dress, the man looked nothing like Doranei. Isak thought it a fair assumption that under Veil's long dark hair was another tattooed ear.

Carel ordered the guards to dismount, brush down their horses to remove the morning's dirt, and tend to their uniforms—just one morning back in the saddle had taken its toll on the cream cloth. Isak found a handful of oatcakes in his saddlebag and a hard hunk of cheese to chew on as he swapped his saddle from Megenn to the more impressive Toramin. The gelding was a fine horse and superbly trained, but the fiery stallion was Isak's favourite. Toramin's dark flanks were draped in a pure white cloth so that only his head, neck, and hocks were exposed. Isak's helm dangled from his saddle, within easy reach.

Isak turned to see Vesna struggling into his armour for the first time in weeks, chuckling to himself as the man fought to free himself of a snag. Magic might have made the black iron lighter than normal, but it was no less awkward. Tila was already wearing full court dress; she had ridden sidesaddle all morning. Now she perched with practised ease, fastening charms and jewellery to her dress before wrapping a silken scarf artfully about her head.

The wait was much shorter than anyone had anticipated. Isak, lazing on Toramin's back, had been watching first Veil's passage to the city and then the activity on the plain. Veil had disappeared inside the city only a few minutes previously, but a faint chorus of trumpets prompted a double column of horsemen to trot out through the gate and split away to line each side of the road. Once these troops were out and ready, a second fanfare announced another group of horses, this time no more than twenty in number.

In their usual order, the Farlan cantered down the slope. The spare horses and baggage had been quartered with a merchant Doranei knew—Isak knew that this meeting of rulers could potentially be momentous and he saw no reason for either ranger to have to say he was a mile back and looking after the horses when Lord Isak met King Emin for the first time. They might have been stoical veterans, but they didn't deserve to miss out on the fun.

As soon as they heard the fanfare, people arrived to line the broad thoroughfare that led to the city. There was quite a crowd by the time the Farlan neared the centre of the plain, all eyes straining to see the foreign white-eye. As he passed the first few, Isak caught mutters and whispered oaths but he ignored them. He knew as well as anyone that Siulents alone was an intimidating sight, and the enormous dragon-emblazoned charger only added to the effect. Toramin's shoulder was just shy of six and a half feet from the ground; with Isak on top the sight was absolutely awe-inspiring.

Looking ahead, Isak began to make out individual faces in the procession; he tried to fit them to what Tila had schooled him on over the past few weeks. Out at the front was obviously Emin Thonal, King of Narkang, dressed in his own colours. Some white material showed through slashes down the sides and arms, clearly the height of fashion, if the other noblemen were anything to go by. A wide-brimmed hat topped with a feather sat cocked to one side on his head, again echoed by those behind him. Isak couldn't help but wonder, with all he'd heard about this man, whether he chose his dress just to see who would follow.

At the king's side rode his queen, brightly clad in spring colours, on a slender bay. Though she was a little older than King Emin, Queen Oterness was both dignified and elegant, and neither the grey wings in her shining auburn hair nor the faint lines around her eyes detracted from her serene beauty.

The king's bodyguard rode behind the royal couple, a white-eye the size of General Lahk called Coran, who had been the king's closest confidant since he took power. Rumours about the king and his friend persisted as the queen failed to produce a child, despite the white-eye's well-known appetites for the city's plentiful whores. Lesarl's spies had concluded there was little to the gossip; the pair were close through the attractions of power, not of the flesh. Coran was dressed soberly in a neat and functional tunic similar to that worn by Veil and Doranei: not quite a uniform, but enough that Isak knew to look for a bee device and tattoo when he was near enough.

As the two parties converged, Doranei gave a small twitch of the hand and the escorting columns of Kingsguard moved off to drive the burgeoning crowd back from the road. Careful to give the Farlan more than enough room, the soldiers turned their horses halfway out towards the crowd, then turned inwards in their saddles to salute.

Carel growled an order and the advance section of Ghosts split away and fell behind before the two parties actually met. Isak led the remainder a little way into the funnel of Kingsguard, then reined in so he could approach on

foot. Tila had quietly mentioned that it would hardly be seeming for King
Emin to greet his guest from two or three feet lower: there was still a huge
difference in height, but on horseback it would only be accentuated.

Taking that as their cue, both parties followed suit and strode forward to
meet each other. With hands out, palms up, Isak approached the king, who
swept off his hat and executed a deep bow. Feeling awkward, Isak was about
to follow suit when the king stepped forward to grasp Isak's arm in friendship.

"My Lord Isak," King Emin declared in a clear, cultured voice, "please be
welcome in my kingdom."

"King Emin," Isak replied, keeping his voice at a similar level, "I thank
you, and all the people of Narkang and the Three Cities, for the welcome I
have received every day I have spent in your kingdom."

Isak bowed as he spoke. Tila had told him that the Farlan had never officially acknowledged Emin Thonal's self-coronation, so those words made a
significant gesture, both politically and theologically.

Understanding showed in Emin's eyes as he returned the bow.

He looked younger than Isak had expected. He had ruled Narkang for
twenty summers, taking over the city when he was only a little older than
Isak was now, but his hair was untouched by grey, the light tan glinting in
the midday sun. He had handsome features, dominated by a strong nose and
brilliant blue eyes. Looking into those knowing eyes reminded Isak of Lord
Bahl's own piercing stare. He lost himself there for a moment before remembering protocol required him to speak again.

"May I present those I bring with me? Count Vesna, the Lady Tila Introl,
and Marshal Carelfolden, the Commander of my Guard." The king nodded
to each as Isak held a hand back to Tila and she passed him the gifts Bahl and
his Chief Steward had so carefully selected.

"Your Majesty," Isak continued, "please accept these as gifts of friendship, the axe named Darklight—" he held out the wrapped weapon and Emin
immediately loosened the cord to pull off the canvas covering. He lifted it
up: a single-headed axe with a wickedly curved spike on the reverse, made
from a single piece of dusky steel, not black iron but something *other*, with
four rods of steel strengthening the wooden shaft. Cut right through the
body of the blade were five runes: light shining through as their edges
glowed red. The king handed the covering to Coran and slipped one ring-
bedecked hand about the grip. The Chetse had small fingers, so one of the
guardsmen had carefully added extra leather binding to Darklight's grip. As
King Emin flexed his fingers about it, Isak thought they had underestimated,

but the king took a few practice strokes and appeared delighted with the result. He beamed at his guest and passed the weapon back to his bodyguard, who rewrapped it, then cradled it carefully in his arms.

"For your queen," Isak continued, "I offer these jewels, created solely for her and those who share her family line." He handed King Emin a small leather box, which he passed carefully to Queen Oterness.

The queen opened the box as carefully as her husband had unwrapped Darklight, but her gasp of wonder was entirely spontaneous. Nestled inside the velvet-lined container were twelve brilliant-cut emeralds, set in gold, connected by four thin chains of gold to a larger emerald. As soon as the queen touched one of the emeralds, all the jewels started to twitch, and one length of chain reached out tentatively to touch her hand. Snake jewels were famous enough that the queen knew what to expect, but still she looked alarmed as the golden chain began to work its way up her arm. She trembled slightly as the jewels slid with a reptilian movement towards her shoulder, but everyone was watching, so she ignored her fear and gracefully inclined her head towards the largest emerald.

With delicate care the chain wove itself in and out of her gleaming auburn hair, carefully positioning the jewels until the large emerald had wriggled its way to the surface at her forehead. The smaller emeralds now circled her head like a crown. Once they were all in place, they stilled. The queen reached up to touch them hesitantly—they felt like normal stones, normal gold, except for an almost imperceptible warmth.

She smiled at her husband, then curtsied deeply to Isak. "You honour me," she said. "I do thank you, for me and for my daughters to come."

For a moment Isak glimpsed the sadness in her eyes and recalled the couple were still childless, but then Queen Oterness smiled, and it lit up her eyes. Isak smiled back and inwardly sighed with relief. He hadn't been sure the snake jewels were right—they'd startled him when Tila had shown him how her grandmother's set of sapphires worked—but Tila had promised him that once over the initial discomfort, any woman would adore such a gift. The jewels had some property imbued in them that seemed almost to enhance beauty. Certainly Queen Oterness was almost glowing now.

Isak had decided not to offer the last gift, the book, publicly. A *Murder of Cardinals* was an account of the Malich affair, written by Cardinal Disten, the man who had exposed the plot in the first place. Isak suspected that King Emin would disappear with the book and pore over it for hours, probably with his curious friend Morghien, at the first opportunity.

Now King Emin bowed again, and said, "My Lord, your generosity overwhelms us. I fear I have nothing to offer a man so blessed with gifts as you, but the freedom of my city and realm are yours, as is my lasting friendship."

Isak smiled: this was all going well. The host should offer nothing but friendship, and since that was what Isak had been sent to win, he was pleased. His first attempt at diplomacy was not going too badly, at least so far.

He indicated his retinue and said, "We look forward to exploring the beauties of your city; thank you for your kindness."

"And," continued the king, "if such a friendship results in sufficient trade to require an embassy here, I would be delighted to offer you the former duke's residence in perpetuity as your home away from home; a little piece of Tirah in Narkang."

From the murmurs, Isak guessed the offer was both unexpected and generous. He bowed again, not sure if he should do or say anything else, but the bow seemed to suffice.

The king was speaking again. "But I have been remiss in my introductions. Lord Isak, allow me to officially present to you Queen Oterness."

The queen held out her hand and Isak took it gently, as Tila had taught him, and kissed the silk of her glove.

"My bodyguard and friend, Coran," he continued, indicating the people as he spoke, "my Prime Minister, Count Antern, and the Chief Councillor of the Public Assembly, Morten Deyl."

Isak inclined his head briefly to each one. Coran looked like a thug with the brains to realise he was nothing without the king. Count Antern looked every inch the sly, ruthless politician that Lesarl had described: the man was utterly loyal to his king and had profited enormously by it. The only unknown quantity here was the Chief Councillor: Morten Deyl had recently been elected to head the Public Assembly. He'd come from almost complete obscurity, but his first year in office had resulted in a host of allegations and rumours. To Lesarl's fury, he had still not discovered who had engineered the vote.

Isak noticed the Chief Councillor's narrow eyes never left Eolis the entire time, even when he bowed. Whatever else he was, the man was a coward.

"Now, my Lord, I'm sure your companions are tired from the journey. Apartments have been prepared in the White Palace for you and your staff— and this afternoon I thought the public baths might be an excellent place to visit. Even if I do say so myself, I think you'll agree they really are quite magnificent." His enthusiasm was infectious and Isak was not the only one who found himself smiling at the thought of such a luxury after their journey.

Isak stood on a balcony above the courtyard of the palace, surveying the neat beds of red, orange, and white flowers that lined the white stone walls. There was a surprising absence of guards—the whole palace felt genteel, elegant; Isak thought it was overly relaxed, and definitely vulnerable. Huge, ornate golden cages standing on pillars all about the grounds housed a multitude of extravagantly coloured songbirds whose voices filled the palace. Isak recalled what the Seer of Ghorent had said: he could well imagine how beautiful the grounds would look when thousands of butterflies arrived. The network of gravel paths, ornate fountains, and marble statues was a far cry from the hard-packed earth and tired, worn grass of Tirah Palace's training ground. What few guards there were wore gold-plated armour and appeared to be as ornamental as the songbirds.

"He must be very sure in his power," Isak commented to Vesna. "This place is wide open to attack."

The count had been very glad to get out of his armour now that the formal introductions were over; their overtly militaristic dress felt rather uncomfortable in these refined surroundings.

"He's designed the place carefully, that's for sure," he replied. "Look carefully: those walls, for example—the top piece is wooden. I'd wager that a unit of men with hammers could knock out the pins, drop them down inside the wall, and be there to man the battlements underneath within minutes. Did you notice the ground outside the outer wall? It's not solid. That's just a layer of earth over boards, no doubt covering a deep ditch. And these apartments? They form a ring, accessible only from the inside. If the main wall is breached, Emin has the higher roof of this ring to turn that pretty courtyard into a killing ground."

Isak looked around once more. In place of a defenceless fancy palace with a sculptured garden, he now saw a classical two-wall castle. He pictured the king himself, and his feathered hat: the absurd headgear hadn't detracted from the man's coldly brilliant eyes that looked as if they saw everything.

"That does seem to be the theme of this city," he agreed. "I wonder what else we'll find lurking under the finery?"

"I'll keep my eyes open in the public baths, watch out for the smiling and the harmless, as my father would have said." Vesna took a bite from an apple and leaned against the balcony, looking up at his Lord.

"Yes, I'm sure you'll find something to look at there. All those married women bathing . . . Tila won't speak to you for a week," Isak teased.

The designers who turned Narkang's half dozen natural hot springs into one of the great wonders of the Land had created three smaller chambers alongside the main public bath. The first was reserved for soldiers; the king's habit of ennobling his supporters meant many of the city's rich élite were scarred veterans. The smaller chamber afforded them a degree of privacy, and allowed the younger generation to mingle with military heroes. King Emin hoped lessons learned by the older soldiers would be passed on not only through training, but by talking.

The second was for women only, so unmarried girls were not on public display, as they would be in the main bath.

The last, the smallest, was a private bath chamber reserved for the royal couple. Few had ever been invited into this sanctuary; it was a rare honour. Since Doranei had been the one to bring Isak's invitation to join King Emin there, it was clear that there was real business to discuss—business that needed to be kept private.

They were summoned to the courtyard an hour or so later, to find King Emin and a line of litters ready for them. His entourage was smaller; the only new-comer was a rather harassed-looking man, unevenly shaved and obviously uncomfortable in his dress uniform. The man couldn't have been more than thirty summers, but from the way he was shifting from foot to foot it looked like he could think of far more productive ways of spending his time than sitting in the public baths with some foreign dignitary.

"Lord Isak, this is Commander Brandt of the City Watch. I know you have your Ghosts, but it will be Commander Brandt's responsibility to ensure they are not required. You have the freedom of the city, but I'm afraid you might find a rather troubled Brandt trotting along behind."

Isak smiled. That made sense: Commander Brandt might have started out as one of the ambitious noblemen of the Kingsguard, but he'd obviously had the shine rubbed off by years of chasing criminals. "He's young to be Commander of the Watch," Isak commented. There was a tense pause and then the Krann grinned at Brandt. "I assume that means he's good at his job, so I'm delighted to have him on hand."

Relief flushed over the commander's face. At King Emin's gesture, the Krann made for the litter with the largest bearers. Most of them had a half-naked man at each corner, their skin oiled, jewellery hanging from their ears and about their necks. Each bearer had curious leather thongs hanging from their wrists. As Isak stepped towards his litter he saw four more bearers move up discreetly to share the weight.

Tila had warned him that litters were the normal choice inside the city walls, but Isak doubted that the bearers had ever had someone of his weight. He tapped the edge of the frame before sitting down, glad at least to feel a strong metallic frame under the cloth. Satisfied the litter at least would bear him, Isak made himself comfortable.

The bearers allowed him a moment to settle, then carefully wrapped the leather thongs about each handle and lifted. A slight grunt came from one of the men, but none wavered. The man on the back-right corner checked his team to make sure they were not about to drop one of the most powerful men in the Land, then they stood ready while the rest of the party did likewise.

Mihn ignored the litter and stationed himself on Isak's left, steel-shod staff held as a walking stick. A small bag hung from his shoulders, tied tight to his back so the book and scroll it contained would not restrict his movements in case of trouble. Commander Brandt took up his station on Isak's right. His hand rested on the rapier at his hip; his eyes checked out every other figure in the courtyard.

King Emin waited until his guests were sorted before he climbed into his own litter, then the whole procession set off, quickly finding a natural rhythm. They shuffled with surprising speed, out under the peaked arch and into the city. Each litter had a thin bamboo framework hung with silk so the passenger could draw a curtain and block out the city, but Isak was far too interested in seeing Narkang. Tirah was a grey city, all ancient stone and brooding clouds. The buildings in the main streets were tightly huddled, and many of the canopied walkways on each side had evolved into covered arcades. Narkang was completely different: life took place in the wide avenues, and the streets served as extra space for the hundreds of taverns and stalls.

It was hard to see much of the buildings surrounding the palace, but Isak got the impression that most were centred on large open courtyards. Gates opened as they passed, people crowding outside to watch the royal procession. There were fruit trees laden with blossom, clay tiles, and colourfully painted shutters on the tall windows: they all combined to make the city look bright and friendly—an appearance that belied the iron bars crossed over every accessible window.

"Commander, I hear you have a simple job policing this city," Isak said, leaning forward slightly.

Commander Brandt gave a snort of laughter, but as he opened his mouth to retort he caught the smile on Isak's face. "In what way, my Lord?" he asked, anxious to hear the young Lord's reply.

"Well, if Narkang is all controlled by the Brotherhood, then surely whenever a crime has been committed you just arrest one of the leaders."

Brandt laughed, but Isak saw him stiffen too. The mention of the Brotherhood had triggered the reaction Isak was seeking.

"It's not quite so simple," the commander said. "The Brotherhood might have great influence over what happens here, but it's still a long way from controlling all activity in the city. I think that if it tried that, the leaders might well wake up to find Coran explaining how this would not be an entirely good idea."

"Coran?" Isak asked, then he recalled, "Ah yes, the king's bodyguard. Tell me, do the Devoted have a significant presence here?"

Brandt opened his mouth, but said nothing—maybe he didn't know what to say. He looked over the crowds, looking for distraction to excuse himself, but saw none. Reluctantly he returned to Isak, who was waiting impassively. "They do, my Lord. The Knights of the Temples are far older than this kingdom, and in some part it has been the maintenance of those links that has prevented all-out war in these parts, not just recently, but for hundreds of years."

"So they're popular then?" Isak's tone was cold.

The commander understood, and ignored the question as best he could.

"They are traditional, Lord Isak—that's perhaps the best way to describe it. In some families boys grow up knowing they are expected to join when they leave childhood. The Knights that rule the cities are sometimes seen as overly strict, perhaps, but they have strong sympathisers among the ruling families."

"And your own?"

Brandt frowned, but didn't hesitate to reply. "Certainly in my family. My father was a member, my elder brother, Suzerain Toquin, is a major in the Order. My sister is married to a colonel, who may one day be vying with my brother for the post of Knight-Cardinal."

"And you?" Isak wondered whether the king was playing a game, setting a Knight of the Temples to guard him.

"My father didn't bother with me. I was too far down the line of succession. He thought a watchman might be of more use to the family than a priest. Not that I regret it; I'm truly married to this city and the laws that keep it. That, I think, is enough ambition for any man."

Isak nodded, lost for a moment. It was easy to envy Commander Brandt if he spoke the truth: he knew his city, and loved it like a mistress. He could see his purpose and pursue it; his successes and failures were clear and immediate. Isak lacked that luxury. He'd never even seen most of his nation. The flag, the tribal characteristics clear in a man's face, the Farlan dialect—were these things enough for someone to love? Wars had been started over nothing more than one man's fits of pique—did it even matter what was real under the weight of history's tide?

"An ambition fit for any man," Isak agreed at length, and with approbation. Now he lay in silence, wondering about the course of his life, playing with the ring he wore on the middle finger of his left hand: a shaped tube of silver an inch long engraved with his Crowned Dragon crest. Farlan men did not generally wear signet rings, ever since Kasi Farlan, young and impetuous then, had lost his temper with the older and more skilful Koezh Vukotic. He had lost his little finger and signet ring in the subsequent duel.

"Commander, do you have a son?"

The man looked startled at the question, but answered, "Yes, my Lord. My eldest is a boy, nine winters."

Isak pulled the ring from his finger and held it out to the man who, after a slight hesitation, took it. He inspected the engraving.

"Give this to him," Isak said. "Tell him to look at that dragon when he wonders what the future holds—and not to dream too hard. Tell him never to forget that he's just a man, like any other."

The commander tucked the ring carefully into a pocket before replying, "My Lord, that's good advice for anyone—a boy of nine or a king."

Isak nodded sadly, unable to meet the commander's gaze.

The rhythmic slap of the bearers' leather-sandalled feet and the swish of their linen skirts on their bare legs marked the procession's steady progress into the heart of the city. The pungent scents of waste, smoke, food, and sweat swirled all around. A line of brown-coated watchmen kept the people back as the crowds swelled, all eager to see the foreign princeling. The houses were wooden here, and closer together, though still prosperous-looking. They all had roofs of the distinctive purple-slate tiles.

Up ahead Isak caught sight of what had to be their destination: an imposing stone building that looked down upon the whole district through massive vaulted windows. The two-storey-high apertures lined both of the longer sides, and each contained a bronze statue, taller than Isak, that watched the streets below. He could see three: Ilit carrying the Horn of Seasons; Belarannar, Goddess of the Earth, with ivy curling about her shoulders; and, in the centre, Vasle, God of Rivers, for the baths were dedicated to an Aspect of the river God.

They entered a wide courtyard, in the middle of which stood a statue of a woman clothed only in sheets of rushing water. A brass plaque on the plinth she stood upon gave thanks to Baoliss, daughter of Vasle. A large copper bowl half filled with water sat at her feet; coins, jewellery, and small figurines had been left there as offerings and thanks.

"My Lord," Mihn's soft voice barely carried above the bustle around them, "it might be sensible to leave a generous gift with the Goddess. This place is her only domain; she might find your presence threatening."

Isak thought for a moment, and quickly agreed; his encounter with Morghien had left him wary of divine sensibilities. A handful of gold emins would be a small price to mollify Baoliss; he had enough to worry about already without upsetting a Goddess. He patted his pockets for a suitable offering, but he'd not come prepared. He whispered to Mihn, who nodded and ran over to Vesna's litter. Another short conversation and he was back with a small but heavy leather pouch, which he handed up to Isak.

Isak reached out and tapped a bearer's arm. The man gave a short whistle and the litter bearers stopped, but before they could lower the litter, the white-eye had slipped his legs over the side and was standing.

Ignoring the staring faces, he approached the stone figure and carefully poured the emins into her bowl, silently thanking Vesna for having the forethought to provide himself with local currency. He smiled to himself: typical of the king to name the coins after himself! As the emins splashed in, Isak felt a presence at his shoulder. A shiver ran down his spine as a whispery breath floated over his ear, then vanished. The echo of a giggle wafted up from the gravel, and then he was alone, with just a vague feeling of a smile touching his skin. That was enough to reassure him.

"My Lord," called King Emin. The queen and Coran stood behind him, both with an air of anticipation. Count Antern seemed to have disappeared somewhere; Isak couldn't see him in the crowd of faces. The Krann took one last look at the statue and bowed almost imperceptibly, then cast around for his own retinue. They had gathered at an appropriate distance behind him. Isak and his party joined the king at the marble-pillared entrance and followed him in.

Isak stared at a massive, beautifully intricate mosaic that showed the God Vasle leading a torrent of water down a river towards a column of elves. He had no idea if this was some famous battle.

He turned his attention back to the long hallway, trying to ignore the stares from those sitting on the sofas and chairs that lined the room. At least a hundred people sat, or stood facing them. Isak recognised the hostile expressions, even if the faces were unknown.

There was a wide range of dress and colour, but Isak noticed a good many red sashes bearing the crest of the Runesword of the Devoted, and several clusters of white-shawled women. One of the parties of women included a man in their group, though the others appeared to have male escorts at the side.

As King Emin and the Krann began to walk down the hall, talk recommenced, though Isak noticed the women in white watched silently. He began to feel rather like an insect that had crawled onto the best carpet: a particularly large and interesting insect, but still not one they intended to touch.

King Emin, for his part, appeared to notice nothing. Nodding to smiling faces as they presented themselves, he swept down the corridor with all the confidence of a crowned monarch. This, Isak thought in passing, was what Tila had been trying to drum into him.

And here was the first lesson. The king commanded the room immediately, dominating the attention of all, secure enough to merely note those faces that didn't smile at him. The tangible air of confidence Emin brought with him made up for the fourteen inches he conceded in height to Isak. Even the brisk stride he had adopted to keep up with Isak's long legs contained no element of rush or hurry.

The corridor led to a small arched doorway, similar in style to the main entrance, but blocked by a brass-bound door. On either side stood a soldier of the Kingsguard, resplendent in dress uniforms—but however beautifully etched, the spearheads were still sharp, and lethal. Off to the left lounged three more obviously armed men: Doranei, Veil, and a particularly tall man with ash-blond hair and a rough scar down his cheek that spoiled his otherwise good looks.

They straightened as their king approached, and the guardsmen pulled the doors open to display a circular pool some eight yards across, steam gently rising from the surface. The walls were tiled in tiny ceramic pieces: this mosaic detailed a scene of feasting and relaxation and stretched all around the chamber, disappearing behind a partition the height of a man that ran along the wall opposite the door.

Marble nymphs sprawled at the edges while another statue of Baoliss sat at the far end, a trickle of steaming water running from her hands into the pool. Busts of the Gods sat in alcoves, the eyes of each picked out in expensive colour: sapphires glinted from the blank face of Nartis, gold shone from Death's cowled head. It was the brilliant emeralds shining from the Lady's perfect features that caught Isak's attention. She was a curious choice, for the Lady was not of the Upper Circle. He didn't doubt that the king had a good reason for her presence.

Doranei and his colleagues marched straight in and headed for the far wall, where there were three high windows, about six feet off the ground. Without breaking his stride, Veil raised one foot and placed it onto a ledge that Isak could now see running the length of the wall, two or three feet high. From there he leapt easily up onto the sill, a dagger drawn but hidden, and peered through the open windows to the outside wall. His search for spies satisfied, he gestured to the others.

Doranei retrieved a pole from one corner and passed it to Veil, who used it to hang heavy pieces of linen attached to rods over the open windows, obscuring the view for any outside observer, but leaving the room still light enough to see each other's faces. Isak thought it rather excessive, but this was Emin's city.

"Lord Isak." The king stood by the wall that sectioned off part of the room and beckoned him over. "I'm afraid we don't have time to enjoy the comforts of these restorative waters. Perhaps you would take my word that they are excellent and follow me?"

Isak gave the man a quizzical look as he disappeared behind the partition. Coran stood back impassively, just far enough to permit Isak's passage. He looked around: Doranei and his colleagues—Isak guessed the scarred man was one of the Brotherhood too—waited on the other side of the pool.

With Mihn close behind, Isak followed the king behind the partition to find a polished wooden bench opposite a small stone shrine at the far end. The shrine, the height of a normal man's chest, had empty slots for incense sitting before an icon of each God of the Upper Circle.

"Excessive piety has its uses," commented Emin as he indicated the shrine. "Would you be kind enough to move that to one side? It should go very easily for one of your strength; it pivots about the right-hand side."

Isak looked suspiciously at the shrine, but he could detect no magic anywhere so he nodded and gripped the sides carefully. The shrine did indeed twist to the right with almost no effort. The wide base moved aside to reveal a hole in the ground. Isak peered in, but he could see nothing. The king smiled and bowed in mock thanks, then stepped past the Farlan Lord and crouched down to the hole.

"The city worries that I have some distressing skin condition. I spend many hours at the baths, so they naturally fear the worst. My doctor is well paid to possess a creative imagination, and by half a dozen others to reveal all he knows. He's starting to enjoy it now, I think."

He smiled and dropped through into the black depths. The Krann turned and caught Mihn's amused expression. He still couldn't see anything, but if the king had taken that fall so easily, how could he not? Another lesson, it appeared, whether intentional or not: find out how deep the hole is before you show it to anyone else! Isak reached a hand out into the space before him and concentrated. It was easy now. Within a few seconds a faint blue glow began to emanate from his fingertips, then it increased in intensity, creeping out to caress the smooth walls of the tunnel below and the floor, perhaps seven feet down.

Emin waited casually to one side, one eyebrow raised theatrically at Isak's use of magic. "Come, my Lord, time is a-wasting."

Isak dropped down, followed by Mihn, and then Coran lowered himself down carefully and deliberately. Isak was puzzled until he saw Coran drop the last few feet onto his right leg. Interesting, Isak thought: given the recuperative powers of most white-eyes, either that damaged leg was a recent injury, or it had been a very severe one.

The king reached out and touched his fingers to a rope that ran all the way down the side of the wood-beamed tunnel. With the light Isak still brandished it was unnecessary, but Emin still trotted his fingers along the rope as he walked off down the slightly sloping tunnel, followed by Coran and then, with a shrug, Isak and Mihn.

As Emin chattered idly away, the hole quietly closed up behind them.

CHAPTER 30

"**Y**OUR MAJESTY—"

"Please," interrupted the king, "that's a little formal for these surroundings, don't you think? Call me Emin—at least when there's no one around to sniff at the breach in protocol!"

"Of course," Isak said. "What I wanted to know was why you use the 'heart' rune."

Emin turned, the weak light casting a strange shadow on his face. "For the Brotherhood?" He shrugged. "A whim, nothing more. Did Fedei tell you that?"

Isak nodded.

The king didn't seem at all irritated by the Seer's revelation, merely curious. "My only requirement was a basic design that could be recognisable, even when so small. I decided on a core rune because they are very simple, and chose 'heart' because it can mean 'kernel' or 'stone' in certain contexts, like a cherry stone, for example. I thought that apt for Narkang: rich and sweet, but under the surface not so vulnerable. If an enemy takes too great a bite, he'll break his teeth, I promise. That's all, nothing more sinister." He laughed. "Why?"

Isak shook his head. "No reason; it just struck me as strange."

"As does much in this life, I find. Ah, here we are."

They had walked several hundred yards and now the tunnel ended abruptly at a wall set with iron rungs. Isak could see a square wooden shaft with slivers of light creeping through the gaps between the higher planks. The rungs were no more than finger-thick steel rods, bent into two right angles and hammered into the rock. Isak tested the first gingerly after Emin had climbed up, but it was clear they went deep. By the time Isak reached halfway up, the king had exited through a trapdoor and into what looked like a cupboard.

Isak peered through at floor level and wrinkled his nose at the thick odour of dust. Squeezing his arms and shoulders through the hole, Isak raised himself up into the small space, brushing away a musty-smelling cape as it stroked his face. He wondered who owned it, and where they were—it didn't seem fitting that a king should own something so frayed. Then he grinned and reminded himself that he wasn't the only one with a previous life. The king had taken his throne by force; maybe this cape was a reminder of sorts. The door stood ajar and Isak paused for a second, listening to the voices, before pushing his way into the room.

"Captain, we have a visitor. Could you please tell Antern to come up, and any of the Brothers who might be around? Our newcomer and the librarian might also want to meet my guest. I suspect most are in, no?"

"They are," confirmed a gruff old voice grumpily. "I was up here trying to find some peace and quiet."

"But again I have confounded you, my apologies. Ah, Lord Isak, please make yourself comfortable."

Emin gestured to the empty room as he ushered out a bulky man with silver hair. It was luxuriously furnished, with a large oak desk dominating one end, eight armchairs in a half circle before it. Paintings adorned every wall, landscapes, for the most part: a distant village surrounded by hills, a vista of the city busy under the summer sun. Isak went to a window and looked out through the leaded glass. In the distance he could see the copper dome of the Public Assembly building glowing in the afternoon sun.

"This is the Di Senego Club. A small gentlemen's club of no great importance to the would-be power brokers of the city," explained Emin as Mihn and Coran emerged in turn from the cupboard.

Mihn checked the door, then went to inspect the windows. Apparently satisfied, he took up a position by the door with a view of the whole room. The king moved behind the desk and unbuckled his sword belt, hanging the gold-hilted rapier from one of two large hooks protruding from the wall.

"Please, my Lord, take a seat. A few associates of mine will be coming up shortly. I know we have important matters to discuss between us, but these are men Morghien and I trust."

Isak found himself a chair directly opposite Emin and unbuckled his own blade. The weapon rested comfortably in the crook of his arm as he sat down. He turned to Mihn, suddenly remembering the final gift, and pointed at the backpack.

He turned back to the king. "That reminds me, your—Emin. Morghien gave me a scroll to give to you, and I have another gift from Lord Bahl. A gesture of goodwill that he didn't wish to be quite so public." Mihn pulled the bag from his back and retrieved the items, then placed both scroll and book onto the desk.

"Mihn has told me what he knows about Morghien, but perhaps you know more about what he wants with me?" He knew he sounded a little whiny, but he was a little fed up with being the object of everyone's interest.

Emin fixed his piercing blue eyes on the Krann for a moment, then nodded. "Of course, though the whole story is too long to relate." He picked up the scroll and waved it in Isak's direction. "Can I assume you've read both of these?"

"Of course. They wouldn't have been given to me otherwise."

"Good, that will save time. As for Morghien, after his experience with the Aspect Seliasei, he wandered the Land and picked up one or two more passengers, and one of those incidents led him to be taken on as acolyte to a minor mage. They went on an expedition, organised by a group of scholars who had become acquainted through a shared study of the Mage Verliq's works. The expedition was to the ruins of Castle Keriabral, Aryn Bwr's own fortress. It fell during the Great War, under somewhat mysterious circumstances. They were escorted by a half legion of Knights of the Temples."

"And what did they find? All the Seer told me was that Morghien was the only one who survived."

Emin hesitated, hearing distant voices. "Coran," he asked, "could you ask them to wait on the stairs for a minute?"

The white-eye nodded and left, closing the door carefully behind him.

"It is something Morghien is unwilling to discuss," Emin told Isak. "It was five years before he felt able to share any of that experience with me. I hope you can understand that he would not like me to divulge such information freely."

He paused for a moment. His face looked haunted. "All you need to know is that two men survived to walk back to Embere. They would not talk about their experiences, other than to say that they had looked Azaer in the face, and heard his dreadful voice. One was Morghien. The other was the son of one of the expedition's leaders, a talented young man named Cordein Malich—"

"Malich?" interrupted Isak and Mihn as one. The king nodded gravely.

"Malich. The young man who became the root of so many of your troubles. In exchange for his life, Malich made a pact of some sort."

Isak sat up straight, a frown on his face. "So who, or what, is Azaer?"

"Another mystery—and in my opinion, the most dangerous one. Among the members of this club are some of the finest minds around, academics and mages, but all we have discovered so far is that there is neither God nor daemon called Azaer. The last man who worked on the problem must have been getting somewhere, for Azaer decided to make an example of him. He was haunted by his own shadow and died, with his wife, in a locked room. I cannot and will not ask anyone else to face such a death again.

"Even so, it continues to snare others, victims of chance whose deaths serve no purpose that I can fathom beyond Azaer's own amusement." The king leant forward on his desk as he spoke, his knuckles whitening.

Isak pointed to the book on the desk. "According to Cardinal Disten, the man who wrote that book, Azaer was not really worshipped as such. Malich was a necromancer, he dealt with daemons. Cardinal Disten says he invoked Azaer's name as a warning, a threat to others."

Isak felt a little foolish; Emin surely knew far more than he did, but he gave no sign of impatience.

"Then that in itself is instructive," he said, contemplatively. "Daemons require worship from their followers as Gods do. From what I can work out, Azaer encourages only fear, causing misery and pain whether his—its—name is mentioned or not. It's a subtler mind at work than a daemon, and I think perhaps, given how infrequently he acts, it is reasonable to say his power is weaker too, more suited to encouraging others along a certain path than creating the path itself. Azaer lives in the shadows—" He paused as Isak flinched, but the Krann said nothing.

After a moment Emin continued, but he was watching Isak carefully now. "Azaer lives in the shadows, manipulating events, perhaps even thoughts, but why, we don't know. Those foolish few we've found worshipping Azaer have treated him as a daemon or a God, but generally it's been an individual, out for personal gain, rather than a huge group of people. My suspicion is that Azaer tolerates such a use as long as his name is associated with fear."

"So what does he want with me?"

"The same as the Gods, the same as the Knights of the Temples, and probably the White Circle too. And right now I'm afraid we have more pressing concerns than even Azaer poses." He raised a hand to ward off further questions and called out, "Coran, bring them in please."

Isak turned to the door as it opened to admit a group of men, varying in age. The white-eye took up position by the wall at Emin's desk. The first two men into the room were so engrossed in discussion they didn't even notice Isak, until a third gave a strangled squawk at the sight of him.

"Gentlemen, please come in and find yourselves a seat," called Emin in a schoolmasterly tone. They turned to the king and collectively mumbled assent. From their clothes, Isak realised they were noblemen, but none of them looked at him with the suspicion he'd been greeted with at the baths.

"Lord Isak, may I introduce you to some friends of mine? The two elderly conversationalists at the front are Norimin Dele, Chief Librarian of the College of Magic, and Anversis Halis, my uncle. I'm not entirely sure why he's here, so we will ignore him for the time being, until he cannot keep himself from talking any longer and Coran throws him out."

The librarian gave a throaty chuckle and patted his companion on the shoulder as Halis dismissed his nephew's words with an abrupt wave of the hand and sank into an armchair. From the glare Coran was giving Halis, it might be less of a joke than Emin was making out.

"Norimin, how goes your search for the Stigmata of the Last Battle?"

"Ah, well now!" the librarian exclaimed with enthusiasm, "we have several interesting reports to follow up on—a young woman in Cholos has apparently had bouts of bleeding down the centre of her skull since the spring of last year. One of our friends has agreed to bring her to Narkang, so I hope to be able to bring her to the club and investigate matters further."

"Excellent, I look forward to it. Please, take a seat. Next, Lord Isak, we have two rather more reputable men—in that they were founding members of the criminal organisation that so plagues this city. Sir Creyl and Marshal Dorik of Tohl. Sir Creyl is also Commander of the Brotherhood."

The two each gave a respectful bow and found chairs opposite the older men.

"And Counts Alscap, a longtime ally, and Antern, whom you have already met."

These men bowed also. Antern positioned himself closest to King Emin, while the large, ruddy-faced Count Alscap was content to sit beside Isak and eye him suspiciously.

"Count Alscap is one of the newest members of our club and thus knows less of our activities than most," the king added softly. "I hope to persuade him that his influence could be better employed here than for further increasing his already impressive fortune."

"Well, he's not convinced of that, and is in no rush to discover more—but he *is* in the king's debt and willing to be of what service he can," Count Alscap said to Isak, his voice deep and rather abrasive.

"Well," declared Emin, realising they were now all staring curiously at his guest, "I hope my news will be sufficiently mundane for you, Count

Alscap. Antern, Creyl, and Dorik know this already, but for those of you who do not, you may have noticed that this year the Spring Fair is going to be the largest yet. Every tavern, inn, and stable is already full; some enterprising spirits have even erected tents as temporary inns."

He looked around the room. So far no one looked that interested. "That in itself is not a problem," he went on. "However, it has come to my attention that there are more men coming in than have taken lodgings."

Isak saw Count Alscap and the two older men sit up straighter.

"Too many of the wagon trains have too few wares, and too many attendants, if you pay the attention some public-spirited thieves do."

"Have they been able to investigate the wagons?" asked Isak cautiously.

"No," replied Sir Creyl, leaning forward in his seat, face flushed purple with anger. "Two of our boys were caught and flogged to death by the guards. No local man would dare do that, not go up against both the law *and* the Brotherhood. As soon as the watchmen arrived they were bribed to ignore it, a good amount too. Fortunately for us, they quietly took the money and left to report it immediately to Commander Brandt. We encourage our watchmen to appear open to such offers."

"Lots of men, wagons that they don't want thieves to investigate—who's planning the rebellion then?" Isak looked round at the assembled faces, but they were all turned to the king.

The king cleared his throat. "As far as we can tell, it's the White Circle. We've identified a number of known mercenary captains among the men coming in, which the Devoted would have no need for, even if they weren't noted for executing mercenaries at every opportunity."

"But that's not like the White Circle, they've never led or funded an uprising anywhere," protested Alscap. "They've always used influence and money to get what they want. Even the war in Tor Milist—they may be the guiding force, but they're neither paying for it or fighting it. Why would they change tactics now? Their detachment has worked well in the past."

Everyone was nodding in agreement, though Isak wasn't quite sure what they were talking about: the White Circle kept cropping up, but all he really knew was that it was a sisterhood of rich women and Lesarl had not been able to infiltrate it—unless his beautiful assassin had managed to inveigle her way in by now. Everyone knew Helrect was run by a woman, Siala, a duchess by marriage—but she used no title, to underline the fact that she ruled without her husband's participation.

"True enough," replied Count Antern, "but Narkang is rather greater a prize. Three months ago they brought a man into the city—we think he's to be the leader of this uprising. Most mercenaries will take money from women, but not orders, and none of the men associated with the White Circle here are capable of leading an army of any sort."

"None still alive, you mean," muttered the librarian, Dele, darkly. "I can think of several men who'd have done it well enough before they contracted 'sudden illnesses' soon after their wives decided to join the White Circle."

"That bastard Jex," bellowed the king's uncle suddenly. Half the room flinched at his unexpected outburst.

Halis muttered an apology as his nephew said, "Correct uncle, Herolen Jex. It took us a long time to discover who he was exactly, but even without his history, it's clear he could fill the role perfectly." He looked at Isak. "You probably won't have heard of Jex: he was a pirate captain from Vijgen, apparently quite famous if you have time for pirate tales, but he is both ruthless and intelligent for certain."

"In any case," Count Antern said, "the end of the Spring Fair would be the logical time to attack. All of our informants agree that's the day. Half the city will be drunk, and they know the king will have to be out on the field to reward the winners of the tourneys and tilting."

"So what's your plan?" Isak's question cut to the point and silenced the room.

All heads turned to the king as he stood and leaned heavily against the desk. His head was down as if scanning a map or battle plan. Slowly, he lifted his cold eyes. "An educated guess would put their numbers at one and a half thousand men. The normal strength of the Kingsguard in Narkang is five hundred. This has been doubled over the past few days, carefully enough that I doubt they have noticed. This still leaves us at a disadvantage, for all that their mercenaries should be inferior to my Kingsguard.

"I have a man who should have reached Brodei Castle by now. Reinforcements will arrive sometime around the end of the fair. What we have to do is be ready for the assault and fight a running retreat to the palace. Once inside, they'll not have the time, nor the skill to break us."

"Jex is an arrogant man," added Antern severely, "but he's no fool. He knows the running retreat will be our instinctive reaction; the king is never unguarded. We expect him to divide his force with the bulk attacking the king, and perhaps a third at the city gates to cut off any breakout we might be planning."

"What if they close the gates? Barricade them? Even with troops in the city you'd be dead before they fought their way through and opened the gates again." There were murmurs in support of Isak's objection, but Emin merely smiled evilly.

"Then they will have a deeply unpleasant surprise. For the duration of the fair the gates remain open. This is, of course, to encourage the debauchery and excess that my people expect and require. While I can hardly be enthusiastic about that, it is convenient that the Gatekeepers do not have to be in residence, as they would normally. I don't know whether our little traditions are known to the Farlan, but the opening and closing of the gates are normally accompanied by a small ceremony. Nothing overly complicated, but significant nonetheless."

"And the point?" interrupted Isak.

"And the point, my Lord, is that it is merely a pleasant little tradition that the folk of the city have grown fond of over the years. Without one of the Gatekeepers there the ceremony will naturally be omitted, and the reason for it will become apparent."

"A magical lock?" All heads turned to Mihn at his suggestion. Emin shook his head.

"Not quite. I must admit the inspiration came from tales of the black gates of Crafanc, though we have employed the idea in a different way. I must admit I'm keen to see how well it works, since we've not really been able to test it out. What isn't public knowledge is that the Gatekeepers of the city have all been ordained Priests of Death. If a priest opens or closes the gates, all is well. If anyone else does so, the daemon bound within the shrine above the locking mechanism will be released."

A gasp ran around the room. Even the two men of the Brotherhood, Sir Creyl and Marshal Tohl, looked shocked. The Chief Librarian shuddered. Isak had to suppress a chuckle. It was just the sort of evil idea he was beginning to expect from Emin.

"Please, calm yourselves. It is perfectly safe for the citizens. The daemon is restricted to the gatehouse and we will have none of our people inside for the entire fair. Watchmen will be guarding the gate, of course, but I believe the duty is known as a retirement post since it is essentially ceremonial. They will surrender before pointlessly laying down their lives."

Isak looked around at the men in the room. Mihn had a thoughtful expression on his face: but he was quite as calculating and dispassionate as King Emin. Antern and Coran had obviously heard nothing new, but the others were completely unsettled.

"What role can I play?" Again Isak brought a sudden hush to the room.

A smile crossed Emin's face. "I appreciate the offer, my Lord. At the risk of sounding crude, you are the most effective killer in our midst. While your men are few in number, each and every one would have an honoured place in the Kingsguard, and that would make a nice surprise for Jex—but it would also make you as important a target as me. I would be more than grateful if you did find an opportunity to kill Jex, but please remember that there are witches and mages within the White Circle. Keeping yourself alive might prove complicated enough—"

He broke off as a clatter came from the cupboard. Coran immediately pushed away from the wall he was leaning against and advanced, hand on hilt. Isak shifted his body so Eolis was in an easier position to draw, but as the door crashed opened it was a panting Veil who tumbled though. He held a lamp in one hand. It was clear from his gulping breaths that he'd sprinted the length of the tunnel.

"Your Majesty, you must return to the baths!"

Emin, apparently ignoring the urgency in Veil's voice, reached leisurely for his sword as he asked, "What's happened?"

"Herolen Jex, my Lord. He's challenged Lord Isak's man to a duel."

"So tell me what happened," Isak said quietly. They were sitting in his apartments at the palace, large, airy rooms that were sumptuous even by Farlan standards. The style was almost opposite to what they were used to: smooth white walls instead of the grey stone of Tirah. Highly polished stone, inlaid marquetry, and etched metal decorated almost every piece of furniture, even the candelabras, and doors and panels were beautifully carved into intricate designs.

Carel stood with his head low and hands clasped together. "My Lord, it was my fault. I'm not used to being around noblemen. In the barracks, things are simpler—"

"No." Tila placed herself between the two men and glared up at Isak. "It was that man Jex at fault. He was insulting me and Carel stepped in to stop him."

"And Jex took offence at what he said and challenged him to a duel?" the king asked. He was lounging on a long sofa, a thin cigar clamped between his lips.

"Well, the Marshal was not wholly tactful, but Jex was looking for an excuse."

"So now you have to fight him?" Isak did not shout, but his friend still shrank back. "Carel, in case you've forgotten, you retired from the Ghosts years ago. You can't fight a man like Herolen Jex at your age."

His companions looked back at him, confusion on their faces.

"How do you know him? I'd not heard of the man." Vesna put down the empty glass he'd been restlessly turning in his hands.

"The king told me." Isak turned back to his aging friend. "That's hardly the problem now. Carel, you're not going to fight this man."

"He doesn't have to," answered Vesna before Carel could speak. "I am."

"And he accepted? I suppose he would," mused Emin. "He'd not have heard of you. Jex is too arrogant to refuse a duel without good reason. Well, there is at least a little good to come out of this. I assume you asked for a full joust when given choice of weapons?"

Vesna nodded. A man with a long-standing reputation as an adulterer didn't survive long without being a good duellist—with any weapon. Vesna was not just a master adulterer, he was a hero of the Farlan Army, and his reputation both on the battlefield and at a formal tourney was well deserved. With any luck, the pirate Jex would probably have never tilted in his life.

"Unfortunately, it also creates a problem. I assume the duel is to be in the morning?"

"No, my Lord," said Tila. "I'm afraid I couldn't think of anything fast enough to stop the duel, but for what it's worth the duel will happen *after* the fair."

"What?" To Tila's surprise, the king's face lit up. As she looked at Isak she saw similar excitement.

"It was the only excuse I could think of to put off the duel. I hoped it would give you time to find a way to stop it. I told Jex that you and the king had already made a wager on the fair, five hundred gold emins that Vesna would win the tilt. I banked on betting law being the same as in Tirah: since his duel puts a wager of yours at risk, if Jex wants to fight immediately, he has to provide the money, because he's forcing you to default." She blushed. "He didn't look like he had five hundred emins to hand."

"My dear," purred Emin, rising and taking her hand, "if I were not a married man I would be on my knee to you this minute." He kissed her palm with affected reverence. "I could not have asked more of you if I'd orchestrated the whole thing myself."

He stood up and craned his head around Isak's massive frame to attract Coran's attention. "Go to Herolen Jex. I believe he is one of Duke Forell's guests. Tell him the duel will take place after the presentation of the prizes at the fair. That should relieve them—I'm sure the others know about Count Vesna's ability."

"Others?" asked Vesna, his coming duel forgotten as his suspicion flared.

"I will take my leave and let your master explain. Oh, the excitement of the Spring Fair . . ." He was almost dancing as he left the room, Coran at his heel as ever. Only a thin trail of smoke and a line of confused faces remained.

Isak suspected that was a frequent happening.

CHAPTER 31

IN THE GREY GLOOM OF EARLY MORNING, the soldier's shifting feet on the cobbles sounded oddly loud. The night had seen rain clouds roll in from the ocean and with them had come a cool mist and rain, nothing heavy but still not what most had hoped for the coming Spring Fair. His muscles felt cold and stiff after long hours of guard duty. He stared out over the damp empty street, another still, silent part of the city. It was too early for most of Narkang's citizens; only a few distant sounds, some mysterious, most mundane, haunted the empty streets. Even the dawn chorus had yet to rouse into action.

His partner was in the guardroom above, warm and comfortable, seated by the arrow-slit window that overlooked the approach to the palace. The solider opened his mouth to call up and demand they change places when a movement caught his eye. In the inky lee of one house, a cloak fluttered out from the shadow. The soldier flexed his fingers round the shaft of his halberd. Someone was watching him. He hawked noisily and spat on the ground, the saliva glistening in the half-light. A tap-tap came; almost inaudible, but enough to be sure his partner was alert to the possible danger.

The figure remained in the shadows for another ten heartbeats, then slipped round the corner and moved stealthily along the wall. His long cape covered most of his body, but the breeze held it open for a moment, long enough to make out bronze scale-armour and a red sash with markings of rank—an officer of the Devoted.

Tonight has just got more interesting, thought the soldier. The Devoted and the Kingsguard found themselves at odds more often than not. The officers of the Devoted were usually recruited from birth and title. No man in the Kingsguard went anywhere unless it was on merit. He reached back and rapped his knuckles on the door behind him. At night the gates to the palace were, of course, barred. A low door in the left-hand gate provided the only access until the king was awake. The soldier heard the bolts drawn back as he kept scanning the street beyond. From here he could see no one else, neither companion nor pursuer, but when the hurrying figure crossed the open stretch of road, the soldier kicked back against the door to open it for him.

"I—" The man's voice broke off as the guard jabbed a thumb towards the door. He hesitated for a split second, then nodded and ducked down to step through the small aperture. Staying in the street would expose the visitor, and he was clearly trying to avoid notice. The guards behind the gate could deal with him. The soldier flicked his upright halberd through two well-practised circles and returned his attention to the fading gloom of the streets.

As the officer came through the door, two pairs of boots and two gleaming sword tips welcomed him. He froze, then gently brought himself upright to match the unfriendly gaze of a Kingsguard soldier. The second moved around him to nudge the door closed again and restore the bolts. Only once the gate was secure did anyone speak.

"So, Major," said the soldier opposite him as he noted the markings on the Knight's scarlet sash. "What can we do for you this fine night?"

The man looked about the fine courtyard before answering. Even in the murky light the White Palace was beautiful. The roses were black shadows, the gravel paths soft grey, and the host of statues loomed like resident spectres.

"I must speak to the Krann of the Farlan."

The soldier gave a short laugh. "Oh well, excuse me a moment while I drag him out of bed by his ear."

"It is a matter of utmost importance."

"I'm sure it is," drawled the soldier. He regarded the earnest face of the major, a young man for his rank, and sheathed his sword. "It's always important to pious bastards like you lot, but the Lord Isak might not agree. Got a nasty temper on him, I hear."

"Then wake one of his men and let him decide. I need to be out of the palace before the city wakes."

The soldier sighed and scratched at his neck idly. "I'm not so sure you'll make that, but I'll go and wake the commander of the Krann's guard. You can wait in the guardhouse there."

Isak sat on the side of his bed, rubbing the sleep from his eyes. Eolis rested on his thighs. The Kingsguard who'd eventually brought Major Ortof-Greyl to him had spoken first to his senior officer, then to one of the black-clad King's Men who prowled the palace at all times. Finally someone decided it was probably important enough to wake the Krann.

Carel scowled at the major. The marshal looked ruffled and irritable. He'd not bothered with a uniform, but the curved blade that he'd named Arugin was ready at hand. The sword reminded him of an arugin, a marsh harrier, for the blade's smooth, silent stroke was like the black bird's gliding flight, and the sword, though made of black iron, had a curious white shimmer, almost like pipe smoke, that resembled the bird's white-tipped wings.

"My Lord, we must speak in private," the major insisted again.

"I have no secrets from these two," replied Isak, nodding towards Mihn and Carel. A sudden pang of sadness hit him: that wasn't quite true. Mihn had seen the scar on his chest, but had been given no explanation, and he had kept it hidden from Carel, his oldest and dearest friend, because Carel would demand answers, and Isak didn't know yet what those answers were.

He decided to compromise. "You can leave," he ordered the man of the Brotherhood hovering behind the major. The man didn't move for a second, then he bowed. His face remained steadfastly blank as he marched from the room, Mihn close on his heels to ensure the man had no chance to listen in.

"So, Major, why are you here? I thought you people were keeping your distance from me."

"I—It is true that the Council are unconvinced that you are the Saviour—"

"Well, how did I persuade them of that? No one else seems to believe me." Isak gave a bitter laugh.

"That is not why I am here. What I came to tell you is that the Knights of the Temples are not as united as you might believe."

Isak stopped laughing and leaned forward, listening more intently.

"Our Order is going through significant changes. While the old guard remains in control of the Council, the younger generation grows stronger every year."

"What are you telling me?"

"That very soon the Knights of the Temples may not be so hostile towards you—but that is not the main reason I demanded to see you at so inconvenient a time. There is a group of men within the Knights, of whom I am one—" He stopped, trying to compose himself.

He was less than thirty summers, Isak guessed, and young to be a major. He was obviously finding the situation daunting. Isak smiled. "I'm listening, Major," he said encouragingly.

The major swallowed and, almost whispering, said, "We are few in number, but we know a secret that even the Knight-Cardinal is ignorant of. We believe we have proof enough that you are the Saviour—or if you are not the Saviour, you will be his champion when his coming is nigh."

"His champion?" wondered Isak aloud.

Mihn looked noncommittal, as usual. The Harlequins did not bear the official history of the Land, but they were impartial recorders of most events. Isak assumed the mention of a champion was just Devoted doctrine, since Mihn offered no other explanation.

"So you want an ally when you try to take power?" Carel didn't bother to disguise the scorn in his voice, but the man looked genuinely hurt by the suggestion.

"Not at all. We hope it will be less of a taking of power, and more of a shift in values. I come to tell you that we will bring you a gift, something that should convince you of our genuine motives. It is under careful guard, so we haven't yet managed to secure it, but within two weeks we shall. The head of our group suggests you and your men, however many guards you wish, of course, meet us at the Ivy Rings on Silvernight. It is an abandoned temple of standing stones, a week's ride from the city."

"As simple as that? Do you think I'm soft in the head? You'll have to give me a reason to believe you or I'll break your legs and pack you back off to Piety Keep." Isak didn't bother to disguise his anger, but then he paused.

Calm again, he asked, "What's this secret you've hidden from the Knight-Cardinal?"

"It would mean nothing to you, it is merely the circumstances of the finding of the gifts we offer you—though he is unaware of what we offer. I myself do not know."

Isak didn't bother trying to unravel the words, which made little sense to him. The major obviously thought whatever it was would go over his head. "Try me."

The man swallowed nervously. "Very well. The gifts—what we will offer to you—were brought back by a man of our Order from an expedition into the Elven Waste years ago—"

"To Keriabral?" Isak had a sly smile on his face as the major's expression turned to one of bewilderment.

"You've heard of it? But he was the only survivor—How could you possibly know?" There was near-panic on his face as he ran the names of possible traitors in his group through his head.

"There were two survivors," Isak said, "well, three with this new one. If we carry on at this rate there'll have been no one killed there at all." Isak's comment drew a furious look from Carel: every soldier feared dying on a field far from home. Your family and friends might never know how or why you died, let alone where: to be lost without burial or the administering of rites was what petrified most men going into battle. It was not something to be belittled.

Isak shot him a look of apology.

"I had no idea," whispered the major. "The man was sent back alone, soon after they arrived at the castle—he was a woodsman, an expert, able to survive almost anywhere. He made it back to Embere and found an escort to accompany him to the Fortress of the Devoted. When he heard that the others had never returned, he hanged himself in guilt at having abandoned them."

"Not much of a secret, considering the consequences if your own leader finds out."

"There are ramifications that would cloud our purpose in this Age."

Isak laughed. "How convenient. Well, I'll think about what you've said and let you know."

"My Lord, this is a matter of the utmost secrecy; we can afford no contact or the Council will put a stop to everything. If the Knight-Cardinal knew about this, he would have us all killed and take the gifts, perhaps even try to kill you."

Isak sat back with a sigh. For a few heartbeats he didn't move, then he looked to both Mihn and Carel. Neither took the opportunity to speak.

"I still have to think about this," Isak said. "Count Vesna will be wearing a lady's favour for the joust. If it's red on the last day, I will be there. White, I refuse. That gives you enough warning?"

"It does, my Lord," Major Ortof-Greyl said, rising. "I thank you for your time." He bowed low, then followed Mihn out.

Carel sat down next to Isak, their concerned expressions almost identical.

"I though life could not get any more complicated." There was no wry humour in Carel's voice, just fatigue. He was beginning to feel his age. "I'm assuming that you'd have told me if you ever believed yourself to be the Saviour, or anything else. So what are we going to do about all those who think you are?"

Isak scratched at the stubble on his cheek. "I don't know. I just hope we can avoid too many people dying over it. I've never had much of a plan for my life, certainly nothing so grand as becoming Lord of the Farlan. That was surprise enough." He sighed heavily.

"If we have to go to war over a lie, or over the misinterpreted ramblings of madmen, then perhaps the Land would be better off without me."

Carel turned in shock, but he saw nothing more than weary resignation on Isak's face. He placed a hand on Isak's huge shoulder. These days, whenever he touched his boy, it didn't feel quite like flesh under his palm. It made him uncomfortable, but he put that aside for Isak's sake. "Then let's make sure it never comes to that," he said quietly.

CHAPTER 32

THE DAY OF THE SPRING FAIR came too soon for the brooding Krann. He'd told the others about the major's visit, but they'd not been able to provide the answers he'd hoped for. Tila pointed out that the Devoted had been founded on decent principles, so there had to be some true men within their ranks.

Vesna worked from the other side: he thought it was a trap, and wondered whether it could truly be an ambush. The Ivy Rings were halfway between Narkang and the Fortress of the Devoted. While killing or abducting Isak was a risky venture, it was certainly feasible: it was no secret that the Devoted considered Siulents and Eolis too dangerous to be at large in the Land.

That would be a dramatic move, and one that would mean they'd have to abandon their strongholds in Emin Thonal's kingdom, but if they thought the prize worthwhile, it wouldn't be beyond the Devoted.

"The Ivy Rings? Who in the name of Vrest's beard told you about them?" Emin actually looked surprised when Isak asked about the temple. They were sitting on a high terrace looking out over the city, overlooking the tents and banners of the Spring Fair. The morning's rain had lessened and Isak had joined Emin for the midday meal.

The king was dressed as resplendently as ever and Isak could see no trace of the strain that he was surely under. In two days his life and city were to be threatened, yet he was relaxed and at ease.

"I overheard a conversation, that's all."

"Then it must have been an odd conversation." Emin sounded curious. "Few people like to talk about the place. But since you asked, the Ivy Rings are a disused temple, once dedicated to Belarannar, but few people go there these days. They're in Llehden, a strange place."

"Strange?"

"Yes, strange." Emin sniffed. For a moment he became reserved, serious, before he forced the mood away. "A friend of mine was lost there a few years past. The shire is a reasonable size—no towns, but a number of villages that are prosperous enough."

"And the lord of the shire?"

"Does not exist. There's not been a Lord of Llehden for generations. As I said, strange things happen there and folk prefer to steer clear. The inhabitants aren't hostile to outsiders, but they live under rather different rules. I have yet to find a tax officer who is willing to go there for me—at least more than once," he added darkly. Emin's smile was ambiguous, not angry, but he clearly didn't relish his lack of control.

"Llehden is like an island: the region feels much more isolated than it actually is. If you go there you'll find the landscape feels—well, *sharper*, as if natural magic influences the environment and folklore and myth have a greater grip on reality. The Gentry, Coldhand Folk, Dead Man's Wives; these things are much more common there. Unless you have a reason to go, I would suggest you avoid Llehden. A place like that has a natural balance to it. I doubt it would welcome you."

"So not a great sight-seeing destination then," Isak said quietly, and changed the conversation, asking instead about the origins of the Spring Fair.

Emin smiled, relieved, and launched himself into a potted version of Narkang's history.

On the second morning of the Spring Fair, Isak awoke to see a single bright shaft of sunlight piercing the shutters of his room. The gloom of previous days had dissipated and as he opened the windows, he was met by a warm sea breeze. Yesterday the air had been full of the murky tang of seaweed and sodden driftwood. Now he could taste the life and energy of the waves. It put a smile on his face as he pulled on Siulents and belted Eolis around his waist. The blue hood of Nartis went into his belt. He felt no need to retreat behind it today, but with so many people out on the plain he wanted to be able to relax without worrying how much people could read in his face.

They went out early. Isak elected to ride so he had horses at hand in case things became desperate on the last day. To justify being the only nobleman on horseback, he toured the fair, using Toramin's great bulk to dissuade people from approaching. Tila accompanied him, riding sidesaddle on Megenn. The saddle was actually a normal one, but with tightly wrapped blankets they had managed to construct something that was comfortable enough for her to ride. If it came to a mad rush for the gates, Isak wanted Tila to be safe. Her own mare was fine for travelling, but Megenn was bigger, faster, and battle-trained.

The entire city seemed to have descended to the plain. A riot of noise, bustle, and activity surrounded the Farlan as they trotted past open kitchens, acrobatic displays, parties of minstrels, and a host of weird and wonderful games. Vesna was naturally at the jousting fences, watching the competition and preparing himself for his first match. He'd been drawn against a commoner who'd won the morning's competitions. It was traditional for a few peasants or apprentices from the city to be allowed to cross lances with the noblemen. The king provided armour and horses, and any victory—rare though they were— would win the man a personal congratulation from his monarch.

Vesna was hardly worried by the tall, ruddy-faced youth who was ecstatic just to be scheduled to face the legendary count. He was more concerned about two men wearing the colours of the Devoted: the Kingsguard champion and a wealthy knight of the city, who'd made a point of coming to greet him. Vesna had noted the tattoo on his ear as they spoke.

As the man departed, casting one last avaricious look at Vesna's ensorcelled sword, Vesna had felt a sudden pang of unfamiliar nervousness. *Fool*, he chastised himself with a grin. *Fall in love and you're suddenly a shy little boy again. There's a reason a man of the Brotherhood made a point of coming to see you now, because you're that good. Just remember: these people know your name for a reason.*

Isak found himself enjoying the fair far more than he'd expected. He loved the exotic, sometimes bizarre foods on display; they were mainly drawn from the ocean and though he recognised little of the samples offered up by beaming cooks, he'd made significant inroads on his hunger long before he was due to eat with the king. The further in they went, the stranger the sights became.

He lingered for a long while to watch a hedge wizard in ragged robes perform a meagre repertoire of tricks. Unsurprisingly, the audience was mainly young children, but Isak was fascinated by the display, mean as it was. By watching the movements and tasting the changes in the air, Isak quickly understood how the man was keeping the children enthralled. His abilities were minimal, too minor perhaps even to have been trained, but Isak greatly enjoyed the invention.

When the display was over, Isak beckoned the man over and gave him a gold emin. He was overwhelmed by the hedge wizard's thanks, which he shrugged off, a little embarrassed at having caused such an emotional scene. Tila raised an eyebrow at his generosity, but Isak just grinned. He had enjoyed the theatrics as much as any of the children there.

"He taught me something. That's worth a coin." Isak held his hands together and copied one of the wizard's unintelligible phrases, and a pair of flame wings rose up into the air before dissipating. The girl smiled at the joy on his face, trying not to show the sudden sadness as she remembered he'd never been allowed this sort of fun before. Sometimes it was hard to remember the Krann was only just out of childhood, for all his size and power.

"Come on, my Lord, we should be going back to the pavilion," she said finally. Isak was dining with the king in the royal box, in one of the two massive pavilions erected down either side of the jousting field.

"Tigers first," he declared. "Emin said there would be a menagerie of animals, and I'm guessing it'll be downwind of here. I'm seeing a tiger before I do anything more." He reached out and took her hand, giving it a squeeze of brotherly affection. Tila could do nothing but laugh at the anticipation on his face as she trotted after him.

"So, my Lord, do you still think your wager is safe? Emin pointed with his cigar to the knight taking the crowd's applause. The young man shone in the sunlight as he wheeled his horse about, waving to the crowd. His visor was up and Isak could see the beaming face of a youth about his own age. As the new—and youngest-ever—champion of the Kingsguard, Emin had gifted the knight with a gold-inlaid suit of armour. The helm had been fashioned into the cherubic features of one of Karkarn's Aspects, a boyish smile with one blood red tear falling from his right eye, an image that was often used by the Harlequins for their masks.

"He's good, but he can't have come up against a man of Count Vesna's ability," answered Tila for her Lord.

She blushed as Emin smiled at her and asked, "You've seen much jousting, my lady?"

"My brother lives for it, your Majesty."

"Then perhaps you would judge the next two men as they parade? Thank you, my dear. Lord Isak, while your most capable advisor prepares my next wager, perhaps we should peruse the crowd." He selected a sweetened prawn from the plate between them and nodded his head to the opposing pavilion. Isak followed the movement, his eye going straight to a group of people taking seats opposite them.

It was hard to stand out in a crowd of rich noblemen and women, but Herolen Jex had managed it. Dressed in red and white, he glided along the walkway ahead of five others. All eyes were on him. The tanned skin of a Western Islander had darkened further with a lifetime under the sun. Isak could easily imagine this man striding the deck of a ship: Jex walked as if he owned the pavilion and all those in it. His glittering smile swept down the rows of people, and they seemed to feel it touch their skin. A whole line of noblemen rippled around to meet his gaze, before lowering their eyes as if he were royalty. The man might have been an enemy, but Isak couldn't help admiring Jex's presence.

Isak glanced at Emin while this procession was going on. The king's eyes were narrow and focused. He was smoking his cigar in his usual languid fashion, but he seemed oblivious to the smoke passing in front of his eyes. Isak looked back to the other pavilion: Jex seated—and looking directly at them. The pirate was sprawled over two seats, one arm running down the backrest and his boots resting on the one in front. It was causing significant discomfort to the man in front of him, but he didn't appear to be objecting.

Jex matched stares with Isak and Emin, then slid his boots back onto the boards below. Leaning forward, he plucked a cigar from the hands of the hapless noble in front, sat back, and began to puff away at it in mockery of the king. Emin gave a slight nod in acknowledgement, which Jex returned.

Isak just pointed to Count Vesna, preparing for his next joust, and made an obscene gesture at the pirate. Jex threw his head back and laughed loud enough to hush half of the pavilion, taking no notice of the curious looks he received.

Similarly, Isak ignored both the groan from behind him and his political advisor poking a leather-shod toe into her Lord's back.

They watched the jousting for much of the afternoon. The gathering opposite them was in a constant state of flux, but they soon noticed a pattern in the way Jex's companions were moving about. The man just sat still and waited for reports to be collected and brought to him. When Vesna easily toppled his third and last opponent of the day, Jex affected a yawn and threw a coin onto the sand as the count dismounted to take his applause. The crowd hushed immediately—the whole city had heard of the coming duel.

Vesna pretended not to see the throw, idly discovering the coin at his feet a few seconds later. Both pavilions craned their heads forward as he bent to pick it up. The Farlan hero held it up to the light for a moment, then turned towards Isak and, with affected delight, held the silver piece up for his Lord to see.

The Krann raised a thumb in approval, knowing Vesna's self-deprecating humour well enough, and the whole crowd began to laugh. Beaming from ear to ear, Vesna walked back to his page with a jaunty step made even more comical by the constraints of his armour.

The crowd laughed even harder, but Jex failed to join in.

CHAPTER 33

"I SAK, IT'S TIME TO DECIDE." Tila couldn't tell if he'd even heard her speak: the frown on his face was more pensive than angry.

Still Isak didn't react. They had been talking endlessly about the Devoted major and his news, right into the early hours, and now it was the last day of Spring Fair and no one was convinced they knew what the right thing to do was. Isak wasn't sure he trusted the earnest young major; there was too much he didn't understand. And yet . . . And yet it was too obvious to be an ambush. Isak's company might not be large, but his men were Ghosts and it would take more than a single regiment to overcome them, especially if they were already on their guard.

Then there was the added problem of Lord Bahl: he wouldn't wait for his Chief Steward to come up with evidence; he would just attack. For all their power, the Devoted stood no chance against the Farlan Army.

And there was another worry: King Emin. Emin and that dangerous little smile of his—in some ways, that was the only reassurance Isak had. The Narkang king was clever, and he wanted the Farlan to know it. If he were Isak's enemy, he would not have shown so much of himself. It was obvious there was more involved, but Emin had dropped enough hints for Isak to be sure his plans were suitably grand in scope, and needing Farlan involvement, not enmity.

He sighed, deeply, and turned to Tila. "The red."

Tila held up the red silk scarf that she'd bought the previous day, then knotted the white about Megenn's reins. Vesna nudged his horse closer and she tied the red scarf about his arm, already clad in black iron. The count had been permitted to wear his enchanted armour after the king had ruled that it was no less awkward than unensorcelled plate, and would not give him an unfair advantage. The count wondered if he also agreed so the expected finale would be all the more dramatic: the Lion of Anvee darkly glittering in the sun, facing the shining form of Emin's champion, the youth nicknamed the Sunbee because of his gold-plated armour. The contrast of misty black and glittering gold would certainly be good fare for the dozens of minstrels and storytellers out on the plain this day.

"Are you sure?" Carel looked far from happy at the decision.

"We can ask the king for an escort, surely?" This was a question Isak had wanted to avoid: he didn't want the king to be privy to all his secrets, in case he had misjudged the man—the last thing he wanted was to leave open the opportunity to blame any "accident" on the Knights of the Temples. Isak could see from Carel's and Vesna's reactions that he wasn't the only one concerned about how much they were trusting the king.

"From what I've found, the Ivy Rings would be a bad place for an ambush, no matter how isolated. As for Emin, I think we can trust him, but who knows—there aren't that many Farlan I can trust completely. "Knowledge is power"—Lesarl's favourite phrase." He laughed hollowly. "And *a wise man knows more than his closest friend.*"

"That's true enough." Vesna gave the scarf a tug to check it was secure. "But you can take this too far sometimes."

Isak looked down at the ground, refusing to look his bondsman in the eye.

"Sometimes a man needs secrets. It doesn't have to be because of a lack of trust."

"It seems to happen more often these days," said Carel. "Morghien, for one—you've said less than Mihn about him. What's going on, Isak?"

"Enough!" he roared suddenly.

Tila flinched and looked away, but Carel didn't even blink: Isak might be powerful now, rich even, but he was still the boy Carel had practically raised.

"Not enough!" he bellowed back. "Do you think yourself so wise now you can do everything alone? I'm not here to run your errands. If you expect me to be some meek little courtier, then you can shove my title and Arugin up your arse."

Isak didn't reply, but clamped his jaws tightly shut.

Carel gave an exasperated snort and clouted the Krann round the head, ignoring the gasps from onlookers. "What's wrong with you, boy? Is the magic rotting your brain, or has all this Saviour talk gone to your head?"

This time Isak gave a snarl and swatted Carel's hand away, then reached out and grabbed a handful of his tunic and physically pulled him from his saddle. He brought Carel's face up to his own.

Tila screamed and grabbed at the huge fist, but Isak shrugged her off without a glance.

"Go on then." Carel croaked. "Hit me. Prove to the whole Land you're nothing more than an animal. Perhaps I did waste my time on you. Maybe I should have given you to that mercenary on the road after all, rather than gift the Land another monster with more power than sense. You're just one man, Isak. Whatever gifts you have, however big you are, you're still just a man. You can't fight a war alone—you'll fail us all."

Isak's fist quivered as fury coursed through his body and the hot scent of rage filled his nostrils. Carel looked into his boy's cold eyes and, for the first time, he felt a pang of fear. The white-eye's face was flushed red and his lips were curled back in a snarl. Sparks danced from his tiny black pupils.

The only sound Carel could hear was the savage rush of Isak's breathing as he struggled to speak. "Don't fail me, boy." The words were little more than a whispered prayer, but they doused the fire instantly.

Isak jerked in shock, accidentally shaking Carel like a rag doll. He looked around at the others clustered around him, then, with a stunned expression on his face, he lowered Carel to the floor. He clung hard to the pommel of the saddle and bent low over Toramin's neck, trembling uncontrollably. Carel reached a hand out to steady himself against the horse's shoulder, panting as hard as Isak.

The Ghosts had formed a circle around them as soon as Isak started raising his voice, warding them from curious onlookers, but they themselves were casting panicky looks at their commander and their Lord.

"I'm sorry." Isak sounded as weak as a kitten, but human once more. Carel coughed, then reached out to Isak. Though he had no strength to squeeze Isak's hand, his words were clear: "I know you are, lad."

As Carel filled his lungs and breathed deeply, colour returned to his cheeks. He held onto Isak's hand and looked up at him, worried. "But one day, my boy, it might go too far; you might not be able to pull back in time. If you want advisors who care about you and not your power, remember what that means. It might not be my place as a loyal subject to ask what puts that hunted look on your face, but as your friend, I'm going to, whether I can help or not. If you keep everything to yourself, it'll drive you mad."

Isak lifted his head, eyes filled with sadness. "I know, but Carel, I don't understand it myself. As for explaining it to you, I wouldn't know where to begin. I'm not even sure there is a beginning." He still looked shamefaced, but held up a hand to ward off further questions. "If we survive today, I promise I'll tell you all I can. I owe you that, I know that, and much more."

Carel looked at him for a moment, then nodded, satisfied. "That'll do, boy. I'll be waiting." He reached out an arm and Isak helped him back on his horse.

Now Isak turned to the others. Tila was visibly shocked, as was Mistress

Daran, who was ineffectually stroking the green silk sleeve of Tila's dress, as much to soothe herself as her charge. Isak opened his mouth to speak, but the words went unsaid. What could he say? That it wouldn't happen again—that he, a white-eye, would never lose his temper again? He tried to catch Tila's eye, but her long hair hid her face.

Touching his heels to Toramin's flank, Isak restarted their advance on the jousting arena. The sun spread thick golden warmth over the trampled grass. Plump cloud rode smoothly on the brisk wind as they raced over the Land. The plain was already crowded and a chorus of songs, shouting, cheers, jeers, and laughter filled the air. The public galleries for the jousting were already full as people jostled for a better view. Clearly word of Tila's bet had got around. Five hundred gold coins—emins or any other currency—was a fortune. The people of Narkang wanted to cheer their champion.

Isak watched as a group of children squabbled over a pair of makeshift lances. The two boys who won out each had a cape fixed about his shoulders. One wore black, the other yellow. They were just about to perch on the backs of the two who were being the horses when a smudge-faced little girl noticed the Farlan. She gave a shriek of excitement and in a matter of seconds, the column had grown a tail of wondering eyes and dirty faces, all marvelling not at Isak, but at Count Vesna, resplendent in his battle dress.

Isak tried to smile but couldn't. He knew they were hanging back from him because they were scared of him, and he knew they had reason to be.

"My Lord is well?" the king enquired as Isak took his seat. As the previous day, the queen was absent and Count Antern filled the chair beside the king. To excuse her from the violence likely to follow, the queen had been forced to spend most of the fair secluded in her chambers, apparently suffering from a severe headache.

Isak gave a curt nod and the king pressed no further. His pale face told enough of a tale, enforced by the way Mihn was fussing around his master, pressing him to eat. At first Isak refused anything other than a mug of tea, but soon he started picking idly at the delicacies piled high on platters.

"The count is well rested, I hope," Emin prompted, looking at Carel and Tila, both of whom looked as wan as their lord, but they both nodded firmly.

"Most certainly, your Majesty," the young woman told him, adding sternly, "he will prove more than a match for Sir Bohv."

As she spoke, the knight himself trotted out to greet the crowd. He was a particularly tall man, standing a good two inches over his Farlan opponent. He had a friendly, open face, and the wild excesses of his carrot hair were checked by the red-stained helm that matched his armour. Though the knight was a devout member of the Knights of the Temples, he remained an individual, in this case displaying a fine sense of humour. His colours were yellow and azure, but as an affectionate nod to both himself and his Order, Sir Bohv's armour was painted bright red.

"I hope so," the king chuckled. "If I'm to win this bet with Lord Isak, I'd hate for any man but my champion to claim victory over Count Vesna."

"After yesterday's performance, your Majesty, I believe your Sunbee should try to be rather less ornamental."

Emin laughed at the truth in her words. His champion had been a hair's breadth from serious injury, too busy playing up to the crowd as he tilted against the knight with the Brotherhood tattoo.

"But he is young, and such folly is understandable, wouldn't you agree, Lord Isak?"

The Krann grunted; he'd been deep in his own thoughts. Emin's smile sparked a flicker of irritation, but he suppressed the feeling and inclined his head to concede the point.

"Unfortunately, the poor boy may find his follies catch up with him soon enough," continued the king. The twinkle in his eye could not fail to arouse Tila's curiosity.

"And what follies are these, your Majesty?"

"I gather his celebrations lasted well into the evening yesterday—and now it appears he is expected to be wearing no fewer than three favours on his arm today, and that leaves him in a pretty pickle."

Tila smiled at the notion, until she imagined Count Vesna riding out with three scarves on his arm. "Your Majesty seems most amused by a situation that cannot fail to distract his champion."

"It has to be a matter of some concern for him, that's true—but then I realised there was a way to avoid this situation."

"Oh?" Her smile fled.

The king smiled even more broadly. "Well, as my champion, I could solve matters easily by commanding him to honour the queen and ask for her favour."

"But the queen is not here," Tila faltered.

"Exactly my problem," the king replied brightly. "So who could my champion legitimately ask, I wonder? As my representative, he would have to pick a lady of sufficient import, perhaps make it a gesture of goodwill—"

"Oh no, he can't—You can't . . ."

Emin clapped his hands together as if the thought had only just struck him. "But of course, a visiting dignitary! Ah, Lady Tila, that is a generous and wise offer."

"But Count Vesna already wears my favour. It would be unseemly for both men to—" Tila's protestations wilted under Emin's relentless smile. The glitter in his eyes showed how much he was enjoying himself. Even today, he had time for games.

"I'm sure the count will understand—a gesture of friendship between nations, that's all. And you would be saving three delicate young ladies from terrible heartbreak."

"I—" She sagged, conceding defeat, trying to ignore a vision of Vesna's expression as she publicly handed her favour to the Sunbee, who for all his swagger, was a remarkably handsome young man. "If Lord Isak agrees, then I would be happy to help," she said, hoping Isak would leap to her rescue.

But Isak was still lost in his own thoughts: now he was staring at the figures opposite him. He could smell more than one mage out there. The woman seated beside Herolen Jex, Duchess Forell he assumed, was returning his scrutiny. Isak felt sure that she knew what he was looking for, that she could feel his presence questing softly out. She was a tall woman, and his extraordinary sight enabled him to make out her proud, imposing face; her hair and eyebrows were oddly dark against her skin. The typical inhabitants of Narkang had pale, sandy-brown colouring, but it looked to Isak as if the women of the White Circle were marking themselves out by dyeing their hair a dark reddish brown.

Isak found his eyes drifting away from the duchess and up to the woman sitting behind her, who was draped similarly in a white shawl, although arranged so that it covered almost her entire head. As Isak stared curiously, the woman looked up and met his eyes; in the shadow of her shawl, Isak could hardly see her face at all. When she smiled at him, he felt it rather than saw it. A cold tremble slithered down his spine. Amidst the clamour of the crowd, he heard only her breathing. Through the radiance of sunshine and the glitter of a thousand reflections, he saw only the darkness of her pupils. Isak's head began to throb as though it had been suddenly plunged into icy water.

"My Lord?" Tila's voice cut through the fog, startling Isak enough for him to break from the hypnotising stare. Seeing his alarm, Tila reached out and laid a hand on his arm. The touch brought him back to reality.

"I'm fine," he said to Tila reassuringly, then, turning to the king, "Emin, who is the woman sitting over there?" The king made no sign that he had noticed Isak's public informality. He followed Isak's gaze.

"That's Duchess Forell," he said, a questioning look on his face.

"No, I meant the woman behind her, the one with her head still covered."

"I'm not sure. I think I've spotted all the titled women of the White Circle, so she cannot be particularly—unless that is Ostia."

"Ostia?"

"A name I've heard—nothing more, unfortunately. Maybe her name is some kind of pun, that she's come from the east, but it's so obviously bad that it must have a greater significance. Why?"

"She keeps her face almost entirely covered, and she's not moved since they arrived. Some of the women have been sent off to fetch or deliver messages, I'd guess, and they're all dripping in jewels and thus I'd assumed titled—but she, who looks like a commoner, just sits without even speaking."

"A good observation," the king said. "Can you tell if she's a mage?"

Isak shrugged. "There's something strange about her, I know that much."

The king sat back and whispered in Coran's ear. The man nodded and moved off up the tiers as Isak returned his attention to the impending joust, which was just about to start.

The two knights cantered past each other, saluting each other with their lances. Sir Bohv's visor was raised and he offered the count a smile too. Vesna gave a twitch of the helm in reply, but the roaring lion decoration made that appear less than friendly. As they reached opposite ends of the fence, Sir Bohv flicked his visor down and both men yanked their steeds about, kicking their spurs in hard. The crowd collectively drew in breath until the two men met and a massive cheer raced around the stands. Both men hit: Vesna's lance glanced off Sir Bohv's shield; the knight's scarlet shaft shattered against the count's shoulder plate.

The second pass was more decisive. Sir Bohv, saluting with his new lance, was greeted with a roar of applause from the public stand. He trotted round to see Vesna standing high in his stirrups and ready to come again, and off they both charged. The Farlan hero kept himself high until Sir Bohv had almost reached him, then dropped down to present as small a target as possible.

Sir Bohv had expected the change in position, a standard ploy, and lowered his lance to match it, but at the very last instant, Vesna threw his body as far forward over his horse's neck as he could, bracing his shield against his body. The lance slid over the surface and away—but Vesna's, with a terrific crash, slammed into Sir Bohv's gut and threw him straight out of the saddle. Commoners and nobles alike all leapt to their feet, bellowing, clapping, screaming, and stamping.

Isak's fist tightened at the dull thump of Sir Bohv hitting the ground. His nerves were on edge already and the jousting was just another reminder of the imminent combat. Though his friend's victory paled when compared to that, he stirred his massive hands to join Emin's applause.

"Excellent strike," the king murmured.

Vesna reined to a halt and wheeled his beast in a tight circle, holding the lance aloft to acknowledge the crowd before urging his horse over to the knight's prone form. A tirade of obscenities made it clear the injury was not mortal and the crowd cheered again as Sir Bohv was helped up, clutching his ribs, to congratulate the victor.

The count looked less than friendly a little later as he was forced to watch the Sunbee swagger over to the royal box and request Tila's favour. She made no reply, but held out the white scarf for a page to tie around the man's golden-shining arm. In the bright sunlight it was hardly noticeable against the fantastic armour, but as Vesna stroked the red scarf on his own wrist, he could see nothing else. Tila's impassive face went unnoticed, as did Emin's satisfied smile.

The Kingsguard champion had won his own first bout of the day easily. His opponent, a noble of similar age, picked himself out of the dirt and stiffly bowed to the golden knight. With the formality over he turned and departed without a second glance.

"They were childhood friends," explained the king. "They grew up as neighbours, but one took the gold, the other the scarlet. Now they cannot even shake hands. But we have more important matters to discuss than the sad realities of life. After the final joust, I will announce the duel is to take place. I expect Jex to find some dramatic moment then to signal the attack.

"The Kingsguard are spread all around. We have a third of our men in the arena itself, dressed as watchmen, tradesmen, and servants. The others are in small groups, running stalls or just milling about. The mercenaries are further away—close, but not sufficiently so that they will attract the attention of any alert watchman."

"So your men will intercept Jex's mercenaries. Even if there are too many of them it will disrupt the attack and let us fight our way out."

"Exactly. But remember: our sole aim is to get to the palace and survive the night. They have enough mages that we must take any opportunities that might come up; we must not linger for anyone. I have a man with orders to break the hinges of the gate so that Count Vesna has a chance to fight his way out. As for you, Lord Isak, my mages will protect you as well as they can at the beginning, ready to counteract any magic used against the royal box, but it will not last long because I'm not staying to fight. I suggest you do the same. You are the best fighter on this field, so let Marshal Carelfolden and Mihn bring Lady Tila in your wake. If you reach the city gates and they are half closed, do not worry. Even if the daemon is released, it will let you pass."

Even now Isak's curiosity overrode the urgency of the situation. "Why wouldn't the daemon attack us?" he asked.

"The covenant that binds the daemon protects the gatekeepers by causing the daemon to actively fear them," he said. "Simply put, the principle of counteraction means the more it fears our people, the stronger it will be against anyone it doesn't fear."

"But we're not gatekeepers," Isak objected. The last thing he needed was to have to fight daemons as well as Jex's mercenaries.

"No, but you have been touched by your God, and the daemon can sense this. That's what it fears. As Chosen of Nartis, your contact with the divine has been stronger even than those ordained as priests."

Isak looked up at Mihn. The small man opened his hands in a half shrug. He had no objection against the king's logic.

"What about your reinforcements?"

"On their way. I cannot risk their arrival until the White Circle mages are fully committed. Duchess Forell is a rich and powerful woman, but she's not much of an opponent. There must be someone else behind this. The White Circle is a group that rewards success and this is their boldest venture. Their leaders will be here somewhere, to claim the prize when it's won."

"That woman, Ostia?" Isak asked.

"Perhaps." Emin said no more. Instead he busied himself with a loose thread on his coat where one of the red-lacquered buttons on his oversized cuffs had snagged and torn off. As he picked off the broken thread and brushed it to the ground, there was a metallic sound that caught Isak's attention. A lavish exterior, something sharp underneath: King Emin was beginning to be almost predictable.

They talked of inconsequential things as they picked at food, and drank watered wine for the sake of appearances. Isak tapped a finger on Eolis as he wondered how he himself would have organised the coming attack. Beside him, Mihn looked as though he had a slight humpback, where Isak's shield was hidden beneath a long cloak. The king's mages would be little use against a crossbow, and Isak couldn't wear Siulents' larger plates without being obviously ready for battle.

Isak let his eyes drift over the crowd. High in the far stand he saw the Devoted major, sitting alone and scrutinising the royal box. When Isak met his eye, the man nodded slowly and deliberately and though Isak made no gesture back, the major appeared satisfied, for he rose, wrapped his plain brown cloak about his body, and quietly departed.

A cheer broke from the crowd as the king's herald stood. Vesna pushed himself to his feet and strode purposefully towards his horse. He ran a hand over the horse's jousting armour, tugging at straps and the saddle until he was satisfied that all was in order.

Resting his arms on the worn saddle, he looked down the jousting fence to where the Sunbee was being helped to his feet. Once upright, the cocky youth took a turn before the public stand, waving to an adoring public with Tila's scarf fluttering from his arm. Vesna looked down at his own favour, touching the red silk, then looked to the royal box, where he locked eyes with Tila. Her steady gaze told Vesna that she'd been given no choice, and he accepted that—but he still intended to teach the boy a lesson.

Once he was in the saddle, Vesna's eyes didn't leave the golden knight for an instant. The first pass decided nothing. Both lances glanced off their targets without troubling the riders. On the second, the Sunbee came close to unseating his opponent as his lance exploded in a shower of splinters on Vesna's shield. The count was rocked back in his seat, but he had years of experience behind him and managed to keep his seat—although he was pretty sure that if they had not been using tourney lances, Vesna would have found himself lying in the mud with a shattered shoulder.

As the Kingsguard champion waited for a second lance, Vesna studied the ground carefully and carefully guided his horse a little further away from the rough fence separating the clashing riders. The Sunbee took a moment to collect a few last cheers from the gallery behind and then snatched his lance from the air as his page tossed it up.

Vesna smiled. The boy was undeniably good, but he was careless when it came to watching his opponent. In a contest of narrow margins, victory was in the details. His horse responded perfectly to his touch, sprinting forward to close the ground faster than normal, and the younger man wasn't able to react in time. Vesna felt only a glancing impact on his shield as he watched the padded tip of his own lance slam squarely into the Sunbee's midriff.

Screams and cheers erupted all around as the Kingsguard champion was catapulted over his horse's rump. The pandemonium made Isak reach for his sword, even as he rose to cheer the victory. The foreigner might have triumphed, but still the people gave him thunderous applause. Raising his lance high above his head, Vesna turned and saluted each section of the crowd individually before trotting to the centre of the arena and formally saluting Isak and the king.

That done, Vesna dismounted and hurried over to where his opponent was lying flat on his back. The king's doctor was kneeling at the man's side, but as the count reached them he took the ashen-faced Sunbee by the elbow and gently helped him up. His wrist was broken and his pride bruised quite as much as his stomach, but he had the good grace to shakily offer the white scarf Tila had given him.

Vesna laughed and clapped the man on the shoulder, his black mood dispersed. "Don't worry, boy, you'll mend soon enough," he said cheerily. "It'll remind you to pay more attention to your opponent next time." He turned his attention back to the adoring crowd, who seemed completely indifferent to the fact that their own champion had been humbled, and by a foreigner at that. Even the noblemen and the well-to-do townsfolk clapped and threw flowers at Vesna's feet.

They only began to quieten when the king's herald rose from his seat. Isak noticed the White Circle looked unmoved by the swell of sentiment. Sitting at their heart, Herolen Jex was eyeing the Farlan hero intently.

"Your Majesty, my Lords, Ladies, gentlefolk," cried the king's herald, rising from his seat, but he was cut off by the king, who touched the man on the shoulder. He jerked around in surprise as the king gestured for him to sit.

King Emin moved forward and began, "My fellow citizens of Narkang," pausing as a fresh cheer came from the public gallery, for the king was well loved by the common folk; for the prosperity he'd brought to the city and the pride he'd given them in it and themselves. Narkang had been little more than a town when Emin Thonal took control—and now the Krann of the Farlan, the Chosen of Nartis, came begging for their friendship. It was easy to cheer the handsome king whose genius had been proven on the battlefield, a man who never shirked the danger of his own bold schemes.

The king looked around at his subjects, basking in their enthusiasm for a few more seconds before raising a hand to calm them. "Since this Farlan rogue has badly inconvenienced my purse, I do not find myself much inclined to let him catch his breath. There is an extant matter of honour between Count Vesna and Herolen Jex—it will be decided here and now by knightly combat."

All heads turned to the opposite stand, where Herolen Jex was lounging in his seat, sipping from a tall silver goblet. He made no reply, but watched Vesna as he collected his blade from a page and strapped it on. The count remounted and stood ready.

"I thought the mêlée was still to come," Jex replied at last, pausing for long enough to make it insulting before adding, "your Majesty." His voice was deep; more measured than Isak had expected from a pirate. A sharp intake of breath ran around the pavilion.

"It was, Master Jex, but I have changed my mind. I believe I have that right since I am king and this is my kingdom." His voice had become significantly sterner.

All about the arena people gripped their seats and looked anxiously at the Kingsguard below, but the soldiers didn't move. Jex appeared to consider the king's words, then shrugged and tossed his goblet away. Standing, he let his cape fall back to a flash of fantastic colours as the sun hit his armour. The cuirass, shoulder plates, and mail had been etched into a pattern of scales that glittered blue and green in the sun; it looked like a reptilian second skin, as arresting and ornate in its own way as the Sunbee's dazzling gold-plate. The pirate straightened his sword belt and then raised his helm to place it on his head. "In that case, your Majesty, I think I will amend that small detail." Jex gave a dismissive flick of his hand and a woman screamed on his right.

Out of the corner of one eye Isak caught sight of a man levelling a crossbow. As the assassin fired, Mihn dived in front of his lord with his shield raised, while Coran, moving even faster, brought up a large rectangular shield from behind the throne. His huge arm shuddered as a pair of loud thwacks echoed out.

Isak watched the moment of realisation on Coran's face as he focused on the steel bolts in front of him; one was only a whisker from his eye, having almost passed clean through the steel plate. There was a moment of perfect silence, then chaos erupted everywhere.

Eolis leapt joyfully into the sunlight. As Isak pulled on his helm he felt a growl rumble up from his gut. Now was the time for bloody murder. He cast off his humanity and replaced it with a cold silver face. Magic ripped through the air from all sides as people scattered and ran or drew weapons. Bursts of light flared around the royal box as Emin's mages defended them, giving them time to retreat—but already Isak was preparing to attack: his fingertips were prickling with rushing energies.

Through the thin eyeholes of his helm, Isak could see people moving like leaves in the wind. He sensed where the first attack would come from, even before the man rose from nowhere to swat aside the nearest Kingsguard with a mace. The bulky mercenary laughed as the soldier crashed down and, wiping the blood from his face, he raised his weapon high to call his men to him. Isak leaped over the rail separating them and onto the lower platform where the mercenary stood triumphant. He stabbed Eolis down into the man's throat, then kicked the corpse away and waited for the next man to come at him.

"Isak," bellowed Carel from behind him, "we're leaving! Get back up here!"

The soldier beside Isak started to step up to the royal box, then his downed comrade gave a cry of pain and he stopped to help the man. Isak reached down and picked up the wounded man, passed out from the pain of his shattered shoulder, and passed him up to Carel. The other Kingsguard scrambled up beside him.

Carel breathed a sigh of relief as Isak reached up to return to the royal box, but as his fingers touched the rail, the white-eye felt a sudden weight hit his shoulders. Carel's face changed to a picture of alarm as Isak sagged, then slammed forward into the frame of the stand. He remained pinned there, with his head and shoulders over the edge at Carel's feet, but when Carel reached down to grip Isak by the shoulder, he burned his fingertips as he touched Siulents.

Isak felt small sparks of energy flicker over his body as he tried to raise his head. A red burst of pain shot down his neck and squeezed the air from his lungs. The pressure increased, until all he could manage was a low moan. The crushing ache in his bones stifled everything else, while the cloying rush of magic raged uncontrolled over his body. Isak felt the Land groan and shudder beneath him as he fought to remain conscious.

Suddenly, without warning, the pressure lessened and Isak opened his mouth to take a deep gasping breath—but he barely had time for one desperate wheeze before he was jerked up in the air like a puppet.

He caught sight of Carel's frantic expression for the briefest of moments, then the air whistled past his head as he was pulled away across the jousting arena. He felt a pavilion loom up behind him, then a burst of pain as he hit it. Then there was only darkness.

CHAPTER 34

Through the numb folds of an empty place, he felt the gentle caress of a hand on his cheek. Images appeared in his mind's eye, people and places he didn't recognise, though memories of them rose in his thoughts. Only the patient brush of delicate fingers kept them back. The comforting touch spread warmth down his cheek, over his neck and chest, and into his limbs. Slowly the warmth made him aware of the rest of his body, the crumpled and broken lines of his skin. The scar on his chest glowed bright white, casting threads of light out into the darkness.

"Isak, you must wake."

The voice stirred a memory as deep as instinct, but no more. He didn't mind. The soft syllables of her voice drove away the pain and he wanted no more than that.

"Isak, you must fight."

The name sent a tingle down his spine. He resisted, but something deep inside stirred. The tang of blood danced about his teeth.

"Isak, wake now. Help is coming."

Unbidden, his chest rose as he took in a huge gulp of air. The musty warmth faded from his skin as daylight began to sting his eyes. He recognised his name now, as he did the pain that flooded back in. The taste of blood grew thick in his mouth.

"I think the prophets were wrong."

Isak, hanging limp in someone's arms, winced at the sudden brightness. As his senses returned, he realised that he couldn't recognise the accent of whoever had just spoken: her Farlan sounded almost ugly, as if she were pronouncing each syllable with contempt.

"Why do you say that, Mistress?" came a whining reply.

"How could it be so easily captured if it is to be the weapon we believed? Ostia?"

"I can tell no more than you, Mistress," replied a third voice. Isak forced his eyelids open. Duchess Forell stood to one side, hands clasped anxiously to her chest. The woman who had just spoken, Ostia, was beside the duchess, a little oasis of serenity and calm amidst the scattered ruin of the pavilion behind. They were inside the jousting arena, Isak thought, but all was still, even the few remaining soldiers were standing motionless as they watched the proceedings.

All three women wore plain white capes of the White Circle over sumptuous dresses of purples and blues, studded with gems and woven with silver and gold.

"It is young, young enough for training."

Isak focused on the speaker, blinking in surprise as he took in her remarkable size and the colour of her skin. A female white-eye. Her white hood was up, but Isak could see that her face was rust coloured. It put him in mind a little of Xeliath's smooth chestnut colouring, but dusted with red.

"Let it stand by itself," the woman commanded. Isak felt the supports disappear from under his arms and he sagged. As his eyes drifted down the length of her body, he stiffened with shock: she was cradling a Crystal Skull, her long fingers clamped protectively about it so that both eye sockets were covered. The Skull itself was small, unassuming, its surface dull, but Isak could still feel the looming weight of the Skull pressing down on his throbbing temples.

So *that* was how he'd been overcome earlier: the Skull was powerful beyond anything he could ever have imagined—and even now it was holding him captive with terrifying ease.

Isak tried to look around the arena surreptitiously. He could see no sign of his companions, just a scattering of bodies that looked dead. He could hear the distant clash of weapons.

"They abandoned you." The strange white-eye sneered at Isak. "They broke and ran, but they will not get far. Shall we see which ones still live?"

She looked at the woman Isak thought was Ostia, who nodded. He could sense it as she began to draw magic, looking out towards the city with an enquiring expression, until a frown crossed her face.

"What is—?" Suddenly she yelped and clutched at her head. "By the pit of Ghenna, what was that?" she shouted.

"Well? What happened?" the white-eye demanded angrily. Clearly her own skills were limited, however much strength the Crystal Skull could lend her. Isak concentrated on Ostia: to be able to spy on the city gates was an amazing feat; to get close enough to be hurt by the daemon was astounding. Isak wondered if Bahl would be able to do that.

"Clever bastard," mused Ostia. She ignored the white-eye's vocal impatience, but a few moments later, said, "I doubt anyone will have managed to close the gate on the king—a daemon has just incarnated in the gatehouse."

Isak chuckled. "Not as clever as you thought? What a pity."

A quick spasm of pain ran through his body as punishment. The white-eye hissed with anger. "You will not think so when you have been bonded to me. Then you'll be as eager as a dog to deal with the problem of the king."

As she spoke, Isak blanched and his eyes went distant and fearful. He felt as if he were watching an arrow speed towards him. Suddenly he convulsed violently and the two guards gripped his arms again to stop him falling flat. The strange white-eye looked to Ostia for explanation.

"I don't know, but I suggest you stop whatever it is you are doing to him."

"I'm doing nothing," she said angrily and took a step back as Isak fell to his knees and began to shake.

Isak.

The world swam beneath his feet. Without warning he retched, splattering the contents of his stomach all over the churned ground. The white-eye twitched her dress in distaste as vomit stained the hem, but she didn't retreat. She stroked the Crystal Skull musingly: this was no trick, that much she could tell.

Isak, can you feel it? Oh Gods, can you feel it? Xeliath's voice echoed loud in Isak's mind.

"What is it?"

A storm rushing over the Land. Nartis himself, coming to lay his blessing upon you. Panic rang out in her voice, panic and euphoric delight. *Lord Bahl has gone to the Palace on the White Isle, gone to embrace his doom.*

Isak felt the Land tremble through his palms. He felt hot sunlight on his skin, and the chill of stone corridors on his fingertips. As the cold bit into his toes, he recognised the place all too well.

The stone wall was freezing as he put a hand against it to steady himself. He looked out onto the unnaturally empty beach and recognised where he was. A single sun-bleached rock sat on the smooth, flat sand, far from the listless encroachment of the tide. He turned from the window and let the faint breeze in the corridor carry him away like a dandelion seed. His thoughts were on the man he knew was about to die, a man he called friend. The man he had feared to tell his dreams to.

He was awake this time, and he knew not to fight the tide of where he was going. His bare feet whispered warnings on the smooth floor, but he ignored them and pushed onto an arched doorway ahead. As he entered the domed chamber his strength almost failed as the immense weight of age inside encircled him.

He dragged his shivering limbs to the statue ahead and one final effort brought his head up to rest on the pedestal. He froze at what he saw before him.

Lord Bahl stood in the centre, as he always had in the dreams, even when he had been just a nameless face. He looked imperious, potent, as magic and anger coursed through his body. He danced and spun with deadly breathless grace when the dark knight attacked, but each strike was met and countered. A deep laughter rumbled through the chamber and Bahl's blows grew faster and more desperate.

Then an opening came and the unknown knight lashed out, faster than Isak could follow. The legendary hooded face dropped and rolled away in a burst of crimson. Isak moaned out loud, as he had every one of the dozen times he'd dreamed of this death. Only this time it was true. Despite everything, it had come true—and he had never warned his Lord . . .

Guilt seeped into him like poison, and his tears fell like acid on his cheeks.

The knight turned at the moan, his fanged blade rising to meet another challenge. The black armour was of ancient design, and fantastically ornate, with beaded ridges and swirls of silver. The knight's hand was naked, fully exposed to the air, and as pale as a corpse's. The monogram at his throat— the entwined letters K and V—made it clear whose armour this had once been, and which legendary warrior had slain Lord Bahl.

Isak stood, and this time he found Eolis in his hand, but when he looked down at it, he saw the blade was as thin and unsubstantial as morning mist. He struggled to raise the weapon, but despite his fury he could manage to advance only one step. He sank to his knees, exhausted, shaking with grief. Looking at his hands, Isak saw that they were hardly visible in the reflected light, like the sword in his hand, and they were growing fainter with each passing moment.

Kastan Styrax chuckled malevolently and dropped his guard. A trail of blood—Bahl's blood, Isak thought with a near sob—spattered on the stone. He gave Isak a mock salute and turned, his broadsword resting on his shoulder as he walked away.

He called out to Isak across the hall, "Another day, boy."

"Mistress, the ceremony will not work if he's unconscious."

"Then I will wake it up. Ah, it is already."

Isak opened his eyes to find the white-eye staring down at him. The duchess stood hunched at her side; Ostia was marking out a circle on the ground with her toe.

"Ceremony?" he muttered through his daze.

"Yes, dog, ceremony. Dangerous animals must be tamed if they are to be of any use."

New strength surged into Isak's limbs. The air tasted sweeter as he took a deep strong breath. He felt the dizzying miles of air above him and the heavy security of earth and rock beneath his feet. A smile crept onto his lips, despite the death of his friend and Master. His veins sparkled with life as clouds rushed overhead to celebrate his ascension. The day had been clear and fresh, but as Isak sucked in each joyful lungful of air, he drew the storm closer.

Isak could feel Nartis now, not as the terrorising deity of his dream, but as a brother, a father. The air shuddered as the God's divine gaze broke through the clouds and settled like a crown on Isak's head. The God's strength was there to draw on; his anger loaned fire to Isak's drained limbs.

"My people have a saying," Isak began.

The women stopped what they were doing and narrowed their eyes at him. Isak looked from one to the other, lingering on Ostia for the longest. Suddenly she recognised some change in the air. Concern blossomed on her face as she felt Nartis. Isak could feel his own strength growing, and he saw in Ostia's eyes that she could see it too, but she ignored it, as though it was unimportant to her cause.

It confirmed Isak's thought that Ostia was not the enemy—or maybe it was just that she had no intention of making an enemy of Nartis. Either way, it was one less problem, and now Isak saw how to deal with the others. He grinned at the white-eye above him.

"They say that only a fool tries to cage a wolf."

The white-eye stared back at him, then snorted in derision, quickly echoed by the duchess.

"Stupid creature," the white-eye said. "You call yourself a wolf? Ha! You are a beast, yes, but no one is strong enough to resist this ceremony, whatever grand statements you might make about your spirit."

Isak continued to grin as his strength grew with every second. He could feel Nartis touch every inch of his skin as the power of divine blessing filled his soul. This was what it truly meant to be a white-eye, to have every fibre humming with rapturous energy. Ostia took a careful step back.

"I'm peasant stock," he said. "We don't make grand statements."

"So?" She tried to affect boredom, but for the first time he could hear slight uncertainty in her voice.

"Wolves never travel alone."

She didn't even have time to take in his words. Her eyes widened as a jolt of pain hit and her body went rigid. Her mouth fell half open in a scream that never came. Without breaking stride, Mihn danced past her falling body, smoothly tearing Arugin from her back and bringing it up to meet the guard on Isak's right. Isak spun to his left and slammed his palm into the other soldier's throat. He felt a snap as something gave way under the blow, then reached down to grab the man's sword from its scabbard. The man's skin was also rusty-coloured; Isak briefly registered that his armour was unusually shaped and coloured.

He turned to see Ostia dive gracefully past, gathering up the Crystal Skull as the white-eye fell, then rolling back onto her feet like a street acrobat. Duchess Forell grabbed at the artefact as she straightened up, but Ostia easily slipped the Skull through the duchess's grip, then lashed out with her foot.

Isak thought he heard a bone break. The duchess collapsed, screaming in pain.

In his peripheral vision, Isak caught sight of a man—a mercenary?—darting forward and he turned and lunged, using his unnatural strength to drive through the man's shield and into his belly. He wrenched the blade violently out, snapping it clean in half, and threw what remained at the nearest soldier to give himself enough time to gather up the mercenary's sword.

Now the other mercenaries hesitated. Isak glanced at Mihn and saw two corpses lying at his feet. Tears streamed from his eyes as blood dripped from a weapon he'd vowed never to use again.

Then Isak felt a pulse of magic ripple out from the Crystal Skull as Ostia snarled something. He hurried to find some defence against the spell, whatever it was, before he realised it wasn't directed at him. Tendrils of energy rushed in all directions as crimson claws appeared in the air around the remaining mercenaries. They died without a sound, leaving only three figures standing amongst a heap of twitching corpses.

Isak could feel Eolis, his shield and helm off to one side, drawing him to them. He kept a wary distance from Ostia. "Who in the name of the Gods are you?" he asked.

"Not in the name of the Gods." She smiled hungrily, looking around at the corpses, and Isak saw elongated teeth behind quivering lips. She tugged her shawl over her head with a gloved hand. "Do you not recognise me?" There was a tenderness in her voice that gave him pause; it reminded him of Xeliath.

"Should I know you?" he asked again, but as he said it, Isak felt a quiver of recognition. Not who, but what. She was fair-skinned, with dark hair, but with her wide face and small features she was clearly not Farlan.

The teeth, and the dark patch of skin that had blossomed on her cheek, burnt by the touch of sunlight, he realised. Finally, a name came.

"Ah, I see it in your face," she said. "My name is Zhia Vukotic—but you do not know my face. I had wondered, but no matter."

"Why did you kill your men?"

"If you can guess what I am, then you surely know I need no reason to kill, even by your standards." She gave a mocking laugh. "Yes, boy, I know that's not what you meant. I killed them because they would have proved an inconvenience; they were loyal to the Circle."

"And you're not? I don't understand."

"Evidently. Can you guess who they are? Or are you really so dim-witted? Then I should put you out of your misery now."

"They—I've never seen anyone like them before."

"Then I will explain. Your man has just killed the Queen of the Fysthrall. This is the Age of Fulfilment and the banished have returned. They have changed so much. Once they were so wonderful . . ." Her voice trailed off, then she shrugged. "Now is not the time. The White Circle is their cause, not mine."

"So why are you involved? Because they were once your allies?"

"Nostalgia? Hah." Her laughter echoed with the weight of years. The memory of the island palace stirred in Isak's mind. Zhia had the same weary, timeless quality about her. He forced down the memory of Bahl's death. That was for later; he could not let himself grieve yet.

"I leave the obsession with the past to my brother. In any case, they are far from what we once knew. They had no idea who I was, other than that I possessed more skill and knowledge than any other of the Circle. The temptation of a Skull was easily enough for me to play the part of a quiet and faithful servant. I didn't expect taking it to be quite so easy."

"That was the only reason you were with them?"

"You're showing your innocence now. With an eternity ahead of me, playing at politics keeps me busy even if it comes to nothing." Zhia shrugged again, taking care not to dislodge her shawl and expose herself to the sun's touch. "If it serves a future purpose, all the better."

"Future purpose?"

Her garrulousness was making Isak suspicious. They were the very definition of foes: Isak was blessed even beyond most Chosen; Zhia with her brothers, was cursed above all others.

"Time is of the essence for Narkang's king. I suggest you find a way to join him." She blinked, then curled her lip with impatience as Isak still didn't appear to understand. "Look, boy: the Fysthrall are far more your enemies than I. They have one ambition, to take revenge on the Gods who banished them. Understandably, thanks to the Saviour prophecies, they see you as a threat to these plans—and it appears you feature in their own prophecies. You are—or have—the key to ending their exile."

"So they are who the Saviour's supposed to fight?" Isak wasn't sure he wanted a true answer to that. Like most, he had assumed that there was some cataclysm to come, so the creeping worry of disaster would be lurking on the horizon until it actually happened.

"They believe so, but they are intellectually insular. I suggest you would be better off having a care of your own shadow more than you do the Fysthrall. Your friend the king is the man to ask about the Saviour—he has written some excellent essays on the subject. The man is obsessed with history—and making his own mark upon it. Now, return to your friends."

Isak sensed her disappointment with him, but he couldn't work out whether it was because he wasn't all that she'd expected, or because Siulents had brought back old and unhappy memories.

"So what's your part in this now?" he asked offhandedly.

"Don't banter with me, boy, it's beyond you."

"You said their cause was not yours," he explained hurriedly. He was more than aware of the angry prickle of magic surrounding her. "What do *you* want—it's obviously not my death."

"Nothing *you* can give me, but it should be easy enough to guess, if you have *any* imagination. Enough of this. Go."

He didn't wait to be told again. His friends needed him. Isak saw the main arena gate lying flat as Emin had promised, and bodies—Kingsguard, mercenaries, ordinary people, both noble and peasant—lying everywhere. He couldn't see Vesna's distinctive armour anywhere among the fallen, so presumably he had made it through.

A group of horses stood tethered to a rail at the back of the public stand, nominally guarded by a mercenary who'd walked out to a rise in the ground to see what he could of the fighting. The unnatural vigour of his ascension was still running through Isak's limbs, and his aim was true as he threw Eolis thirty yards to impale the man. Like a hunting dog, Mihn padded away to retrieve the sword. As he returned, Isak saw the streaking of tears on his face.

"Thank you," he said as Mihn handed him Eolis. He caught Mihn by the shoulder and held him there, forcing Mihn to look him straight in the eye, though the man could hardly bear to lift his head.

"I am your bondsman," he said, quietly. "It was my duty."

"That's not what I meant," Isak said. "I know you don't fear death, as a sensible man should—and dying bravely would have been easy there, even though I saw how fast you were: you're as good a swordsman as I've ever seen. That must make it hurt all the more."

"I needed Arugin. Dying bravely wouldn't erase my shame. Your cause is my life as much as my penitence."

It was hard to argue with him, but there were things to be done. Isak made a mental promise that he would continue this later and then turned his horse towards the city. "Come on, we need to get to the baths. The man who builds one tunnel builds many. I can't see Emin's reinforcements, so this could get desperate, and I don't intend to watch from the sidelines."

CHAPTER 35

"LOOK ALIVE, THEY'RE COMING AGAIN."

Tired eyes and bloody faces lifted automatically at Vesna's voice. The black knight's reassuring presence meant they nodded grimly and tightened their grip on their weapons. The walls were manned by Kingsguard, bolstered by watchmen and palace servants, but without a real-life hero in their midst they might well have been broken by the hardened troops attacking. They murmured encouragement to each other and straightened their backs.

"Have you left some for me then?" bellowed Isak with forced humour. Vesna whirled around, relief washing over his features as he hurried down from the battlements. He sheathed his sword and took Isak's arm.

"Gods, you're alive," he said, thankfully. "When they said you'd been dragged from the royal box I thought you didn't stand a chance. I was going to go back, but Tila—and Mihn—said—"

Isak held up a hand to stop him. "Enough, Mihn was right. He'd not have got past the guards with company. How are we doing here?" Isak waved to the walls as shouts came from the other side.

"There's more than we expected, some regiments of mercenaries I've never seen before. Yeetatchen, or something—wherever they're from, they fight like daemons. The king's at the main gate—the lowest part of the wall is to the northern side of the gate."

"Where's Carel?"

"He's fine, he's with the king. I'm commanding the running repairs, but the bulk of the attack so far has been up by the gate. We've been able to contain those few trying to sneak their way in, but it's pretty tight." He stopped as he suddenly realised what was strange. He looked around. "How in the names of the Upper Circle did you get into the castle?"

Isak smiled and waved the question away. "King Emin is a man who likes to have secrets. If you need me, send someone and I'll come with the storm on my heels."

"And in your hands too, I hope!" he laughed. A shout from the wall attracted his attention and he ran back up the stairs, calling over his shoulder, "Be safe, my Lord."

Isak and Mihn ran to the main gate, stopping briefly as a servant appeared with the rest of Siulents. Mihn helped Isak to strap it on as screams and the clash of steel rang out from the left of the main gate. He could see soldiers clustered on the wall, the longest stretch between towers, with a rise of ground outside. As Isak approached, he noticed the changes that Vesna had predicted upon their arrival. The count had got it absolutely right: this was no longer an indefensible pleasure palace, but a place of war.

The air above the walls shuddered as a blazing light burst into life, blinding the defenders momentarily until it snapped out as suddenly as it had appeared. From the nearest tower, fire stabbed out in reply and crashed down on the other side of the wall. Isak heard the thump as it hit and distant screams.

The wall shook once, twice, and Isak felt magic beat against the stone. They were trying to punch a hole in the wall so they could pour men into the palace. The white-eye leapt up the steps, sliding on his helm and shield as he ran. One of the Kingsguard on the wall turned at the sound of metal on stone.

Delight flowered on his face when he saw the silver giant and he called out, "Lord Isak!"

More faces turned and saw and took up the call. Isak waved acknowledgment, but headed directly for the group of dark figures with King Emin at the centre. The curved edge of Darklight glowed at Emin's back, illuminating his golden armour. Even in the middle of battle, the man looked composed and at ease. His palace had shaken off its delicate image; the king had no need. It made Isak wonder exactly what would ever cause that to happen.

"This is a fine toy you've brought me, Lord Isak," Emin called, raising the axe in salute. "Doranei found you, then?"

Isak nodded his thanks—he had been quite right in thinking Emin would have a number of tunnels for his private use. The path to the public baths had been clear and when they'd arrived, Doranei had stepped out of the shadows, armoured and sword drawn. Some furtive sneaking through deserted streets and a second tunnel brought them inside the palace and once past the welcoming sword tips of the Kingsguard, a huge stone block had been moved over the trapdoor, just in case Isak wasn't the only one to work out the king's predilection for secret tunnels.

Carel hugged Isak briefly, then turned to Mihn and clapped him on the shoulder. A warning shout erased any thought of conversation as Mihn word-lessly handed Arugin back to the veteran Ghost. There was a clatter of lad-ders, and through the crenellations Isak could see untidy clumps of soldiers waiting to scale the walls and attack.

One of Emin's men leaned out to aim a crossbow down at them, flinching as an arrow hit the stone beside him then skewed wildly upwards. Isak nudged the man aside, a young watchman wearing ill-fitting armour and an apprehensive expression, and leaned out over the wall.

Holding his shield against arrows and the dying sun, Isak squinted down the ladder. The first man was only a few yards off. Isak took in the scene, then a flurry of arrows prompted him to haste. With a muttered apology to the sword, he used Eolis to cut away one side of the ladder. The enchanted edge sliced through the iron rods bound roughly to the top like a hot knife through butter and the ladder lurched and fell.

A howling war cry pierced the air as Isak pulled himself back to relative safety. Two figures, flailing madly, flew through the air towards the wall and landed safely on the walkway: Isak recognised the distinctive shapes of Fys-thrall as the warriors began to strike out with furious purpose.

The king raised Darklight, but before he could move, Coran had rushed from his master's lee. Bellowing like an enraged bull, he swung a huge mace above his head, slamming it square onto the shield of the first man. Sheer animal strength smashed the man off the walkway onto the gravel path below. The second Fysthrall half turned at the sound of the impact, and his error cost him his life as one of the Farlan guardsmen brutally decapitated him.

A Kingsguard stepped into the space they left, ready to hack away at the ladder, when an arrow flew almost clean through his throat. The impact sent him collapsing backwards, pawing weakly at his neck. Coran ignored the dying man's feeble wails and stepped over to crash his mace down on the head of a mercenary emerging over the wall. A second mercenary right behind was ready; he pushed his colleague's corpse out of the way and stabbed wildly with his spear, trying to drive the white-eye back.

As Coran gave ground, another Fysthrall landed on the walkway. Doranei darted forward and trapped the man's sword between his own axe and sword, then stamped hard into the side of his knee. The king's man jumped back again as Coran swung up the butt of his huge mace and caught the Fysthrall under the chin, knocking him back over the battlements to fall amongst his own troops.

"Bloody mages," spat Carel. He was unscathed, and looked younger now.

He swung Arugin with ease. "They keep tossing these dark-skinned monsters at us; bloody things don't know when they're dead."

Isak didn't have time to correct the veteran as more mercenaries rushed up the ladder. They fought with desperation, and their numbers kept increasing. Isak could feel magic billowing on the wind as blood flew and lingering screams haunted every shadow. He ducked a wildly swung axe and ran the man through, pushing him back off Eolis and over the wall. A sword glanced off his cuirass and he lashed out with his shield, feeling the hard edge crunch into teeth and bone.

There was no time to see how anyone else was faring. He caught glimpses of Emin, shining in the firelight, a dark trail following his axe, and he could hear Coran roaring above the clang of steel and the howl and sob of death. Isak followed the white-eye's lead and threw himself at the attackers. Cutting and stabbing with furious abandon, he closed the few yards to where men continued to spill over the walls. His guards, close behind, drove off the mercenaries to give Isak the respite he needed.

Putting a hand on the stone wall Isak steadied himself, opening his senses and drawing magic in. He could feel the bank of ladders set against the wall and the image of a flame appeared in his mind. Stretching out his hand, Isak felt the fire grow there. The flames rose and expanded as the climbing mercenaries shrieked in fear. Leaning forward he dropped the still-expanding fireball over the wall. It engulfed one man, who screamed and threw himself backwards, flailing desperately as he fell to earth, but the unnatural fire was not yet finished. With malevolent purpose the flames licked out, and where they touched, they stayed, until they had crept slowly out to mark every one of the siege ladders.

The climbers, seeing the fate of their fellows, tried to escape, fighting each other to get away. Some fell, the flames already devouring their clothes; others stared futilely, almost mesmerised, at the fire flashing slowly down towards them.

"Isak," called King Emin, "can you see their mages? The wall's weakening."

As the king spoke the wall shook again, as though some invisible giant pounded its fists against the stone. Isak gave the fire one last burst of strength and released it to surge down the walls, wrapping everything in dancing orange sparks. The ladders were all alight and for a brief moment they had no one left to fight.

"We need to stop them breaching," Emin told Isak. A thin line of dried blood ran down his face and lay in sticky trails on his armour. "I don't know how much longer the wall will hold, but if they had any sense they'd realise throwing more soldiers onto the walkway would win them a breach anyway." Amidst all the chaos, the king still sounded calm and in control.

Isak leaned out as far as he dared behind his shield. He knew Siulents was an obvious target now the sun was fading. An arrow sped through the gap he'd left and skimmed off the cheek of his helm. He flinched and withdrew. He had an idea of the ground outside the palace; that would have to be enough; the rest was magic. He knew roughly where the king's mages had been attacking; soon he could sense the enemy as they readied themselves for another assault.

The clouds above were stirring restlessly. They'd been massing since Bahl's death, swarming to salute the new Lord of Storms. Isak could almost feel their animal nature: giants of the air yawning and stretching, growling with barely contained anger. He could taste the anticipatory pressure in the air. Both attackers and defenders felt a tingle down their necks and glanced nervously at the sky.

As the first bolt of lightning crashed down, the soldiers near the enemy mages scattered. Isak perceived what appeared to be their scent on the wind as though it were the musk of a frightened deer. There were three, women, but Ostia was not among them. One was gathering her defences, trying to form a shield about herself, so Isak concentrated down on her first, urging the energy in the air to focus on the ground at her feet. With an enormous effort she managed to redirect the bolts of lightning towards her companions. They, feeling Isak's gaze on her, had backed carefully away, constructing their own defences as white daggers of light smashed down all around them, but one was too slow. She was caught in the teeth of the storm, lashed brutally and cast aside. The third survived for a moment, but she had forgotten about the king's mages; in seconds she was consumed by their fire.

Isak felt a weak note of confidence in the woman he had first targeted as her shield held against the storm. He smiled.

Now Isak pushed his hands together, driving his senses out as the Land obeyed his commands, willingly responding to the touch of the Chosen. Isak could feel earth between his fingers; he could smell the trampled grass. As he spread his palms out, the Land followed his guidance and ripped apart underneath the mage.

She fell, all defences gone, confidence supplanted by horror as she lay crumpled and broken, looking up from her grave at a raging sky. A whimper escaped her lips. She reached out to touch the walls of earth on either side, recoiling from the damp soil as though it had scorched her. Fear paralysed her. Isak closed his hands again.

The defenders had a little time to rest as the mercenaries drew back in disarray, but Isak didn't want it: time brought back the human part of him, the part that thought and mourned. It was cowardly, he knew, but he wanted to escape from his responsibilities, to hide behind the beast that came out in battle. That side of him didn't care who was dead or alive, who was Lord and who was servant. He kept silent about Bahl's death, though guilt gnawed away inside him.

He told himself he had never quite believed that palace by the shore to be real. Even after he'd recognised Bahl, he had refused to accept it. He had deliberately shied away from warning Bahl—he knew the old Lord wouldn't have listened, for Bahl had half craved the release death would bring, but still it would have meant acknowledging too much. Normal people didn't have premonitions of the future, not even the Chosen. It meant Isak was different, and he was as afraid of that as he was of the dark knight who he himself would one day have to face, and that cold face he'd one day stare upon as he died.

"Isak." Carel approached carrying a skin of wine and some ripped pieces of bread. "Get something into your stomach, boy, it'll give you strength." The old man handed Isak a chunk of bread. It looked rather pathetic in his huge hand, but he recognised the need to eat something, however small.

"What's wrong, lad? Are you injured?"

Isak shook his head. He didn't know what to say. He was keeping more and more from the one man who knew him better than anyone; one of the few people he knew he could trust absolutely; it was beginning to look like there was never a good time for the truth.

"My life has become more complicated," Isak eventually managed.

Carel frowned, then squatted down next to Isak with his sabre resting on his shoulder so he was close enough to whisper. "What happened in the arena? Something Mihn said?"

"No, we don't have time right now—and anyway, none of it matters if we don't survive today." The dark corner of his soul wanted to laugh. *If this is all true then it doesn't matter what you do. You'll not die here unless the dark knight appears, and he won't. You know who he is already. You're just too scared to face the truth. Go and cower behind the battlements, watching others die and waiting for your time.*

"And that's it," Isak said aloud. "There are others, and they matter. Perhaps they matter enough that the truth shouldn't be hidden."

"Isak? What are you talking about, boy?" Carel sounded bewildered, perhaps worried Isak was losing his mind.

"Nothing." Isak dismissed the question with a wave of the hand and stood upright again. Now that he'd made his decision, Isak felt new purpose filling him. "Call the battle hymn. The enemy is coming."

"Ah, Isak, lad, that's only supposed to come from Lord Bahl, from the Lord of the Farlan. They'll sing it for you, but . . . it'd be wrong. People might think you meant rebellion." Carel sounded anguished as he spoke, his loyalties torn.

It seemed strange to Isak, but he knew the pride Carel set in those few lines of verse.

"Better that it would, but I *am* Lord of the Farlan now." The catch in his voice was unexpected. "Carel, Lord Bahl died this afternoon. Pass the word on. Tell them to sing to Lord Bahl's honour—I'll not have a defeat as his memorial."

The word spread quickly. The Farlan soldiers seemed to sag at the news, as though the rock their lives had been founded upon was now gone. Lord Bahl had led their grandfathers and their great-grandfathers into victorious battle. He was the eternal hero who arrived bearing the vengeance of the Gods. And now he was dead. The cornerstone of their nation was suddenly, unexpectedly, gone.

Only Carel, striding amongst them, stopped men from dropping hopelessly to the floor. Whispering fiercely in the ear of one, clapping a firm hand on the shoulder of the next; one by one he roused in them the love they'd had for their Lord. In the heat of battle, their passion burned with sudden and terrible intensity. Cold fury showed in their eyes as they waited for the enemy. The battle hymn came softly from their lips. Now they were angry.

When the enemy came, it looked a final desperate attempt. Any remaining mages of the White Circle had fled in fear of Isak, but a division of Fysthrall warriors led the attack. They didn't look human in the firelight. Their blue-green scaled armour glowed eerily, and they seemed to jerk and shuffle as they raised the ladders.

As Isak watched them come to an accompaniment of the whistle of arrows, the sight of them evoked an elusive memory of glinting bodies and huge bronze war hammers shining in the light of an unnatural fire—but he couldn't remember any more. Faces and names eluded him as the present intruded on his thoughts.

Scores of arrows kept the defenders down as the Fysthrall swarmed up to attack. White-eyes stood on the tops of the ladders while they were being raised, ready to leap over the battlements the moment wood met stone, when they started striking out with fierce abandon, brandishing their long-handled battle-axes. The first Ghost to come within range was caught in the armpit, the bronze-inlaid blade cutting deep, but it caught on the inside of his cuirass and fell with the man. The Fysthrall abandoned his axe and pulled a pair of short swords from his belt. He started trading blows with Carel before Ghosts on either side impaled him.

Elsewhere the white-eyes didn't fall so easily and brutally cut the defenders down . . . but the battle hymn of the Ghosts was taken up by the Kingsguard now and it echoed down the wall.

The captain of the Fysthrall white-eyes charged up and over, heading straight for Isak, screaming a challenge as he battered a path to the new Farlan Lord.

Isak waited for him, sword and shield forward to meet the enchanted axes in the captain's hands. The Fysthrall white-eye roared at Isak and began to rain blows down on him. With bodies piling up on the ground and more men coming up the ladder there was little room to move, but Carel managed to slip around to cut at the back of the Fysthrall's leg. The blow glanced off his armour, but it distracted the white-eye enough for Isak to start his own attack.

Now using all his speed and power, Isak hacked away, until Eolis caught the shaft of one axe and sliced through. A burst of red appeared as the magic in the blade suddenly ran wild and, in a cloud of light, the uncontrolled energies wrapped themselves around the captain's arm. Isak heard the sizzle of burning flesh as the man cried out in pain and lowered his guard. The next blow sheared through his throat.

Isak carefully kicked the corpse off into the palace gardens and looked around, spotting Carel as the old man cried out. Throwing himself forward in controlled fury, Isak struck off the offender's arm, then smashed his shield into the man's face. The Fysthrall screamed in agony, but the cry was cut off as Eolis punctured his heart.

The enemy held a small stretch of wall now and were trying to drive a wedge through the Farlan Ghosts. Isak ploughed in, swinging wide strokes they couldn't avoid, so crowded together were they. A sword got through his guard, but was turned by Siulents, and in a heartbeat Isak had kicked out and heard the crouching man's neck snap, all the while he was stabbing through another man's breastplate into his heart.

"Isak," King Emin called, a way behind him, "we're being swamped. Pull back to the keep." As he spoke, another tremor ran though the wall. Isak looked around in confusion. He turned aside the last man's sword and watched agony flower on his face as a Kingsguard stabbed him in the ribs, then stopped and opened his senses. He couldn't feel any mages in the area, but the walls shook again and he realised they wouldn't hold for much longer.

Looking over the battlements he saw the reason for the wall's shaking: a battering ram was being backed away from the wall for another run. Its brass head glowed with magic. It appeared the enemy did not trust any of the king's gates now: they would come in through the walls where no daemons were lurking, waiting to cause even more death and destruction.

Isak smiled grimly, they were probably right not to trust the gates. He cut away all the ladders he could reach again, then shouted back, "We're going." He turned to Carel, worried by the way the old man's face was contorted in pain and fatigue.

A horn was sounded and immediately all King Emin's men and Isak's own party turned and ran for the nearest stairs. Isak gave Carel a shove, but he stumbled and was caught by one of the Ghosts, who grabbed his arm and helped him on. Mihn didn't move, waiting for Isak.

"Go, I'll follow once everyone is off," he said, waving Mihn away, but the small man didn't move. "Do what I tell you!" Isak shouted, wanting him clear. "Get down those stairs now!"

Mihn frowned at Isak for a moment, trying to work out what he was going to do, then bobbed his head. "I'll wait for you by the gate, but I'll not go in until you do."

As Mihn left, Isak saw men of the Brotherhood run down the walkway towards the advancing troops. Each one carried bottles with burning rags in the neck. They threw them down the walkway and as the bottles smashed, the stone caught aflame, creating a barrier to protect the fleeing soldiers. That done, the King's Men ran, collecting up the few stragglers yet to leave, cutting down the last few enemies, until they were on their way to safety.

Isak watched them join the crowd clustered around the keep's gate. The wall shook again; it was about to crumble. The pop and grind of splitting stone screamed in the air. He ran to the head of the stairs; they were running out of time. The wall would give in the next few blows and Emin's troops would be caught in the open and slaughtered as they gathered at the small gate of the keep, waiting for space to move to safety. Behind him the wall groaned and lurched. Two huge blocks of stone fell inwards and crashed down. Isak grabbed at the battlements as the walkway shuddered underneath him. He looked around: the flames were still too ferocious to cross. There might still be time.

Carel was halfway across the palace gardens when he heard stones falling and he turned back to see Isak balanced precariously, ten yards from the breach—and then only five as another piece collapsed. Through the gap he could see pike heads, black against the firelight behind. Any more and the mercenaries would walk straight in. He looked around and saw how many were fighting to get into the keep—and here came Count Vesna's companies sprinting towards them from the rear of the palace, desperate to reach the gate in time.

Carel turned back to look at Isak, then drew Arugin again as four men ran towards them from the nearest tower, outstripped by the solders who'd been there. They stopped dead as he stepped forward. Unarmed and dressed in bright colour, they had to be the king's mages.

"You four, do something to help him."

One looked over at the silver figure on the walls. Isak was kneeling down on the wall with his shield raised above his head. The stairs were within reach, but he wasn't looking at them.

"Help him?" another replied incredulously. He was young, little older than Isak himself. His orange and blue robes were expensive; they'd have looked impressive this morning, no doubt. Now they were stained and scorched. "We've got to get away," he explained.

"What?" Carel asked. "Why?"

"He's calling down the storm, using his magic to bring it to him. The lightning will follow anything drawing magic. Please, let us pass!" He sounded desperate, as if he were pleading with every remaining ounce of his strength.

Before Carel could reply, Commander Brandt appeared. "What's he doing up there?" he asked. The watchman seemed furious more than anything else. His battered armour was covered in blood, but if it was his own the man didn't seem to have noticed.

"Buying us some time. If they breach it now we'll be slaughtered."

Brandt looked back at the men fighting to get into the keep, then at Isak.

"He's not going to manage it alone. Look." Brandt pointed to the intact side of the wall where the mercenaries were slowly making their way forward, throwing corpses onto the roaring flames to smother them.

"You." Brandt grabbed the oldest of the mages. "The enemy were throwing men up onto the walls by magic—can you do that?"

The man looked blank for a moment, lost in panic, then his face cleared. "I think so, Commander, it's a simple spell. With four of us together, yes."

"Good." Brandt drew his sword, causing the mage to shrink back in fear. "Then get me up there now, or we're all dead."

"We'll need time—"

"You don't have it. I know about magic: draw as much as you can and get it done. If I'm still here in half a minute I swear you'll be the first to die."

The mage opened his mouth to object, then looked again at the bloody sword and slammed it shut. He walked around Brandt until he could see Isak over the commander's shoulder. Taking hold of an object at his belt he took a deep breath while the other mages stepped forward to place their hands on his shoulders and lend their strength. He closed his eyes, almost giddy with the rampant magic in the air. The mage's eyelids shuddered with panic as he felt the power flowing in from the other mages. It felt like an age as he lifted his trembling hand; the energy inside was scorching his fingers as it waited to be released—and then, suddenly, the magic took over and his palm slammed against Brandt's cuirass. He felt the raw power blossom all around and the commander falling away before unconsciousness enveloped him.

"By the eyes of Fate, who's that?" The Kingsguard pointed over the battlements as they watched a figure land heavily a few yards from Lord Isak.

"Gods, that's Brandt," muttered the king as the figure clambered to his feet. A line of mercenaries were inching towards him. "Don't just gape, you fools, help him!"

Those soldiers with bows began to fire down on the figures edging cautiously towards the commander. Flames dripped from the walkway as Brandt started slashing wildly at the lead soldier, who was nearly upon him. The man slipped on the bloody stone and landed on a burning patch, setting his own clothes alight.

As Brandt jumped back, the man pulled himself up and fled back towards his own troops, who shrank away from the burning soldier. The commander found his footing on the now-sloping walkway and backed away from the flames to where Isak knelt, motionless. The burning man was flailing madly at his comrades, then he tripped on the corpses at his feet and set them alight too.

"What's happening?" demanded Carel as he appeared in the narrow doorway and barged out to where King Emin stood. Sheer exhaustion made him put pride to one side and reach for Doranei's shoulder to steady himself; instinct was all that was keeping the veteran Ghost going now, for his arm was bleeding badly and he was ready to retch from fatigue. But Carel was a professional, and his boy was still out there. Somehow he found the strength to continue.

"Lord Isak seems to be casting some sort of spell." The king pointed upwards. "Look at the sky—that's not natural." They all looked at the angry clouds roiling in the air above Isak. Even the gigantic silver-clad white-eye seemed insignificant against that brooding mass of violence.

"The mage said he was calling down the storm."

"Well, it looks like it's about to hit."

The wall shook again, a deep rumble that rose to a tortuous cracking as a ten-yard stretch ripped away and collapsed inwards. Isak hadn't moved, but everyone could feel the pressure in the air mounting. They knew something had to give soon. Near to him, Brandt attacked the advancing troops with reckless abandon, putting everything he had into a furious volley of blows.

"He's trying to take on an entire army," cried one young Kingsguard soldier, "but he's just a watchman."

"Just a watchman, boy?" roared the king, anger flaring from nothing to a holy terror. "He might be saving your life!"

Brandt took another blow on the shield and lunged up at his attacker's throat. The man fell, but another stepped forward and caught Brandt on the shoulder. He reeled, crying out in pain, but the sound was lost as a bolt of lightning crashed down onto the tower where the mages had stood. For a moment the men on the wall were frozen in time, as were the figures scrambling through the breach and spilling out into the scarred gardens. Then the tower was struck again, then the wall, then the ground, again and again. The storm was upon them, called by the Lord of Storms himself.

"*As the shadows rose and the enemy appeared on all sides, Nartis spoke to the heavens. The storm obeyed his call and unleashed its legions—and he rained terrible fire down upon that place of death,*" intoned Carel. There were tears in his eyes as he spoke. A few Kingsguard men turned with questioning faces as the air was split with fire and the voice of the storm raged unchecked, lashing down one bolt after another.

It was a quotation every Farlan knew, and it came from the legends before the Great War. King Emin saw the Ghost beside him mouth the words of a prayer, then he turned to gain a last glimpse of Commander Brandt, struggling hopelessly against two attackers. Then the burning white light was all he could see, pierced only by the screams of the dying and the very earth itself trembling.

CHAPTER 36

"AND SO IT BEGINS." His thoughts stirred lazily, as if moving against the heavy current of a river.

"What do you mean?"

"The banished have returned. Soon you will command an army of the Devoted. Prophecies are stirring and you're at their heart."

"I've never wanted this."

"What do you want? Can you fight what must come to pass?"

"I don't know, but I don't want a war that could tear the Land apart. If the prophecies of this Age are colliding, who knows what destruction could result?"

"Sometimes peace can only come about through war. You cannot sit and do nothing when others strive to conquer and destroy."

"That's not the same as being the Saviour people expect."

"The life I am trapped in is one of premonitions and possibilities. I can sense some of your future because it's a future I will share. Dark clouds are gathering, forces you cannot control. I've seen you dead while a horror takes your place and leaves you mindless; living like an animal; cast into the Dark Place while the Land goes to ruin."

"So what can I do? Let the Devoted pledge themselves to me when I meet them in Llehden?"

"Llehden? Who suggested meeting there? It's a place of great power; I can't imagine the Devoted being welcome there. They must be desperate to keep the meeting secret. When you go there, you will meet the witch of Llehden. She may be able to help you."

"What help could some village crone give me?"

"The Land is slipping out of balance, driven by power used without thought given to the consequences. The witch draws her power from the Land itself, where there must be balance in all things. I believe she will not stand aside and allow that to be destroyed, and that she will recognise your own need for balance. I sense she will show you a path through darkness."

The darkness brightened. Isak felt his limbs, tired and aching, and his eyes caked with tears. Wakefulness insinuated itself, sharp and insistent, though he longed to sink back into the sanctuary of sleep. He felt a bed beneath him, damp and clammy after the cool cradle of empty air. The buzz of conversation stung at his ears before calming into words and voices he recognised. Slowly, he returned to the Land and its cares.

"We should let him sleep."

"He needs to be up, so people can see him."

"How did he survive?"

"How do you think? His first hours as Lord of the Farlan—Nartis could hardly fail to watch over him, especially during a storm. What I want to know is how he did what he did. It wasn't just using his magic to create lightning, he actually called the storm onto him. It scared the shit out of the king's mages, and then—"

"But what about his arm?"

"That I can't explain. Reckon we'll need a mage or maybe a priest to explain that."

Isak suddenly gasped for air, as though surfacing from water. The people around his bed jumped back in surprise—he'd been as still as a corpse. Now his heaving gulps of breath sounded like a return to life. Looking up, Isak focused on the roof above. He was in the palace, some corner of a lavishly decorated hall. With an effort he brought his mind into focus: was this the Queen's Hall? It wasn't the main audience chamber; it was a smaller and more elegant room.

"How do you feel?"

Isak had to suppress a laugh at Tila's question. He had not taken stock of his injuries yet, but he did know every bone and muscle in his body hurt. Lifting his head from whatever was supporting it caused a sharp spasm of pain to drive deep behind his eyes and his vision wavered and blurred.

When he opened his eyes again, Tila and Mihn were kneeling at his side, hands on his chest and forehead to keep him still.

"Careful," Tila warned him softly. "The wall collapsed under you; you fell quite a way."

"What happened?" Isak croaked.

"What happened?" Carel repeated behind her. Isak forced his eyes to focus on his old friend. He saw a battered and weary face, bruised and still bleeding a little down the left-hand side. His arm was in a sling, wrapped in grubby bandages. "Don't you remember bringing down the wrath of the Gods on those soldiers?"

"I—No, I remember flashes. That's all."

"Flashes is all there were, boy!" A glint appeared in Carel's eye. "A whole damn lot of them, more lightning than nature ever cast down in one place. We still don't know how many you killed, but it was hundreds. They had crammed near every man they had into the breach. You had your shield in the air and it attracted the lightning, then channelled it down onto them."

Isak could feel a dull throb in his hand, but it was mild compared to how the rest of his body felt. He carefully lifted his shield arm—and fought back a scream. To his absolute horror his left arm had changed completely: it *felt* the same: same size, and weight, but instead of his usual healthy colour it glowed an unearthly white, shining in the bright morning sunlight. The skin was perfectly smooth, and unbroken by even the slightest scratch. It looked as if every drop of blood, every hint of colour, had been leached from his arm. Panicking, he raised his other hand, but that looked normal, although grazed and bruised after the battle.

"It's only the left one," Tila said softly, soothingly, but her expression betrayed her alarm.

"How far up does it go?" He tried to twist his head sideways to get a better look, but the effort made him wince in pain and he let his head slump back on the pillows.

"Just beyond the shoulder," Mihn said, appearing behind Tila. "It ends abruptly—it looks like you've dipped your arm in paint." He betrayed no emotion now. Isak remembered seeing him fighting on the wall, wielding only his staff. Mihn had surpassed even the men of the Brotherhood for agility and speed. He'd not been hurt, avoiding even the smallest cut, though his tears had flowed freely. He'd vowed never again to use a sword after he failed to become a Harlequin, but he had broken that vow to help rescue Isak from the White Circle; that was one more shame he felt on his soul.

Dipped in paint: that was an accurate description, Isak thought: the bit he could see wasn't translucent, not drained of colour at all, just purely white. He remembered how the lightning had curled lovingly around his arm, its burning bright light first warming his skin, then seeping down to the very bone. Now he looked closer, he could see the fine hairs, and two moles on his forearm, still there, but snow-coloured. Although he healed exceptionally fast and almost inhumanly well, he had one scar, from when he'd fallen from a tree and nearly lost his arm: now that was barely visible. Isak stared at it in fascination. Blue veins were just visible under the skin. His arm wasn't damaged, just touched by the divine.

He reached for Eolis, lying at his side, and touched the edge of the blade against his forearm. Despite the battle it was as sharp as ever: he watched, mesmerised, as a trickle of scarlet edged its way down his arm. The contrast against his skin was shocking.

"If you've quite finished?" Tila sound exasperated. "I've just bandaged every wretched cut on your body and you want to make more? Don't mind me, will you."

Isak looked up at the girl, grinning wider as a reluctant smile crossed her own lips. Her once-elegant green silk dress was now torn and stained with blood, and frayed at the edges where she'd ripped off the flounces for bandages and run a knife from thigh to calf to free her legs enough to move properly.

As he took in her appearance he realised with a jolt that his own chest was bare. His hand immediately went to the scar there.

"Ah, yes," Carel said quietly, "and then there's that. What in Nartis's name is it, boy? Why didn't you bloody tell me about it?" Though the words were harsh, his voice remained at conversational level.

"King Emin saw it too," commented Vesna, moving into Isak's field of vision. Isak was pretty sure the pained expression on his face had nothing to do with the crutch he was resting on.

"Did he say anything?"

"He did, my Lord, and I hope it makes more sense to you."

Isak narrowed his eyes at the formality. Clearly the count was hurt that he'd not been deemed trustworthy enough to tell.

"He said he wondered why you'd chosen it."

"That's all?"

He nodded.

Isak suddenly felt as though all the energy had drained from his body. He sagged back onto the bed. He didn't even have enough strength to feel guilty yet.

"Well?" Carel demanded.

"Please, not today. There's too much to do, too many to grieve for." Isak coughed feebly, taking a moment to recover his breath again. "Can you leave me alone for a while?"

None of them looked happy, but Isak's fatigue was obviously not put on just to get out of an awkward conversation. They moved away silently and crossed the hall to join Mistress Daran, who was supervising the nursing of the wounded Ghosts lying there.

Isak lay back and tried to identify the points of pain in his body. Once his headache had calmed a bit it was easier, using his supernatural awareness, to ensure that no great damage had been done. He had no broken bones; nothing had got past Siulents. There were deep bruises from where axes and swords had pounded against his armour, but his weakness was mainly from the overuse of magic.

A faint smile appeared on his lips as he remembered wielding the power of the storm. A tremor of that power still rang in his bones: an echo of the divine.

After a few minutes of staring up at the beautifully painted ceiling, listening idly to the distant voices, he began to feel a little stronger. Gingerly he lifted his head and raised himself up onto his elbows. The pain had dulled a bit: now it felt like an awful hangover—albeit one that affected his soul as well. His huge body felt heavy and awkward; even the smallest movement was an effort.

At last he managed to get himself out of bed. He stood there swaying as Mihn dragged over a chair for him so he could sit with a little more dignity. Isak caught sight of Tila, Carel, and Vesna, watching from a little distance, allowing Mihn to help his Lord. Tila sent someone off to find food and in a few minutes a servant appeared with a platter and a steaming jug of tea. Isak wrapped his hands around the pot, huddling over it to breathe in the warm vapour.

"Where's my brother's body?" The booming voice made Isak flinch as it echoed through the hall. A broad man stormed in through the far end of the hall, ahead of a small group of people. In stark contrast a tiny man, a palace official by his dress, was trotting behind, trying to keep up. His hands were clasped anxiously together as he pursued the larger man.

"My Lord, Suzerain Toquin, if I could please speak to you alone—"

"Damn you, man, no, you can't!" the man snarled, casting a contemptuous look at the servant. His scarlet and white tunic was immaculate and expensive. Suzerain Toquin's face reddened with rage as he looked down the hall, then spied Isak and strode on past the women in his group trying to calm him down. One had a young boy clutching at her skirts.

The nobleman glared at the white-eye as if daring him to complain about the intrusion. Isak recalled the name: Commander Brandt's brother, and he remembered Brandt's heroic actions on the wall, and his final sacrifice. Suzerain Toquin could hardly be faulted for being angry.

Isak pulled himself up as straight as he could and said, "My Lord, you must be Commander Brandt's brother. I apologise for not getting up to greet you, but I've been in a bit of a fight."

The man scowled, mollified slightly by Isak's respectful tone.

"You must be the Dowager Countess Toquin?" Isak continued, looking at the older of the two women in the suzerain's party.

She gave a small curtsey; her tearstained eyes never left Isak's face.

"You, madam, must be Lady Toquin." He smiled gently at the younger woman and turned to the boy. "And you are the son Commander Brandt spoke of so proudly." The woman bobbed her head and clutched the boy closer; her grief was almost palpable, but it didn't look like the boy had yet fully grasped that his father was never coming home. He was only nine, Isak thought, too young to fully understand what had happened yet.

"Come here, Master Toquin," he said softly, and beckoned to the boy.

His mother tightened her grip for a moment, then released him and gave him a little push forward. Brandt's son took a few steps towards Isak, unafraid of the white-eye until he closed on him and realised just how big he was—even hunched over in his seat, Isak towered over the boy.

Moving slowly so he wouldn't take fright, Isak pointed at the ring hanging from a leather thong around the boy's neck. He had no idea whether this was how one treated children this age, but the boy looked ready to flee back to his mother at the slightest provocation. He was a thin child, looking more like his mother than his father to Isak's eyes.

"Did your father give you that?"

The boy nodded.

"Did he tell you it was mine?"

Another nod, then the boy's trembling hand reached up and touched the silver ring about his neck. "Do you want it back?" The boy sounded understandably upset at the thought of returning his last gift from his father.

Isak chuckled, but it turned into a painful wheeze that almost caused the child to bolt. "No, it's yours to keep, and maybe even to give to a son of your own one day. Do you remember what your father told you when he gave you the ring?"

"He said that we're all men, and nothing more. But that didn't mean we shouldn't try to be as good as we can." The boy recited the lines carefully, making sure he remembered every word.

"Good. You must always remember your father when you look at it, and remember that he died to protect others. He saved my life, your father did—

and probably the lives of the king, the queen, and everyone else in the palace. Always remember that your father was a hero, and not just a hero, but one worthy of the Age of Myths."

The boy nodded miserably. Reality began to sink in and his lip trembled. He tightened his eyes against the welling tears.

Isak reached out and gently nudged the boy back towards his mother. Lady Toquin knelt and sobbed unashamedly into her son's hair as he buried his face in her neck, her scarf bunched tightly in his little fists.

Isak drew himself to his feet, wincing slightly, but unable to remain still now. "I don't know whether you have any traditions of your own, but the commander's body would be welcome at the Temple of Nartis if you wish it. He deserves a hero's grave."

Suzerain Toquin blinked several times as he took in the offer. From his reaction, Isak assumed few were permitted interment in the temple here. Isak didn't care what objections the priests might have—he couldn't imagine even the most senile refusing the new Lord of the Farlan. It might still be a matter of heated debate whether Nartis's Chosen was in fact the head of the entire cult, but even the most fervent secessionist could guess King Emin's position on the subject.

"Thank you, my Lord," replied the man stiffly. "My Order requires burial to be completed before sunset, which the priests may object to, but if that is possible, we would be very happy to accept your offer."

"It will be arranged for this afternoon, when I go to sacrifice at the temple with the king. Burial under moonlight is preferable because Nartis attends, but I must grow used to being his representative in the Land anyway. It will be done as you wish. Until then, if you would excuse me—we have much to do here."

"Of course, my Lord. You do my brother a great honour. Thank you." The suzerain bowed and turned, looking deflated now his anger had dissipated. It was a less imposing man who left to grieve, one arm supporting his trembling mother, the other around his nephew, who was clinging tightly to his mother.

"The commander's body has been found, I assume?" Isak murmured to the small palace official once Suzerain Toquin had reached the door of the hall.

"I, ah . . . It has, my Lord, but it was, um, badly burned."

"Then find a casket, and nail it shut so no one can view the body. Mihn here will go with you. You are to get the body prepared and down to the temple. Explain to the priests what is going to happen, and ensure they are ready for the commander's funeral this afternoon. Mihn will hurt anyone who gets in your way, and continue to hurt them until they agree to help. If they still do not agree, you will be lifting the casket over their corpse. Understand?"

The servant stared at Isak, quivering slightly at the coldness in his voice until Mihn grasped him firmly by the arm and led him away.

It was late afternoon by the time Isak and the king managed to extricate themselves from the chaos of the aftermath. The shadows had begun to lengthen as a line of litters started out from the temple quarter, back through the shocked silence of the city streets to the palace. Mounted soldiers clattered along on either side of the gently swaying litters. Isak watched the faces of those he passed: the bloody and the scared, the tired and confused.

King Emin's reign had brought more than a decade of peace to the entire kingdom. A professional navy dissuaded even the raids of the Western Isles pirates. War was something that happened in other countries.

Now, talk of the Saviour and rumours of strange events in Raland that had left part of the city aflame had restored to Narkang a grim uncertainty that everyone had devoutly hoped would be a thing of the past.

Emin had insisted they use the litters to go to the temples as a symbol of normal life for the rest of the city. It seemed to work, for the procession brought people out of their houses despite their fears and the risk of more fighting. Even with the dead at the palace—the Fysthrall soldiers who'd not died at the breach had fallen on their swords—there were hundreds of people still unaccounted for.

Fleeing mercenaries tried to hide in alleys and sewers, but Narkang's criminals, directed by the Brotherhood, had dealt with them, leaving corpses all over the city. Herolen Jex's body had not been among them so far, but King Emin was still hopeful.

The arrival of the relief troops, delayed for several hours by White Circle mages, had helped matters, but still there were too many questions unanswered. The first Emin had asked himself when walking in the corpse-strewn gardens with Isak: *Why had this happened?* Getting together a division of men, secretly, showed organisation and determination. There had to be a purpose behind attacking such a powerful nation, but too much didn't make sense.

Emin concluded—because he could see no other explanation—that the massive effort had failed through bad luck.

Isak decided not to voice the opinion that sense might not have played too great a part; privately, he thought that prophecy might have supplanted practicality when the Fysthrall came to make their plans. Perhaps worse, prophecy itself had been supplanted—or more likely, perverted.

There was a commotion up ahead. Isak leaned out past his bearers to see what was happening.

Vesna, walking alongside, stepped away to get a better view. "There's a carriage up ahead," he reported.

"Can you see who's in it?"

A burst of magic shivered out from the direction of the carriage—nothing aggressive, but enough to announce a presence.

"A woman," Vesna said. "Her hood is hiding her face."

Isak eased himself off the litter and set off without another word towards the tall black carriage blocking the road. He moved awkwardly to begin with, his muscles still feeling stiff and sore. Ahead he could see soldiers crowding around the coach, gesticulating to the driver and to the woman leaning out of the open door. A young lieutenant was crouching beside the king's litter, talking in an urgent voice, as Isak passed.

"A friend of yours?" Emin climbed out of his litter, pushed past the lieutenant, and joined Isak.

"I think I met her yesterday, at the arena."

"Really? Well then, her departure may be swifter than she hopes."

"I doubt that; she's stronger than I am. She didn't fight at the palace though; she had her own reasons for being with the White Circle."

A rare moment of surprise flashed across the king's face, but he asked nothing further as they made their way to the carriage. The guards fell back quickly, glad the problem was no longer theirs.

"Ostia." Isak received a thin smile in reply, but Emin's flamboyant bow was received with much greater warmth.

Zhia Vukotic gave the king a coquettish smile from the shadows of her hood. When at last she spoke, her voice was rich and smooth, the rounding of her syllables sounding cultured, old. "King Emin, it is a shame we've not met already. I have greatly admired the way you govern your city."

"Yet you appear to be leaving it," the king countered.

Zhia's smile widened further under the canopy of her silk hood, wide enough for Emin to see all he needed to recognise her.

"I would address you by your proper title, but I doubt you are currently using 'Princess,' so I hope you forgive the informality," he added.

"Easily enough; such trappings are behind me now and the names I am called these days tend to be less than kind."

"Lady, it was the will of the Gods to make you thus; in this company I shall certainly not cast slurs on one's nature."

Isak gave a snort at the comparison but was ignored by both.

"Well, you were discreet in your living arrangements," continued Emin. "I had no idea you were in the city. If you admire my politics, then I am flattered. Your reputation precedes you."

"As does yours. During the months of enduring the White Circle's childish games, I frequently wished we could have been introduced. I've not met an adequate Xeliache opponent for years—not one with a true understanding of strategy. Considering your rise to power, I think you would provide me with true diversion, for a time at least."

"Xeliache?" Isak asked. The word sounded disturbingly familiar.

"Xeliache, the more accurate name for Heartland." Emin didn't take his eyes off Zhia. "It comes from the core runes Xeliath, meaning heart, and Eache, meaning the Land."

The vampire smiled, something akin to desire in her eyes. Isak looked from one to the other, but they were oblivious to his presence, too caught up in the prospect of a challenging intellectual conflict. He was glad. The connection between "Xeliath" and "Heart" had stunned him into dumb silence. He'd not suspected, but it made sense. The threads to his life connected—he should have already guessed this.

"My Lady, the next time we meet, we will find time for a game," the king promised.

"And if we are leading opposing armies?"

"Would you really not have the time to spare?"

Zhia laughed, a seductive, velvety sound. "My kind always have time to spare. Very well, your Majesty. When we meet again, we will play. I hope it will not find us enemies, though."

"Can we be anything but? You can hardly have failed to notice the bees on my collar."

"Indeed I did not. Nor did I overlook the fact that you made no effort to cover them and save me a small discomfort. As for an enmity, that depends on others. My family has no wish to take your crown, but we cannot speak for the whole Land."

"Which others?"

"But of course, you'll not have heard," Zhia purred.

Emin's eyes narrowed; he was fully aware of the advantage over him that she was enjoying.

Isak was barely listening now, until he realised the importance of Zhia Vukotic's news.

"I hear the Temple of the Sun is in flames. The Menin have returned from the East and Lord Charr rushed out to offer battle. His army was slaughtered and there were too few soldiers left in Thotel to defend it. The city fell to the first attack. The Chetse have been conquered." Zhia smiled at them both and pulled the carriage door closed again. "Until we meet again, your Majesty, my Lord." She inclined her head gracefully and tapped on the carriage partition.

CHAPTER 37

TEN DAYS LATER, as sullen clouds lingered in the sky, the Farlan party made their way towards Llehden. The death of Lord Bahl had cut short their stay in Narkang, for time was now against them. The spectre of civil war was growing stronger every day Isak was absent from Tirah.

The group riding towards Llehden was much depleted. Three Ghosts too badly injured to ride had been left behind, and more than half of those who had saddled up that morning had injuries that promised to make the journey miserable.

Eight of their number had died in the battle, and their bodies had been cremated. After some debate, the funerary urns had been placed in the Temple of Nartis, on display beside Commander Brandt's tomb. None of the men had had much in the way of family, and the temple seemed to have become a memorial to the battle's dead. The Farlan were seen as the city's deliverers, and their dead were being treated with reverence by the population.

The light was strange, dull grey, more low autumn than spring. Half the day had already passed and the oncoming dusk was preying on Isak's mind. He'd been born this day, on Silvernight, eighteen summers ago. His mother had gone into labour as the light began to fade, and as Arian's sparkle etched every surface she had screamed her pain and fear to the uncaring night. The trees glowed ghostly silver, standing careless guard as her blood had flowed: the terrible haemorrhaging that came with the birth of a white-eye. Isak had been born coated in the life's blood of another. It was one death he felt the guilt for deep in his bones.

A twisting river, the Meistahl, writhed its way northeast, marking two-thirds of Llehden's shire border before it joined the Morwhent five miles from Narkang. The far side was marked by a line of gigantic pines that ran for more than thirty miles down towards a deep, still lake. Huge, broken round boulders lay scattered under those trees, making it hard to pass that way on horseback.

"They're called twilight stones," King Emin told Isak. "If you come from that way at dusk you'll see the gentry standing on them and watching the sun fade. It's the only time you'll see them—unless they want you to."

"You've seen them? I didn't realise they actually existed."

He'd expected Emin to smile at his ignorance, but the king's mouth had stayed set while his blue eyes glittered. Isak had debated long and hard before telling King Emin where they were going, and why, but he eventually decided that he would find out sooner or later, and with the Land on the cusp of war, it was better to show some trust.

"They are not part of our Land; few of us are part of theirs. They care nothing for the Gods and less for men, just for the woods they live in. They're the soul of the forest," he said. "I don't know whether they even conceive of themselves as individuals. What I do know is that you don't cross them. Your new Devoted friends might find themselves in real danger if they come across the gentry. I don't believe the Order approves of free spirits, and the gentry have short tempers."

There was only one bridge across the river, which ran too fast to ford. Major Ortof-Greyl was waiting for them on the far side, sitting high and still in his saddle. He was wearing partial mail and some kind of uniform, but it looked ceremonial: wide scarlet sleeves and trousers detailed with mother-of-pearl and a fox-fur hood.

At the bridge Megenn shied away at first, staring down at the dark silent water and twitching his ears nervously. None of the horses seemed very happy about entering the shire, but with calming hands and gentle voices they were coaxed over. The wind shook the trees as Isak crossed, as if the forest shied away for a moment and then reached out to embrace him. Isak scowled, but he was glad enough for their cover when he reached it. Isak ignored the major as he rode alongside and tried to engage the brooding white-eye in conversation. Only when Vesna plucked at the man's sleeve and frowned did the major move ahead and allow the grim silence to return.

There had been no mention of Isak's birthday, other than Tila's delicate kiss on his cheek and Carel clapping a knowing hand on his shoulder as they breakfasted—that was all Isak needed, to know that he had friends to remember it, and that they knew him well enough to not mention it.

Ahead of them, the third moon, Arian, sat high in the sky. Arian appeared for a week every three years, and the middle day of that week was Silvernight. For two days either side, the night was merely a little brighter, but everyone knew they were bad days to be abroad. There were tales galore of all the evil deeds of the past three years that had risen up from the ground in this week. True or not, there was no doubt that spirits and unnatural creatures certainly roamed the Land when Arian was high; no man of sense would enter open country. Each time Arian appeared, there would be fresh tales of horror and murder told in the taverns and inns and whispered at hearths and bedsides. It was an unchancy time.

For all that, Silvernight itself was so enchanting that every town and village held a festival to celebrate it. On that middle day every surface touched by the bright moonlight appeared to be coated in silver. It was impossible to resist the lure of being outside after dusk, and unlike the days before and after, no fell creatures stirred that night, so it was a time of safety as well as joy.

As they travelled further into Llehden, the light began to wane and open ground gave way to increasingly dense woodland. Hawthorns stretched their twisted branches out towards the road, fat oaks rustled their brittle twigs, and yews reached down low to cover the ground about themselves with a concealing skirt of night. They saw few creatures. A solitary kite passed overhead and small birds and early bats darted past their eyes, but only a bandit lynx had paid them any attention. The large cat watched them lazily from a high elm, paws hugged about the smooth bark of the branch. Isak could see tufts of grey fur protruding from the cat's chin like the wisps of a beard. Coppery streaks on its back meant the lynx disappeared when it dropped down into the twilight of the undergrowth, long before the soldiers approached. No sound reached even Isak's keen ears. The lynx just melted away to add another set of eyes to the shadows all around.

The road was nothing more than a wide track, overgrown and old, but easy enough to follow as it threaded a path through the trees. They passed a few isolated farmhouses looking dark and abandoned, though cattle lowed from the barns. Even for a farmer, Silvernight meant society and merriment. Only Isak was unmoved.

Two hours of travelling took them deep into the ancient heart of the woods. The last vestiges of day gave way to silvery twilight. All along the road the trees leaned close over their heads, the moons casting a flurry of leaf shadows underfoot, until the path opened out and became the neglected approach to a large stone house. Tall weeds almost obscured the low wall that surrounded the grounds, a hundred yards of lawn gone to pasture, and at the back, a darkened building that looked derelict.

The gates were gone and as Isak reached the gap and looked down the driveway he reined in and stared.

Major Ortof-Greyl had started on down the road when he realised his party were no longer following. They had stopped before the open gateway. The old grey walls, set against the black background of a tall laurel hedge and the encroaching trees on each side, shone in the moonlight. Crawling trails of ivy reached up the cracked stone wall. Isak set off down the driveway towards the house, his companions following behind. In an open window on the upper floor he saw an owl, bright in the moonlight and as still as a statue until Isak was only twenty yards away. It suddenly stretched its wings out and hooted, breaking the evening silence. The owl's haunting call prompted a strange chattering sound to ring out around the grounds as voices echoed from the shadows.

Isak turned to look around, unsettled by the sudden stir. He drew Eolis half out of its scabbard. He couldn't feel any other presence nearby, not even what was making the noise—then a woman, swathed in a long dark cape that covered a long robe that looked black in the moonlight, stepped out from the trees. She called out in the Narkang tongue.

"They're welcoming you," Mihn translated, unbidden.

"What are?" Isak felt immediately ashamed that he'd shown his blade, even half drawn—it was traditional not to draw weapons on Silvernight, whatever the reason. Old soldiers swore that Arian would burn and corrode the surface of any blade exposed on this magical night. He looked down. Eolis shone all the more brightly, unearthly, and dangerous.

"The gentry," Mihn said softly after she had replied.

Isak looked more closely at the woman, who appeared to be no more than thirty. She had long dark hair creeping out from under her hood, and piercing, knowing eyes. She stood so still it was as if she were of another place and time, set apart from worldly concerns. Isak could see a soft smile on her face.

"I thought they had no interest in men," he said through Mihn.

"They don't, but they welcome you as a brother."

"Have they told you that?" Isak asked.

When Mihn translated Isak's words, her only reply was a sniff of scorn.

"Are you the witch of Llehden?"

"I am a witch," she said.

A figure stepped out beside her. It had the shape of a slender, lithe man, but little else was human. Its pale, hairless skin drawn tight over harsh features reminded Isak of the mercenary Aracnan. The figure—the gentry—had sharp, narrow eyes that looked completely black in this light—almost the complete opposite of Isak's own white eyes. The gentry looked poised either to attack or flee, but neither impulse showed on its impassive face. It wore a robe of stitched leaves, tied at the waist by a switch of what looked like willow. Its feet were bare, and the large toes of each were pushed in the black soil where it stood.

By the time Isak had finished studying the gentry he realised there was a group of them; they had arrived as silently as wraiths. The first, their representative maybe, regarded Isak. He remembered the king's warning that the gentry had short tempers. If they truly were greeting him as a brother, then sitting atop Megenn and staring down at them was probably deeply insulting.

Isak pulled off the silk mask and slipped from his horse, dropping lightly to the ground.

The gentry shot him a grin, flashing long canines, and bowed low, though keeping his eyes on Isak all the while. Isak found himself bowing too, almost as low, which produced another predatory smile. Then it spoke in a barking chatter, firing sounds out through the night that were echoed out by the unseen gentry still among the trees. Without waiting for a response, the figure turned and darted away. All around, Isak heard sudden movement and glimpsed shapes flashing through the slivers of moonlight between the trees. He guessed at least fifty gentry had gathered.

The witch arched an eyebrow. From her expression, Isak was sure she'd never seen the gentry act like that. *They say that they will escort you to the Ivy Rings, where soldiers wait. They call you a friend of the Land. That the soldiers still live is a gesture of respect for you.*

His surprise at a voice appearing in his head must have shown as the corners of her mouth curled into a smile. *How?*

I am a witch. Your heart is not the only one with abilities.

You know of her?

I have heard her in the night. A song of fears; for you and for the Land. She feels your pain as her own.

My injuries?

The pain of your future, and of your soul. There is a storm on the horizon, one you feel in your blood, but it is wild and uncontrollable. So much is drawn to your light that you will make your own future only if you can control that storm. Consider your choices well, for they will impact on the whole Land as much as her.

What is your part in this?

I care nothing for the plans of Gods or the pride of men. I am a witch of Llehden, bound to the Land and bound to protect its balance. Those who need help will find it in me; those who need haven will find it here. That is the bond I gave for the powers I bear. Go now. Events are waiting upon you. When my help is needed, it will be given.

When it's needed?

You are not here to see me; now is not the time for that. All I know is that a time will come when you will need a light in dark places. Then, young dragon, you will need my help.

And you'll give it so freely? It doesn't sound like you even know what you're committing to. Isak tried hard not to sound insulting in his head.

No one can see the future exactly. Those who see furthest and with the greatest clarity are prophets, and that is the source of their madness. I can feel an echo of the future, no more. Until that time when you need a light in dark places, I do not need to understand more.

And what am I supposed to do until then? Even in his head he sounded petulant; he tried to control the anger he always felt when things were beyond his control. Now was not the time to lose his temper, particularly not with someone who might save his life in some way.

Control the storm, find a way to channel its power and chain it. I can feel the Land inside you, entwined with magic, and struggling to find its own balance. The price of my power is to use it when others have need of it; it may be that the price of your power will be the need of the entire Land.

But—

No more. You have your future to meet now.

My future?

The witch turned and walked softly away until she was swallowed up by the silver-tinged darkness. When at last she replied, it was soft and distant, but he could feel a fond humour in the words. *Our future always lies ahead of us, but sometimes it stops and turns around to look us in the face. All things have their time. Remember that, young dragon.*

"So what happened back there?" Vesna asked quietly.

Isak rode on unheeding, his eyes vague, his cloak hood hiding his face from Arian's light, pondering the strange meeting. The ranger Jeil trotted ahead, following the gentry who were now leading the way. Megenn, unguided by Isak, trailed after the others at his own pace.

Isak could see nothing but the image of the witch. It was hard not to trust her, but Isak was beginning to doubt altruism in anyone. Was she another player, entering the game? If so, to what end? She had no kingdom to protect, no border to expand—did she have a greater goal than that?

The witch did not offer to guide them herself; Silvernight itself was a time for human festivities, when witches and the spirits of the night kept quiet. The Finntrail would leave even the weariest of travellers alone, the Coldhand folk would ignore an open barn door, and witches by tradition stayed at home. She had gone outside her house only to speak to the gentry, and nothing but an urgent plea for help would draw her beyond the boundary wall before dawn.

Mihn had muttered something under his breath, part of a nursery rhyme maybe, but when Tila had asked, he said it was just the ending of an old poem. She pushed Mihn until he agreed to repeat it.

Reluctantly, in a subdued voice, he recited, "And even the snakes and the gentry shiver, when the Llehden witch comes riding by."

Tila shivered. She understood his reluctance now.

"Isak, what happened?" Vesna touched his Lord on the arm, startling Isak from his thoughts. "With the witch, why were you just staring at each other?" Vesna looked smaller in the bright moonlight, but perhaps he was just overshadowed by the glow of Siulents.

"We were talking," Isak admitted, and then added, surprisingly, "I'm sorry. There's so much I've not told you, all of you."

Carel looked resigned and unsurprised, but Tila was furious that there was yet more she didn't know. Even Mihn stared darkly at his Lord, his silent criticism the hardest to bear.

"I know how you all feel," Isak started, "but it can't be tonight. Tomorrow, or when this week is finished and the Land returns to normal."

"With the Menin invading the west, normal won't be for many years," muttered Carel.

"I meant when Arian goes away," Isak clarified. "This light hurts my eyes—this light hurts much in me. Then I'll explain what I can to you."

"About the scar too?"

"About the scar," confirmed Isak. "And the dreams, and anything else you want."

Major Ortof-Greyl had been riding ahead with Jeil, but the murmur of voices behind stirred his paranoia. He looked back nervously, even more embarrassed when Tila shot him a dazzling smile. Isak sneered at the man, who was everything he despised: pious, privileged, educated—he'd probably been closeted away from the Land and taught by priests. And all those honed combat skills and a fine scholarly mind: everything blurred before the smile of a pretty, young girl.

Ortof-Greyl awkwardly returned her smile. The beads of sweat on his brow shone in the moonlight.

As Isak watched the major turn back to the road, he saw that the tree line was receding, giving way to pastureland. Rustling grasses shimmered and rippled slowly. The track dipped down, following the contours of the earth, towards a stream. The major's horse instinctively turned to the water, but was pulled back onto the right path, up the slope and to a copse of tall oaks on the peak of a small hill.

Now there were signs of human life. Six hobbled horses stood by the trees, under the supervision of a soldier who waved and beckoned them in. The scarlet of his uniform looked black in the moonlight, his steel shone brightly. From either side of the copse, drawn by the sound of hoofs, trotted a squad of knights, moving slowly so as not to appear aggressive, but as the gentry began to yammer and hiss, every horse stopped dead, fearful of the voices from the shadows.

"You might tell them not to come closer. The gentry seem to object to your presence," Isak said, deciding he agreed with the forest spirits. The smug piety of the Knights of the Temples was grating—all the more so for the violence the Order had done over the years, always in the name of the Gods. Lord Bahl had said once that religious law was nothing more than an obscene collection of misinterpretations. Bahl had never been the most forgiving—or accountable—of rulers, but he had never hidden behind religious dogma to justify his actions.

Before the Great War, the Gods had been closer to mortals, making mistakes, lying and cheating each other, playing tricks and breaking promises. Since then, myths and stories of the Gods had been used to justify all sorts of strange, sometimes barbaric laws, from the stoning of wildfowl on prayerday to the summary execution of people whose bedrooms overlooked a temple entrance. The people of Vanach, Farlan's neighbouring state, were in the grip of religious law; the people there were rumoured to be living in both poverty and terror. That had been a good enough reason for the Chief Steward to recommend the longer southern route around Tor Milist to Narkang—the disputed lands between two avaricious rulers were preferable to the wilful madness of folk living according to scripture.

"The presence of those creatures pollutes this holy place." The major kept his head low as he spoke.

Isak couldn't tell whether he was repeating by rote or trying to hide his disgust. Free spirits like the gentry were considered blasphemous and unclean by the Devoted. Isak couldn't help wondering why the Gods themselves did nothing to stop them if this was such an obscenity.

"Gods, look at them," breathed Carel in wonder.

For a moment Isak looked around, thinking the gentry had come out into the open, then he realised Carel was staring at the huge weathered standing stones past the trees: roughly hewn blocks of moss-speckled granite. The forbidding stones looked almost dull in the moonlight. All but one of the outer circle were still standing erect, towering ten feet or more into the sky. Thick trails of ivy snaked up their sides, somehow reaching from one stone to the next until it crowned the forgotten temple. The ivy looked black and sinister; Arian's light seemed to slip off its waxy surface and down onto the twigs and acorns that littered the ground. It illuminated two yards of ground inside the ring before the second circle of standing stones, half the height of the outer ring, rose to cast yet more shadows.

"The outer stones are called 'the Soldiers.' The inner ring stones are 'the Priests.'"

Isak nodded absentmindedly at Mihn's words, scanning the copse until he could make out four men in the centre. Again, they were trying to appear relaxed and nonthreatening. It made Isak's palms itch.

"The soldiers are supposed to have murdered the priests during a ritual," Mihn continued quietly. "They waited for them to fall into a trance before creeping up and slitting their throats. They were supposed to be protecting the priests. There is disagreement about whether this was a just act or not, but murder certainly took place here."

"And Belarannar turned them all to stone?"

"No, the soldiers escaped."

"And the act was justified." The major's voice was fierce as he glared at Mihn, his hand hovering close to his blade. He had turned back to find his charges. "The monks were consorting with daemons, using human sacrifices in the most evil of rituals. The soldiers were men hired to protect the monastery, but they could not ignore the truth. They founded our Order to continue the struggle against the enemies of the Gods. These stones remind my Order of our origins."

Mihn didn't reply, but dipped his head to acknowledge the major's words.

"Penitence is a wonderful thing," declared Isak. He caught Vesna's eye and forced a smirk. The count smiled in return. Major Ortof-Greyl kept his mouth firmly shut and endured the jibe silently.

Isak climbed down off his horse and entered the copse on foot. He could feel the weight of Arian's gaze lift from his shoulders—perhaps he was happier here in the shadows. The gentry, spirits that were usually seen only at twilight, when the Gods rested, had accepted him as a brother. What about the other creatures of shadow? Would Azaer now see him as kin or foe?

"You're worried about that, aren't you?" Isak hadn't meant to speak aloud, but it was quietly done and Mihn was the only one close enough to hear. Still, he kept quiet as he continued to speak in his head, *Are you scared of finding yourself on the wrong side of this war? What if the real you comes out only in battle? What if you are the monster you've always feared? Do you trust yourself to be a good and just ruler?*

He didn't know how to answer these questions, but they lingered, for if forces on both sides had affected his life, there would be darkness in his soul as well as light. Deep inside, he recognised the truth in that.

Moving through the trees, touching the trailing ivy as he went, Isak felt the temple, slumbering. The ground was still consecrated, whatever had happened here: it was still special to a Goddess of the Upper Circle and there would always be an echo of her presence there.

And all around, Isak could feel the gentry stirring, leaning gently with the wind as they stood as patiently as the grass. It was only when they moved that he could feel them at all; unlike humans, there was no resonance of their presence so they just faded into the background of wood and earth, leaving a faint air of expectation, like scent on the breeze. He envied them that, the peace of being so completely a part of the Land that they could just step back into it and disappear.

"Lord Isak," called someone from the heart of the temple in precise, educated Farlan. A portly older man stepped out through the inner circle to meet them, moving like a man many summers younger. As he neared, Isak could see he was a general.

"My Lord, I am Jebel Gort," the man said, a dazed smile on his face. It took Isak a moment to realise that this general of sixty or more summers was slightly awestruck.

"And them?" Isak gestured to the three other men, who had not moved. Two, though looking well into middle age, were obviously fit and strong; they wore swords at their hips. One man was of western stock, with a wide nose and sloping forehead; Isak suspected he was from Vanach. The other was Chetse—though he looked strange with short hair and a rapier at his waist. The only Chetse Isak had met was one of the wildest of their kind; this man looked like a doll in comparison. The third man was younger, a tall, hard-faced individual who might have been from Narkang. He stood a little further back.

"These are General Diolis, General Chotech in the middle, with Major Irien back there," General Gort said. "Major Ortof-Greyl has explained that we are not here as officials of our Order."

"He told me something that I didn't believe," Isak said, "but you didn't bring any mages with you, and I think the gentry would have dealt with any army—"

"The gentry?" the general cut in. "So that's what's been making such an infernal racket at night."

"They were probably arguing about how they wanted to kill you. In any case, I've been brought to a strange place that I don't much care for; to meet people I care much less for, for a reason I don't believe, and on my birthday. Consider me annoyed and get to the fucking point."

The general's face was in shadow so Isak couldn't see his reaction, but his reply was certainly measured. "Very well, my Lord. Our group is small, restricted to men we can trust to pursue the true aims of the Order. The Knight-Cardinal is certainly not one of those—he doesn't care much about the death of his nephew, but it gives him a pretext to want your head. He has aspirations to be the Saviour, and he positively drools at the thought of your weapons. The other members of the Council are growing tired of his megalomania. Two Councillors are expected to retire this year and when that happens, it is almost certain that General Diolis and General Chotech will take their places. That gives me the majority I need to have the Knight-Cardinal replaced, and when I do so we can begin the process of reminding power brokers like Telith Vener and Afasin just what our Order's strength should be used for."

"So this is a coup, dressed up in doctrine."

The man shrugged. "What we do today will, I am certain, demonstrate that we do not lust for the power." Without giving Isak time to reply the general stepped forward and knelt before Isak. The other three moved quickly to follow suit, Major Ortof-Greyl stepping swiftly past Isak to kneel behind his superiors.

Isak looked at his companions in bemusement. They said nothing. Vesna was smiling as if it was all just a joke. Carel, Mihn, and Tila just looked puzzled.

"Lord Isak. Here, in our most sacred temple, we pledge ourselves to your name and banner, to perform those tasks the Gods will require of you as their Saviour. I swear to take control of the Knights of the Temples only to serve your will, and the will of the Gods. When it is needed, I shall provide you with the army of Devoted soldiers spoken of in the prophecies. To prove our faith, we have brought you gifts to aid you in the Age to come."

The major jumped up and ran to a flat altar-stone in the centre of the temple. Isak had hardly noticed the brass-bound box. It was no more than a foot across, but the major picked it up reverentially. He returned with the box held out before him, his arms tense, as if the weight of the box was nearly too great for him. The general remained on one knee as he accepted it and turned it towards Isak. There was a thin film of sweat on his brow, but anticipation shone in his eyes as he lifted the lid and held it out for Isak to see.

The other Farlan gasped as the contents shone as bright as Siulents in the moonlight.

Isak was speechless, trembling all over. At first he was too afraid to believe what he was seeing, then a primal hunger flared inside him, sparked by the eerie glow coming from the box. He felt the damp touch of pain as his hand clenched so hard he drew blood.

The rest of the Land faded away and he lost himself in the smooth lines of the two Crystal Skulls. For a moment he could do nothing, hear nothing, as he stared dumbfounded at what was being offered to him. He knew their names at once. Unbidden, the memories rose in his head: Hunting and Protection, the Skulls Aryn Bwr had forged for himself that together made him stronger than any mortal—the weapons that had killed Gods.

With the heady beat of blood pounding in his ears, Isak slowly fought for control of his senses and at last reached out a shaky hand. The world grew heavy and textured as his fingers neared the box. He spread his hand to touch both at once. He expected them to be cold, until he felt the power they contained. They were warmer than his fingers—he could see a little wisp of steam curl away from the surface of one. Then they were hotter still, then suddenly scorching. A wrench of burning pain gripped his arm, growing fiercer with each passing instant. Then the world went black.

ENDGAME

Isak awoke to a place of dark twilight, lit by faint stars that faded away when he looked directly at them but glittered fiercely at the edges of his sight. The air was thin and dry against the back of his throat; it tasted of long memories, bitter and empty. He could see neither trees nor standing stones now, only undulating rocky ground in all directions, underneath a dawn sky of unbroken slate-coloured cloud. Kneeling, Isak removed his gauntlet and touched the desiccated grey dust underfoot. It felt dead to his fingers, not like the sand of a desert, but like a wasteland that had been drained of all life. It gave him a hollow feeling inside, as though a part of him was now missing.

Pulling his silver gauntlet back on, Isak noticed it had lost its lustre. The silver had faded with the light and now it looked plain and dull, like weathered iron. It was still his armour, yet somehow diminished; when he checked, Eolis was the same. He pulled off his helm and the blue silk hood and drew in deep gulps of thin air. His muscles were weak and stiff, and no matter how hard he tried, he couldn't seem to shake off the fatigue.

"I've been waiting for you."

Isak whirled around, hand on sword, to see an armoured figure standing ten yards away. The knight had a blank helm hiding his face and the teardrop shield on his arm was turned away so Isak could not see the design on its surface. His sword was drawn, but held behind his back; the pose reminded Isak of some of the formal duelling positions he'd seen Vesna practise.

Isak could see from the knight's stance that a challenge was being offered. The air of menace was all too apparent. He drew his own weapon and planted his feet securely, a shoulder width apart and with one slightly ahead of the other, just as Carel had taught him so many years ago.

"Where am I? Who are you?"

"You are nowhere, caught in a moment between your past and the future." The voice was male, rich and subtle, like King Emin's, but with an accent he couldn't place. Everything about the knight was threatening, even his words; *your* past, but only *the* future, as if there was no place for Isak in that future. The thought chilled him, this wasn't the black-armoured knight of his dreams—the one Isak *knew* would one day kill him—but it reminded him of Morghien's warning: that Isak would have to face a death of the mind. A sudden sadness crept over him. To die in this empty, dead place was somehow worse than any other fate he could imagine.

"What do you want from me?"

The knight hadn't appeared to expect that question, but for reply, he raised his shield and brought his sword around to point it directly at Isak. Realisation came with a jolt; the knight was wearing Siulents, and carrying the same blade Isak had in his hand, not copies, but as real as those Isak himself carried, similarly dimmed yet unmistakable.

"What do I want from you, boy? Everything, all that you are. Part of me has been with you all your life to make of you the tool I need for the years to come."

"All my life?"

"Certainly. Events needed to be guided, my investment protected. That priest of Larat, for example—he could not be allowed to rummage around in your head."

"So what happened when I touched the Skulls?"

"I doubt you would understand even if I told you," the knight sneered.

"So the prophecies of the last king are really true? You denied Death's judgement?" Some part of Isak demanded proof, despite the growing dreadful certainty in his gut.

The knight eased the helm from his head and let it drop to the ground. He shook his silvery, almost insubstantial hair loose. It accentuated his thin jaw and sharp cheekbones. Aryn Bwr's strange beauty made him look delicate, but far from weak; Isak suspected he had a whipcord strength that could strike like lightning.

"All this for revenge?"

"Don't think to pity me," the elf lord spat. "You know nothing of my cause, nothing of the war I fought. My time has come again, and this time I will not fail."

In a heartbeat he leapt forward and slashed up underneath Isak's shield. The white-eye hardly saw the blow coming; he barely caught it in time. A second overhand cut flashed past his head as Isak twisted sideways and slashed wildly to deflect a cut to his exposed legs. Somehow he battered Aryn Bwr's blade away.

Isak scrambled backwards to give himself some space, but the elf pursued and struck again and again. Even Isak's unnatural speed was barely keeping up with Aryn Bwr.

The elf stopped suddenly and gave Isak a cold smile. "Strange, when I was looking out through your eyes you seemed faster than this." He attacked again, not looking for a killing blow, but content to drive Isak back, confusing and unbalancing the young white-eye, always stepping back at the last moment when Isak could almost feel the bite of Eolis at his neck. He took the moments of respite gladly, then lunged at the elf with every ounce of strength in his massive body.

Aryn Bwr rode Isak's clumsy attack like a willow branch flexing in the wind, then thrust hard. Isak caught the blow on his shield, and as the blade cut down it forced the shield into his shoulder with jarring force.

Isak tried to retaliate, but again the elf stepped around Isak's thrust. This time he smashed his shield down onto Isak's wrist and pain burst through his hand as something snapped under the blow. Worse, Eolis was knocked from his grip. Isak gasped and reeled; he didn't even see the elf punch forward with Eolis's hilt. The blow connected and stars flared before his eyes.

He fell, sprawled at the last king's feet. Aryn Bwr stared down at him with contempt. "Is that all you have? So it is true, they made you weak; weak enough to be one they could control."

Isak struggled up onto his elbows. "What do you mean?"

"You do not know?" Aryn Bwr laughed. "Boy, you are not even the first Saviour this Age has seen, and you are his inferior in every way. Dare you deny it? You see him in your dreams; you've known him your whole life."

"The Saviour? Then—" Isak could not begin to find the words for the questions he wanted to ask.

"Then what happened? Azaer happened. Azaer encouraged their vanity, urged the Gods to be their own undoing, to be divided and distrustful of each other, while I returned to power. The Gods made their Saviour the greatest of men, perhaps even greater than me, but before long the Saviour began to question why he needed to serve any master."

Isak lay on the floor, overwhelmed by what he was hearing, but not so dazed that he did not desperately search for a way to escape. He knew it was futile: Aryn Bwr had been the supreme warrior; he had killed Gods. He had fallen only to Karkarn, the God of War himself.

The elf sheathed his weapon and reached down to haul Isak up. Bringing him close, the last king stared deep into Isak's eyes.

Isak returned the look, staring into pale, gold-flecked eyes as though the answer would be there. He felt a fog about his mind, enveloping his thoughts and slowing draining the strength from his body. The heavy sleep of the grave called to him, drawing him in to its embrace, but as his strength faded and his mind weakened, understanding suddenly unfurled in his mind like a bud bursting into a flower.

"Now I know," Isak said calmly.

Aryn Bwr hesitated, eyes narrowing as he tightened his grip on Isak. He had felt the change in Isak's mind and a flicker of uncertainty crept onto his face.

"Tell me, elf, can you remember your own name?"

The last king said nothing.

"Your name. Can you remember it?"

"I—" Uncertainly blossomed into loss, then fear. Aryn Bwr's true name had been struck from history, and like the Finntrail in Morghien's mind, that loss weakened his spirit.

"Can you remember your death?" As he said that, Isak felt the grip on his throat falter and weaken. "Oh yes, that you can remember, that pain is still inside you. You're dead; a memory barely beyond Death's reach. Without name or form, what are you now?"

Isak smiled and raised his left hand, though his arm was sore, numb from the fight. Despite his feebleness, Isak took hold of Aryn Bwr's wrist and prised the fingers from his throat. Lifting his right arm, the hand twisted and curled over the broken wrist, Isak spread his fingers as best he could in front of his enemy's face and remembered what he'd done to Morghien. Under his touch, the weaves of magic parted like morning mist.

The last king shrieked and writhed in Isak's grip, but the white-eye felt his strength rush back into his body. Now the elf spirit was helpless to resist. Isak forced down the snarl that built in his throat as he embraced the magic all around and gathered a storm of power in his hand, determined not to submit to the rage in his belly as he had outside Lomin.

Reaching out with his mind, Isak cast a net of magic over the dead king's soul and savagely bound it, ripping it from the body it had tried to inhabit. Aryn Bwr howled with terror.

The elf's soul, held tightly in Isak's grip, was a feeble thing now. The shadows darkened as Death's reach crept closer. Aryn Bwr renewed his screams and struggled futilely until Isak pulled the soul away from the darkness and into himself, where part of it had hidden to avoid Death's constant watch.

Isak stood alone and breathed deeply; the air was fresher now and the weariness had left his limbs. Even the pain was gone now, for the damage was not to flesh and bone but to the product of his mind. The sky was lightening, and faintly the scents of heather and wet grass came to him, smelling wonderful to him after the dead land.

In his mind Isak held the spirit of Aryn Bwr, but gently now; the time for force was over. There was no way for the elf to wield power over him anymore.

What have you done? Isak felt the elf's voice in his mind, soft and pained, but tinged with fear.

I've survived; just like you've taught me to every day of my life.

What will you do with me? Aryn Bwr knew he was closer than at any other time to the final retribution of Ghenna's deepest pit.

I'm not going to kill you, if that's what you mean. I think I can find a better use for you. If the Land looks to me to be the Saviour, then I think I'll need your brain.

You were never meant to be Saviour—

I know, Isak interrupted with a smile. *"In silver light born, in silver light clothed." That was never intended to be me; that was your rebirth tonight. Except now it's not going to happen. All things have their time; remember that, my chained dragon. Your time has passed.*

You've broken history. Destiny had you die this night. Do you realise what that means?

Isak stretched and felt a cool breath of air drift past his face. He could feel himself returning to the temple inside the trees, to the life that was at long last his own.

It means we make our own future now. It means no prophecy fits what is going to happen. All we have is ourselves.

He smiled. The Land awaited him.

Dramatis Personæ

Afasin—White-eye general of the Knights of the Temples

Alscap, Count Teb—Narkang nobleman

Alterr—Goddess of the Night Sky and Greater Moon and member of the Upper Circle of the pantheon

Amah, Suzerain Duril—Farlan nobleman

Amanas, Quitin—Keymaster of the Heraldic Library of Tirah

Amavoq—Goddess of the Forest, patron of the Yeetatchen tribe, and member of the Upper Circle of the pantheon

Antern, Count Opess—Advisor to King Emin

Anviss—God of Woods, also known as the God of Lonely Places

Aracnan—An immortal of unknown origin

Aryn Bwr—Battle name of the last king of the elves who led their rebellion against the Gods, his true name having been excised from history

Asenn—Goddess of Rain and Snow, daughter of Lliot

Atro—White-eye Lord of the Farlan, Lord Bahl's predecessor

Azaer—A shadow

Bahl—White-eye Lord of the Farlan

Belarannar—God of the Earth and member of the Upper Circle of the pantheon

Berard, Captain Heyn—Commander of the garrison of Ghorent

Brandt, Commander Toquin—Commander of the Narkang City Watch and younger brother of Suzerain Toquin

Carasay, Sir Cerse—Colonel of the Tirah Palace Guard Legion

Carel (Carelfolden), Betyn—Formerly a sergeant in the Farlan Palace Guard, now a mercenary

Cerrat, Jeco—A novice chaplain in the cult of Nartis

Certinse, Cardinal Varn—Younger brother of Suzerain Tildek, Duchess Lomin, and Knight-Cardinal Certinse

Certinse, Knight-Cardinal Horel—Commander of the Knights of the Temples, younger brother of Suzerain Tildek, and Farlan by birth

Certinse, Sir Dirass—Knight of the Palace Guard, third son of Suzerain Tildek

Chalat—White-eye Lord of the Chetse tribe

Charr—White-eye Krann to Lord Chalat

Chirialt, Dermeness—Farlan mage

Chotech, General Tethat—Member of the Knights of the Temples

Coadech, Suzerain Eyan—Lord of Narkang's most easterly suzerainty

Coran—White-eye bodyguard of King Emin

Cosep, Harle—A Farlan Swordmaster

Creyl, Sir (Creyl Cuder)—Advisor to King Emin and founding member of the Brotherhood

Dancer—Farlan nobleman and member of the Chief Steward's coterie of secret advisors

Danva, Suzerain Woral—Farlan nobleman

Daran, Mistress (Mistress Amari Daran)—Tila Introl's chaperone

Death—Chief of the Gods and head of the Upper Circle of the Pantheon

Dedev, Borl—Farlan ranger

Dele, Norimin—Chief Librarian of the College of Magic of Narkang

Destech, Guret—A lieutenant, one of the mercenary Tochet

Dev, General Chate—Highest ranked of the Chetse generals and Commander of the Ten Thousand

Deyl, Morten—Chief Councillor of the Public Assembly of Narkang

Diolis, General Nemhar—Member of the Knights of the Temples

Disten, Cardinal Fesin—Famous member of the Cardinal branch of the Farlan Cult of Nartis

Doranei, Ashin—Member of the Brotherhood, one of King Emin's personal agents

Elierl, General Brinn—Farlan general posted to Lomin

Eraliave, Cortuneo—Elven general who predated the Wars of the Houses

Farlan, King Deliss—Famous Farlan king, father of Kasi Farlan

Farlan, Prince Kasi—Legendary prince of the Farlan, in whose image white-eyes were created, and after whom the lesser moon was named

Fedei, Wisten—The Seer of Ghorent

Fordall, Invriss—A mage from Lomin

Fordan, Suzerain Leren—Farlan nobleman

Forell, Duchess Karo—Ranking member of the White Circle in Narkang

Gaur—Half-human warrior from the Waste, Lord Styrax's most trusted general

Genedel—A dragon

Gerrint, Adjutant Pirav—Chetse soldier of the Lion Legion, General Dev's adjutant

Gort, General Jebehl—General of the Knights of the Temples, member of its ruling council

Grast, Deverk—Former Lord of the Menin who instigated the Long March to their current home and tried to wipe out the Litse tribe

Halis, Anversis—Narkang academic, King Emin's uncle

Horen, Councillor Jan—Head of the town council of Ghorent

Ilit—God of the Wind, Patron of the Litse tribe and member of the Upper Circle of the Pantheon

Ineh—Deceased Farlan white-eye, lover of Lord Bahl

Inoth—Goddess of the Western Seas, Lliot's eldest child, she replaced him in the Upper Circle of the Pantheon

Introl, Anad—Gatekeeper of Tirah, member of the city council and Tila's father

Introl, Tila—Krann Isak's personal maid and advisor

Isak—White-eye Chosen of Nartis, Krann to Lord Bahl

Jeil—Farlan ranger

Karkarn—God of War and Destruction, patron of the Menin tribe and member of the Upper Circle of the Pantheon

Kerin, Swordmaster Orayn—Commander of the Swordmasters and Knight-Defender of Tirah

Kinbe, Count Nayer—Farlan nobleman from Lomin

Kulet—Former white-eye sergeant in the Palace Guard

Lady, the—Common name of Fate, Goddess of Luck

Lahk, General—White-eye general commanding the forces around Tirah

Larat—God of Magic and Manipulation, member of the Upper Circle of the Pantheon

Larim, Shotein—Menin white-eye mage, Chosen of Larat and Krann to Lord Salen

Leferna, Priata—The commander of the White Circle forces in Tor Milist

Legana—A devotee of the Lady, a Farlan agent

Leitah—Goddess of Wisdom and Learning, sister to Larat, who died in the Great War

Lesarl, Chief Steward Fordan—Principal advisor to the Lord of the Farlan

Lliot—God of Water, member of the Upper Circle of the Pantheon until he died during the Age of Myths, whereupon his domain was divided up among his five children: Inoth, Turist, Shoso, Vasle, and Asenn

Lomin, Duchess Feya—Wife of Duke of Lomin, mother to Scion Lomin, sister to Cardinal Certinse, Knight-Cardinal Certinse, and Suzerain Tildek

Lomin, Duke Koren—Farlan ruler of Lomin

Lomin, Scion Karlat—Son of the Duke of Lomin and grandson of Suzerain Certinse

Malich, Cordein—A necromancer from Embere

Mihn (ab Netren ab Felith)—Wanderer from the coast north of the Great Forest

Morghien—Drifter of Embere descent, known as the man of many spirits

Nartis—God of the Night, Storms and Hunters, patron of the Farlan tribe and member of the Upper Circle of the Pantheon

Nelbove, Suzerain Atar—Farlan nobleman

Nemarse, Duke—Ruler of Raland

Nostil, Prince Velere—Aryn Bwr's heir, first owner of the Skull of Ruling

Ortof-Greyl, Major Harn—Member of the Knights of the Temples

Salen, Lord of the Hidden Tower—Menin White-eye, Chosen of Larat

Seliasei—Aspect of Vasle that now possesses Morghien

Selsetin, Suzerain Pelan—Farlan nobleman

Semar—Former Lord of the Farlan, designer and builder of the Tower of Semar

Sempes, Duke Faral—Ruler of the Farlan city of Perlir

Shalstik—Elven prophet who predicted Aryn Bwr's return

Sheredal, Spreader of the Frost—Aspect of the Goddess Asenn

Shoso—God of Northern Seas, son of Lliot

Shotir—God of Healing and Forgiveness

Solsis, Count Juren—Farlan nobleman from Lomin

Sorodoch, Teche—Chetse mage-smith

Styrax, Kohrad—White-eye son of Lord Styrax

Styrax, Lord Kastan—White-eye Lord of the Menin

Tebran, Suzerain Kehed—Farlan nobleman

Thonal, King Emin—King of Narkang and the Three Cities

Thonal, Queen Oterness—Queen of Narkang

Tildek, Suzerain Esh—Farlan nobleman, father of Sir Dirass Certinse, elder brother of Knight-Cardinal Certinse, Cardinal Certinse, and the Duchess of Lomin

Tiniq—Farlan ranger, twin brother of General Lahk

Tochet, Dechat—Chetse mercenary, former General of the Eastern Tunnels

Tohl, Marshal Dorik—Member of the original Brotherhood, the criminal gang

Toquin, Suzerain—Narkang nobleman

Torl, Suzerain Karn—Farlan nobleman

Triena—Goddess of Romantic Love and Fidelity, part of the linked Goddesses who together cover all the aspects of love

Tsatach—God of Fire and the Sun, patron of the Chetse tribe and member of the Upper Circle of the Pantheon

Turist—God of the Southern Seas until he was killed during the Great War

Vasle—God of Rivers and Inland Seas

Veil, Arin—Member of the Brotherhood

Vener, General Telith—General of the Knights of the Temples

Veren—First God of the Beasts, killed during the Great War

Verliq, Arasay—Mage and academic, who founded a small nation in the east, later conquered by Lord Styrax

Versijt, Lord Aliax—Famous Yeetatchen ruler who almost conquered the Farlan

Vesna, Count Evanelial—Famous Farlan soldier from Anvee

Vilan, Count Peran—Farlan nobleman from Torl

Volah, Scion Sohn—Farlan nobleman

Volah, Suzerain Abse—Farlan nobleman

Vrerr, Duke Sarole—Ruler of Tor Milist

Vrest—God of the Beasts, member of the Upper Circle of the Pantheon, formerly an Aspect of Veren before Veren's death

Vrill, Duke Anote—Menin white-eye general

Vukotic, Prince Koezh—Ruler of the Vukotic tribe, cursed with vampirism after the Last Battle

Vukotic, Prince Vorizh—Younger brother of Koezh, cursed with vampirism after the Last Battle, and subsequently driven insane

Vukotic, Princess Zhia—Youngest of the Vukotic family, cursed with vampirism after the Last Battle

Xeliath—Yeetatchen white-eye who has the Skull of Dreams fused to her hand

ABOUT THE AUTHOR

TOM LLOYD was born in 1979 in Berkshire. After a degree in international relations he went straight into publishing where he still works. He never received the memo about suitable jobs for writers and consequently has never been a kitchen-hand, hospital porter, pigeon hunter, or secret agent. He lives in South London, isn't one of those authors who gives a damn about the history of the font used in his books, and only believes in forms of exercise that allow him to hit something. Visit him online at www.tomlloyd.co.uk.